WHAT PEOPLE /

My gratitude to those who reviewed this nov~. ~ing with my editor, Alice Peck, who said, "This is my type of booo.; provide invaluable feedback and direction.

John L. Palmer, KTCH, KCT, 33°, Managing Editor, Knight Templar Magazine (June 2009): "Unlike most fiction about the Templars, this exciting historical novel has been painstakingly researched...the detail is incredibly accurate, so if you are interested in the day to day lives of the ancient Templars, here is presented an opportunity to learn about them and to have a fun read at the same time..."

Jim Cox, Editor, Midwest Book Review (Summer 2009): "A truly riveting novel from beginning to end, this is the stuff of which Hollywood blockbuster movies are made!"

Knight Templar Jim Russell, KofP, Texas: "...(a) perfect storyline to be savored...a balance of historical fact and esoteric knowledge that has seldom been brought to the public's eye. A must read for the modern Templar..."

Ron Holland, International Bundesbrief Society (Swiss heritage): "...enjoyed the attention to detail...many of the (same) conclusions I (arrived at) in over a decade researching the Templars."

William C. House, Editor, Reversespins.com (May 2009): "...a fascinating book...the action takes place during the crusades in the late 13th century. The Templars and a secret organization have vowed to protect the pilgrims but they have a deeper, hidden spiritual quest as well. It is this last search, that makes *The Templars, Two Kings and a Pope*, compelling historical fiction unlike any other."

Neal Watt, Texas: "Grigor Fedan has written a great read based on his studies of the Templars and medieval history...I believe my brother Masons will find great interest in Mr. Fedan's book."

Mike Akers, California: "...if you love the middle ages, this is the book to read, if you really want to know·and understand the Templars, this is the one to read."

Dustin Collins, Washington: "One of the best books I have ever read..."

Lora Cline, Arizona: "I finished it in two days...I couldn't put it down...it touched me profoundly."

Jack McCallum, Tennessee: "I hope to see it one day in a first rate movie. It's that good!"

Peter Leever, The Netherlands: "I enjoyed it tremendously. I gained insight into the Templars' tactics, weaponry and hierarchy. Thanks for all the pleasant reading hours."

Carter Diggs, Virginia: "Thank you for sharing your book...it's like you had inside information."

Dwayne Young, U.S. Navy: "I finished the book for the third time...I highly recommend it."

Beth McKenzie, Reviewer, MyShelf.com: "I approached this book as a student of the middle ages, as a member of a Masonic family, as a person interested in Gnostic teachings and finally as an uninformed reviewer. When you read *The Templars, Two Kings and a Pope*, as every person seeking spiritual enlightenment will be drawn to do, you will be delighted with an intricate midrash for seekers in the 21st Century."

THE TEMPLARS, TWO KINGS AND A POPE

A Historical Novel of Spirituality and a Covert War

Hafiz Press

Library of Congress Control Number: 2008911845
Fedan, Grigor

The Templars, Two Kings and a Pope

Book Design by Margaret Strubel
margaret.strubel@gmail.com

AUTHOR'S NOTE

I wanted the truth about the Knights Templar. Did they really meditate, were therefore deeply spiritual but also fierce warriors? What really happened to them?

I spent five years doing research and found more than I had bargained for. I focused on a critical period in their history, between 1288 and 1315 and discovered a surprising story of a secret war, but also of expansive spirituality at a time of fanaticism, greed, and brutality.

The Knights Templar were officially around from 1119 to 1312; warrior-monks who achieved notoriety in the Holy Land for their fighting skills and in Europe for their financial abilities. They were also rumored to be wealthy. In the period I studied events came to a boil: they were thrown out of the Holy Land by the Turks in 1291, and in 1307, the French king and the pope imprisoned and tortured them supposedly because they had adopted heretical practices. It's likely that the French king just wanted their money. That's what historians tell us. But the legends claim that the Templars survived by settling in Scotland and Switzerland under the guise of a secret society, "The Brotherhood." The Rosicrucians' "History of the Brotherhood," published in 1614, and other esoteric groups since then have claimed a direct connection.

I sifted through the scholarly accounts as well as the myths. It wasn't easy; there was much contradictory information, and even renowned scholarly works had flaws. Some neglected to mention the crucial link between Pope Clement V and the French king, or seemed confounded about the Templars' military hierarchy, mystical practice, their tactics, or which weapons and armor were in use at the time, or ignorant of the relationship between high-skill and discipline to training; all of which would have an impact on the interpretation of events. I eventually arrived at a credible version but was left with a host of questions. The Brotherhood did not originate as a result of the French persecution but dated back to the beginnings of the Order. Why? The Templars clearly had a mystical practice, but where did it come from? There were many references in the legends to a mystical "treasure." What was it? Rebel armies in Scotland, Flanders, Aquitaine, and Switzerland used telltale Templar tactics. How come? Evidence suggests the warrior-monks had foreknowledge of their demise. Who told them, and why didn't they resist? I knew that if I could answer those questions I would have a good story to tell.

Then I made two significant discoveries. First, that the Brotherhood's reason for being was to safeguard their Gnostic practice, as was the case with other groups. After reading up on Gnosticism, things made sense, such as the Templars' flag, called *Beauseant*, "To Be Whole," also their battle cry. Spiritual wholeness was a goal in Gnosticism, a mystical path of Jesus and his disciples according to the recently translated ancient documents, the Nag Hammadi Library. But this was an original version centered on meditation, what Jesus taught and the Templars inherited and found in today's Kabbalah, Sufism, and Mystical Christianity rather than the sect that evolved over the centuries. The second discovery involved a largely unknown historical figure, Lord Otto de Grandson, England's chief diplomat, royal counselor, and without doubt, a member of the Brotherhood, who was active around the time the Templars were rounded up by the French king. Following his trail provided the rest of the answers I was after. The Templars' apparent destruction was just one more chapter in a covert war that started in 1294, three years after they left the Holy Land. It was Lord Otto de Grandson who learned early on of the French king's plans for empire and maneuvered the Brotherhood to fight him, using a mystical treasure portrayed both as the Ark of the Covenant and the Holy Grail—the means to talk directly to God, and a physical link to Jesus—and I surmised that it had to have been a Gnostic manuscript written by Jesus. I now have no doubt that such a document existed, and that it was the catalyst for the Templars' survival.

The Templars, Two Kings and a Pope is the novelized reconstruction of the Brotherhood's secret war against Philip IV. It begins in 1290 when Lord Otto de Grandson launched his scheme to stop the French king. It involved a prophecy, the search for the Jesus Gospel and the covert wars in Aquitaine, Flanders, and Scotland. It culminated twenty-five years later with dramatic seminal changes that transformed the world in the upcoming centuries. This novel is also a study of life in the Middle Ages in Europe, and an honest portrayal of what it was like to be a Templar, back when the predominant religion was Catholicism and the language of the nobility in Britain and of the Templars was the *Lingua Franca,*the language of the Franks, French.

I dedicate this book to

sincere monks and nuns

of all faiths.

PART ONE

CHAPTER I

[1]

The late afternoon London fog, thick and slow, crept down the Strand and came over the wall in back of the garden enveloping trees, shrubs, and flowers. Through a windowpane in his second-floor solarium, Lord Otto de Grandson watched as his roses became diffused in the white mist. He loved the heavy fog; it reminded him of his childhood and how it used to slither down the craggy Alpine valleys and make everything soft and dream-like.

Then he heard a beggar's bell asking for alms out on the Strand. The rhythmic ringing yanked Otto out of his reverie. He listened again, this time with full attention. That was no ordinary beggar. It was urgent news. He counted the rings: one-six, meant Vespers; one-two-three, meant Grey Friars; one-one, meant today. Otto listened two more times for confirmation, and there was no doubt: he was to meet a courier that evening at Vespers by the Grey Friar's abbey in the city.

He walked over to a side table, picked up a codex he had just bought by the Franciscan Roger Bacon and sat down to read. For a while he just stared at the words. What could be the urgent message? It had to be from France. Maybe Cantor de Milly had run across a letter from King Philip with a concrete time-line when the French would declare war? Or maybe…Otto stopped himself. He would just wait and see; there was no sense speculating. He read the Aristotelian text until he came to a word the copier had omitted from an otherwise powerful sentence. That was annoying. He resolved to make the correction the following day. Then he noticed that the servants had started lighting the oil lamps and candles throughout the house. He put the book down and called for his hauberk of fine German chain mail and sword belt. After a groom helped him put them on, he draped a heincelin over his shoulders against the evening chill. At the bottom of the stairs he announced to anyone listening, "I'm going for Vespers at the Grey Friars."

When he stood under the appointed elm in the abbey's garden shrouded in foggy twilight, he turned his gaze to the monks and worshippers rushing to church, and sure enough, eventually one among the many hooded parishioners cut away from the crowd; then slowly, as though going for a stroll, circled the sundial, touched the nearby statue's right foot, and casually made his way to the tree.

When the man came close and uncovered his head, Otto recognized the immaculate goatee, hooked nose, and thick, knitted eyebrows. "Cantor! What are you doing here?"

Blood-shot eyes stared at Otto. "I couldn't trust a courier with what I have to tell you, my Lord," Cantor whispered tensely in his Languedoc French. "The time has come for you to fulfill your promise."

"What happened?"

"Three days ago, at the royal palace in Paris, I overheard King Philip order his ministers, Flote, Nogaret, and Marigny, to set the French Scheme in motion." Cantor paused, apparently trying to control the emotion in his voice. "I saw all four of them go into the sitting chamber without their clerks and attendants and knew it was important. So I hid in the next room pretending to write a letter should anyone walk in, but no one did and I listened by pressing my ear to the connecting door. Marigny is going to finish off the Scottish royal family; Flote is to send men to Acre to create an incident that will break the truce in the Holy Land with the Turks. Nogaret's job is to get rid of the pope. I heard it all, clear as day."

Cantor's face settled into a grimace. "The French will have everything in place, my Lord. They plan for Acre to fall to the Turks in the spring of 1291. By then the Scots will be both without a king, or an heir to the throne, and there'll be a new pope, a puppet of the French."

For Otto it was all like a bad dream, one he had reviewed in his mind many times. Now that it was happening, he discovered he was actually relieved. The wait was over; it was time for action. "I can understand why you decided to come in person to tell me, but we have known…"

"The French are no longer just making plans," Cantor interrupted. "You must understand that now they are going ahead with their scheme! They have to be stopped!"

"I know, Cantor. I know. But I promise your efforts will be rewarded. Don't worry, King Philip will never conquer Europe."

"How will you stop that monster? He's just as ruthless and ambitious as his father and grandfather, but far more capable. I know him much better than you, my Lord. Believe me, this French king can become emperor."

Otto looked at the man's exhausted and anxious face. In all likelihood he had not stopped to rest or eat for the past three days. "From the day you alerted me to the French Scheme twelve years ago, I have been hard at work…Cantor, we made a bargain. You fulfilled your part, and on my honor, I will fulfill mine."

Cantor shook his head. "Please tell me how you are going to stop Philip's killers from starting a war with the Turks or doing away with the pope and Scottish royals."

"No one can. I could try and stop a French army, but not a determined killer. But I have a plan of my own once the inevitable happens."

"But I rushed over…"

"I'm sorry, Cantor, but I have to focus on what's possible. My plan will work."

"If you think that your King Edward can stop Philip, you are wrong. The French can raise an army several times the size of the English."

"Yes, I'm painfully aware of that."

Otto decided to tell Cantor everything, to give him hope; after all, the man had risked his life for the past twelve years, not to mention his present journey. "I'm going to arrange for the Knights Templar to fight the French."

Cantor's eyes flickered with either surprise or delight. "How will you do that? Part of Philip's strategy includes destroying the Templars. Are you going to save them? But how? The way Philip has it set up, there's no way."

Two weeks later Otto looked up from a parchment he had been studying as one of his clerks escorted Lord Ralph Hengham and the shire reeve, Sir Ian, into his work chamber at Westminster Palace. In the morning light coming through the narrow windows behind him, Otto tried to read their faces for the good news he had been hoping for. They both seemed pleased with themselves, and Otto's spirits rose. He dismissed his clerk with a nod, stood from his worktable and extended an open hand for the two men to approach.

Sir Ian seemed particularly excited. "William is going to Abissey Castle this summer for a week," he blurted out, forgoing social amenities.

At the words, Otto's attention shifted from studying the shire reeve's drab attire to his face. The sheriff—as they were now called—stared back at him with a glint of pride in his eyes. "You didn't think I had the means to arrange it, eh, brother?" he said.

Otto laughed as he stood and came around his worktable. What the man lacked in manners he made up with results. "I have never doubted your ability to influence people, Brother Ian. Maybe one day you can come and work for me."

"Leave the good shire reeve where he is, Otto," interjected Lord Hengham, stroking his elegant beard, "you've got enough spies working for you."

"So I'm finally going to meet William!" Otto said, pointing to the chairs in one corner of the room. "After all these years of waiting!" Otto signaled for his friend Ralph to sit next to him, and Sheriff Ian in one of the two chairs facing them.

After exchanging pleasantries with the two men, Otto decided to get to the point. "Somehow we have to convince William to leave the Cistercians and join the Templars. Any ideas?"

"We know what's at stake," Ralph Hengham said in a ponderous tone, and Otto knew that the king's chief Justice was about to go into one of his lawyerly tirades. "Without William we can't find his uncle John, Without John, there is no Jesus Gospel, and without the Gospel the Templars won't have any reason to fight the French king..."

"We know that, Ralph," interrupted Otto, "so let's hope that William is like his uncle, in which case the Brotherhood's troubles might soon be over."

Ralph nodded ever so slightly at Otto, and then turned to face Sheriff Ian. "You've kept an eye on William all these years Brother Ian, and you know him best. How can we convince him to become a Templar in the Holy Land? "

"He'll be at Abissey for about a week, that's all," Ian said, nervously switching his body in the chair and making his cheap chain mail rustle. "Each year, at summer's end, around the Feast of St. James, William's abbot sends a friar named Jules to raise money from local barons. I interceded through Bishop Gregor so that William accompanies the friar this year. That's the best I could come up with."

"And we appreciate it, Brother Ian," Ralph said soothingly. "But we'll need more than a week with William. Perhaps all we can do is meet with him and gain his trust. Then, next year..."

"Next year?" Otto exclaimed. "Ralph, William just turned twenty, and can now join the Templars. For God's sake, man, let's not waste any more time! Caesarius' prophecy says that the Templars will be driven out of the Holy Land by the end of the century. That can be anytime now!"

"What do you suggest, Otto? Force William into becoming a Templar?"

"No, of course not. I'll travel to Abissey this summer using the upcoming meeting of Parliament as my reason. I'll tell King Edward that I need to make sure the earl of Abissey is on our side. Then Brother Ian can use some excuse to introduce me to William. Of course, Ian, I don't want William to know who I am."

"Don't worry brother. I'll figure it out."

"Well, then," said Ralph, "should we succeed in convincing the lad, we should then be willing to offer him the funds necessary to travel to Outremer and join the Templars."

"Yes, of course," said Otto.

Ian shook his head vehemently. "No, no, no. Please. I thought you understood."

"Understood what, Brother Ian," asked Ralph. "Certainly you would want to make it easier…"

"Don't you see? The Caesarius Prophecy surfaced right when we needed it. That's what John taught me long ago, that those who have the inner power would manifest whatever is needed." Ian's eyes shone, and he appeared to be gaining in self-assurance, as though the words were giving him substance. "The Prophecy," continued Ian, "came because of John, he needed it. Without it he couldn't have gone searching for the Gospel. And now the Prophecy is pointing the course for his nephew. William must manifest what he needs to be in harmony with the forces behind the Prophecy, and to learn that he's like his uncle."

Otto realized that it would be useless to argue with Ian. *So be it*, he thought. If the lad couldn't raise the funds, he and Ralph could always intervene without Ian's knowledge. "Very well, Brother Ian. You seem to know what you are talking about. We'll let William fend for himself."

Ian seemed to relax. "You'll see, brother; you'll see how it works."

Otto smiled at Ian and nodded. "I look forward to our joint effort."

Ian took the hint and rose to his feet. "I'll see you at Abissey in four months, Brother Otto." He then wished them *Beauseant* and left the room.

When he heard the sheriff's steps fading down the hall, Otto turned to Ralph. "He is totally sold on the Caesarius Prophecy, eh?"

"Well, you heard him. 'The power of the Prophecy,' indeed! Selecting him twelve years ago to tell the brethren about the Prophecy was sheer genius. By now no one dares dispute its legitimacy. The French count who gave us so much trouble is now a believer, as is Bishop Gregor who has become an expert on Caesarius of Heisterbach and his prophecies. All thanks to Brother Ian's efforts. I'm just amazed that John was convinced as well, otherwise he wouldn't have taken off after the Gospel."

Otto took a long, deliberate breath. "Well, God bless them all."

"Let's just hope that William can find his uncle…I wonder, though, if William is truly up to the challenge. When we received that letter from John telling us that William could find him, we decided that it was because William was much like him. So…what should I look for in William? You told me you met John once. What was he like?"

"Yes, I met him once while in Acre," Ralph said. "I don't know how to describe him. I can't tell you exactly what it is he has, but I think you'll know if William has it as well. John's mere presence is awe inspiring, he's very serene in demeanor, but you realize that it must come from deep inside, and you feel as though you've known and loved him all your life. I've never met anyone else like him before or since. I think you'll just have to go with your instincts. If there is a Jesus Gospel, I'm sure John found it, and if William is anything like him, he's sure to follow in his footsteps."

"Very well, very well," Otto said absentmindedly. So much depended on William, so much, and the notion had always made him uneasy, from the beginning. But of course, he could always stop the process and implement his alternate plan. *There is time, there is enough time.*

"So much depends on William, Otto," Ralph said as though reading his thoughts. "What if he turns us down, or fails, what then?"

"We'll cross that river when we have to. William will come through for us, I'm sure of that."

[2]

Looking after a depraved friar was not the life William had envisioned for himself as a novice monk. Those innocent notions had ended in one painful moment, and now here he was approaching the familiar meadow, wearing the Cistercian white habit he had once coveted so much, and leading the friar's horse by the reins as his sandaled feet kicked up the road's summer dust.

But for now all is well, he told himself. *There's no temptation for Brother Jules.*

The place was just as he remembered, William noted as he tugged on the reins. He ran his gaze over the grassy expanse ringed by trees and took in the old giant oak with the huge trunk and two main branches reaching up toward the sky. The stream gurgled some fifty feet away, hidden behind a line of pine trees and a few boulders. Over the years he had stopped here at least four times with his father and brother, along with a handful of servants, on the way to London. At that moment he heard Jules cough, and William longed for the past, for any past rather than the here and now.

He recalled the last time he saw the meadow on his way to enter the abbey a little over two years before. Then he couldn't wait to don the habit and start what he thought would be a quiet life of prayer and contemplation among devoted monks. William shook his head. He had been so naive!

He wiped the perspiration from his forehead with his free hand, looked up at the sun and figured they had another three hours before dark. They could make it over the next hill, but the meadow looked cool and inviting. William was hot and sweaty under his heavy habit, and remembered that the brook ran clean. Perhaps if nothing else they could replenish their water bags and water the horse.

"Brother Guillaime, we'll stop for Nones here," Brother Jules said in French.

William led the way to the old oak wishing the friar would speak English and call him by his English name, now that they were no longer in Normandy. He found French irritating; it grated on his ears. Maybe it was the sight of the old oak, or just the sound of his superior's voice, or maybe that he just yearned for a simpler time.

William searched for a place to graze the horse and spotted a healthy patch of clover and wild oats by a large rock. He stopped the horse and took a rope from the saddlebag, tied the hackney to a tree, loosened the bridle then pulled the bit from its mouth.

"I don't remember this meadow. Are we getting close to Abissey Castle?" Brother Jules asked struggling to slide off the saddle, his face glistening with perspiration, heavy lines showing the fatigue from the day's journey.

"At our pace it will take us two more days," William waited for Brother Jules to come down from the horse then loosened the saddle's cinch. If it were up to him he could make it in a day but he knew Brother Jules could hardly move, even though he had ridden the entire way. William looked down at his dusty feet and bent down to rub a blister forming on his left heel. He made an effort to sound cordial. "There's a monastery on the way. We can spend tomorrow's night there if you wish." He knew he should pray for him, rather than wishing him gone, never born.

Brother Jules slumped down on some dry grass, with his back resting against a tree trunk. "Oh no, we'll find an inn. Brother, fetch me water for cleansing."

William reached for the two almost empty water bags looped together by the horse's neck and headed for the creek.

When he skirted a boulder he saw the two peasant boys chatting under a tree and his heart sank. Of course! That's why Brother Jules wanted to make camp. William had not seen them since noon and had hoped they had made headway or turned off somewhere.

As he came near, William desperately tried to figure out what to do about the two. He now realized Jules had kept the horse's pace to within sight of the boys, ever since spotting them that morning. William pretended to inspect the water bags as he stood a good distance away from the boys, who glanced furtively at him a couple of times, whispered to each other and continued to eat, ill at ease. He thought of ordering them to leave but was within earshot of Brother Jules. The two were barefoot, dressed in homemade trousers and tunics, rags really, of rough linen. The younger one was fair, eight or so, and without doubt the one who had caught the friar's fancy. There was little question in William's mind of

Jules' intent, not after what happened the previous night at the inn when he had
stared at the serving boy, in fact had appeared mesmerized by that very blond
child with pale blue eyes. Jules had seemed unable to take his gaze off of him,
eating his food absent-mindedly, and seemed to become agitated whenever the
server approached them, gawking up and down the young body.

Perhaps that had been the reason their abbot had ordered William to accompany Brother Jules on this year's trip. "Look after him," he had been told,
thinking he was to watch for his safety. Now it made sense.

William decided there was nothing he could do at the moment except keep
Jules away from the children. He grabbed the bags' straps in either hand and
headed toward the uneasy boys on his way to the stream behind them. When he
approached they quickly rose to their feet and bowed.

He reached the slow moving creek, shed his sandals, uncorked the leather
bags, and walked into the shallow waters. He picked up the bottom of his habit
and jacked it up to his waist to avoid getting the coarse wool wet. For a moment
he relished the feel of the water on his legs and the soothing sounds around him:
the flowing creek, the breeze, rustling leaves, bugs skimming the surface, and
the birds singing up high on the branches. He bent over, sunk the water bags
and started muttering a prayer asking for guidance. Why couldn't the world just
let him be? All he ever wanted was to pray in peace, away from all the sins and
ugliness.

But for now, how was he to protect the children? He was but a novice, and
Jules a senior friar whose orders he was sworn to obey without question.

"What's taking you so long?" he heard Jules yell, and William decided to
pray for humility and acceptance, and for God to protect the two boys.

William made his way back to their camp. When he went by the two boys,
they again stood up and bowed.

He filled Brother Jules' bowl from a water bag, and brought it to him, avoiding eye contact.

"Very good, Guillaime. Now fetch me the drying cloth."

William watched as Brother Jules dried his hands and then used the now
moist cloth to wipe his pale neck, arms and feet.

"The abbey couldn't survive without me," Jules said as he dabbed his forehead
with the cloth, " these trips of mine are what keeps the place afloat and people
like you fed." He tossed the cloth by a tree with a flick of his wrist. "Fortunately
for the abbey, my family is rich and powerful...we have ruled Brabant for over
two hundred years..." and the friar continued with his oft-repeated litany of how
closely his people were associated with the French royal family and how, had he
been out in the world, he would be in line to become the duke of that province.

Now it was just a matter of time before he became a bishop.

The sad part, William realized, was that it was all true. He looked down at the rotund figure with dough-like flesh and wished with all his heart that he would die, let out a groan, clutch his chest and die. That would be just. Why would God let it be otherwise?

"Oh, my, by all that's holy!" Jules exclaimed, looking at his right hand. "My ring, where's my ring?" At this the friar rose, walked over to the horse and anxiously reached for the backpack.

"You have to help me look! This is very important!" yelled Jules.

William loosened the straps behind the saddle and brought the heavy pack down to the ground, opened it and turned it over, emptying the contents. The friar's belongings, "the direst necessities," came tumbling out. William foraged through underwear of various thickness, bags of powders and bottles of potions, even a box of jewelry, and his own items: an extra habit and his only luxury, a *braie* he wore from his days as a squire and the object of ridicule from the other novices who considered underpants an affectation.

They spent some time looking, but there was no ring. Jules appeared anxious, nervously throwing things around, looking under the same items several times.

Heaviness in his heart told William what would come next.

"I must have left it at the inn last night. Brother, you have to go back and get it right now before some thief finds it!" Jules said, out of breath, as he looked at William wide-eyed, his almost-non-existent eyebrows frozen in an arch. "Anybody can use the ring to sign important family and Church documents on my behalf, you can't imagine the consequences! But what would someone like you, raised to be a mere knight know about these things?"

All William ever remembered writing on behalf of Brother Jules were requests for money to his family. Granted, some of it was handed over to the abbot but most destined for the purchase of "dire necessities" and apparently lavish meals, probably at the inn near the abbey.

"Brother Guillaime, I order you to go this very instant," Jules said extending a sausage arm in the direction they had just come, "and don't stop until you reach the inn and find my ring!"

William studied Jules, his jowls flapping in his excitement, and was certain that if he tore off the friar's habit and undid the pouch where he kept his money, he would find the ring inside. He had noticed that through all the wild gesticulations, Jules' attention kept going back to the spot behind the boulder where the two peasant boys sat eating.

Taking his time, hoping for someone else to stop by the meadow, or for a storm, anything, William picked up the horse's rope, a water bag, and started for the creek.

"Ride the horse as hard as you can!" Jules yelled.

William took some time to water the docile beast and momentarily thought of ordering the two boys to come with him, but under what pretext? And how? He had but the one horse. He could take one boy with him but two stood a better chance against Jules. William ran his hand along the animal's neck to determine how tired it was but the horse was young and that day's slow pace had hardly produced a sweat. He had no excuse; he had to obey Jules. The boys were in God's hands.

He fixed the saddle, refastened the bit and halter, mounted the hackney and on the way gave Brother Jules one last look. The friar stood by their pack of belongings, his feet wide apart, hands on his hips. Reluctantly, William dug his heels into the horse's sides and sent it into an easy canter, toward the inn of the night before.

William wasn't sure how long he rode, but after a while he recognized the bend on the road and the beginning of the fir forest. A few feet further down was the turnoff to the Jewish village.

At that moment the abbot's words came back to him: "Look after him!"

He brought the horse to a halt, his gaze fixed on the path leading to the village.

What was he supposed to do? The abbot's instructions could have meant many things and after all he had received specific orders from a superior—Brother Jules. And he had taken an oath of obedience, a sacred oath.

But what would happen to the boys? Hadn't he also taken an oath as a knight to care for those who couldn't defend themselves? He could keep riding on to the inn, where he would not find the ring, and then return to the meadow, apologize for returning empty handed, and pretend that nothing out if the ordinary had happened. But if he turned around and defended the boys, Brother Jules' ugly secret would be exposed.

Then he would have to bring the case to their abbot… and Brother Jules' word would be against his. The abbot would have to pay heed to Brother Jules; after all he was a highborn, a man of great rank.

William realized he had been staring without seeing, his eyes riveted on the ruts on the pathway to the Jewish village, ruts made by so many carts over the years. He felt a jolt to his heart and at that moment the old grief was back: Jacob!

That had been another time in his life when he stood by and allowed evil to take its course.

At the thought, William felt a surge of rage, turned his horse around, dug his heels hard and released the reins, prompting the hackney into a gallop. He would have hell to pay in this life, but not in the next.

But the meadow was empty. The backpack and belongings were still strewn by the oak and a few paces away the meager possessions of the two peasant boys—bread and some dried meat—lay on two old kerchiefs along with a water jug.

A sick feeling in his gut told William he better hurry.

He rode around the meadow at a brisk pace, scanning the surroundings. Of course Brother Jules would want to hide from view with the boys, but where? William's attention was drawn to a large boulder on the other side of the creek. He dismounted, ran toward the rock and as he got closer heard muffled cries.

Without breaking stride he came around the boulder and found the undressed fat man standing, a naked boy on the ground beneath him and the other boy tied to a tree.

William reached for the friar's back, his hands dug into flesh, then he pulled the heavy body back and made Jules tumble down.

Lying on his back, Jules appeared stunned and stared up at William. "Brother Guillaime!" Jules said with fear in his voice. "By God, how dare you attack me! These are mere *villeins*, can't you tell?"

William glared at Jules. "You…evil, horrid man!" He then turned his attention to the cowering little boy on the ground. William bent over and gently picked him up, brushing away the twigs and dirt that clung to his thin back. The boy clutched his hands to his chest, shaking with sobs, tears and snot running down his face. Yes, he was but a mere *villein*, a peasant, and would likely die an old man barely in his thirties, underfed and overworked, his life indentured to some farmer, weaver, or tanner.

William embraced him, trying desperately to undo the harm done to the young soul who perhaps did not fully understand what had happened. He then looked him over for signs of sexual violation but realized he didn't quite know what to look for.

"How are you, young lad? What did this man do to you?" he asked in English.

"Oh, for goodness sake, nothing happened!" Brother Jules exclaimed in French.

"Is it true that nothing happened?" William asked the child, who continued sobbing, averting his eyes. William inspected him and could see no signs of rough treatment anywhere. He felt relieved that he had arrived in time and no physical violation had taken place. He let loose of the youngster and went and untied the other sobbing boy.

He then turned to face the friar.

Brother Jules had knelt on the ground, his face looking up at the sky and began intoning a heartfelt prayer. "I thank you oh, Lord, for my Brother Guillaime, without whom I would have gravely sinned against you…" he continued, his prayer becoming more impassioned, calling himself a "worthless sinner." He then picked up a branch and proceeded to beat himself with it, first on his naked back but then all over, with greater force as he went on, until he drew blood and great welts formed all over his face and body.

William watched him, his anger subsiding, feeling respectful of Jules' act of contrition.

He turned to look at the children. The younger one was now dressed and the sobbing had stopped. The two ran to where they had left their belongings and William watched them leave the meadow as fast as they could.

Brother Jules lay prostrate, face down on the ground, arms and legs spread out in his final act of surrender to the Almighty. William knelt beside him and proceeded to pray, reciting the Paternosters of the office of Nones. He prayed with gratitude that he had arrived in time to save the boys and that obviously he had been an instrument of the Lord in changing Brother Jules' sinful ways. All is well, William told himself as the tension in his chest lifted. Now he felt guilty for thinking of Jules as evil; the friar was greatly flawed but obviously very devout.

That day and the following, the penitent Brother Jules kept on praying and whenever they stopped punished his flesh again to the point where William felt sorry and wanted to stop him. Jules' face, arms and legs showed nothing but welts, bruises and bloody wounds. But the friar kept up the self-flagellation, punctuated by prayer and mournful declarations of his horrid nature. "I'm but a monster," he said repeatedly between sobs, and then beat himself even harder.

In late afternoon of the second day after leaving the meadow, they came within sight of Castle Abissey perched on a hill in the middle of a small valley that was dotted with half a dozen white huts, each surrounded by a field defined with a low stone fence. They were going past one of the huts and a heavy smell of burning dung wafted through the air. Cooking smoke poured from the only opening, the door. It appeared as though itchy pigs had rubbed away the white wash on one spot of the squat, thatched-roof structure, exposing the hardened mud and some of the wooden lattice.

William could hear the yells of shepherds gathering their flocks in the distance, and the sharp barks of their dogs reverberating through the still air.

Brother Jules came down from the horse and insisted on furthering his penance by walking the rest of the way barefoot, humbly staying behind the hackney.

William continued on foot, leading the horse by the reins, for it wouldn't be seemly for him to ride with his superior on foot. They slowly covered the half league or so to the fortress and in the twilight watched as the heavy doors opened before them into the outer bailey, where the commander of the guard met them accompanied by two armed men.

William was about to speak when Brother Jules ran out panting from behind the horse. "Oh, my man, grace fall upon you, please protect me!" he said in heavily accented English.

A bewildered William could only look on as Jules continued: "Please let me see your lord, tell him I implore his protection from this crazed man who attacked me most savagely!" Jules said as he pointed wildly at William, then turned to face the commander. "I am Jules of Saint Simeon, count of Laverne, brother of the duke of Brabant, and presently a humble Cistercian friar serving at the Abbey of Sobern. Your lord knows me well."

The officer, who had been studying the friar's wounds, ordered his guards to arrest William, who stood in silent surprise, and as his hands were shackled, looked at Jules and noticed a quick flash of satisfaction in his eyes.

The soldier holding William by the shackles seemed unsure. "This isn't right," he said hesitantly.

The commander came to stand but a foot from the guard then brought his face to within inches of his subordinate's. "Sergeant," he said in a rough whisper, "one of the earl's friends, the brother of a duke, has been attacked, and he's told us who did it. That's all we need to know."

The guard took William to the dungeon, while the officer escorted the limping and moaning Brother Jules in the direction of the castle keep.

[3]

Otto stared at Sheriff Ian, going over what he had just heard. "William is in the dungeon because he attacked the friar to protect two *villein* boys, but the friar claims William attacked him out of envy of his nobler rank?"

"Yes, brother," replied Ian. The two spoke in hushed tones as they walked along the main hallway on the ground floor on their way to the dungeon, for all around them were signs of Castle Abissey bedding down for the night, as knights, servants, and minor guests gathered in the great hall to find a place to sleep. The early ones had located the best spots with reeds or hay free of dirt, grease or food droppings, which they piled up to make mattresses. Others were busy shaking their blankets to rid them of as many lice and fleas as they could. "That's not like William at all," continued Ian. "Besides, I can tell the friar hurt himself using a stick. I've seen injuries in my life, and that's plain to me." Ian stopped and held Otto by the arm, then looked him in the eyes. "I'm sure the friar would have killed the two *villein* boys had it not been for William."

"This entire affair is quite astonishing," Otto said. "I don't know what to make of it all. I'm glad to hear that William finally arrived, but now he's a prisoner? That's bizarre. But you say we can visit him in his cell and talk to him in private?"

"Yes, of course, brother; that's where we're going right now. I have access to the earl's dungeon, and with your authority we should be able to do anything we want. But we best hurry, the friar will try to do away with William any way he can."

Ian led the way down the narrow stairs leading to the prison cells under the castle. "The earl of Abissey is not a powerful baron, so he must stay in King Edward's good graces," Ian said as he made his way carefully. "Brother, you could demand just about anything and the earl would trip over himself trying to comply." At the bottom of the stairs they found a guard who handed Ian his torch, and he guided Otto through a maze of corridors to a guard's post, a small room with spy holes to the four adjoining cells. Ian pointed to one of the holes. "I thought you may want to observe William first, before meeting with him."

Otto bent over and looked through the slot in the stonework. The sole source of light in William's cell came through a metal grill on his door, a torch casting a grid pattern on the opposing wall. To the left was a cot of rough timbers and next to it Otto saw a young monk kneeling on the damp stone floor, a likely knight judging by his big, strong body and noble bearing; of black hair and dark complexion. In the young man's pleasing features he discerned strength but also that peace that only the very devout have.

Otto noted that William was praying. Not pacing, not hitting the walls in anger, not any of the myriad of things people did when unjustly imprisoned, but in an apparent state of grace. It was obvious that circumstances had brought out William's true spirit. He was a sincere monk, and without question, Brotherhood material. The fact that he was willing to sacrifice everything to protect two *villein* boys was proof.

After some time Otto heard footsteps outside, then the sound of a key opening the door of William's cell. In walked a guard and a rotund monk. Otto asked Ian in a whisper whether that was Brother Jules.

Ian peered through the slot. "That's him."

Otto followed the proceedings with keen interest. Jules ordered the guard to wait outside the door.

"I've come to offer you my services as confessor and to extend my forgiveness," Jules said, loud enough for the guard to hear.

William continued praying.

Jules sat down on the cot and switched to a whisper, inaudible to the guard but one Otto could make out by pressing his ear against the opening. "They will execute you in the morning. The earl has no patience for those who assault men of noble rank."

Jules fumbled in his habit and produced a knife, which he placed on the cot beside him. "I've taken pity on you and decided to let you end your life by your own hands. After all, you were a knight, and your station deserves a more dignified end than to be flailed alive and quartered by horses in public view."

Jules rose, and louder now, intoned the rites of absolution ending with a prayer. He then left in haste, perhaps unsettled by William who had not moved the entire time.

Otto couldn't keep from chuckling. Jules was indeed a horrid man, but you had to admire his cunning. The average twenty-year old might have believed Jules' threat, that the earl would execute him for such an offense. In reality, local barons would not dare touch a member of the Church and could only refer him to his abbot. Jules had used the confession excuse to gain access to William, but only priests heard confessions; obviously the guard wouldn't know that. Then the whole thing with the knife. That was brilliant. Chances were that William would attack a guard with it to try to escape and most likely be overwhelmed by the guards who might kill him in the process. Desperate men did such things. How Jules would explain the presence of a knife in the cell after his visit was something else. Perhaps he was desperate himself and was taking inordinate steps to ensure William died that very night, before he could tell people what happened on the road. It was clear Jules didn't know that Ian had already talked to William.

Otto pulled away from the spy hole and approached Ian who stood a few feet away. "You say Jules was planning on killing those two boys? How do you know?"

"Every year, around this time, we've found at least one crucified child."

"Oh my! But of course, now I remember. You brought the matter to the Brotherhood a while back…it has been going on for several years. It makes perfect sense. After having his way with a boy, what better way to silence him than to crucify him? That way the Jews are to blame." That was one of the infamous crimes the Jews were blamed for through the centuries, crucifying Christian children. In addition the Jews were suspect of poisoning wells and causing mass famine. "That friar is very clever…and evil." The Brotherhood would have to deal with him; they couldn't allow a man that wicked to go on. But first things first. "William is indeed an admirable young man, and thanks to Brother Jules, he's probably ready to leave the Cistercians and could be talked into joining the Templars. But you have to do it."

"Me? But…"

"Ian, this incident is a godsend. William knows what the friar was planning to do with those boys and he's in turmoil; disappointed in his order, and questioning whether he made the right choice. If you escort him back to his abbot, you'll have about eight days to convince him to join the Templars."

"I suppose…"

"Yes, Ian. First, go into his cell and let William know that you are involved. And please remove the knife Jules left behind on the cot. I will speak with the earl. This is the king's affair because the friar is a foreign highborn and the earl will assume that I'm trying to avoid an incident with the French court. I'll notify the earl that you will escort William as your prisoner and the friar as his accuser back to their abbey in Normandy. However, as soon as you can arrange it, let's make Jules disappear."

"Yes, Brother Otto," Ian said as he turned around and headed out the door.

Otto watched as Ian entered the young man's cell.

"William, It's me, Sheriff Ian."

At this William rose.

"You will be sent back to your abbot to be dealt with, along with the friar." Ian said as he bent over to pick up the knife from the cot. "I will be escorting you both."

[4]

Once the sheriff left his cell, William took a moment to compose himself. He was still reeling from Jules' visit; the friar's sickness had been so obvious, his intentions transparent. William let out a sigh. The prison cell was quiet, and now he could pray for as long as he wanted without interruption.

He prayed, and once again felt a sense of grace, and he focused on the joy growing in his heart. He knew that all would be well as long as he could feel that; nothing else really mattered.

The following morning, William was brought before the earl who stood surrounded by a number of guards in the inner bailey on top of the stairs leading to the castle keep. Two steps below him stood Brother Jules, his scant hair slick with oil, looking rested and at ease. He turned to look at William and seemed upset, but then shrugged his shoulders and stared at the earl with a faint smile on his face. Sheriff Ian was to one side of the stairs, waiting with arms folded.

"William Montfort," said the short and thin earl still wearing his night robe, "you have heinously assaulted a man of high birth." William noted the pleasure on the friar's face at the words. "But it's not for me to mete out punishment, that is your abbot's responsibility. I am ordering the sheriff to escort you back to your abbey."

"No!" Exclaimed Jules.

The earl turned to the friar. "Jules, this is an inconvenience, but you must go as well to bear witness against your subordinate, this William."

Jules approached the earl and whispered anxiously in his ear, but the earl kept shaking his head. Jules resumed his place and stared at the ground until the earl dismissed everyone and William was escorted back to his cell.

That afternoon William heard from the guards that no one could account for Jules. By evening, the earl ordered an extensive search and during that night his soldiers looked throughout the castle, in farms, in the two neighboring villages, but found no trace of the friar.

Before sunrise a guard escorted William out of his cell to the outer bailey and handed him over to the sheriff.

"It'll be just the two of us, William," Sheriff Ian said as he led him to the friar's horse. "It appears Brother Jules decided not to go back to the abbey but make his way in the world."

They started out of the castle with the sun peeking over a hill, William riding his horse, his shackled hands in front of him holding the reins. He was relieved that he would not have to bear the friar's presence but was concerned about other potential victims. Well, he had done all that he could. Obviously no one had believed his story, and William doubted the abbot would, but that was fine, he was at peace. He would suffer whatever punishment with gladness; it was as though the Lord had given him this one chance to make up for Jacob by protecting the two boys. William imagined that his abbot would sentence him to solitary confinement with only bread and water for a few months. No duties except prayer. That would be grand. And after that? Well, that was in God's hands.

At noon they stopped at a crossroads. "We'll rest here," the sheriff said as he dismounted. "I'm waiting to meet someone, then we can go."

Eventually a party of about twelve men on horseback approached them. The man heading the group wore a houpellande, a robe much like William had seen on his own earl, but fancier yet, for this one was made entirely of scarlet cloth, which he had seen before in thin strips in ladies' dresses. The man rode a beautiful white palfrey of smooth gait, the type of riding horse William had only heard about. Two clerks and several men-at-arms followed the obviously important lord, who stopped and dismounted.

The sheriff and the lord ambled far from the road, as though going for a stroll, the sheriff respectfully falling behind.

[5]

Otto turned around. They were safely out of sight and earshot from his clerks and guards. "How did it go with Jules?"

"He resisted, but is unhurt," replied Ian. "He'll be safe in a prison cell in the island by nightfall."

"Good, my friend. We've done well in the sight of God. I'm just glad we caught him. What about William? Have you talked to him?"

Ian shook his head. "Not yet, brother. I was waiting until we gained some distance from the castle and any prying ears and eyes."

"Ian, you realize the events of these past days were a miracle? Make the best of this journey. Please.

"Mention John to William and convince him to become a Templar. Don't mention Hafiz Mountain or the Jesus Gospel, it's too early for that. You may tell him of the Caesarius Prophecy if the need arises.

"I already sent an urgent letter to Bishop Gregor requesting that he contact William's abbot so William can transfer to the Templars. The abbot will be made to think that William is being forced to join the Templars as punishment."

"I'll make sure that William is ready."

"We also need someone to guide his steps once he becomes a Templar."

"I would choose Brother Hughes," Ian said without hesitation. "Both of us served with William's uncle at Tortosa."

"I take it Hughes is a member of the Brotherhood and not just a Templar?"

"Of course. And he's a tough and capable man. He'll protect and guide William like no one else. I recently heard that he's now a commander."

Otto nodded. "I'll make the arrangements so that Commander Hughes meets William in Outremer. That's a relief. I was concerned about William getting killed in combat…"

"If you knew John, you wouldn't say that." Interrupted Ian.

"Why? William will be fighting. You are telling me that John can protect him?"

"He might, but that's not what I meant. If William is anything like John, nothing can happen to him, unless he allows it."

"Really? How does that work?"

"I don't know, brother. I just know it does. I was with John in many battles and the only time he was wounded was to teach me a lesson. The man is beyond our understanding."

Otto sighed. "Sounds like quite an amazing man. *Beauseant*, Brother Ian."

"*Beauseant*, Brother Otto. Until we meet again."

[6]

William, sitting cross-legged on the ground with his back against a tree, watched the sheriff and the lord approach the group. The lord's men, some of whom were supposed to be guarding him but had ambled about, quickly scrambled to stand by their horses.

William noticed the lord scrutinizing him as he came near. When their eyes met the lord seemed to smile ever so subtly.

"I beg your leave, my Lord," the sheriff said as he bowed.

The lord did not respond but waved his hand in dismissal. He then climbed on his horse and rode with his entourage on the way to London.

After they were gone, the sheriff walked to where William sat. He undid William's shackles and smiled. "William, I am a friend of your uncle John. We served together as Knights Templar in Outremer."

"My uncle? You knew my uncle John?"

"Yes, son. Let me introduce myself." He extended his ungloved hand. "I'm Sir Ian Duval, in the king's service as shire reeve of Devonshire.

"And by the way, William, you are not a prisoner. I believe your story."

As William took the sheriff's hand he studied the man. He noted that Sir Ian was perhaps in his forties, had gray hair, a well-lined face with a number of scars. His eyes caught William's attention, for they were kind, and he seemed a frank and honest man, of lean body and medium height. He wore an old but service-able hauberk of mended chain mail under a green tunic. A heavy, well-maintained sword hung inconspicuously by his side, as though a part of his body. His head was covered with only a mail hood. There was no helmet, nor shield. Either he had become careless, or was particularly skillful and sure of himself. There was no sign of his family's heraldic coat of arms. His warhorse was an aging Percheron he treated with familiarity. Obviously man and beast knew each other well.

"At what point did you believe me?" William asked.

"From the moment I laid eyes on you. Not only did I remember you, but I also heard the friar's tale and sensed it was false."

"Have we met before?"

"When you were a child. I visited your father once and helped place you and your brother at the earl of Sheffield's household."

William and Sir Ian walked their horses in silence for some time. They were in no hurry now, William thought.

For the following three days, in casual conversation, Sir Ian told William about his uncle—how they had met as young men in the Holy Land, how they fought together for seven years, and forged a close friendship. In his eyes John was a saint, an extraordinary man of mysterious ways, whose purpose in life seemed to be on a higher plane. Ian described how John healed people with his hands. "A friend of ours was dying after being poisoned. John touched his stomach and within a day our friend was well. And he healed many others. But he performed other amazing feats. One time he walked unarmed and alone into a Saracens' camp, and they were so impressed by him that their emir became his friend."

"You talk about him as though he's dead. Did he die?""

Sir Ian stared at the ground lost in thought. "He went on a mission eleven years ago and never made it back, but we received word from him and know that he's alive."

"Where? What happened?"

Sir Ian shrugged his shoulders. "He's an amazing man. You'll meet him one day." Then he told more stories about him, and that led to talk about the Templars and their strict code of honor, as well as their discipline and devotion. "Death in battle," Sir Ian told William, "becomes unimportant, just another thing that happens, and honor and duty is all you care about; you realize that the dedication and devotion reflected in your actions is enriching you beyond measure."

"A life of discipline and devotion is why I became a monk," William said. "But I can't stay in an order that allows people like Brother Jules to be a part of it." In saying this William knew he was uttering words he had not yet told himself. "And I know there are at least two other friars just like him."

"Yes, I know the story," Sir Ian said. "The other two friars are also rich, noble, and waiting for a chance to go somewhere more comfortable, but meantime living a life with as much luxury as possible while they 'put in time' for appearances' sake. The abbot and the Cistercians have to make accommodations to survive and that includes making room for the rich and powerful who want the Church for their own ends.

"You won't find that in the Templars."

It occurred to William that Sir Ian was trying to recruit him, and he thought about what becoming a Templar would mean. They were monks, and that was grand, they had a reputation for honor and discipline, but also as fierce warriors, and that meant killing. And that was a dark thought. Maybe he could join them as a scholar.

He noticed a man and a woman coming on foot in their direction, carrying bundles on their backs. "I have a notion that Brother Jules didn't just leave on his own accord, did he?"

Ian shot William an appreciative glance. "You are right. He's in a place where he can't harm anyone. The Templars have a prison on an island not far from here where they keep criminals like the friar; those that the world put up with because of their power and influence. They'll try to change Jules' ways through prayer."

"I've never heard of anything like it." William noted that the couple carrying firewood hugged the side of the road in deference to Sir Ian, although still a good distance away. "Is that what Templars do? Does that mean that you are still a Templar?"

"I no longer wear the habit—the surcoat with the red cross—but once you take the oath you always remain a Templar. Now I serve in secret. There are many of us in key places. What happened with you and Jules involved four of us. We took care so both you and Jules ended up where you belong."

The couple never lifted their eyes from the ground as they went past, apparently concerned about making eye contact with a knight.

Things started to make sense to William...the lord's smile, Ian's flowery descriptions of the Templars for the past three days and the constant talk about his uncle. It wasn't merely the talk from an elder to someone trying to decide what to do with his life. "Where I belong? Does that mean you and the other Templars have plans for me?"

"Yes."

"So you being at Abissey with that lord, that was planned?"

"Yes. We wanted to find a way to talk to you. But when we learned that you had been made prisoner, the opportunity was clear. I would escort you to your abbot and on the way talk you into joining the Templars so you can search for your uncle."

In utter surprise, William laughed. The proposition was too direct and blunt, the premise bizarre. "You are hoping I will become a Templar and go to the Holy Land so I can find my uncle John?" The words when spoken did sound peculiar, but he felt excited like never before. William stared at Sir Ian in wonder. It was all so odd. "Why would I be able to find him? Why can't others look for him? Where is he?"

"I don't know William. He sent us a letter after he disappeared saying that he couldn't make it back, but that you could find him. That was over ten years ago. We've been waiting for you to come of age ever since.

"His ways are beyond the rest of us...if he believed you alone could find him, that must be the case."

Sir Ian mounted and William followed suit. It was close to noon but the day was overcast and cool. The road ahead meandered down into a valley. Two boys trotted past them also carrying firewood, apparently trying to catch up with the couple and William knew they would soon tire and have to stop. He blessed them in his thoughts and hoped they would be forever safe.

Sir Ian pulled out some bread and dried meat from his saddlebag and gave half to William.

William ate the chunks of heavily salted dried beef and the bread that was by now stale and hard. He often wondered how smoothly things had gone in his life and had marveled at his good fortune: first as squire when he sorely needed a horse, and his earl had suddenly offered one; then as a knight when the earl gifted him armor; and then when he wanted to become a monk and the earl agreed so readily. Now it was clear: Sir Ian had gone to a lot of trouble for him, and it was touching that he cared; most surprising though, was the reason why. Sir Ian was part of a society of powerful men who tried to do good in the world, and they needed him.

At the realization, William's heart felt even lighter than on the day he decided to become a monk. It was as though destiny had mapped out a course. He couldn't be a Cistercian anymore; that was behind him, and becoming a Templar was certainly worth considering. "I assume," William said, "that back when I asked the earl of Sheffield for his leave to become a monk and he agreed, you had something to do with it?"

"No, lad, for that I chose a former Templar who is the earl's superior and someone he greatly admires."

William smiled broadly. "It's so unbelievable that all of these people whom I've never met want to help me!"

"That's because I told them you would become a Templar and find John."

"What made you so sure I would accept?"

Sir Ian smiled. "You will. In fact, you just did."

And William realized Sir Ian was right. Somehow he would have to reconcile his soul with killing. Knights don't become scholars, they remain knights; and something inside told him he had to find his uncle John. But just as important, he knew that Ian was the kind of monk he would want to be near. If there were more Templars like him, then that's where he belonged. Besides, his uncle had chosen the Templars, and he was a saint.

"Sir Ian, why do you and the others want to find my uncle? Obviously you have gone to a lot of trouble to make sure I do. But why me? "

"I know you have many questions, William. I'll tell you what I know, but we have time, lad. Things will become clear in due time. I promise."

They rode for some time, chatting about a cloistered life, and the friends they had left behind. Sir Ian held the reins loose, allowing his horse to set its own pace. "I saw you here and there over the years, William. You seemed like a happy child, were you not?" he asked suddenly.

William shook his head and instinctively looked up to find a magnificent hawk with wings outstretched. "I felt different from those around me: my parents, my brother Richard, the other squires. I wanted nothing to do with war and violence, but in their eyes those things were as natural as that hawk flying overhead carrying a rat. When people go to fairs they are used to games where cats, dogs, and pigs are clobbered, strangled, stoned, shot with arrows…and they think it's all very amusing. I cried for days after my parents took me to my first fair, and my father wanted to beat me because he thought I was so strange. In my eyes the world is sick. Do you understand what I'm saying?"

Sir Ian had been staring at the bird with its prey, now disappearing into a clump of trees. "Did you have any friends, someone who thought like you?"

"Only one person, a Jew named Jacob."

The road was now empty of travelers. In the distance they could hear a farmer calling his cows.

"You befriended a Jew?"

"Yes. Of course I had to keep it secret, but he was the one who taught me to read and write."

"You know how to read and write?"

"Yes. The other squires used to tease me by saying that I had all the makings of a merchant."

"You are a most unusual man. Please do tell me about Jacob."

William stared at the ground "He was a cobbler who lived in the Jewish village off this very road. My father's lands were within his rounds and he would stop first in the village and then come by our house. Jacob would drive his cart by the river on the other side of an apple orchard from my father's manor, so as not to disturb us. He traveled with his family, a wife and two children, a daughter about my age and a son about a year older. He would spend whatever time he needed to make or fix our shoes, gloves, and saddles, always using the best leathers. For my mother he made shoes so soft, they felt like butter in your hands and light as feathers.

"One day—I must have been around seven—I approached his cart to watch him work. I noticed his daughter sitting by his side reading aloud from a book. I got curious and looked over her shoulder and was mystified by the words on the page which she could decipher with such ease. The story she was reading was very interesting. It was about a warrior who after many adventures comes home disguised as a beggar, so his wife doesn't recognize him. She has many suitors, because her husband is presumed dead. She still loves her husband and decrees that he who can draw his bow will marry her. Everyone tries, but it is a big bow and requires great strength. Everyone fails except for her husband.

"I was enthralled by the story and asked if I could come back to hear some more stories.

"Instead, Jacob started to teach me how to read—I mean at that very moment. And I came back every day. Two weeks later, as he was about to leave, he handed me the one book his daughter was reading and told me I could keep it until he came by again."

"A cobbler who was also a scholar. Don't you think it odd?"

William patted his horse's neck. "I eventually learned that's not uncommon for Jews or Muslims. Only Christians seem to be terribly ignorant. However, Jacob was unique. He had been sent to Spain as a child by his father to live with his uncle, and was trained as a physician. Jacob returned to England to live with his family but could only work as a cobbler, his father's occupation, because Jews are forbidden from engaging in the higher trades."

"Go on."

"The next time he came he had books for me; not scrolls, but codices; fine vellum sheets bound in covers. Oh, how I loved to read! I had to hide the books in the barn, way up high in the loft where no one but the bats and barn cats would go. And so it was I learned to read in French, English, Greek and Latin. To this day I can read Greek and Latin but I have never spoken them.

"Jacob also showed me how to use an abacus. After that I was learning mathematics, but not just the counting of merchants, but geometry, and what the Arabs call 'al-jabr.'

"He taught me for five years. My family was unaware, at least not until much later when all of us squires were told to attend talks in the wintertime by visiting scholars who talked about math, natural science, the arts, music; that's when everyone found out just how much I knew. While my brother Richard and the others were struggling with the basics, I was trying to engage the scholars to find out if there was anything they could teach me that I didn't already know. There wasn't.

"Mine were the secrets of the ancients, their knowledge, their stories, their poems, the beauty of so many minds and I wondered how and why there had been such people, so great, and why there was no one like them anymore.

"Jacob said such was the fate of Christianity, to live in the shadow of greatness, for the Christians had abandoned learning in the fanaticism of the fourth century, but not so for Jews and Muslims who inherited the rich trove of knowledge from the Romans."

"What happened in the fourth century?" Sir Ian asked.

"It was all because of the then Roman Emperor, Constantine," William said. "He was an astute politician who wanted to strengthen his grip on power. He decided to first have the Church declare that Jesus was the Son of God, the only son of God. We now take that for granted, but actually that was a major step that changed the world...at the time many considered Jesus a rabbi, a spiritual teacher, but Constantine wanted Jesus to be much more, as great or greater than any pagan god. He aligned himself with a Christian sect that held his views, and declared the others heretical. That accomplished, he proceeded to make Christianity the official religion of the Empire. Oh, there was the usual tale of how he had won a battle through divine intervention; but at any rate, he consolidated his power because by then Christians were numerous. Constantine also defined the New Testament of the Bible—the four gospels—and ordered that all other gospels, well over a hundred, be burned, because those said that Jesus was human. Christian hordes started ransacking the great Roman libraries, going after everything that was not the official Bible, destroying the knowledge accumulated by the Greeks and the Romans over all those centuries. However, Christian monks in charge of the Library of Alexandria took what they could to the desert and handed it over to the Arabs."

Ian stared at William and appeared thoughtful, not shocked or amazed as William thought he would be.

"It seems Jacob taught you a lot."

They came over a hill and found a shepherd with his flock blocking the road. The man tried anxiously to get his animals out of the way. William dismounted, gave his reins to Ian and helped the shepherd usher his animals through a narrow gate in the stone fence. When they were done, and while the man kept bowing awkwardly at him, William noticed Sir Ian's approving gaze as he mounted his horse.

"Yes, Jacob taught me a lot," continued William. "But it wasn't until I was twelve that he had me read the most important books. I recall two in particular, one by the Muslim Averroes and the other by the Jew Maimonides—both lived in Spain about a hundred years ago. I was impressed and saddened by reading them: impressed by their wide knowledge and wisdom and saddened because those were the kind of people we didn't have and I wondered what our lives would be like if we did.

"Since then I have read books by some noted Christian scholars—Saint Augustine, Peter Abelard, and the Dominican Tomasso di Aquino—all truly brilliant, but their writings seemed trite compared to the likes of Averroes and Maimonides. Even the stories literate monks read at the abbey were silly adventures and romances, nothing like the intricate and wonderful stories I read as a child.

"I asked Jacob where he got his books and he said from the Arabs in Spain who had all the books from the ancients, all the knowledge on earth."

"But books are very expensive, how did he get to own them?"

"Oh, he didn't. He told me that books were passed around within the Jewish community. He thought I deserved to read them as well."

"Sounds like a wonderful man whom you loved deeply. What happened to him?"

William felt a lump in his throat and knew he would break down if he tried to talk. He got down from his horse, took the reins in his left hand and walked down the empty road that stretched in between two wooded hills. Sir Ian followed on his horse. After some time William felt composed, stopped and turned around to look at Sir Ian. "I was fifteen at the time and had come home with my brother for Michaelmas. At the breakfast table I heard from my father that the Jews had kidnapped and sacrificed another Christian boy. My father said the Jews did this for their secret rites, catch a Christian child and crucify him or her, and they did this often, for children were found thus from time to time and people knew what had happened."

William took a deep breath. "That afternoon town folk came to our house with pitchforks, axes, and sickles, ready to raid the Jewish village in retribution. My father armed himself and joined the other knights, merchants, farmers, and peasants, and marched on to the Jewish village.

"I could only watch them from my chamber window, knowing full well that Jews did not commit such crimes, because I knew one such Jew and he would never, ever, possibly do such a thing. But all I could do was pray, other than that I did nothing. I did nothing."

"William, I understand, and I'm sorry. Was Jacob slain?"

"Yes, along with his family. I ran across his cart the following day on my way back to the castle. My brother, who was riding with me, pointed to the cart and the bodies strewn around it and laughed, saying how we now needed to find another cobbler."

"I don't know that you could have done anything to prevent the killings, William. You were but a boy."

"I already knew how to wield sword and lance."

"Would you have wielded them against your own kin?"

William resumed his brisk walk. "I think not. But at least I could have stood before them, stopped them, and perhaps I could have reasoned with them."

Sir Ian spurred his horse, passed William, blocked his path and turned to face him. "William, you went through a lot at a young age. I can understand what you were seeking in the abbey. You are right; the Jews are innocent of such crimes, and I know because I have dealt with many as a Templar and some I can call 'brother.' There are also Muslims I can call thus."

William stared at Sir Ian. "But the Templars fight the Muslims in the Holy Land and the Dominican inquisitors go after Jews. They are considered enemies of Christ, enemies of the Church."

"Do you believe that?"

"No, not even as a child before I met Jacob. It's never been a truth for me."

Ian smiled at him. "That's part of the reason why we want you to join us."

William walked in silence for some time, and then spoke, almost as if to himself. "If the Jews are not to blame for the crucifixion killings of Christian children, then who is committing those horrible crimes? And why?"

"Oh, son, I'm afraid you already know the answer."

William looked Sir Ian in the eyes, his gaze searching, pondering.

"Oh, my Lord, have mercy!" he exclaimed. "Of course. That's what Brother Jules was planning to do with the two boys to keep them quiet; otherwise he would have a whole village coming after him.

"I wonder how many times that's happened?"

"Much too often, my friend, by many others like Jules. I am willing to wager that when the young boy was found crucified, which prompted the citizens in your father's fief to kill Jews, someone like Brother Jules was somewhere in the vicinity.

"William, you just avenged your Jacob."

William entered the eatery a short distance from the abbey where he had agreed to meet Sir Ian after seeing his abbot. The public house was better than average, still wattle and daub, but with a wooden floor covered with clean reeds, glass windows instead of shutters or waxed cloth, and tables and benches made of hardy oak rather than fir. It was past dinnertime and just a handful of patrons sat drinking ale, beer, cider, and hot, spiced wine. Ian had picked the one table by the window and William noticed that he had ordered meat pie, roasted apples and ale for both.

Sir Ian looked up. "Are you now Sir William?"

"I am," William said as he took a seat facing Sir Ian and looked self-consciously at his new attire: a tunic, hose and shoes the draper brother had given him. "I have some friends I wish I could have said farewell to, but the abbot made me swear that I wouldn't."

"And you are not to mention anything about Jules to anyone."

"Yes, I swore to that as well."

"But he released you from the Cistercians. Was that difficult?"

"I had to promise that I would join the Templars, that way I remain a monk."

Ian pulled out a pouch and handed William six gold coins. "This is enough for a hackney, a cheap sword, and some provisions for the road," he told him. "You will return home a poor knight but a knight nevertheless."

Sir Ian took a long, thoughtful sip of ale from his mug. "You have until April to board a Templar galley bound for Outremer. This is August, so you have seven months at home to outfit yourself and raise the money you need. I figured three hundred English pounds would do to buy a quality hauberk, a sword, a destrier with saddle and mail protection, your space in the galley, plus the hundred and fifty pounds of gifting every knight is expected to provide when joining the Order."

William stared at the coins in his hand. "I need to join some tournaments, then. My father doesn't have that kind of money."

Sir Ian appeared to be thinking and kept shaking his head. Then he smiled broadly. "Many have tried to make their fortunes that way, but few have succeeded. No matter, I'm certain you'll find a way."

He sipped his ale in silence for some time. "You did a great service by helping us catch Jules," he said. "Unfortunately the world is full of people like him. And that's one of the main reasons the likes of us join the Templars, to seek refuge from such people… but also to fight them. And fight them you will. Great things await you in the Holy Land. I believe you will find your uncle and do many things you can't yet imagine, but that will be just the beginning. Your real challenge will be to help the Templars survive."

William took a bite of pie then washed the greasy taste with the dark and bitter ale. "Help the Templars survive? Me? Why do you say that?"

"Because of a prophecy by a famous seer, Caesarius of Heisterbach."

William pinched pieces of pie absentmindedly. "He was a Cistercian monk, a scholar who wrote about miracles…but yes, he made some predictions…mostly about the end of the world, I think."

"This is a secret prophecy he gave only to us. It's very important, William."

"Will there be war?"

"There's always war. No, that's the least of our worries. There are forces gathering for the destruction of our Knights Templar."

"By whom? And why?"

Sir Ian cleared his throat. "According to Caesarius, by the end of this century all Christian armies will be driven out of the Holy Land by the Turks, and shortly after, the Templars will be attacked by the French king. And that is why we are asking you to search for your uncle, before any of that happens. He has the means to save the Order."

"What does my uncle have that can save the Templars?"

"I don't know, William, but he does. Very important people believe this."

"Why would the French king want to destroy the Templars?"

"It's nothing new. It has happened throughout history. The world at large lives in darkness, but there is always a group endowed with great understanding and they are persecuted for it. That's what happened with the Cathars. They were a peaceful people who lived in the Languedoc region of southern France a hundred years ago. They believed that God resides within all of us, and that we can be one with Him without Church or priests, by simply going inside. They too had embraced Jews and Muslims. For this, the pope and the king of France saw to it that most of the Cathars were killed three decades ago, in 1254. The Templars were able to save some by hiding them. There are still a few in small villages in the Pyrenees, but the Dominican inquisitors are determined to kill them all.

"The Sultanate of Granada is the only place left where Jews, Muslims and Christians live in harmony, where people can believe and practice what they wish, but it's just a matter of time before they too are conquered by the fanatics…either Christian or Muslim."

William nodded. "Jacob told me about the Cathars and Moorish Spain. You say that I will find that type of tolerance in the Templars?"

Sir Ian started on a roasted apple with obvious relish. "Not all Templars," he said in between bites. "I'm talking about a group within the Order. They, like the Cathars, believe we all have God inside and that we are all brothers."

Sir Ian stopped eating and looked at William with concern. "You must keep this a secret, William."

"I promise, Sir Ian. I'll keep what you told me to myself."

"Wait until one of your uncle's friends approaches you, and talks as we have, openly about all matters. Then you can speak freely."

"You mean a member of the group within the Templars you told me about?"

"A friend of your uncle's. Until then don't say anything to anyone."

Ian stood and extended his hand. "*Beauseant*, William."

William shook Sir Ian's hand. "Be whole?"

"It's the Templars' salutation and battle cry, as well as the name we've given our flag, the black and white. In time it'll all make sense to you."

[7]

Otto walked into the chief justice's chambers at Westminster Palace, as usual, unannounced, dismissing Lord Hengham's clerks attempt to follow protocol by showing him in.

He found Ralph at his table amid a mountain of documents. Two big oil lamps burned bright, throwing shadows on his patrician features.

"You look very pleased with yourself, Otto. Success?"

"Beyond my dreams, Brother Ralph," Otto said as he sat on a chair across the table from his friend. "Two days ago I received word from Brother Ian. William is on his way home to gather funds for his journey to Outremer."

Ralph chuckled. "Let's hope that Ian is right, and he can manifest what he needs. But otherwise, we'll step in, right?

"Of course."

"Well, then, let us pray that William survives being a Templar. Have you thought what to do should he die in combat?"

Otto smiled. "You should hear Ian's answer to that question, Ralph. Apparently if he's anything like his uncle John, that can't happen."

"Oh, my. The power of the Prophecy, eh? But seriously, between you and me, suppose William gets killed in combat. According to Ian that will prove that he's not like his uncle after all…and leaves your plan in shambles. What would you do if he dies?"

"Ralph, that's always a possibility for any of us. We do the best we can and leave the rest to God." Otto felt a twinge of remorse, which he disguised with a knowing smile. There was no way he could divulge his alternate plan.

Ralph leaned back in his chair and bit his lower lip, a sure sign of concern, thought Otto.

"Just curious, Otto. Do you ever feel guilty for concocting this whole affair?"

Otto shook his head. "Only briefly, at the beginning, eleven years ago, when we learned that John had gone looking for the Jesus Gospel and then disappeared. The thought that such a good man might die because of a plan of my making bothered me beyond imagining. But then again, the French must be stopped and we need the Jesus Gospel to do it, you know that, Ralph. Otherwise what would become of the Templars? The moment they get thrown out of the Holy Land they would lose their reason for being; no longer fighting for a holy cause, they would become just another contemplative order. Then the French king could round them up like sheep."

"You are right on that regard, Otto. But we lied to the Brotherhood, and used that poor shire reeve, Sir Ian, to do our dirty work. I feel terrible!"

"Ralph, how else could we have alerted the Brotherhood about the French king's ambitions? Had I walked into a Brotherhood meeting and simply told them, they would not have believed me, and because I'm one of King Edward's close friends and counselors, they would have had reason to suspect my motives. The Prophecy was the only way."

Ralph played with his signet ring, apparently still ill at ease. "I still think we should try and stop Philip at this early stage. Surely we can send Templars to protect the remaining Scottish royals…and, Otto, the moment you learn that the French have sent their agents to Acre, why, we can be on the lookout…"

"Lookout for whom, Ralph? We know that Flote won't be stupid enough to send readily recognizable Frenchmen to Acre. And do we know their targets? I assume they'll go after prominent Muslims in the city, but whom do we protect?"

Ralph raised his hands in frustration. "I think you want war, man! I think you want to face King Philip once and for all and get it over with."

Otto got up from his chair and went to the window behind Ralph to stare into space. "Ralph, my friend, please believe that I have nothing personal invested in this."

"I'm not contemplating such a horrid thought, Otto. But I think you are not telling me the whole story."

Otto turned to face Ralph, feeling resigned. "So be it, my brother," he said and inhaled deeply. "I want to fight the French because I believe in my heart that I can defeat them, and that I'm the only one who can. But I must do it while I still have vitality and my wits about me, because this will be a long and hard battle.

"The French have reason to fear our King Edward. If they declared war at this moment, Edward would have the barons of Aquitaine to add to his English army, and he could also bring the Scots to his side. That would make him a formidable foe. They also fear the Templars; they could rally the other military orders and they are rich. So it makes sense that the French want our king fighting the Scots, while they take Aquitaine away from him, and maneuver the Templars out of the Holy Land and within their grasp. Then, when they set up a puppet pope, he can order the destruction of the Templars, and at the same time, bestow the Holy Roman Empire's crown on Philip.

"If at this stage we prevent the killings of the Scottish royals and the breaking of the truce with the Turks in the Holy Land, the French will just wait for another opportune moment. I want them fully engaged in their scheme; I want to bog them down until they cry for mercy. Then I want them so utterly defeated, they'll never try anything like it again!

"And for that I need the Brotherhood, and through them, the Templars; and to enlist them I need the Jesus Gospel. You know that."

"And you are certain that the Gospel, if it really exists, will say…"

"Ralph, my friend. It's a Gnostic text, written by Jesus, stating that we don't need priests for our salvation."

Ralph thought for a moment, contemplating the window behind Otto's shoulder. "Well, yes, a classic Gnostic text would say that." Ralph sighed. "But let us suppose the worst, that William can't find his uncle nor the Gospel…"

"In that case I will go myself and search desperately, and if I die trying, so be it."

"But surely you are not serious. Those brave souls the Brotherhood sent before John were never heard from again. Be reasonable, Otto. Even if Philip does become the Holy Roman emperor and conquers Europe and the Holy Land as you told me, that's not the end of the world."

Otto shook his head. "According to my spy in the French court, Philip will then launch the ultimate crusade."

"What does that mean? A crusade to end all crusades?"

"Yes, my friend. He will give the Christian fanatics their dream of a Christian only world, by massacring all Jews and Muslims everywhere."

"Good Heavens! Are you sure? No, but of course you are. But then, won't that be enough to motivate the Brotherhood? What do you need the Jesus Gospel for?"

"Ah, Ralph. How can I possibly prove it? No one will believe me until it's too late. The French Scheme is so outlandish...I even had a hard time convincing you. But a French king and a pope persecuting the Templars, after what happened to the Cathars? That's another story. However, given the Templars' disregard for pain and death they would just as likely decide to become martyrs. Most of our brethren are like Ian, Templars. You've heard them at Brotherhood meetings...all that talk about honor, duty, and dying a good death, remember? But imagine what would happen should the Brotherhood have the Jesus Gospel in their possession! They have been looking for it for two hundred years, and if they are convinced that the French king would want to destroy it, they'll go after Philip with every Templar under their command!"

"So why don't you just fabricate a Jesus Gospel, as you did the Caesarius Prophecy?"

"You mean..."

"I mean come up with a credible text. Jot down some likely things in Greek or Aramaic that Jesus might have said, and make sure it specifically states that there is no need for a Church, priests, nor dogma. Just a classic Gnostic message of finding God inside oneself."

Otto couldn't believe what he was hearing, and he studied Ralph's expression for any hidden meaning, but found only concern.

"Ralph...that's impossible. Only a Christ-like being could write something that would pass muster by William and others like him. And Christ-like beings don't get involved in subterfuge. They don't lie."

"But if we have a fake Gospel we wouldn't need the likes of William, would we?"

"You forget that we need someone to lead the Templars on a holy cause. The gospel has to be real so William believes in it and is empowered by it, and if the quest to find it becomes the stuff of legend, so much the better."

Ralph gave Otto a sad smile. "Yes, of course you are right." Then he sighed. "We need someone like John. Too bad he never made it back. And we need the actual gospel. I pray it all works out. I pray William is indeed like his uncle."

"Amen to that."

CHAPTER II

[1]

Shortly after the sun rose, William left the inn on an old and gentle horse he had bought the day before, along with a cheap sword. He headed northwest toward the coast through the Normandy countryside, feeling as though he was living someone else's life. How could it be that he was no longer a Cistercian monk? How did it happen?

The road was full of tradesmen with wares. William approached a man on a cart with bolts of chalons and damask cloth. "Where is everyone going?" William asked.

"To the Fair of Troyes, of course," the driver said studying William. "That's where honest men head this time of year to earn a few *livres*."

William got out of the clothier's way, wondering whether he looked less than honest, and for the following ten leagues to the town of Arras had no choice but to meander among the carts and horses packed full of merchandise, for the road was narrow and bordered on both sides by hedgerows. He arrived by the city's gates by early afternoon and looked for a public house to eat dinner. Arras was no different from other small towns grown crowded within its protective wall, its mostly wattle and daub structures sprouting added stories below thatched roofs, and every inch of space fully utilized. The narrow streets were filthy with sewage thrown from windows and droppings from a multitude of horses, waiting to be flushed by the next rains. And it was noisy, the walls of mud and sticks did little to block sound, but the canyons formed by the tall houses amplified everything. There was a hum of so many voices, coughs, shouts, cries, and barks, punctuated by the hammering of smithies. A smell much like that of dirty clothes mixed with urine and the all-pervading smoke of cooking fires, a combination that hung in the stagnant air...how could people live like that, William wondered. Maybe they felt safe from bandits and invading armies behind the city's walls, but at what price?

William found a busy eatery stall on a side street selling pies and bowls of pottage of questionable ingredients and baskets with smoked salmon, cheeses and breads. People all around him were busy pointing at items, yelling orders, shoving money, and William found himself being pushed out of the way. He shook his head in frustration and forced his way through the crowd. He saw angry faces turn in his direction, but when they noticed his size and the sword by his side, were quick to yield. Feeling annoyed but hungry, William settled for the salmon and a loaf of bread, and ate while walking his horse back to the main road. As a monk he never got shoved around—in fact was served first and never paid for anything—and in his former life as a knight had commanded respect. He realized he had a choice: either avoid busy places, or relearn how to assert himself.

The next town was Saint Omer, possibly two hours away now that traffic had thinned down to the occasional wagon.

How his life had changed! From the moment he confronted Brother Jules he felt as though he had fallen down a steep hill and had rolled and bumped along, landing at last in a different existence, dazed and confused. He knew it was best to adapt to who he was: a knight once again. However, the sword by his side felt foreign to him, as did the new clothes on his skin. William missed the comforting feeling of the heavy, rough habit …a sort of cocoon. He had a hard time meeting the glances of travelers as knights were supposed to, his inclination was to stare at the ground and pray. He knew he would miss the abbey and those he had grown fond of. William's best friend had been Brother Benjamin, a kindred soul, not learned in books, but sweetly devoted. Their walks in the garden after Vespers would be no more.

William let go of the reins—his hackney was not bound to be unruly; it absolutely refused to go faster than a trot—unsheathed his sword and studied it. Not German or Italian steel, for sure: the surface was pockmarked with tiny pits and it was rusting in places. It had been sharpened recently, but the edge had a number of gouges. A heavy blow against something hard might just snap it in two. Oh, well, he would just have to avoid doing that.

As William handled the sword to get accustomed to its feel and weight, the realization that he was going back home started to sink in. He envisioned his mother's surprise when first seeing him… at the very least that was worth the trip. He would have to tell her that he had to leave again, and that would break her heart. His father would pressure him to assume his role as the first-born and his brother would want him to be more like his friends: rowdy, violent, and lewd, and to stop embarrassing him with his "saintliness." And there was Farwell, the earl's son, who enjoyed schemes that embarrassed and humiliated people. Yes, he would have to face them all over again…and the killing. He would likely end up killing someone at the tournaments, and that was a heavy thought.

He would also have to face temptation. In the abbey monks punished their flesh when thoughts of sex invaded their minds, but William had learned that his best defense was to stop the thoughts before they took hold. He wondered how that would work around women on a daily basis.

He slept that night by his horse, hidden behind a hedgerow two fields away from the road. In the morning he climbed over the earthen embankment lined with trees and shrubs, and meandered along a lane until he came to the main road.

By midmorning William arrived at the boat in Calais just in time to watch it being loaded. That was a relief. On the way over he and Sir Ian had spent two days waiting for the ferry to show up. William went up the plank, walking the hackney behind him. He was met by the shipmaster who extended his hand. William dug in his pouch and produced a gold *livre* coin. The English shipmaster gave him back three ten-schilling coins. On impulse William stacked the coins on his hand and noticed that one of them was smaller. Someone had filed away some of the gold from the edge. "This coin has been clipped," William said handing it back.

"You want to get across?" the man asked with a harsh look.

William was taken aback by the shipmaster's manner. He sighed and went onboard. He didn't want to be a knight just yet; challenging people with a sword could wait, instead he tossed the illegal coin in the sea and let matters be.

William found that the longer he rode the more responsive his mount became. By the time he approached the meadow with the big oak, the old hackney didn't seem to mind the occasional trot and they were making good time. However, he still dismounted on steep slopes and took frequent breaks.

He studied the bay horse. It was a common Chapman, the type used by tradesmen. It seemed healthy, and someone had been sweet to it, for it had a good disposition.

He entered the fir forest and went by the lane leading to the Jewish village, where a lone cart creaked its way towards the road, but still a good distance away. He decided to walk trailing the horse behind him, and studied the ground, knowing that Jacob had passed that very spot countless of times. He uttered a prayer for his old Jewish teacher and thanked him for all that he had done. On impulse, William turned his head to his right, and he saw Jacob, walking by his side, smiling. William felt a lump in his throat as he contemplated the familiar bushy black beard, the corkscrew lock of hair that fell on his ample forehead, his kind face, and wide smile. Jacob had his head tilted to one side, as though wait-ing for the answer to one of his scholarly questions.

William stopped and stood for a moment enjoying Jacob's presence after so many years. Then, with sorrow and joy, bid him goodbye and promised he would never forget him. Jacob's crinkly eyes became moist and his lips moved in silence, pronouncing the blessing William remembered so well.

He arrived at the meadow as the sun was about to set. The old resting place would no longer remind him of the carefree days when he camped out as a boy but of the evil Jules.

William found a group of guildsmen by the big oak, potters and tinsmiths by the looks of their wares and their clothes. Their one-horse wagon was filled to the brim, and a heavy cloth cover stretched tight over the top. The five men eyed him with suspicion, and he assumed they were trying to determine who he was, for he had no hauberk, helmet, or shield, had a cheap horse and sword. He could well be a highwayman. To assuage their fears William walked over and undid his hood so they could see his shaved tonsure on the back of his head and know that until recently he had been a monk. "The Lord's blessings on this good day," he said in English, "I'm heading home."

The five men seemed to relax. "We've heard of highwaymen about, Sire," said a short stocky tinsmith judging by his tunic, "and would counsel the gentleman to be cautious."

William guessed the tinsmith was trying his best to sound cultured.

The following morning as William prepared to move on he saw the men hurry to try and follow him. They now knew him to be a knight, and wished to trail behind for protection. That would be fine.

For the first few hours of that day's journey, William felt ill at ease with the guildsmen and sorely missed being alone, but kept his horse's pace so they could follow. By late morning the men broke into song with ballads of beautiful maidens, great romances, and of heroic deeds of long-forgotten warriors. Some of the songs were rather racy, and they laughed heartily. When the lyrics became brutal and nasty, William asked them to sing something else. Surprised, the men obliged.

At noon, William stopped and the tinsmiths and potters did as well, keeping their distance of about ten yards behind. They built a fire and shortly after, as William sat eating the bread and dried mullet he had bought in Dover, a potter brought him a bowl of hot pottage, made with onions, cabbage, spinach, a dab of lard dissolving in the middle and unknown brown and black spots—some of which appeared to have legs—floating about. There were also globs William tried to ignore. He thanked the potter, and proceeded to slurp the smelly concoction with faked delight as his travel companions watched appreciatively.

Early in the morning of the following day, they came to the top of a hill overlooking a valley and William's home. At the sight of the farms and a village in the distance, the guildsmen begged his leave and proceeded on down the hill.

William studied the familiar landscape below him. To the left, and some two leagues away, he recognized his family's home, a three-story manor, with a protective wall around it, flanked by a lush pasture and an apple orchard, and surrounded by wheat, barley, and produce farms. He remembered every tree, every hill, every creek and pond, every house in that valley and most of its people whom he knew by name. His great-great-great-grand father, who had fought alongside William the Conqueror, had been fortunate to get the fief and it had passed to the eldest son over the generations.

William had been in line to inherit. Normally, someone in his younger brother Richard's place would have been much relieved when William became a monk, but not Richard. At sixteen, and already a big burly man, Richard had cried like a babe and followed him for much of the road to Dover and only turned back when William reminded him that he was worrying their mother.

William loved his family dearly, and yet they were so different from him. And they loved him as well, but saw him as troublesome; someone they had given up trying to understand long ago. "What does a knight need with learning from books?" Besides, he had always protected animals, scolding a peasant when he mistreated an ox, or stopping a fellow page from beating his horse with a stick. That one time William had picked up a stick of his own and struck the boy with it until he swore not to do it again, much to the amusement of their earl, who had stopped his horse to watch. "Young William, you will be a menace with a sword," he had told him. William recalled that the earl of Sheffield always seemed to remember his name and always had a gift for him on his birthday.

As William approached his father's house in late morning, he was still trying to decide what to tell his family. It was close to dinner, and they'd all be home. His fear was that his father would try and keep him, renewing the arguments of old, trying to change his very soul. His mother would chime in quietly that his father was getting on in years and that they needed both sons to take care of the fief.

William dismounted when he came to his home's drawbridge. The guard dogs announced his presence as he crossed the front gate. He was met by a smiling servant who took his horse. Then the front door of the house burst open and out came Richard, a surprised look on his face, big arms outstretched. William was lifted off the ground in a bear hug.

"Willy, Willy, what are you doing home?" his brother asked as he dropped him in front of their mother, Lady Claire, who stood at the door with a smile on her lips and the nose twitching she did when fighting back tears. Her hair, daintily kept under a toque had a few gray streaks, but her handsome fine features and hazel eyes were as warm as ever. William kissed the offered cheek and was escorted inside by her gentle tug on his arm.

He was led to where his father sat on a bench in the great hall, facing the one window, savoring a cup of hot, spiced wine. Sir Lawrence appeared momentarily surprised, then looked his eldest son up and down.

Outside the window William could see his mother's flowerbeds, and beyond, the open area for household animals and the shops built against the tall, thick perimeter wall. To his father's left stretched the long dining table and beyond, the main fireplace. The back wall of the large room was occupied by cupboards full of earthenware, glasses, goblets, jugs of wine, and the treasured cinnamon, pepper and nutmeg; all securely locked.

"William, what's this? Have you come home for good?" Sir Lawrence said with expectant eyes.

William hesitated and then swallowed hard. "No, father. I now belong with the Knights Templar. I am to stay home for seven months, with your permission, and then will take my leave for the Holy Land."

Sir Lawrence stared at his cup, playing with the deep red liquid, rocking it from side to side. "You seem to think that you can do what you wish with no regard to family duty."

William squatted in front of his seated father and was aware of his mother and brother standing behind him.

"I'm sorry father, but I can only be a monk. Joining the Templars was a decision I arrived at with my abbot's counsel. He deemed that my training as a knight was being wasted in the abbey. He released me on condition that I transfer my allegiance to the Templars."

"But William, there are so many dangers in Outremer," his mother said in French behind him. William turned his head and looked up at Lady Claire's anguished face. "You could fall off the edge of the earth, as some have done when a storm blows their ships off-course. And if you arrive safely, you may not die in battle but be captured and be kept as a slave by the Saracen who have potions to convert you to their evil faith."

William knew better than to try and dispel the myths. "Yes mother, there are many dangers. But I will travel on a big ship, crewed by Templars who know their way. I will be fighting, but for Christ, and this family will receive many blessings for it."

Sir Lawrence glared at his wife. "Woman, it's all your fault. You kept me from raising him proper." Then he noticed her tears. "Go do your crying some-where else."

Lady Claire turned away and William heard her quick steps going up the stairs.

"Well, William." His father said shaking his head and staring at the flowers outside the window. "I suppose your uncle would be proud of you."

Hardly a word was spoken at the dinner table and William felt badly for hurting his family, but he knew he had no other choice. He had gone through a similar path two years before when he announced he was leaving the earl's service to become a monk. The difference was that this time his father had appar-ently given up on him, and his mother had perhaps accepted the inevitable.

They were eating the main meal of a non-fish day, this time, roasted veni-son with cabbage, peas, and juniper berries, served on trenchers—slices of day-old bread that would be fed to the animals but that at the abbey were given to the poor—accompanied by fresh bread and butter. William watched his mother daintily feeding herself with her hands and then wiping her greasy fingers on her trencher, while Richard and Sir Lawrence used their sleeves. At the abbey, the monks rinsed their hands in water bowls in between courses.

Sir Lawrence broke the silence by clearing his throat. "As long as you are in my house you will assume your dutiful position, is that clear?"

"Yes, father."

A short time later, while they were still eating, a servant brought William a tunic with the family colors: red background with a white chevron crossing the front. The elderly groom, who had served the family for as long as William could remember, also gave him the black metal solid bar medallion that identified him as the eldest son. Richard, William noticed, had continued to wear the second-son's crescent medallion.

"Willy, are you going to spend your time reading and praying, as you used to?" Richard asked while smothering a slice of bread with butter.

"No. I need to outfit myself. I have nothing but that old horse I rode and a cheap sword I bought for the road."

"Don't count on me for anything," Sir Lawrence said.

"I won't, father. I intend to ask our lord for my needs. I must train as well for I've lost my fighting skills." Before becoming a monk, his training had been a challenge. He had enjoyed the physical part of it, but not the competitions where he feared killing someone; had only defended himself and was criticized for being timid. William wondered how he would react this time around with his new resolve.

That afternoon he walked alone along the familiar riverbank and apple orchard, remembering who he was before becoming a monk, but feeling a loss inside, as though someone dear to him had died, and William realized it was the devout Cistercian monk he thought he was going to be for the rest of his life. In the middle of the fruit trees he sobbed quietly; then knelt down and prayed.

When William got home the grooms were laying out a supper of cheese, bread, and wine as the two maids carried water in sloshing pails up the stairs to the bedchambers. Well, he might as well enjoy the luxury of finding a bowl of water for cleansing by his bed. But William knew he would miss getting up with the other monks at daybreak and filing out to the well outside to wash before Matins.

Theirs was a modern household modeled after the latest trends. The sons shared a chamber, as did William's parents, on either side of a chimney that shed its heat into the solarium, the family's sitting room. The servants shared another big room on the ground floor; but most of William's friends when he had been a squire slept with their parents, and even the servants. William was grateful for his mother's good sense as he made his way to his own bed, separated by a curtain from Richard's.

The next day he saddled the Chapman horse and made his way to the earl of Sheffield's castle, accompanied by his brother. They rode through the village and William saw no changes in the familiar huts; a pig or a goat always tied in front, the tailor's shop with clothing prominently displayed, the one tavern already well attended.

Richard had taken pains to dress. He had foregone his tunic and instead sported a form-fitting doublet that because it only came down to his waist, called for a codpiece over his privates. Richard's skin-tight black hose showed off his well-muscled legs and behind. A flowing white bourrelet covered his head, and pointed shoes his feet. A most unusual attire for someone who two years before would rather be naked than without his hauberk, and made fun of the "dandies" who wore such clothing.

"You have taken to fancy dress, Richard?" William asked.

Richard blushed. "Oh, it's nothing. I promised to visit with my ladylove."

"Ladylove? Are you planning to wed?"

"It's all set for next summer," Richard said with excitement. "You remember Elizabeth, a lady at the earl's court, don't you?"

William recalled a smart and vivacious girl, the younger of two daughters of Sir Leonard, who had a fief not far down the road.

Richard patted his horse's neck. "I, too, need to enter tournaments so I can earn enough for a house of my own. I'm good, brother. Last spring I rammed through two visiting knights. They had to carry them away, blood all over," Richard said laughing. "After I get settled, I plan on going to war.

"When King Edward invaded Wales," Richard went on, "ten knights from our court went with him, and you should hear the great stories they told. I want to go next time he invades. It has to happen, Willy. If not, there's also talk about the pope raising an army to liberate Jerusalem.

"Maybe the two of us can meet in Outremer, slaughtering the enemies of the Lord, and we'll both become heroes, come back with great honors. Then King Edward would make us both earls and gift us rich lands to govern. That would be grand," Richard said with a big smile looking at his brother for approval.

William noticed they were now going through their earl's game reserve, a wonderful thickly wooded hollow he remembered exploring with his friends as a child. "What happened with the other squires who were not knighted with us?"

"Of the twelve men we apprenticed with, four have not been able to become knights because of the cost of equipment," Richard said in a somber tone. "I feel bad for them. They can't enter tournaments without being knighted, and they have no other means for raising money."

Richard continued talking about their friends, anecdotes of little import and William could tell his brother was trying to reacquaint himself with him, so he went along with the chatter, making comments and asking questions.

As they approached Sheffield Castle, William studied the modern stone structure as though seeing it for the first time. In comparison to Abissey Castle, which dated back to the Saxons, the place was huge, and far more comfortable. For one thing, there were fireplaces in every floor, rather than the typical smoky hearth in the main hall vented by a hole in the roof.

They crossed the bridge over the exterior moat and went through the gate into the outer ward—a space much bigger than the old-style baileys—with stables, smithies, kitchens and servants' quarters. In the center, protected by an interior moat and a curtain wall surrounding an inner ward, was the castle keep, the heart of the fortification; a four story structure, consisting of knight's and squires' quarters on the first floor, the ladies' on the second and the earl and his family's chambers on the top two floors. The only thing William disliked about the place from all the years he spent here, was that the upper floors' garderobes emptied human excrement directly into the interior moat, right by the knights' windows, and at night one had to get used to the splashing noises, not to mention the smell that the twenty-foot wide channel gave off in hot summer days before the rains flushed it to the fields outside.

William and Richard rode up to the inner ward and handed the horses to a groom. The two brothers agreed to meet at the stables by noon. William made his way to the earl's chambers to pay his respects, and Richard went looking for

Elizabeth.

[2]

Earl Orland of Sheffield paced his work chamber as he finished dictating a letter to his bishop. This was the second time in two years he had received a missive from Bishop Gregor, and one could not afford to ignore his requests. Yes, he responded, he was prepared to do whatever was in his power to assist Sir William Montfort, whom the bishop two years before had called "dear to my heart." The new request was to "most discreetly assist him in his quest on becoming a Knight Templar." The means were left up to Orland's judgment. The bishop had thanked him for his kind treatment of the lad over the years, and "the inordinate gracefulness" with which Orland had acquiesced to the young man becoming a monk two years before.

Orland concluded the letter with the assurance he would do everything in his power to please the bishop, "for the perpetual glory of our Holy Church." He waited for his clerk, who stood at the writing desk next to the window, to finish the letter. After it had been read back to him, he affixed his seal, and felt satisfied. A powerful Church official now owed him a series of favors.

Orland would be glad to help William become a Templar and fortunately the bishop had not asked him to sponsor the lad. The equipment alone would cost over one hundred pounds, and the donation to the Order a whole lot more. It would have been an expensive request, and one he would have tried to decline. He guessed that William was on his way home, and that he would show up any day now.

A footman came in to announce that Sir William Montfort was asking for an audience.

Orland laughed and shook his head. It was eerie, he thought as he made his way to the audience room. Such coincidences were rather unsettling, and it reminded him of John, William's uncle. Coincidences always happened around him as well.

Orland climbed up to the dais and his plush blue velvet armchair at the far end of the formal room and took a moment to survey his subjects' coats of arms with pleasure, all twenty-six of them including William's family, displayed all around the room. Orland's seat was strategically placed in front of a large window so that he would be a silhouette to a visitor forced to look up at him from the hard bench ten feet away.

Orland studied William as he entered and noticed with some satisfaction that the lad had maintained his strong body, although he now shuffled a bit, something that would change with training. William's hands looked hard, his handsome face at ease, his gaze peaceful and sure as he looked the earl straight in the eyes, as few men dared do. The lad was like his uncle, one of those rare people with nothing but goodness inside.

Orland motioned for William to climb the dais and stand beside him. Orland was fond of the lad and had missed him, he realized, as he acknowledged his bow with a hand gesture.

Although of difficult nature, William was an honorable man, sometimes a bit too honorable, a quality suited for battle but not for court. Just like his uncle.

Orland listened to William's story, how he left the abbey because his knightly skills were being wasted, followed by his plea to become a Knight Templar. Orland wondered what his secret was. Why would Bishop Gregor care about a knight's son? Perhaps he was his secret bastard?

"I yearn to live as a monk but am trained as a knight, so it seems my destiny would be best fulfilled combining the two," William said earnestly.

Orland went through the motions of asking about William's motivation, his ability to raise the necessary funds, and smiled when told of the unrealistic plan to raise money in tournaments.

"You have my blessing to join the Knights Templar, William," Orland said. "We have two scheduled tournaments, one in the fall and one in the spring.

"I counsel you patience," Orland said. "Plan on raising the funds you require over a number of years.

"You are most welcome to use my training facilities, armor, and any available horse in the stable. As the tournaments approach, we'll see what else you need."

Orland dismissed William, watched him leave the room and felt proud of him. How Orland wished he were his son. How easy it would be to love him. Instead God had given him an offspring who would never walk the same honorable path.

[3]

Over the next three months William trained with his brother Richard. William rode one of the earl's horses, a Forest Horse, not quite as fast as he would have liked, but a strong and able mount. It was good to be astride a warhorse, they were just a few hands taller than the palfreys, but massive, and the best ones—Percherons and Boulonnais—were big enough to push the smaller mounts out of the way but were just as nimble.

Richard's squire assisted both brothers, but that also meant that they had to devote a quarter of their training time to him, sparring, and instructing him. But that was fine, that was expected, and the man was helpful, caring for the horses and equipment.

In time William felt he had regained his former mastery, and then became even better. He knew he now had a determination he had lacked before.

He grew close to Richard. When sparring with others they almost invariably gained the upper hand, but when facing one another, the points were much
harder to score. Richard was the stronger of the two, but William was faster.

They soon fell into a comfortable routine. William and Richard trained hard
from Wednesday to Saturday, and then every Sunday rode home, attended mass,
visited their parents, and spent Monday and Tuesday looking after whatever their
father needed done. Often that meant acting as bailiffs in the borough: overseeing the wind-powered mill operations jointly owned by the farmers and villagers;
meeting with the sheriff to decide on the shire's road works within their fief, or
settling a quarrel between two farmers. On occasion their time was spent collecting overdue rents from tenants. On Wednesdays they would get up early and ride
to the castle, and William knew Richard couldn't wait to see Elizabeth.

On a late Thursday afternoon, following another day of hard training, William and Richard, with their squire trailing behind, approached the appointed
place where Elizabeth and her sister Veronica waited for them. That was their
new routine when the day was done. The two would make it over to the castle's
garden, where Richard and Elizabeth strolled hand in hand until sunset, while
William and Veronica walked behind, providing discreet company.

William spotted the two sisters waiting by the fountain, whispering and
smiling when they saw the two brothers approach.

The brothers dismounted and turned the horses over to Richard's squire,
who had, as usual when they were around the castle, followed a few yards behind.
William smiled as Richard smoothed his hair with his hands, and looked over his
clothes, suddenly concerned about his appearance.

William heard a horse's hoofs behind him, and turned to find Farwell, the
earl's son, on his warhorse, the finest one in the earldom, a fine black Percheron,
his clothes the best money could buy. He stopped and stared at them.

Farwell came down from his charger, handed it over to his own squire, and
approached Richard. He stood in front of him, blocking his path, with a peculiar
smile on his face. "The two love birds are to meet again, eh?"

William noticed that he came up to his brother's shoulders and looked puny
by comparison. Like Richard, Farwell sported a doublet, but his was of gray silk
and was padded to give the "pigeon chest" effect. Over his green hose Farwell
wore a leather codpiece studded with three large rubies. Gold chains, medallions,
and an assortment of jewelry adorned his belt.

"This should make for great sport at the tournament." Farwell said, his blue
eyes sparkling with glee. He stood silent for a while, stroking his waxed goatee
with a smirk on his face, then turned, climbed on his horse and left.

The threat was obvious. Farwell meant to challenge Richard for Elizabeth's hand, not just the equipment.

Richard turned around to face his brother.

"Not to worry, Richard," William told him, "It's a court game, a bluff." But William was concerned. He knew Richard could easily defeat Farwell, but if he killed him, it could be disastrous. The earl would have no choice but to punish Richard and his family otherwise he would be considered a weakling. They could lose their fief; Richard could end up in prison, or worse. On the other hand, Richard couldn't just forfeit Elizabeth, and lose face and his honor. Obviously Farwell was aware of this, and had Richard cornered.

William patted his brother's shoulder and they walked to meet the ladies.

"What was that about?" Elizabeth wanted to know.

"Oh, Farwell making trouble is all," Richard answered. "He's threatening to challenge me for your hand at the tournament."

William noticed Elizabeth's reaction, which may have escaped Richard. She appeared flattered as she glanced at her sister Veronica, then she smiled, and raised an eyebrow.

Both girls were pretty; tall and slender, of reddish-auburn hair, soft, creamy skin and big, brown eyes. William found them appealing and studied them with curiosity. They wore stylish attire: both had long colorful gowns; Elizabeth covered her tresses with a toque—the white flat cloth covered her head and its chin-strap concealed her ears. Veronica wore a veil cinched on top with a circlet. For modesty, she covered her ears with silk cauls.

The four went on for their walk around the fountain and by beds of deep purple, pink, and white flowers, their feet softly crunching on the gravel path. After some time Richard seemed to have gotten over the incident with Farwell and fawned over his ladylove, murmuring softly next to her ear, making her giggle.

Walking slowly behind the two lovers, Veronica tried to engage William, flirting with him, as she did with all the men at the earl's court, married or un-married. But he only answered politely, and found her talk and gestures silly. As usual, she kept at it for a while, but to William's relief eventually gave up and, folded her arms and remained silent for the rest of the walk. He knew she would try again; he was probably a challenge to the very attractive and sought-after young girl. At the end of their walk, as they were about to part, Veronica seemed to accidentally rub her hand against William's, who instinctively recoiled.

Veronica's touch spread like fire through his body and into his loins. He took a deep breath, and began praying silently. He would have to remember not to let her touch him again.

As the brothers were about to leave, Elizabeth gave William a long look.

"I remember that you read, William, and for some time I've wanted to talk to you."

"About what?"

"Books, of course," Elizabeth said surprising both brothers, who didn't know she could read. "I particularly love plays. My uncle used to read them aloud to us, but I have found none in the earl's library and wonder whether you know of any."

"I don't know who may have such books around here," William answered.

"Oh, that's a pity. I so enjoy plays. Next time an actors' troupe comes, let's all go!"

"Elizabeth, you know the kind of people who go to those functions," Veronica said. "Father would never allow it."

That night William lay in bed in the knights' quarters, worrying about Farwell's threat. To the spoiled earl's son and Elizabeth it was apparently all sport, but William knew his brother's intentions were brutally honest. Elizabeth, on the other hand, was apparently fond of his brother, but when a game presented itself, particularly when she could impress her sister and the other ladies, she seemed to get carried away.

Two years earlier, at fourteen, Elizabeth had been bright, pretty, and flirtatious, and followed the older girls who played their sometimes-fatal games of allowing several young men to court them at once. Death in duel was common, and the girl fought over was usually a celebrity for some time. Nothing much had changed, he noted. William remembered that Farwell was always scheming some way to cause embarrassment to someone, usually with mean-spirited jokes or pranks. Now his games had become deadlier.

William knew of at least two cases in which knights had been humiliated by choosing to forfeit a challenge. Not only did they lose their equipment, but became non-entities, ridiculed openly even by squires. One had gone on to become a mercenary in France, the other killed himself. So chances were good that Richard would fight, hoping to disable Farwell. But in a challenge there was no pulling back of swords; the rules of trial by combat came into play and it usually ended in death unless the earl interfered, but that only happened if injury prevented further combat. For someone like Richard, he would have to go for the kill, or risk being killed.

William decided that he had to find a way to challenge Farwell himself. He was sure he could disable him.

On the morning of the tournament, a gloriously sunny Saturday, William and Richard rode palfreys as their squire walked their fully armored warhorses behind them. This was ceremony, and it called for a colorful display. They made their way behind the castle to the pasture that had been converted into the tournament grounds, a hundred by fifty-yard rectangle with an eighty by twenty-yard jousting field in the middle outlined with a string of banners. On the right side of the grounds stood the tented bleachers for the gentry and to the left the uncovered benches for the commoners. All around were vendors' carts, whose sides were open to reveal ale, beer, wine, meat pies, roasted apples and sweet pies. Behind their squire, the brothers were followed by two pages carrying their lances and shields. The brothers circled the grounds parading past both stands, waving at the cheering gentry and commoners alike.

All around they could hear the excited murmur of the gathered crowd mixed in with the snorting of nervous horses. There was a curious feeling in the air, a mixture of all the excitement of a fair—the gaiety of colorful ladies' dresses, heraldic colors on horses and knights, vendors announcing their goods—and the tension of combat, heightened by the whining sound of rotating stone wheels sharpening swords.

William and Richard wore hauberks with padded aketons underneath, covered with tunics with their family's white chevron over a red background. On their chargers—likewise sporting mantles with their family's colors—clanked their heavy suits of jousting armor, a bit over a hundred pounds each of steel, leather straps, and straw padding. William had borrowed his gear from the earl, Richard was using an old well-patched suit of armor that had belonged to their grand father. Both brothers had shields recently painted with their family's chevron.

In the first rows of nobles, amid flags and banners of visiting knights and dignitaries, sat the earl of Sheffield with his wife the Countess Lorena beside him, and the highborn, including a duke from France. There were no dukes in all of Britain, so this was a great honor, a person almost as mighty as a king. There were also two foreign counts. In England the wife of an earl was known as a "countess" so people thought the male equivalent odd. Behind them sat the lesser nobility, mostly knights and their families.

All around the earl sat the court ladies like crisp, bright flowers in their colorful gowns, faces powdered to look as pale as possible, hairlines plucked for the fashionable rounded, high forehead look, hair covered with every conceivable headdress, and wimples, crespinettes and snoods holding in tresses. Each lady had a scarf, ready to bestow as she chose upon a pretender or a challenger, and the ladies laughed happily, pointing out various knights. Several men, including the earl of Sheffield, wore heincelin robes that covered from shoulders to knees, with bourrelets covering their heads. A good number of the merchants in the commoners' stands—both men and women—had equally fanciful attire.

It was so shallow, William thought, but this was his chance to make money. However, he had to protect Richard first.

Near the stands was Farwell, already fully armored and astride his beautiful black Percheron. William had seen him mistreat the animal. He used the spurs needlessly, whipped him as punishment, and punched him for sport, and the poor animal now stood nervously flaring its nose, stomping, and twitching its tail.

William walked over to where Farwell stood and hit him on the side of his helmet with his sword, a common way for knights to call the attention of a distracted squire. "Sir Farwell," he said loud enough for all in the stands to hear, "I challenge you."

It took a moment for Farwell to respond. "And to the death, you idiot!" he yelled.

William did not answer and walked calmly away. He knew that angered, Farwell would want to fight immediately rather than putting it off to the end of the jousts, which had been William's concern. A few moments later a crier announced the first joust "between Sir William and Sir Farwell." The crowd cheered.

Richard's squire and page helped William into his armor and onto his mount. He took his lance and rode to the far end of the jousting field. Farwell was already waiting for William at the other end of the eighty-yard stretch.

First came a word from the earl, exhorting all participants to abide by the rules of chivalry. Then the priest blessed them all and said a prayer for those who would die that day.

William and Farwell faced each other and waited for the trumpet to sound.

William took a deep breath and prayed. All he wanted was to disable Farwell. He just hoped he was good enough so he could hurt and not kill.

He heard the trumpet sound and spurred his horse into a gallop, keeping his lance slightly raised to avoid letting Farwell know where he intended to strike. Farwell on the other hand aimed low, for his belly, which was meant to impale him. William had watched Farwell spar and his opponents invariably let him win. If that was always the case, Farwell had never honed his skills and was probably overconfident.

They came at each other at a full gallop. With a smooth motion William swung his lance and easily tapped aside Farwell's, then angled the tip in between Farwell's shield and helmet and gave him a glancing blow to the chest, all too fast for William's own eyes to follow, for his hands, arms and body had acted without thinking. He felt his lance's tip strike solid and Farwell's body give in. The blow sent Farwell careening sideways and William heard the crowd gasp.

When William stopped his destrier and turned around, he saw Farwell sitting to one side of his mount, his torso hanging down toward the ground, arms swinging limply.

William cantered over, looking and listening for signs of life; then he heard Farwell's labored breath, and he thanked God. He hit him on the helmet with his sword and Farwell rolled out of his saddle and slumped to the ground. He got down from his horse and walked over to the prostrated man. He could hear his groans, and placed the tip of the sword on Farwell's throat, protected only by mail. He turned to the stands to give the earl a chance to stop the match.

The earl took off his hat, granting Farwell his life, but also bequeathing William all of the man's equipment, including squire, page, and grooms. That was a major victory, for Farwell had the best of everything, well beyond a common knight's reach.

William met Farwell's squire who offered him a ransom for all his winnings. He accepted eighteen pounds and ten shillings for everything except the black charger, which he announced he would keep, despite the exorbitant offer of thirty pounds.

As William took off the heavy jousting armor to fight in his hauberk, he realized how relieved he felt. His brother was safe and the earl's son perhaps only badly bruised.

That afternoon knights were to engage in a melee and fight in teams of six. Depending on the opponents, it could become very violent, close to open combat.

But it went fine. William didn't kill anyone and won all encounters except for one, deemed a draw. He came away with close to fifty pounds—quite possibly the most anyone made that day, and about equal the amount his father made from rents in a year. In the past, when William had entered tournaments he had done so reluctantly and had only defended himself. This time, he had to admit, it had been very exciting—he felt exhilaration all over his body, like a tingling. It was gratifying to know he was one of the best.

William wondered how the losers felt. A handful had probably lost their family's fortunes that day. There had been at least two deaths and four other men had been badly hurt and would probably die from their wounds.

The violence from the stands had been kept to a minimum thanks to the constable's men. Only once did a squire and a groom jump into the fray to assist a losing knight.

Through it all William had kept an eye on Richard, and his brother had done reasonably well, winning three matches and one joust, but losing once, which had cost him two pounds. All together, Richard had won seventeen pounds.

In the late afternoon William and Richard, both sore and tired, rode home behind their parents. William sat astride the big black charger he had won from Farwell, and he knew it would take some time for the animal to get used to his touch. It flinched each time he approached it, and pulled away at the sight of a raised hand. William had received numerous offers for the animal, but the beautiful Percheron was supposed to be his—he just knew it.

Richard turned to his brother with a somber look. "I know you were protecting me, Willy, by challenging Farwell, but I can take care of myself," he spoke in a low tone so their parents would not hear.

William sensed the heaviness in his brother's voice, the hurt pride.

"I know you can, Richard. No question. But a defeat from me is easier for Farwell to bear, because I will soon be gone to Outremer. But you must remain behind, and I didn't want you to have an enemy so close to home."

To his relief Richard appeared satisfied with the answer.

"I may be coming with you, brother."

"That's…but why, Richard? I thought you wanted to wed, settle down."

Richard patted his horse's neck, the brutish Samson. "I'm not certain anymore. This morning, before you challenged Farwell, when I asked Elizabeth for her scarf, she refused me, laughed, and said whoever won the duel would get it."

"Was she alone?"

"No, she was in the stands with the other ladies."

"I think she had to keep up the game in front of her friends. She didn't really mean it."

That evening William, along with his family, went to mass. The small stone church with a tall steeple was located in the village outskirts and had been built on a farm owned by the bishop. The long and narrow structure had six tall stained glass windows on each side, each depicting a key scene from the New Testament in chronological sequence from left to right—starting with the nativity and ending with Jesus' resurrection. William watched as people around him looked at the pictures and commented, and he felt sad. That was the extent of the New Testament for them because most were like his own family: illiterate and ignorant.

For this occasion the congregation was made up of only knights and their families, unlike Sunday's mass, when the commoners were in attendance.

The elderly priest congratulated the local knights for "an honorable tourney" and lectured them to limit their "basic natures," to those occasions. "I pray," Father Mathew said, "that one day the needless slaughter will stop." He went on to mention an incident that previous week when a knight killed a young peasant because the boy had looked at his daughter as she went by. "If you keep killing the peasants, who will work the fields? Certainly not you," he said. At this, people laughed. The well-thought-of priest pleaded with them to "at least respect the Truce of God, and do not kill on Sundays." Father Mathew called for the knight who had killed the peasant to compensate the boy's mother for her loss. "She's a widow and the young man was feeding the family. Five pounds would be in order." His sad words hung in the air as he stepped off the pulpit.

The following day at the breakfast table, Sir Lawrence appeared in a good mood, laughing with a friend who had come over to invite him on a hunt.

"Father, do you know of other tournaments held nearby?" William asked.

Sir Lawrence put down a slice of bread and salted sardine to look at his eldest son. "There are only two such tourneys nearby that I know of, William. The others are at least a week's ride away."

Sir Lawrence continued eating and chatting with his friend, and William tried to recall a time when Sir Lawrence had been anything other than curt with his wife and sons. William studied the middle-aged knight of brown hair streaked with gray, the heavily lined face and ruddy complexion, and wondered what made him so cold.

William made further inquiries among the older knights at Castle Sheffield about the two nearby tournaments and found out that the two events and the one the earl sponsored took place the same day, making it impossible for him to compete in more than one. Disheartened, William realized he wouldn't be able to raise the money he needed by spring, and he decided to ride to Abissey right after the local tourney to notify Sir Ian that he would have to postpone his trip.

How much time should he ask for? He couldn't put off his trip for three years, what he needed if he kept winning at his current rate. Sir Ian and the other Templars expected him to travel much sooner than that.

Maybe he could try to make money abroad. William knew that the tourneys in Normandy and Gascony were very popular, and there were several of them. There, he might earn enough in six months. He would just have to fight hard and win every time.

Richard talked constantly about Elizabeth. A week after the tournament he went to see her and it appeared the relationship was back on course, at least judging by his happiness when he returned. She was coming over with her family on Christmas to spend a few days, and Lady Claire got busy setting up the house for her guests, fussing over small details with the servants.

During the winter months the entire household slept in the three chambers with fireplaces, including servants and guests. In preparation for the visitors, who would stay for a week, Lady Claire had the servants spread hay under the dinner table to absorb grease, soup, and other spills, and to "be a home for the fleas and lice our guests will honor us with."

However, four days before Elizabeth's scheduled visit, as William sat with his mother in the family's solarium, Richard came in and announced that everything had been cancelled, not only the visit, but the wedding. Elizabeth was now going to spend Christmas at the castle, for Farwell had expressed an interest in her.

"Did she tell you that herself?" William asked, noting Lady Claire's pained expression.

Richard pulled up a chair. "Yes. I came to see her, and found her in the castle's great hall, visiting with Farwell, her sister, and one of his friends. They were laughing and telling stories. When she saw me, she excused herself and came over, took me by the arm, and told me things had changed, that it was not her fault, but her father had counseled her to take her time and consider all suitors."

"Meaning Farwell," William said.

Richard leaned forward and held his face in his two big hands, staring at his feet.

Their mother moved her chair next to Richard's and gently stroked his head.

"Yes…I guess I never really knew her," Richard told them. "I thought we were of the same mind and heart. But she changed, I can see it's not her father's doing: it is her."

"I am sorry, Richard." William said. He knew how much his brother was hurting; he could see it in his eyes and hear it in his voice. It was clear that Farwell had engineered the entire episode as revenge. William knew that while Elizabeth and her family might be enthralled by the prospects of elevating their social status, Farwell had no intention of marrying her, his future bride would have to be one who would enhance his position, a daughter of one of the neighboring earls. Someone like Farwell never married for love. The sad thing, William thought, recalling the way Elizabeth looked at Richard while on their walks, was that Elizabeth loved his brother. Of that, William was certain.

In the midst of Richard's heartbreak, William's family managed to settle into a quiet life that winter and William renewed his customary long hours at prayer. He missed the discipline and the feel of the abbey, so in the early morning, before the sun came up, he got up for Matins, and in his mind joined his brothers back at the abbey and prayed with them. It was hard to separate himself from his family during the day, especially Richard, for he knew his brother needed his company, but William managed to always excuse himself for at least Matins and Vespers.

Conversations with his family were mostly about the neighbors, or about the fief, if his father was involved. But one evening, at supper, William asked about his uncle John. From Lady Claire he got a sorrowful glance, and from his father a curt answer: "There is nothing to be said. He left."

The following morning William found his mother in the great hall putting away some goblets in the cupboard. She wore her "work clothes," a gray wool gown, her long chestnut hair gathered in a braid down her back, carefully wrapped with a cordet, a simple wimple on her head held by a circlet. Her hazel eyes surveyed the cups she had inherited from her mother, items the servants dared not touch. Lady Claire motioned for William to come near, looked around to make sure no one was about and whispered: "Your father is just hurt over his brother John's absence and never understood him, but he was always fearful for him."

She took a hold of his hand. "John used to pray long hours just like you," Lady Claire said as they walked to stand by the tall window overlooking her flower beds outside now covered in snow, and her sad eyes became thoughtful.

William felt his mother's warm hand, gentle and soft.

"I had just married your father and moved here. Your grandparents were still alive and John was fifteen at the time, five years younger than your father."

"He was a quiet boy, and I became an older sister, although I was nary a year older, and we talked and joked when he was home from the castle."

William waited for his mother to continue while she observed the snow outside, lost in thought. "He told me about his gift and how it worked—told me that knowledge about things just came to him, and sometimes he would have visions. Your grandparents and your father were fearful of his gift, and saw it as a curse, for if someone from the Church found out, John could be in trouble.

"I would intercede when things got bad, such as the time he had a vision at the dinner table and started sobbing and gazing at something we could not see. He was sixteen and skinny, not yet a big man, and it was most unseemly. Your grandfather wanted to beat him, but I begged him not to. John was unaware of it all, and turned to us with tears running down his face. 'I saw him, he talked to me,' he said in wonder. 'Who talked to you?' your grandfather asked, and John replied 'Jesus.'

"When John said that, I knew it was the truth, for there was a sweet feeling in the room, as though a host of angels had descended, and the air smelled like roses, heavenly roses, but somehow I was the only one aware of that, because your grandfather just got angrier. 'Don't say those things, that's heresy! Only saints can see Jesus,' he yelled at him.

"John never spoke to his father about his visions again, but he spoke with me, and he said Orland also knew… He was such a sweet boy, just like you, Willy," Lady Claire said, and her face spread into a smile.

"He also loved animals. Back then I had a dog I had raised from a pup. One day a horse kicked it. No one cared. Your grandfather and father wanted to kill it to stop the whining, but John took the little thing and cuddled it, and soon the crying stopped, and it lay sleeping in his arms. I don't know what he did, for I knew it had broken bones, but in a week's time the dog was going about its business, as usual."

Lady Claire looked down at her carefully manicured nails and sighed. "Then one day, when John was about your age, he left. You were almost a year old. You don't remember, but he used to carry you around and play with you—so unlike a man! When he departed, he had already been knighted, so he took his horse, helmet, hauberk, shield and sword, and nothing else."

"You wailed for days, and your father thought you were sick, but I knew you missed your uncle."

William looked at his mother's loving face, just beginning to show creases around the lips and eyes. He did recall someone other than her holding him with love and tenderness. He definitely remembered the love.

"Months later," she continued, "one of the earl's men came over with a letter, and he read it to us. It was from a Templar master in the Holy Land, and it said John was now serving the Lord with them, to not worry about his welfare, for he was now in good hands. It was a mystery to us how he managed to travel that far and join the Templars with no money to his name.

"That's the last we ever heard of him."

William thanked her, and kissed her cheek. He understood her pain, for she had met a gentler man than anyone she had ever known, one with a loving heart, and she had never forgotten him. William guessed she never would.

Spring came at the end of February that year; the snow disappeared and the ponds and rivers thawed. Soon after, cattle roamed the fields as the grass started to come back. In the first week of March, William and Richard went back to the castle to see about the upcoming tournament two weeks hence.

Riding with Richard into Sheffield Castle's outer ward, William noticed Richard's silence. The brothers left their mounts at the stables and made their way toward the knights' quarters. They were crossing the bridge over the interior moat when William saw Veronica, Elizabeth's sister, standing at the gate to the inner ward, watching them approach.

"Sir Richard and Sir William, I bid you a pleasant morning and beg for a moment of your time," she said as she stood on their path. "I need to tell you about Elizabeth," she blurted out, and by the tone in her voice William knew it would be bad news.

"Elizabeth is quite distraught, sick of heart, her life beyond repair," Veronica said as tears came to her eyes. "Farwell had appeared a most courteous and kind suitor, and it looked as a good match in the beginning. My father was very glad, for it spelled a much-needed change in the family's fortunes." She spoke rapidly, repeating lines she had obviously rehearsed. "My sister was willing to do her part for us, even though she loved you, Richard, with all her heart. I know because I heard her crying at night, and she confided in me about her grief. Farwell had promised to talk to his father about a wedding, and he and Elizabeth started making plans." Veronica's voice was angry now, and tears flowed freely.

"Farwell waited for a time when he was alone with her. He sent me on an errand, and I left them in his sitting parlor, talking about the wedding feast. All seemed well. When I returned, she was alone, distraught, her dress torn and signs of roughness all over."

William and Richard stood in shocked silence.

"He violated her!" Veronica screamed and began to cry uncontrollably.

That was it, the revenge, thought William. By now Farwell and his friends would have spread the news of his conquest: Elizabeth had lost her virginity, and was no longer eligible for marriage. She could now become someone's mistress, or a nun. Her life as she had known it, full of promise and the lighthearted ways of a lady of the court, was over.

Richard's face had turned red. He clenched his jaws and his hand went for his sword. William realized that trouble was inevitable. Knowing Richard, he would want to charge around the castle looking for Farwell. But knowing Farwell, William suspected a trap.

William knew it would be useless to try and reason with Richard, who was beyond words. William considered subduing him, but his brother was stronger, so he decided to do the only thing that would save his family: find Farwell first.

William took off running as fast as he could. On the way he undid his sword belt and let it fall to the ground. Not only could he move faster and more quietly without it, but also he did not want to be armed when he found Farwell. He tried to think while he ran, and made his way into the knights' barracks at a fast clip.

Throwing open a door to the sleeping quarters William bumped into Simon, one of the knights he had squired with, and a good friend of Farwell's. William grabbed the man by the tunic, pinned him against the wall and yelled, "Where is Farwell!"

He noticed Simon's eyes dance with laughter, so he grabbed his throat with his left hand and pushed hard with his thumb into the man's windpipe, as he pinned his chest and arms with his right arm. Simon gagged and his face turned red, his eyes no longer laughing, but desperate. William asked again: "Where's Farwell!" this time right into his face.

"He's…in his sitting room," Simon stammered, his voice barely audible.

"Is he alone?" he noticed Simon hesitate, so he pushed harder on his throat. William waited until he seemed about to pass out, then let him gasp for air.

"I will kill you, right now Simon. I know something is afoot, and I will do anything to stop Farwell. Now tell me what's he planning." William noticed Simon's now subdued look. He had him.

"All right, I'll tell you," Simon said in a hoarse whisper and William released his grip to let him talk.

"Farwell is in his sitting room unarmed, but he has two of his friends, armed, hiding behind the window drapes. He knew Veronica would tell you first thing. In fact, both she and Farwell have been waiting for you and Richard for five days now, spying the road every morning, knowing you would come soon. He expects Richard to come charging in and attack him. His friends will then jump out and slay Richard, claiming they were defending an unarmed Farwell."

A simple plan, from a simple wicked mind. William let go of Simon and made it as quietly as he could up the servants' stairs to Farwell's chambers. William could guess the rest of the plan. Whether Richard survived or not, it would be the end of their family, for the earl would then be forced to confiscate their fief in punishment for the attempt on his son's life. He wouldn't have any other choice; otherwise his authority would dissipate.

William felt a knot in his stomach, and realized it was all up to him. The good thing, he reasoned, was that the trap was set in Farwell's sitting room, a space too small for swinging a sword. However, if Farwell's friends were armed with daggers, he might be killed, for he was not wearing his hauberk.

William came up the servants' stairs into Farwell's bedchamber, which contained four beds lined up along its length, and he went across it to the back door of the sitting room, as he heard Richard's voice resonating in the floor below.

The door was slightly ajar, and he looked inside. To his right and by the window sat Farwell, apparently engrossed in cleaning a tournament helmet, a fancy affair with a brass hawk on top. He seemed oblivious to Richard's angry steps coming up the stairs.

William could see figures hidden behind the drapes and beneath them the tips of boots and sword blades. He tried to visualize a plan of action but had to think fast. His hands were clammy, and perspiration covered his face, even in the cold and drafty castle. Swords would be hard to wield in close quarters and with speed and surprise he could overpower at least one of the men, but he would be left vulnerable to the second. Maybe he could charge the man on the left first, strike him through the drapes, then deal with the one that would be coming at him.

William looked around him and saw a bedpan, the only solid object within reach. He heard Richard come through the door, grabbed the bedpan, hid it behind his back and jumped into the room facing Farwell and his hidden friends, yelling as loud as he could: "Richard, it's a trap, it's a trap!"

He heard his brother stop behind him and saw both men emerge from the curtains, swords in hand.

Farwell jumped to his feet. "Kill them, kill them both," he yelled.

The man closest to William struck at him with his sword. William used his left hand to deflect the blade downward as he swung the bedpan in a wide arc from behind and struck the man in the face. William felt his left hand being cut and the sword strike his left thigh as the man he struck hesitated, then crumbled to the ground, blood pouring out of his shattered nose.

William turned to survey the room. The second man had decided against attacking Richard who glared at him sword in hand.

Richard turned his gaze toward Farwell who had sat down again. He studied William, and seemed to be taking stock of his wounds, then looked back at Farwell, and stood staring at him, studying his features with apparent curiosity. Richard leaned over, extended his left hand and grabbed a clump of Farwell's blond hair, raising him to his feet as though he were a rag doll.

Farwell let out a whimper but otherwise stood motionless and silent, staring at Richard's sword with wide eyes.

"I won't be killing you today, Farwell, but someday I will."

That was strange, William noted, for Richard didn't sound angry; but rather matter of fact. With this he spat on Farwell's face, let go of his hair and watched him slump down on the chair.

[4]

Earl Orland of Sheffield craved to be on horseback chasing deer rather than be dealing with court troubles. Orland sat behind his worktable in his solarium. Farwell, William, and Richard stood before him. Veronica, Elizabeth, and Simon behind them. Generous sunlight came through the windows of the large room and a ray of light beamed on one of the wall tapestries, a hunting scene in a forest. All was silent except for the girls' sniffles.

One of Farwell's games gone astray, Orland thought.

He asked each one, in turn, for their version of events.

"I was seduced by Elizabeth," Farwell told him, staring down at the floor and uttering the words a bit too forcefully, "and I only tried to protect myself from

Richard by asking my friends to guard me. She planned to wed me, and set up a trap with her sister.

"Imagine the pretensions of such a lowborn."

Orland no longer looked at his son, but stared at William's bandaged leg.

Elizabeth in turn, tears streaming, spoke of a rape. "I forsook a good man at my father's urging, only to be subjected to the violent loss of my maidenhood," she said amid sobs.

As each person spoke, it became clearer to Orland that his son had crossed the line from mischief into evil when he lost the joust to William, and at that moment Orland had nothing but contempt for the pathetic fruit of his loins, his only heir.

How he wished William had been his son. But God had given him Farwell instead.

Looking into William's face, he saw his friend John staring back at him and remembered how John, many years before, had warned him of a scheme by one of Orland's cousins to murder him and his father and have the earldom pass to that side of the family.

His father had conducted a hearing much like this one. Though both his cousin and his accomplice had successfully countered all the charges against them, from then on the relationship had been more guarded and any possibility of a similar plot forever averted. But John had been disgraced in the court. Only Orland was certain of the charges, being sure of John's gift of visions, something only those close to him knew about. Orland knew his cousin would seek revenge on the young knight, so he gave John enough money to join the Templars in Outremer.

For Orland, John was the brother he never had. And now he would send his two nephews to join him.

He addressed his son. "Farwell, you have brought dishonor to our family."

Orland sent Farwell to his chambers under guard and told him he would decide what to do next. He stood and walked over to Elizabeth. "I am sorry for what Farwell did to you. But what's done is done and there is no undoing."

He then turned around to face the two brothers. "William, you want to join the Templars in Outremer and need only money for it. Richard, your days in this court are done. I have a wicked son, and there's nothing I can do about it. I'm sorry, but as long as you are here, he will cause you nothing but trouble. I would counsel you to go with your brother. I'm willing to gift you both the necessary funds.

"I will keep your family's fief safe, should something happen to your father. I swear it."

William appeared elated at the words. "Thank you, my Lord. I gladly accept."

"So do I, my Lord," replied Richard.

At this Orland heard Elizabeth's muffled cries behind him as her sister led her away.

[5]

The late afternoon sun was setting behind the hills as the two brothers rode home, and William wondered how different things now looked from that morning when they rode to the castle. He also thought of how things had been ordained for him. Had it not been for Jules he would still be at the abbey, and without him, his brother would in all likelihood have fallen prey to Farwell. So, ironically, he had to be grateful to the depraved friar. Now he also had to thank Farwell for making his trip to Outremer possible.

William felt bad for Elizabeth. It was obvious she cared for Richard and had been Farwell's easy pawn. "Richard," he asked, "do you still love Elizabeth?"

His brother turned in his saddle. "No, she got what she had coming. She welcomed Farwell's attentions knowing full well what he was like. Her heart became greedy and she forsook me for money and position."

"What if I could prove otherwise? What if she loved you, but was prompted by her father as she claims?"

"No matter. She is now a fallen woman."

"So you think she provoked Farwell into raping her?"

"Women have their ways for enticing and she chose to be alone with him. As I said, she got what she deserved. Besides, even if I felt differently, how could I wed a fallen woman?"

William stared at his brother in wonder because when he heard his words they sounded empty, untrue, and William knew that things would turn out differently. Somehow Richard would end up marrying Elizabeth—he could feel them together, sense their long tenure in this life; but Richard would need to change. A lot.

Two months later, William stood next to his brother Richard by a window in the hallway outside the guests' quarters at London Templar House. Richard was mesmerized by the action outside in the ward: six Templars on foot wearing hauberks stood blindfolded with swords in hand, while ten other monks acting as their attackers, came at them from all sides, wielding swords and shields at the ready. The defenders formed a circle and with uncanny precision fended off each blow, time and time again, not allowing the attackers to enter their defensive line.

"I've never seen anything like it," muttered Richard. "How do you suppose they can tell where the enemy is?"

"I don't know, Richard. I suppose we'll be doing that ourselves at some point." William knew his brother was perhaps overwhelmed by it all. That morning during Matins William had noticed Richard imitating everything he did, nervously stealing glances in his direction while pretending to close his eyes in prayer.

"Are you ready for tomorrow, lad?" William heard Sir Ian's voice behind him, and turned around to see him approach along the long hallway, his steps resonating on the stone floor.

"As ready as I'll ever be," replied William as he embraced Sir Ian. They went to sit on a nearby bench. Richard remained transfixed watching the Templars' combat exercises.

"Everything is still too new for your brother, eh?" Sir Ian asked.

"He'll be fine." But William had decided to keep a close watch on Richard, explain things as they came up. According to Sir Ian, Richard was welcome to come along—the Templars were used to knights bringing friends and relatives, for the training weeded out those who didn't belong. Now that they were about to sail to the Holy Land, William worried that Richard would simply not fit in as a monk…as a warrior, yes, but a cloistered life was a different matter.

"You two are fully equipped?" Sir Ian asked.

William unsheathed his sword and held it before the sheriff with both hands. "Look at the quality of the steel, Sir Ian," and he turned the blade in the light to show a flawless surface of smooth, hard steel. "Thanks to our earl's generosity, we bought the best that money could buy—swords, helmets and hauberks, all made in Milan. The hauberks came with a variety of armor plates that can be easily attached to the mail as one desires."

"That's an impressive sword." Sir Ian appeared pleased. "I just saw your horses, those are fine destriers.

"Well, tomorrow you sail. After all you've gone through to get to this point, you must be relieved."

"Mostly anxious and excited. And grateful it all worked out, a miracle of sorts."

Sir Ian smiled broadly. "Yes, quite a miracle. Eventually you'll get used to those."

"What do you mean?"

"Oh, never mind.

"Please remember the reason you are going," Sir Ian said in a whisper. "You will find your uncle. But proceed patiently, please."

The following day, under an early morning sun peeking through thin fog, William stood next to Richard on deck in the ship's bow and watched the crew, two dark-skinned deck hands and three Templars shove the big ship with long poles. The vessel—a big hulk of shiny new wood—was over a hundred feet long and about thirty wide in the middle. It consisted of one big deck with a long covered area down its center where the horses, cargo and passengers were housed. The mast towered from the middle, a forty-foot timber.

On the quay stood the relatives of some of the passengers and Sir Ian, waving goodbye. A woman kept fervently making the sign of the cross at the departing ship.

William felt the pull of the outgoing tide and they glided on to the middle of the Thames. Two Templars then hoisted the sail and turned it to the wind until it billowed out and the ship picked up speed. William had read about their triangular sail called a "lateen," an innovation the Europeans had copied from the Saracen that allowed sailing in any direction regardless of where the wind came from, by simply pivoting the sail using a timber along its bottom, a big improvement over the old square sails that could only go down-wind. Their shipmaster, Brother Roger, a tall and affable man with red hair and beard, commanded the crew in a calm voice. William could now see the red cross—the odd Templar one with all four arms the same size—emblazoned on the canvas and the black and white flag Sir Ian had called the *Beauseant* flying on top of the mast.

William sensed his brother's apprehension as they both stared at the moving shoreline and the vanishing city they were leaving behind, perhaps forever. Through the fog William could make out the shape of the Tower of London at the very end of the city as they went past it.

The fog dissipated by midmorning. The green shoreline of the Thames became dotted with castles, and in between these, square forts—built by the Romans according to Brother Roger, and still being used to protect the city. After a few leagues, the river opened into a bay and the ship hugged the coast to the west. By mid afternoon they spotted the white cliffs of Dover. The ship now rolled in rough seas, and Brother Roger directed his passengers to stand by their mounts. "We don't want those big beasts moving around. Keep them calm until they get used to the waves."

William looked over his black destrier. Though held tight by ropes, William could see that his eyes were wide with fear, and was pulling back on the ropes with all his might. William began stroking the Percheron's nose, talking softly, "All is well, my boy. All is well."

That night, William, Richard, and the four other would-be Templar novices slept fitfully next to their horses, wrapped in blankets against the cold wind, lying on coarse sacks full of straw they had been issued at London Templar House.

The following day after dinner, with no land in sight and nothing but the rough ocean all around them, Richard and the other knights sat around in a circle near the now calmer horses. "What if we fall off the edge of the world?" William overheard a tall fellow, ask. "And what about dragons? My uncle told me of a ship that was attacked by one."

"We can't fall off the edge," William said, who was standing by and listening with amusement. "The world is round. It's like a ball, you see, with no edges."

The tall man laughed. "Just look out yonder," he said shivering with fear or cold, pointing at the horizon all around. "Can't you tell that the world is like a plate?"

"Yeah," added a second one with a thick black beard, wearing his blanket wrapped tightly around his body. "If the world were round, once you came down the sides, you would fall off! Explain that!"

William shook his head. "No one knows why you don't fall off, but you'll notice that the horizon stays the same distance away, no matter how long we sail, and then…"

"We are far from the edge," interrupted Brother Roger, as he walked by coiling a rope. "Very far. As for dragons, I haven't seen one in the ten years I've sailed this route."

One of the other Templars assured them that dragons lived far to the south, so they were safe.

After eight days they entered the Mediterranean Sea. The waters calmed down and the temperature warmed up. After three days of calm sailing, Richard and the other recruits, apparently no longer afraid of the voyage, sat around the deck chatting about their new lives, how they planned on gathering glory by killing many of the enemy. William had no choice but to sit nearby, leaning against a post, trying his best not to listen. Then the conversation turned to monastic life, how much they would be expected to pray, fast, and the vows of poverty and chastity.

"I've been bedding at least one woman a week from the age of thirteen," said a redheaded knight with freckles. "That's going to be the hardest thing for me to get used to, going without sex."

"Yeah, that won't be easy," replied Richard as he turned to look at his brother. "William, you were a monk and went for two years without a woman. How did you manage?"

William looked at the sky. "It wasn't that hard in the abbey because there was no temptation."

"But you just spent seven months around women again. How was that?"

"Oh," laughed the freckled one. "I bet he just went wild in the tavern!"

Richard and the other four laughed, exchanging glances.

William turned his head in their direction. "Actually, I did not. I still considered myself a monk." The snickers died down at the sound of William's tone. "I was tempted many times, but each time I got over the impulse, I became stronger. It's all a matter of stopping the thoughts before they take hold, and I did it through prayer." With this William switched his gaze to the sea.

The would-be Templars stole furtive, inquisitive glances at William. The freckled one shrugged his shoulders.

"Can't wait to slay some Saracen," said the tall one after a pause. "My uncle told me that the pope will raise a new Christian army and then we'll take back the land the enemies of our Lord have taken from us."

"And because we'll all be Templars by then," added the freckled one, "we'll be leading the fight."

Brother Roger came and sat beside Richard. He signaled for William to join the group. "Most of the Holy Land has been lost to the fierce Mameluk Turks now being led by Sultan Qalawun. All that remain are the coastal castles and cities. I don't think anyone will be defeating the Turks anytime soon."

"Turks are a type of Arab?" Richard asked.

"No, they are not. They're not even from the region," replied Brother Roger. "The Turks are made up of many tribes but the ones we mostly fight are the Sajuk and the Mameluk."

"If the Turks are not from the Holy Land, then where do they come from?" asked the man with the black beard.

"They came from the steppes beyond the Black Sea. Starting two centuries ago, the Mameluk were brought as slaves by the Egyptians because they were such good warriors, and they eventually took over the Egyptian army. During the Mongol invasion of 1230 the Turks had to leave their homeland and joined the ones already in Outremer, and now they are pushing all Christian armies toward the sea."

"But the Templars are the mightiest warriors on earth," said the fellow with the freckles, "surely they can beat the Turks!"

"The Turks have a big, well-disciplined army," Brother Roger answered. "The Templars alone can't fight them."

"But the Christian kings have many men," said the tall one, "the pope need only ask them to come to the Holy Land."

"You are right," Brother Roger said. "If the Europeans decided to unite and liberate the Holy Land, they could. But for some reason the kings of Europe lack the will, and the pope keeps trying, but to no avail."

After a silence the freckled one stood up. "Beg your pardon brother shipmaster," he said, "but all of that is just talk. Who cares about Turks and what the kings and the pope are doing as long as we get to fight!

"The more Turks the more we get to slay, that's what I say!" the freckled one chuckled.

Brother Roger sighed, and went to assist a sailor tightening the sail.

William walked away from the group searching for a place where he could be alone. He found an area enclosed by crates where spare ropes were kept. He sat on a coil with the deep blue Mediterranean in front and no one around. Waves lapped against the side of the ship, the sun felt warm on his shoulders and off in the distance he could see a long brown shape, perhaps the African coast. He decided this was where he would spend the remainder of the journey.

It took them six weeks to reach Acre, the main port in the Holy Land. The city occupied a small peninsula in the Bay of Acre. From a distance they could see the massive stone fortifications and tall towers of the city, an imposing presence. Brother Roger pointed out to the recruits where Templar House stood, a strong fort with walls twenty-feet thick at the tip of the city. In the distance, at the southern end of the bay they could distinguish the ruins of the city of Haifa destroyed by the Turks some twenty years before.

CHAPTER III

[1]

William stepped off the ship with his saddlebag over his left shoulder and looked around the quay. Off to the side stood a Knight Templar—Brother Roger had said someone would be there to greet them, and William guessed the man was waiting for the new arrivals. William stopped beside the silent Templar and exchanged smiles, and then he took a deep breath. He didn't know what to expect from that point on, but things so far had worked out fine. Richard seemed capable of making new friends, and William guessed that he would do just that wherever he went, so there was no need to worry about him. But it would be nice to be assigned to the same castle.

When Richard and the others came off the ship, the silent Templar led them on a short walk to the end of the quay, then on along a tunnel through the wall, and down to a city street. Across the way stood a massive fortress, Acre Templar House.

That evening after Vespers William and Richard joined twelve knights, other recent arrivals from Europe and Cyprus, in a meeting hall lined with weapons of all sorts: crossbows, the short and hefty maces used for bludgeoning, the star-shaped caltrops for throwing, lances and javelins, and a few famous swords, rusted but revered. "Admire the weapons, but Templars only fight with sword and lance," a barrel-chested, red-haired commander told them—his rank distinguished by a white mantle draped over his shoulders—"You will be assigned to a Templar castle, and for the next six months undergo training the likes of which none of you has experienced before." The commander's booming voice echoed in the big room. "Most of you won't make it through the first cycle of training and will remain squires, perhaps for a long time. A third will leave before the year is out. But those who become knights, no matter how long it takes, will be forever changed. Then you may take the Templar vows, and wear the surcoat with the cross," the commander pointed to the red cross on the white surcoat he wore over his hauberk.

The following morning William walked with Richard through the busy, narrow, and clean streets of the strange city, awed by all the stores with their exotic merchandise: clothes made entirely of silk; fruit he had read about: oranges, pomegranates, and dates; delicate and elaborate porcelain cups, bowls and dishes, and spicy and aromatic foods served on flat, thin breads. *This is the Holy Land*, William reminded himself, *and this city has been here for thousands of years, long before the time of Jesus*. He marveled at the alleyways cluttered with pedestrians, fancy carriages, carts, horses, and camels, terraces with opulent gardens, women entirely hidden in cloth, men in flowing robes…elegant and clean. William studied the tall narrow buildings made of hard stones with tiled roofs, and touched a well-worn corner and tried to imagine whether Jesus had perhaps done the same.

William observed Richard: his uncertainty overwhelmed by the newness of it all, studying the old buildings, courtyards, and alleyways full of shops, and William wondered whether Richard would be one to leave before the year was out.

They approached a store of rugs and fabrics, a big open area surrounded by columns, the merchandise in neat piles on the smooth stone floor. Richard ran his hand along a red cloth and marveled at its softness.

"Silk from Katai," the vendor said in French, "soft but hardy. Ladies really like it."

Richard studied the man's dark features. "Are you a Saracen?"

"Yes, Sire. I'm an Arab."

William noticed how Richard recoiled at the news and left the store in a hurry, then stood outside staring at the mountains of fancy rugs and fabrics next to the sidewalk. "Why is he allowed to live in a Christian city? I thought all the Saracens of Acre had been slain long ago," Richard said.

"We must learn their ways," said William. "I am certain there are many things we don't understand." He pointed to a man jotting down figures on a tablet. "It's fascinating, Richard. Notice that none of the merchants have abacuses for counting. That man over there is using some sort of squiggles—instead of Roman numerals—he jots them down in columns and counts that way."

"So?"

"Well, it's interesting, that's all."

That afternoon after Nones, William and Richard were told both would be assigned to Pilgrim Castle, a day-and-a-half ride down the coast from Acre.

The following day they rode, led by a Knight Templar named Brother Alphonse. Two other prospective novices, one of them the freckled knight from the ship, accompanied them.

"If we encounter an enemy patrol, our orders are to run," the serious looking Brother Alphonse said as they started out of the city, going south along the bay. It was late May and the air was already hot in the early morning. "Cover your hauberks with a cloak," Brother Alphonse ordered them, "otherwise the mail will get so hot it will burn you."

They stopped their horses to rummage through their packs.

"Watch out for the enemy, but also, watch out for what the sun can do," continued Brother Alphonse, "particularly in the summer. It can kill you. Keep your skin covered.

"Leave a cup of water outside, and you'll see it disappear. The same happens with the sweat on your body. That's why all Templars are bearded and always wear their surcoats' hoods over their heads." Brother Alphonse inspected the recruits to make sure they followed his instructions. "Things are worse in the area south of Jerusalem. That's the start of the desert," he said as William and the others mounted, now safely cloaked with blankets. "If you ever find yourself in that place, what I just told you could save your life."

William studied the craggy but green countryside around him. It was sparser and dryer than anything he had seen before, and he tried to imagine the desert Brother Alphonse talked about, a completely barren landscape. What struck William was the color of the vegetation; it was a peculiar shade of green, and the sun was bright, as he had never seen it, and the air dry, clean, and warm.

The following morning they approached the foreboding bulk of their new home standing gray and massive against the blue of the sea behind it.

Pilgrim Castle was modern and huge, one of the strongest fortifications William had ever seen; its walls even stronger than those of Acre, at least thirty feet thick. It had been built on a tongue of rock protruding into the sea; its tall ramparts sheer with the ocean on three sides, and fronted by a deep moat.

Once in the outer ward, Brother Alphonse had the recruits dismount and walk their horses to the stables. Then he showed them the castle. He led William and the others up the stairs to one of the towers in front. The land was flat all around, except for a hill the Christians called Mount Carmel, a hazy lump to the northeast.

"Pilgrim Castle houses fifty Templar knights, fifty-eight sergeants, sixty squires, a hundred Turcopoles—mercenary Syrian Christian archers—and a hundred cross-bowmen," explained Brother Alphonse in his no-nonsense tone. "Most of the knights, sergeants, squires and Turcopoles serve in either of two squadrons, or are assigned to castle duties as guards or scouts. There are a few other sergeants and Turcopoles assigned to our farms, and they come to the castle every Saturday for Review. The crossbowmen—all of them mercenaries—are here to protect the castle but on occasion go out with the battle group—which is what we call both squadrons joined together for a major battle. There are another ninety-two Templar brothers who are masons, cooks, tailors, smiths, and doctors, assisted by another hundred or so grooms and servants. We have four priests who see to our spiritual needs.

"Our castle is supplied by land and by sea," Brother Alphonse said as he led the group along the rampart toward the west tower. "The ships—mainly from Genoa, Florence, Venice, Cyprus, and Constantinople—have to be unloaded by the two castle boats, which meet them out at sea. The larger items, mainly horses and hay, come by land from Acre.

"Most of our food is grown on local farms, owned by Castle Pilgrim and managed by Templar sergeants, and located next to neighboring villages and towns that used to be protected by local barons. But for the last hundred years—ever since the fall of Jerusalem to the Turks—the area is always teetering on the brink of chaos. We are the ones imposing order around here, but are constantly clashing with local warlords, bandits, and the Turkish detachments sent to harass us."

Brother Alphonse led them to look over the north wall to a nearby town. "That's Atlit, built on land owned by the Templars, about a third of Acre's size. Christians live there, along with a few Muslims. They work in the castle as our servants, and on the farms.

"Pilgrim Castle was last attacked unsuccessfully by the Mameluk Turks a few years ago," Brother Alphonse said as he led the recruits back down to the outer ward. "Since then we have enjoyed a truce in exchange for half the town's rents. Acre has a truce with the Turks as well. Let's hope the relative peace lasts.

"Last year the County of Tripoli—including the Templar castle—fell to Sultan Qalawun, the Mameluk leader— as did the port of Latakia to the north. You saw what Qalawun did to Haifa twenty years ago. Caesaria, a city to the south, was also destroyed at about the same time.

"In the old days Castle Pilgrim was part of the Haifa *Commanderie*, and our seneschal answered to the Haifa commander, a senior seneschal. But the *commanderies*—a complex of castles and forts protecting a city—in the Holy Land are now gone. Now there are only isolated castles.

"What remains besides Pilgrim and Acre are Tyre, Sidon, Beirut, Tortosa, and the Island of Ruad, all to the north and on the coast, defended by Templars, Hospitallers, and Teutonic Knights. Twenty years ago there were more than thirty Templar castles and forts and about as many belonging to the other orders."

William studied Atlit, its narrow streets and houses looked rather quaint. "So we are on the retreat," he said catching Brother Alphonse's attention, "and it seems just a matter of time before the Turks decide to kill us all."

"That's about it," said Brother Alphonse.

That evening William and Richard were assigned bunks in adjoining dorms that slept fifty men each.

William was putting away his gear in the allotted shelf near his bunk when he heard someone behind him.

"My name is Bridon," a voice said in heavily accented French, "and I have the bunk next to yours."

William turned around to find a short, slender man, with wispy brown hair and sparse beard, in a brown squire's surcoat with blue, guileless eyes. "Nice to make your acquaintance, Bridon. My name is William. Where are you from?"

"From Ireland…you noticed my accent, eh? People make fun of me because of it, but I don't care."

Turned out that Bridon had been a squire for over five years. "But this year I'll make the cut and become a knight," he said with a smile. He talked incessantly as William continued unpacking, gushing about the Templars, about Castle Pilgrim, and at great length, about Jesus.

"We are so blessed," Bridon said with emotion. "By just fighting for Christ, we, and our families, receive many blessings; but should we die in combat, we are saved, and go straight to heaven."

William looked into Bridon's innocent eyes, brimming with happiness. "Yes, Bridon, we are blessed."

The following day William and Richard visited the draper brother and were issued brown squire's surcoats, linen, and personal items for cleansing and equipment upkeep. They were given shields painted with the Templars' red cross, and sturdy knives. Their surcoats were very similar to monks' habits, and it occurred to William that once he became a knight, except for the red cross on the chest, he would look much like he did before as a Cistercian monk.

William walked up to Richard who stood in the ward admiring the knife. "So we are supposed to eat with this, but also use it as a weapon?" Richard asked.

"And as a tool, I guess. I like the shields, good and sturdy, but not too heavy."

"Good stuff. And the people are nice. But what do you think of the old men?"

William knew that Richard was referring to the associates, four older newcomers not required to take vows, who were serving time in the Order for crimes committed, and showed no signs of devotion. "We're not supposed to befriend them, Richard. They'll keep to themselves and follow the rules.

"But the rest of the Templars are impressive. There are several highborn who donated all their possessions to the Order. And there are others like me, who had been novitiates in other orders. Have you made any friends yet, Richard?"

"Yes. Last night I had a good chat with the man in a nearby bunk. Very devout, William, even more than you."

The trainees broke into two groups of five each, under the direction of a training sergeant. All sergeants were from the working class, men who took the same vows as the knights, and wore light brown surcoats with the same red cross and a black mantle of command, a garment that hung down from the shoulders to mid-torso. The sergeants who all spoke a quaint mixture of French and their native tongues, salted with the occasional word in Arabic, something that took getting used to, showed them how they were expected to maintain their equipment, and told them to seek quick replacement of sword, hauberk, helmet, horse, or anything that showed wear or damage. The most critical item was the horse; it had to be strong and able, well-trained, and used to its rider. The castle kept two spare destriers—fine Percherons bred in Templar farms in Europe—for each combat monk, in addition to numerous palfreys and hackneys for non-combatants, as well as donkeys and camels for freight.

William found life at Pilgrim Castle more disciplined than at his old abbey. He and Richard were now postulants and followed the rigors of the Templars, getting up on the fourth hour for Matins, then Prime, Terce and Sext all before breakfast. Afterward they went to their duties, training until Nones, at mid-afternoon.

The chapel had a large, vaulted ceiling with two large stained glass windows, one depicting the Virgin Mary kneeling by her crucified son, the other showing Christ ascending into heaven. The cavern-like place was permeated with the heavy scent of myrrh, which clung to the air, sweet and pungent. Prayers were supposed to be said in silence, but monks tended to murmur, and it became a drone, a deep and pleasing sound of devotion reverberating off the stone walls.

Vespers came at sunset followed by the evening meal, after which the monks could work on their equipment and look after their horses. The day ended with Compline when the horologe in the keep's tower chimed the twenty-first hour right before bedtime. Templar monks kept close track of the hours to know which office to pray, and when to eat, sleep or work, and most followed the chiming with their fingers. Some, like Richard, couldn't keep track, so they watched others and followed the throng. All meals were eaten in silence; the only permissible sound was the voice of the scholar-monk reading aloud from the Bible.

On Saturday mornings, all castle personnel lined up in the outer ward for

Review, during which the seneschal called out the names of their comrades who had died that week in combat, named the squires eligible to take their vows of knighthood, and identified those Templars being punished for misdeeds. The occasion ended with a talk meant to inspire them to fight, pray, and avoid temptation. Afterward, they broke ranks and stood about in what was called a Chapter Meeting, an occasion to speak freely and voice concerns. On Sundays they heard mass after Matins and spent the rest of the day in quiet contemplation and fasting, interrupted only by the holy offices.

That first week the trainees were trained to wield their lances and swords until they understood what they had been doing wrong; they learned how to position their bodies for maximum thrust, and how to guard their bodies without a shield.

Walking back from Vespers that first Sunday, with every muscle sore from the rigorous training, William saw Bridon run up to him with a big smile on his face. "Would you like to pray to the Holy Mother, William? Let's pray to the Holy Mother, she'll fill our hearts with joy." Bridon grabbed hold of his sleeve and pulled him along to a niche where a squire and a knight were already kneeling.

William found that the Templars were particularly devoted to the Virgin Mary, but they called her "Holy Mother." He started noticing niches all over the castle.

William sought out Richard whenever he could. One day after training, William found him slumped down in a corner of the outer ward by the stables.

"Tired, Richard?"

"Oh, Willy! This is the hardest thing I've ever done. My sergeant has me maneuvering on my horse, over and over again."

"I know. We are supposed to get to the point where everyone of us acts in unison, and the horses are so trained that they can detect our slightest command. I can now command my horse with a slight touch from my knees."

"I know it's necessary, but it's wearing me down, Willy."

"Keep on, Richard. Next week comes the toughest part of the training. Remember the exercises we watched in London Templar House?"

"Where the monks fought blindfolded? Don't tell me we are doing that next."

"We are."

Two days later the trainees were handed helmets without eye slots, and they could see nothing at all. At first, they were told to simply listen, to pay attention. Then they were made to walk around the outer ward. They all tripped and fell, then were taught to tell where objects and people were by subtle sounds and sensations. The way the wind blew, how sounds traveled and bounced, the feel of reflected sunlight from solid objects; how things smelled; leather was obvious as were body odors. After three days they could smell and "feel" the presence of people, animals, wood, cloth, and even sand and stones.

By the end of the first week William could get around an ever-changing obstacle course. Then, when the trainees formed a circle and others came to attack, he could almost always sense where his "friends" were and where the "enemy" was. He learned to "feel" how Templars fought, and how different it was from those impersonating Turks. Any change in dress, or weaponry became evident. After three weeks he knew that it was possible to fight without seeing, but realized that it would take much practice to get to the point where the sergeants were. When they demonstrated, it was as though it made no difference whether they could see or not. However, after the three weeks, when he sparred using his eyes again, the senses he had honed came into play. He was aware where everyone was at any given time, all around him. He could "feel" the battlefield.

One evening as they walked to their sleeping quarters, Bridon told William that he squired for a knight named Brother Oliver, who according to Bridon, was short-tempered and always angry. "I can't do anything right. Brother Oliver and his sergeant keep yelling at me all the time. Today I asked them if when the time comes you could be assigned to our team as our trainee squire, but Brother Oliver said that our commander won't allow our team to train anyone because I'm so incompetent.

"I don't think I'm incompetent, do you, William?"

"You are just fine at what you do, Bridon. God knows it and loves you. That's what counts."

A month later William was assigned to a knight, and he was much relieved, because the week before Richard had his own knight assigned and for a moment William thought he was being held back. William's training sergeant walked him over to meet his knight, Brother Jeremiah, a four-year veteran. William also met Brother Jeremiah's sergeant, Brother Vincent, and Squire Milton.

"Your duties, Trainee Squire William, are few," said Brother Sergeant Vincent. "This morning we'll be doing battle. Our scouts reported enemy activity in two nearby villages and the marshal decided to send a squadron to each. You'll be assisting Squire Milton with the equipment, but when the combat starts, you are only to watch. I'll let you know when you are ready to fight."

The squadrons fell in formation in front of the castle. William's commander stood in front with his sergeant, squire, and two Turcopoles, and the standard-bearer, a squire. Three paces behind came the first of five lines of knights, four abreast. Behind each knight was his sergeant and squire, and behind these, two

Turcopoles. Then came the other four lines of knights arranged the same way.

William, Richard, and eight other trainees followed the squadrons, trailing a spare mount each.

Once in formation, each squadron went in different directions. William's headed south and by midmorning spotted a village under attack, a dozen stone huts surrounded by a shoulder-high rock wall. The adjoining fields had goats and sheep.

The Templars stopped some hundred yards away from the attackers and two sergeants rode back to the trainees.

"Those are Syrian bandits," Sergeant Vincent said. "Trainee squires, stay here with the mounts and don't move until we return."

William and the other trainees stood on a promontory with the spare horses and watched the knights form a single line, each followed by his individual team of sergeant, squire and Turcopoles, and gallop toward the enemy.

William watched the Templar knights crash into the Syrian line, sweeping men and beasts before them. Each knight's team worked in unison: the sergeant protecting the knight's left flank and the squire the right, while the two Turcopoles defended their team against enemy archers. William was impressed with the precision with which the Templars fought; everyone knew their job and did it perfectly, the squadron truly operating as a single body. After the initial confrontation that lasted but a few moments, the squadron started cleaning the battlefield, working on pockets of resistance, then dealing with the wounded and securing those who surrendered. No prisoners were taken; those who had given up were disarmed and released while the wounded were either treated or mercy killed.

The entire battle was over quickly, the enemy fleeing, dead, or wounded.

When signaled, William and the other trainees rode to the now quiet battle scene to help.

The Templars were left with three lightly wounded sergeants. Two maimed horses had to be put down.

William walked the battlefield staring at the dead. Some still had their eyes open, and save for the wounds, looked as though they were about to get up or speak. He said a prayer for those who would mourn them, and realized that he would be killing soon, very soon. To be a Templar knight one had to be the best, completely fearless, and have no apprehensions; be willing to kill and be killed. A part of him resonated with what he was becoming, a member of the mightiest, best disciplined fighting force in the world. But there was another side of him that recoiled at the thought of such mayhem. When his time came to fight, he knew what would be required of him, a complete abandonment of reason and compassion—everything that Christ stood for.

The following day the squadrons fought Bedouins—nomadic Arabs from Africa—The tactics and results were much the same, a formation that wrapped around the enemy and left them dead, wounded or fleeing.

After that battle, when William went to bed, he noticed that Bridon's bunk was empty, and it remained empty the whole night. Concerned, the following morning he asked the commander's sergeant for Bridon's whereabouts, and was told that he had been wounded and was in the infirmary. "He'll make knight this time around," the sergeant said, " because of how he fought. He was totally fearless, he charged two Syrians head on and continued fighting after being wounded several times. It's a miracle he's still alive."

William visited Bridon in the infirmary and found him chipper, and as talkative as ever, elated in the knowledge that he had finally made the cut.

Two days later William's squadron fought their third battle of that week and William and the other trainees, again told by their sergeants to watch from some distance away, spotted a column of Sajuks approaching over a hill to the west, as their squadron fought, ignorant of the new threat.

The trainees looked at each other, tied their spare mounts together so they couldn't move and ran to intercept the enemy. They fought brilliantly, killing three of the Sajuks and routing the rest. William wounded one man, and was thankful his time to kill had not yet come.

After the battle, their sergeants told William, Richard, and the others that they had disobeyed their orders and would be punished.

That evening, Brother Dimas, the commander of their squadron, called the would-be knights to his chambers, a large room with a huge worktable in the middle and cubbyholes full of maps against the wall. "You disobeyed your sergeants' orders, a very serious offense," Commander Dimas said as his hard gaze studied each trainee in turn. "Always obey a military order no matter what. Obedience is more important than winning a battle or saving a fellow Templar." William felt the commander's eyes bearing down on him and a shudder went down his spine. "Life is but transitory, but your soul is eternal, and we are fighting for our souls, not for our lives. From obedience you will learn loyalty, from loyalty you will learn honor, and with honor you will earn your place in heaven."

As punishment, the trainees were made to wash all the floors of the castle on their hands and knees every day for a month after Compline—while praying. They also were to walk barefoot for three months when not in battle dress, maintain complete silence for two months, and eat only bread and water for a week.

Shortly after Brother Dimas had meted out their punishment, two of the trainees left, including the freckled man from the ship. For the eight who remained, counting William and Richard, their training intensified for the following six weeks. When not accompanying their assigned knights into battle, their military training continued. They were well fed and the rigorous routine made their bodies harder and stronger than they had ever been. They were faster, their senses keener to the movements of their opponents and their brother monks; but overall, their characters were being tempered hard, challenged time and again. They were subjected to intense interrogation meant to break their spirits.

One time they were told to spit on a cross and deny Christ. That day, the trainees were ushered into the chapel one at the time by their respective sergeant, and met at the altar by Commander Dimas.

At first, William couldn't believe his ears, and Commander Dimas had to repeat the order. "Trainee Squire William, I order you to spit on the cross and say that you don't believe in Christ. If you do it, you'll be made knight right away. If you don't, you'll spend the rest of your life in the dungeon."

William stood stupefied. Then he found his nerve. "No, there's no way I will do it. I would rather die."

Those who did spit on the cross failed the test. William's sergeant explained afterward outside the chapel: "When you were ordered to spit on the cross, that was not a military order, and you rightly refused because it went contrary to your beliefs, who you are. You have to be true to yourself or you'll never learn to be true to Christ. That's the ultimate test of your honor.

"You are not to share what I told you with others. I will ask you to swear to that."

"I understand; you want everyone to meet the test on their own accord, but what happens to those who fail?"

"They are not Templar material. They are told to leave. The sergeants, by the way, go through a similar test. We can't force people to be honorable; by this stage in the training either you have it or you never will."

Three trainees left the following day.

The five who remained went into the last phase of their training. They were dropped alone in the middle of the desert with no food or water and learned to endure; were made to engage in mock battles for days on end, far beyond exhaustion and hallucinations, and then expected to fight expertly. The lessons were drilled into them: never surrender, always obey a military order; and live, fight, and die with honor.

"You are fighting for Christ and will die for Him," their seneschal told them during Review. "It's just a question of when."

At the sound of his words everyone in the ward cheered. Some wept.

But as he walked away, William felt empty, phony. No matter how hard he tried, he couldn't quite make himself become a true Templar knight, ready to kill for Christ. He thought of Bridon. That was someone sweet and devout, whose whole ambition in life was simple: pray, love Jesus and the Virgin and fight as a Templar knight. William went to the infirmary to check on him, but when he arrived by his sick bed, he found a very different Bridon, sullen and quiet.

"Don't come near me, William, I have leprosy.

"I won't be a Templar knight, and must leave as soon as possible. That's why the wounds didn't bother me, because I couldn't feel anything on account of the illness."

"Where would you go? What would you do?"

"Oh, I can still be a knight. They are transferring me to the Knights of Saint Lazarus, an order for lepers. They have a castle near Acre."

A week later the trainees' military training ended and William and the others were assigned each to a new knight. They were no longer training squires, but regular squires, members of their knight's combat team. Now it was a matter of qualifying for that final step: becoming a Knight Templar. William had hoped to continue serving close to Richard, but they were assigned to different squadrons. William now squired for Brother Julian, perhaps for a long time.

The following evening, as he made his way to the stables after Vespers, William found a group of squires, gathered in front of the smithies' shop, waiting for new horseshoes, stirrups and other items. Most sat on their hunches on the ground, others stood leaning against a massive rampart.

"Next month Brothers Dimas and Joseph will call out the lucky ones," Squire Alex—a man William knew had been waiting to become a knight for three years—was saying to one of the newer squires. "If you think your name will be called, forget it."

"They mean to teach us humility," Squire Dominic said. "They want to see if we can take the humiliation of having our fates in the hands of the sergeants."

William continued on his way to the stables. He decided that there was no sense in hoping to be knighted soon; he would just do his best.

Two weeks went by and William seldom saw Richard, now that he served in the other squadron, but one afternoon after training exercises, William's sergeant approached him. "You'll be glad to know that your brother Richard will probably be knighted soon. He's done very well. During a battle his sergeant saw him lose his sword in a fight; so he yanked a Sajuk off his horse and used him as a club. The man is incredible."

William was glad for Richard, but felt at a loss, left behind. He was sure he would remain a squire for a long time. There was no way he could fight like that.

William's squadron went out several times that week and in most occasions the enemy ran when the Templars approached them. But during one encounter on a narrow canyon sprinkled with palm trees, shrubs and large boulders, William, who as usual was covering Julian's right flank and was a few paces behind him, realized that they were running into a trap, they were charging into a field where their horses could not charge at full gallop because of the big boulders. Then William saw six Syrian bandits with bows waiting behind a rock, and four of them shot Brother Julian's two Turcopoles, then split up, aiming their arrows at William and the sergeant, while the two others charged at Brother Julian. William instinctively dropped his shield, grabbed his lance with both hands and rode to face the four archers, swinging the long weapon around him. He struck an archer in the throat with the point and felt the butt hit anther Syrian in the chest, then turned his horse to find a third bowman ready to let go of an arrow in his direction. The man shot, William jerked his head to one side as he broadsided the man with his lance and the arrow grazed his helmet next to the eye slot. He then followed up with the lance's butt to the head. The enemy archer collapsed on top of his horse.

William looked around, his senses and body revved up to fight. He saw that the three other Syrians were lying on the ground and that his sergeant was studying him.

"You did well, Squire William. The fight is over, let's take care of our wounded."

The sergeant rode up to Brother Julian whose leg showed an ugly slash. The two Turcopoles lying on the ground appeared to be alive, with arrows protruding from their chests. The bleeding had stopped, so perhaps the brother doctors could pull out the arrows and save them. William picked them up as gently as possible, one hand on their belts and the other by their tunics, and hoisted them up on their horses to take them back to the castle.

As he rode, he realized that he had killed for the first time. The man he had struck in the throat with the lance never got up. Sorrow overtook him and he prayed.

That next Saturday during Review, the marshal presented a list to the seneschal who ceremoniously took the parchment in his hands and prepared to call out the names of those squires selected for the dubbing ceremony. Both squadrons were lined up in the outer bailey, each facing their respective commander, the knights in the first row, then the sergeants, the squires on the third row, and last, the Turcopoles. The smithies, cooks, servants, and grooms stood a respectful distance away. The entire castle was mostly silent—only the snorting and stomping of the animals could be heard from the stables.

William heard the names of two squires called, and the gasps of surprise coming from the two men, and he smiled inwardly realizing how happy they must be. Then he heard Richard's name. *The Sergeant had been right, Richard made it!* There was a long silence, and he thought that was it, they would be dismissed, when he heard his name. William felt his heart skip a beat and couldn't help but look at the seneschal in disbelief. Had he heard right? William looked to the front rows and caught the smiles from his sergeant and his knight, Brother Julian, who had turned their heads in his direction, and it dawned on him that yes, both he and Richard were to become Knights Templar on their first six-month cycle of training.

CHAPTER IV

[1]

Six months and eighteen days after their arrival, William and Richard, along with the two others squires knelt down in the chapel before their seneschal who gave them the kiss of kinship on both cheeks. They were now Poor Knights of Christ and the Temple of Solomon.

"Praised be the Lord," Richard said afterward as they walked through the ward, "we are now Templar knights."

William noticed how much Richard had changed, and it wasn't just the surcoat with the cross. He now had a self-confidence that William knew came from deep inside. During the past four months, Richard had befriended Brother Maurice, a very devout monk about their age who kept company with others like him. They were known as the Hardcores of Pilgrim Castle, given to repeated fasts and self-flagellation to atone for their sins. Richard spent all his time with them and William saw his brother only in passing.

Richard's new friends came to congratulate him, and William continued walking on his own, seeking solitude so he could think. Where was the person who according to Sir Ian would tell him how to look for uncle John? But why not look for his uncle right away? William climbed one of the guard towers and looked out at the vast terrain that spread out in front of the castle. Where to start? He walked along the parapet to the west wall and looked out over the ocean. Then he realized he was trapped: there was nothing he could do at present but be a Knight Templar and kill.

The day after their initiation, the new knights were assigned to one of the two squadrons. William was assigned a sergeant, a squire and two Trucopoles. He immediately took a liking to his sergeant, Brother Albert, a tall and lanky man who was quiet and appeared very devout. He was one of the monks William usually found praying in the chapel in between offices. His lips moved in constant prayer as he did his chores, and he had about him a sweet look of ecstatic devotion.

In one day William had gone from taking orders from sergeants to being their superior. The first time his squadron filed in, William took his position with the other squadron knights.

Next to him stood Brother Julian, whom he had served as a squire. "Brother William, welcome," he said with a smile. Now that they were no longer separated by rank, Brother Julian appeared to William as a different person, warm and friendly, rather than aloof and authoritarian. "You saved my life that day when you attacked the Syrians with your lance. Thank you."

The squadrons left almost every day on patrol along the roads to Acre and Jerusalem and the nearby farms, villages, and towns. Whenever the two squadrons went out together, they were called a battle group and rode under the marshal's command.

William's first skirmish as a knight was uneventful; the squadron chased down a group of Sajuks harassing a goat farm on the road to Jerusalem and captured them. As usual, William found himself tearing off his helmet as soon as the fighting was over, the heat inside it unbearable. He wondered whether that was why so many men had scars on their faces, and why so many had lost an eye to an arrow; but then he was told by Sergeant Albert that the Saracen and the Turks had expert marksmen who could shoot an arrow through the helmet's narrow eye slots.

"The enemy has adopted harassing tactics where they hit and run," the seneschal told them that following Saturday. "They are drawing us to terrains where our horses are useless. Another tactic involves pretending to retreat, only to lure the charging knights into a circle of archers. Their traps are becoming more elaborate. Now they are using sharpened poles against our horses. Be careful!"

On his way to the stables, William thought of using the armor plates he had bought along with his hauberk, but couldn't decide how much to use. He had to be careful not to burden himself with too much weight and the stiffness that came with the plates. He had heard the stories of knights immobilized by too much armor, and he let Sergeant Albert decide where he needed extra protection. William ended up with plates on his back, chest, shoulders, thighs, and knees.

He had to admit that he got goose bumps when charging the enemy chanting the battle cry: "*Beauseant! Beauseant!*" In his Saturday talks, the seneschal implied that the meaning of the words "to be whole" meant that they were to fight and die with the faith of Christ in their hearts, but the explanation didn't sound right to William. How did the flag of equal horizontal black and white stripes symbolize that?

Two weeks after William became a knight, his squadron went out to patrol the road to Acre where they found a column of Syrian bandits. Again, the enemy had chosen a battlefield with small hills and trenches that made a full charge virtually impossible. The Syrians had formed a clump defensive line: armored riders in front with archers in the middle, hoping to decimate the Templars with arrows. Commander Dimas ordered the squadron to charge in small groups of three lances each, three knights and their teams blasting the middle of the enemy line, to break their defenses and neutralize the archers. William knew he would end up killing again that day, given the Syrian's numbers. He rode with Brother Julian to his right, and another knight to his left, and they were the first to strike the Syrians and make a breach in their line.

William was now getting used to the feel and tempo of fighting. It all happened fast, his body simply reacted without thinking, the long hours of training took over, and he knew that if he thought about it, it would slow him down. As if in a dream, as though it was happening to someone else, he saw one horseman impaled at the end of his lance, and then another, then one came on his right flank and was felled by his squire. He felt rather than saw arrows coming at him, and he raised his shield. Two riders came at him, and he fought them: fended to the left, struck to the right, felt his horse surge to one side, slashed one man, back to his left, feinted with the sword, struck with the shield and followed with the sword, and the second man fell.

Then all was quiet and Brother Albert stood to his right inspecting him for wounds.

William looked over the battlefield and saw the bodies of the men he had killed, but felt nothing inside. They were part of the landscape, four bodies among the many. More significant were the fallen Templars, two squires lying bloody on the ground…faces he had seen bowing in prayer that same morning.

During Vespers the images from the battle came back to William, and he saw the four men he had killed, and the scenes kept replaying in his mind over and over, and now he could see their faces and hear their screams, and he figured that's the way it was going to be every time. He tried to pray as hard as he could, trying to dispel the images.

That night after Compline as he went across the dorm adjoining his, William caught a conversation between Maurice and a number of his followers, including Richard. "Did you see him ride right into the group of Saracens?" asked a tall knight. "Jesus would be so proud! He died with so much glory and is in heaven right now sitting next to Him!" William guessed they were talking about one of the squires who had died that afternoon.

He looked at the group and noticed the look of rapture on Richard's face as he listened intently to every word.

"My dream is to die thus!" Maurice said, "gloriously sacrificing my life for Christ."

The group went on with their spirited talk, laying out a path to liberate the Holy Land and particularly Jerusalem, the "clearing out the enemies of our Lord," by slaying all Muslims and Jews.

Then a short and husky man told a story of a mass slaughter of Jews he had witnessed, and the glory that was felt after "the cleansing of our Holy Land."

That night William couldn't sleep, instead he fretted for Richard, and wished his brother would end his friendship with Maurice and the Hardcores, for their talk worried him. Given enough exposure to Maurice's group Richard would end up a fanatic, just like them.

In the morning William found Richard by his bunk. He was busy cleaning his sword, a bottle of oil, grinding sand, sharpening stone, and beeswax by his feet, rags strewn all around.

"Richard, haven't had much of a chance to talk to you," William said with a smile.

Richard looked up, his face solemn. "Brother William, yes. I've little time for talk these days. Busy with the Lord, always busy with the Lord's work."

"I have just been thinking about mother," William said, "how concerned she must be for us, and was planning to send her something on the next ship."

Richard looked at him for a moment. "I have no time for things of the world, Brother William. I would counsel you pray for her, if you are concerned. Christ will take care of her."

Richard had called him "Brother William" and the implication was clear, he was now just another one of his Templar brothers. "Very well, as you wish. May the Lord be with you." William turned to leave and found Maurice standing behind him. William noticed his round face with small features: his nose a mere rise above thin lips and pale cold eyes below very blond, almost white eyebrows. Even his sparse beard seemed translucent. Everything about him was cold and lifeless.

"Brother Maurice, you concern yourself with others' conversations?"

Maurice eyed him grimly and did not respond.

On William's third week as a Knight Templar the Battle Group engaged in a particularly furious battle in front of a small Christian town tucked in a green valley that the Sajuks had attacked and begun to ransack before the Templars showed up. The Battle Group fought for several hours against a superior force, and by noon, with the battle almost won, William saw an enemy officer charge at Brother Albert, who appeared wounded. William had watched the heavily armored Sajuk officer throughout the battle, a fierce fighter who took extraordinary risks. William, who had lost his lance and shield, spurred his horse; the Sajuk saw him, veered away from Albert and aimed his lance at William. William raised his sword high above his head with both hands, knowing he needed all his strength to penetrate the man's armor. With the lance about to strike him, William gyrated his torso to the left, felt the lance brush his chest plate, stood up on his stirrups and brought his sword down on the man's collarbone with all his might. He saw his blade cleave the man almost in half, and felt the sword yanked out of his hands.

William got off his exhausted charger to retrieve his sword and tried to look at his adversary's severed body dangling from his horse, but found that he couldn't. His heart heavy with regret, he wondered how many more he would have to kill. When would it end?

Wasn't he supposed to look for his uncle? When would that happen?

Three days later, Brother Dimas, the commander of their squadron, was promoted to marshal, when the Templar who held that post was transferred.

To replace Brother Dimas, the Templar master had sent Brother Hughes, a fifteen-year veteran. On that day, following Sext and before breakfast, William, along with his squadron, stood at attention in the outer ward, outside the chapel, waiting to meet their new commander.

With the bright sun on their backs, the sounds of horses snorting from the nearby stables, and the smithies banging on hot metal from across the way, the outgoing marshal passed on the battle group's command flag—a two pointed black and white *Beauseant*—to Brother Dimas, who in turn passed on the squadron's flag, a smaller version of the same flag, to Brother Hughes.

Their new commander walked slowly along his squadron, stopping to look at each Templar. When he recognized someone he greeted them, otherwise he repeated their name several times. When he stood in front of him, William thought he saw surprise on his face.

"Your name, brother?" Commander Hughes asked.

"William, brother commander."

"Do you have a surname?"

"Montfort, brother commander."

"Ah, yes," he said and walked on to the next man.

That evening after Compline, the brother in charge of the Turcopoles came by William's bunk, as he was getting ready for bed.

"Brother William, if you please, come with me."

William followed the brother turcopolier to Dimas' former chambers on the third floor. Nothing had changed: the large room was still filled with the same books, maps and coffers. Sitting at the massive table was Brother Hughes. On seeing him enter, the commander invited William to sit down and thanked the turcopolier.

Commander Hughes appeared to be in his early thirties. He had prematurely gray hair, a black beard and thick dark eyebrows. His tanned face seemed chiseled out of rock, all sharp and hard lines. He was of medium height, and sturdily built.

"Brother William, you look very much like a dear friend, Brother John Montfort. I assume you are related."

"Yes, brother commander, he's my uncle," William said and he felt a happy jolt in his gut.

"I thought so. So glad to meet John's kin." Brother Hughes told William how he met John when they were both at Tortosa. "We served in the same squadron," Hughes said leaning back in his chair. "I can't tell you how many times we were surrounded, and had to fight our way out of so many traps." The stories didn't seem all that remarkable to William, but in the telling William noticed Hughes' nature. He was forceful and energetic, but calm, and William found himself feeling very comfortable with the man.

William decided to take a chance. "I believe my uncle became a saint." He saw how Hughes appeared unperturbed by the heresy.

Commander Hughes smiled, leaned forward and propped his elbows among documents on the table. "Your uncle became what you and I are striving for."

"What is that, Brother Hughes?"

"He reached harmony with creation, he gained peace in his heart."

"Brother Hughes, do you know what happened to him?"

"He was made prisoner by the Saracen after a battle, and was never ransomed."

The commander talked about devotion, and he mentioned how the Muslims could also be very devoted, and the Jews as well, and William became aware that Hughes was watching his reaction. Then he asked how William prayed.

"How I pray?"

"Yes, what do you feel when you pray?"

"I pray until I feel grace, then dwell in that glorious state."

Hughes appeared pleased. "We have much to talk about, Brother William."

William took that as a dismissal. "I appreciate the time we spent, Brother Hughes. I would like to come back, with your permission."

"I understand that you read and write, is that so?"

"Yes, brother commander."

"I can make you my clerk, that way no one will question your being here. I read and write, but with you around I can do so much more. Would that be of your liking?"

"Very much so, brother commander."

As he walked to his quarters, William was certain Commander Hughes was the man Sir Ian had mentioned who was supposed to help him find his uncle. William had the urge to turn around and go back when he remembered Ian's words to wait until he was approached, to be patient. He decided to heed them. Maybe he was being tested, tested to see if he was discreet...and patient.

Brother Hughes proved a capable commander, more aggressive than Brother Dimas had been, but still a disappointment to the Hardcores who had hoped for a "commander not afraid of anything." Knights, sergeants and squires ended up serving where they felt kinship, and so it was that the more fanatical Templars of all ranks ended up in the same squadron, Richard's, led by a hard-charging commander. William overheard Maurice tell his followers in his dorm: "All we need is an all out war for the pope and the kings of Europe to raise another army and clear the Holy Land, once and for all, or die gloriously in the process."

That night in their workroom, William asked Brother Hughes what he thought of the Hardcores.

Hughes looked up from a map of Haifa he had been studying that showed the city before it was destroyed by the Turks. "They are in every Templar castle, and when they get a leader, like Brother Maurice, they tend to grow in numbers.

"The Hardcores have a practical advantage over you and me, William. They suffer less, for they question nothing. You suffer each time you kill in battle, don't you?"

William choked when he tried to talk. "Yes, brother, I never wanted to kill, that's why I became a Cistercian monk...but was compelled to become a Templar. All I ever wanted was to lead a peaceful life dedicated to the Lord."

"I know, William. But believe me, your destiny is here," Hughes said as he rolled up the map.

"But why? If I'm so ill suited, then why am I here? And you? You understand me. Why are we here? What's the point?"

"William, you ask the right questions," Hughes said while walking over to the cubbyholes where he kept his maps. "It's like holding a candle in the dark, while all around you people are trying to blow it out. The fanatics are everywhere: Muslim, Christian, and Jew," he said as he slid the map where it belonged. "But the ones with understanding are also present in Muslim, Christian, and Jew. The problem is that fanatics dominate, and as long as they do, we will have war, do you see that?"

"Yes, of course, but I can't change their minds, so what can I possibly do?"

"Become like your uncle."

"Like my uncle. You said he reached harmony with creation. When I look at the world around me and see brutality and I am forced to kill, how can I possibly reach peace and harmony?"

"You will reach that point, but you need help. That's why we are here."

"Who, brother?" William asked with anticipation, feeling that something important was about to happen.

"The Brotherhood."

Hughes walked from the cubbyholes to a large map on the wall that showed all of Palestine. "The Brotherhood is a secret organization that founded the Templars two centuries ago, and still makes the top-level decisions on what happens to the Order. But their most important purpose is helping those with a broader understanding reach a point of 'knowing.'"

"Knowing?" William asked.

"Yes. Through meditation…"

"Meditation?"

"I will explain everything in time, but know that through the practice of meditation you can reach a point of total understanding, what is called 'The Knowing.'" Hughes stopped as if to collect his thoughts. "What survives today of Jesus' teachings tells us that when he said 'The kingdom of God is within you,' he spoke of 'The Knowing.' When he said, 'If thy eye be single thy whole body will be filled with light,' he spoke of meditation. If we were to follow Jesus' original teachings we would also find ourselves in 'The Knowing,' in harmony with creation."

"So 'The Knowing' is a state grace?"

Hughes started walking around the room in slow, measured steps staring at the floor. "I have yet to experience it myself, but John did explain it to me. He said that 'The Knowing' is well beyond the grace we experience through fervent prayer or meditation, although that's the beginning. For some, it's a sudden revelation, for others it evolves over time, but whatever the case, it's the beginning of our soul's journey into the infinite. At that moment there is complete understanding, the knowing of who we are and who God is. That's harmony."

Hughes stopped his contemplative pacing and leaned his arms on the back of his chair. "That's what the knowledge is all about. However, this is not done with our minds but rather with that part of us that we can call our souls, and we feel it in our hearts. John said that the mind then follows along, and it is led by the soul in deciphering what we experience.

"John told me that at the moment of knowing nothing is more important than the feeling of that harmony; but we realize that all the secrets of creation are ours should we want them. Eventually we attain the state of the Christ: we are whole, we are one with God."

"So that's what *Beauseant* really means." Then William took a moment to go over what he had heard. "Did all that originate with Jesus?"

"No, it started before Jesus. It all comes from Gnosticism," Hughes said as he sat down again. "As you know, gnosis means knowledge in Greek and the concept goes back to the ancient Greeks, who invaded the Holy Land before the Romans. That's how Arabs and Jews learned about gnosis. But the Brotherhood took a different route. In olden times, the area in the south of France called the Languedoc was the place where many mystical Jews and Arabs found refuge among those curious mountain people who learned from them and became the Cathars. It was Cathars who started the Brotherhood and that's how the knowledge was passed down to us.

"But the original Gnosis has become corrupt. From even before Jesus' time, Gnosticism became a religion with dogma and ritual; and what Jesus tried to do was preserve gnosis, 'The Knowing' in its purest form. That's what the Cathars practiced, and that's what we inherited."

William asked Hughes to show him what meditation was, and Hughes instructed him to sit still and let go of the world, relax.

"As Jesus said, William, 'The kingdom of God is within you.' Shut out the world and allow what's inside you to show itself."

"But how?"

"Ah! Use your breath; it is the link between the world and 'The Knowing.' Remember Jesus: 'If thy eye be single thy whole body will be filled with light.' Bring your gaze gently to the point between your eyebrows, and your whole being will go there. Then mind your breath, and let it slow down until your thoughts cease, the world is no more and God is within you."

For the following two weeks Hughes directed William to reach within himself and explore the hidden realm he had only tasted during prayer. One memorable evening, William experienced a profound joy, way stronger than what he felt after prayer, and Hughes told him to allow it to expand, that this was it, the beginning of "The Knowing."

William became aware that the quiet, the joyful silence inside did expand, or rather he expanded into it, and he realized that this was what he craved all along, during those long hours of prayer when he felt near something that he didn't quite know how to reach. Now he did. And there was a sense of promise, he knew he would transform, become...something indefinable. "Whole" was just a word, because there was so much more.

"This is so...precious, why doesn't everyone do it?" William asked.

"Not everyone is ready. Most people need rules, priests, and churches, all the tangible and external things, and are threatened by what they don't understand, so they have tried to destroy the path of 'The Knowing,' and branded it a heresy."

"But your Brotherhood protects it, and if they are behind the Templars, then there's no danger of it being destroyed, right?"

"Only as long as we exist. However, if the Templars are attacked as Caesarius predicted…"

"A man named Sir Ian told me…"

"Yes, I know what Ian told you.

"The Brotherhood cannot survive without the Templars. It needs the well-disciplined knights, and the Order's money to protect 'The Knowing,' and to perform whatever actions are needed."

"Actions? You mean like the prison where they keep those horrible people?"

"That and so much more. We have fought secret wars to throw out despots. But our primary duty is to keep 'The Knowing' alive. At present this also involves safekeeping the temporal knowledge the Saracen acquired from the Romans…"

"I know how the Arabs acquired the knowledge from the Romans, but how is that tied to 'The Knowing?'"

Hughes hesitated. "Let's just say that a very important document about 'The Knowing' was included with the books the Alexandria Library monks took with them to the desert."

"Who wrote the document?"

"You'll soon find out. Someone else will explain everything to you, very soon. I'm not trying to be mysterious, only practical. I want you to hear the complete story."

William shrugged his shoulders. "I trust you know best."

Hughes smiled at William. "Well, I suppose you would want to join the Brotherhood?"

"Of course, no question. Thank you." And William knew he had finally found his kin.

"Good to have you, William."

"Does this mean I can now start searching for my uncle?"

"All in due time, my friend. Be patient."

Maurice's group had grown to almost a hundred knights, sergeants, and squires. When Brother Joseph, the commander of the other squadron was killed in battle, they clamored for Maurice to be promoted, which Brother Dimas and the seneschal approved.

"He'll make a capable commander," Hughes commented to William during one of their chats, "and he'll get many Templars killed."

William thought of Richard, and prayed he would be spared. He had heard of rash suicidal missions by the likes of commanders like Maurice, where whole squadrons had been annihilated.

The days went by, filled with violence, and William felt an increasing sense of despair and wondered when he would embark on the search for his uncle. He imagined that Hughes was just as anxious, and that he had a plan. In the meantime, he had to continue fighting…and killing.

The squadrons were reorganized, and Maurice ended up with an all-Hardcore squadron, including Richard. The other squadron, under Hughes, ended up with twelve Hardcores, but there was much to be said for Hughes' abilities for leadership, for his Hardcores respected their new commander and showed clear signs of loyalty, particularly when other Hardcores criticized him.

"When can I start searching for my uncle, Brother Hughes?" William asked one evening as they walked toward the workroom. It had already been almost a month since Hughes had revealed the secrets of the Brotherhood to him.

"Soon, very soon."

"Do you know where he is?"

"No," Hughes answered, opening the door and letting William in first. "But I know what the place is like." At William's baffled expression, he added as he lit a candle. "It's hard to explain, but you'll understand. He is in a place called Hafiz Mountain. Hafiz in Arabic comes from the root word 'to protect,' and it's the same word used to say writing, and learning. You protect knowledge by writing it down, and learning it, see?"

"Where is the Mountain?"

"It's not on any map, so very likely it's just a code name. It's the place where the Christian monks from Alexandria sought refuge with their precious books." Hughes sat down in his chair facing his cluttered table, which he ignored. "The Brotherhood learned about Hafiz Mountain a long time ago, and sent John to find it, but he never came back. In a letter, John told the Brotherhood that you alone could find him."

So that's how it happened. "All of you are convinced that I can find him. But how?"

Hughes snickered. "If I knew that, I wouldn't need you, would I? I would just go and get him myself." Then he stood up to look out the window at the moonlit ward. "Very shortly we'll have a chance to go to Acre. When we do, you'll meet the Brotherhood of the Holy Land. That will be the first step in finding your uncle."

"But when, brother?"

"Soon, William. Be patient."

A week later, a group of pilgrims arrived at Castle Pilgrim. They had been beleaguered by a band of Turks on the road from Jerusalem, and had to run their horses ragged to escape them. Brother Dimas decided to give the pilgrims an escort to Acre, and selected Hughes' squadron.

They left for Acre the following day with the thirty pilgrims, all men, originally from Venice, and arrived a day later without incident. They were to spend a night at Templar House before heading back.

After Vespers, Hughes approached William outside the chapel. "Come with me, Brother William," he said aloud, "I have duties for you."

Hughes led William on foot out of Templar House and down the narrow streets of Acre. "I sent a carrier pigeon with news of our arrival and some people are waiting to meet you," Hughes said as they made their way into an exclusive quarter of sparkling tall houses with numerous balconies, fancy big windows and courtyards behind tall walls—all you could see were the tops of trees and vines pouring over. They came to an alleyway and went up a staircase that led to a well-kept hidden garden and a palace behind it.

Hughes knocked on the door, and an Arab servant let them in. To William's surprise, Hughes addressed the bowing man in Arabic and seemed to speak the language with ease. The servant led them to an upstairs sitting room.

There were about forty persons in the room, some sitting on lush pillows, others in elongated chairs. It was the most luxurious room William had ever seen: an abundance of gold, silver, silk and other soft fabrics of rich colors in furniture, wall-hangings and carpets.

When he walked in with Hughes, the room fell silent. They were led to one of the elongated chairs. Hughes took off his surcoat's and hauberk's hoods, so his head was bare, and William followed his lead.

An Arab with an immaculate small black beard and dressed in black silk robes shouted "*Beauseant*" and the group responded with the same. Then a distinguished looking Templar sitting at the far end spoke: "Brothers, this is our new member, Brother Knight Templar William Montfort." The speaker was tall and elegant in his surcoat, and spoke in a cultured tone. "The nephew of our beloved John," he said as he walked over and handed William a silver medallion showing a dove with wings outstretched.

"This is our medallion. Always show you it to brothers," said the tall man, "and if you lose it, draw the dove on anything handy to identify yourself."

One of those present turned out to be the head of the pilgrims they had escorted. He shook William's hand, slapped his shoulder, and told him: "You didn't know your Brother Hughes could arrange a trip to Acre so conveniently, did you?"

William discovered there were twelve more Templar brothers, five Hospitaller knights, two Eastern Orthodox and at least four Roman Catholic priests, a number of Jews and many Arabs. The tall Templar turned out to be the grand master of the Templars, Guillaume de Beajeu, and he was also the grand master of the Brotherhood. His mantle of command—casually draped over a chair, was full-length and showed one cross on either side of the chest. Everything about him was neat; even the typical Templar unkempt beard somehow looked elegant. William was in awe of the man—he held authority over all Templars, everyone in that room, in addition to many cardinals and possibly even kings.

The Templar knights came over to greet William, and he recognized one as the ship's master who had brought him from London. His full name was Roger de Flor, and he wore a sergeant's brown surcoat with a black mantle. Most of the Arabs were Muslims, and out of the several Jews, one was a rabbi named Joshua Ben-Jashim.

"What we all have in common is 'The Knowing,'" the rabbi said as servants brought snow flushed with pomegranate juice in delicate porcelain cups. "I am a member of a Jewish mystical group and we base our practice on Gnosticism. Jesus was a Gnostic, you know."

There were Druze, Christians and Sufis present according to Hughes, who whispered in William's ear, but they all wore distinctive headdress identifying them as members of their tribes. The Druze wore a black and white headdress, with the ends swept back and tucked behind the neck. The Sufis kept their practice secret and only displayed their various tribe allegiances. One wore a red and white checkered headdress; the other had a plain white.

The grand master rose and looked at William. "I understand you want to find your uncle."

William was nervous in the great man's presence, but the other Templars appeared at ease, and he had watched Hughes joke with him earlier. "Yes, brother grand master," William answered getting up from his chair and standing before the greatest Templar of them all. "Ever since Brother Ian told me about my uncle John."

"So do we, son." Grand master Guillaime de Beajeau turned around and addressed the group. "Now let us figure out how to find John."

The men in the group nodded, then stood and gathered around their grand master and William.

"When we learned of Caesarius' prophecy, finding the Jesus Gospel became our top priority. Fortunately, we already knew John, and his peculiar gifts," the grand master said. "We knew he was the best qualified. We asked, and he accepted. He left on his search for the Gospel over ten years ago, but never came back. However, we have reason to believe that he found Hafiz Mountain.

"We know John's first stop was Jerusalem. Rabbi Ben-Jashim had told him about Jesus' prison cell, the place where the Romans held Jesus before the crucifixion, and John wanted to visit it. A few months later he showed up at Ben Jashim's house in Jerusalem and handed him this letter for the Brotherhood." The grand master walked over to a side table and opened a wooden box encrusted with gems. He withdrew a piece of parchment and handed it to William.

William read the clear handwriting in Greek that started by thanking the rabbi for the valuable information, "and Druze Sheik Dun for the trouble his men went through to stage my capture. I visited Jesus' prison cell and it opened my heart and my eyes as never before. I am certain that I will find Hafiz Mountain and the Jesus Gospel, but I also know I won't be able to leave once I get there.

"I have a request of the Brotherhood, and it concerns my nephew William, who on this day is but a boy. Pray assist him, for he has my gifts and if anyone can find me, he will. Make certain he becomes a Templar and a member of the Brotherhood, and all will be well. There's time, my brothers, for things to happen as ordained."

The letter was signed, "*Beauseant*, In Christ Always, Your Humble Brother, John Montfort."

William handed the letter back to the grand master who carefully folded it and put it back in the jeweled box by his side. William realized the full impact his presence meant to those around him, and why they had helped him.

"His letter mentions the Jesus Gospel," William said, "I never knew Jesus wrote any gospels, brother grand master." At that moment it dawned on William that the Jesus Gospel was the document describing "The Knowing" that Hughes said had been at the Library of Alexandria and was carried by monks to the desert.

The grand master cleared his throat. "Besides 'The Knowing,' that's the Templars' most guarded secret," he replied. "According to Cathar legend the prison cell is key to finding the Jesus Gospel, so the first thing the early Templars did when Jerusalem was liberated during the First Crusade was find the prison cell. Since then, access to the cell has been limited to a select few, for the Brotherhood didn't want the essence of the place to dissipate, but those who have seen it report it's just a hole in the ground, with no writings or signs on the walls that could lead to Hafiz Mountain and the Gospel. But John wanted to see it anyway."

"Why is Hafiz Mountain so difficult to find, brother grand master?" William asked.

"Probably because it requires the type of talents John has, and apparently you have as well."

"Brother, I don't want to sound doubtful, but what makes you so sure the Cathars were right and that there is a Jesus Gospel, and that it is at Hafiz Mountain?"

The grand master took a few steps toward the open balcony, his hands clasped behind him, his princely strides slow and measured, his gaze switching from random objects back to William. "A thousand years ago, Emperor Constantine declared Jesus to be the corporal Son of God, and Christianity the official religion of the Roman Empire. Then he ordered the destruction of existing gospels contradicting his position, mostly Gnostic gospels that said we can all be the sons of God, that we can all reach the same level of being one with God Jesus reached, by going inside. We know that's what Jesus taught, from what survives of his teachings."

Grand master Guillaime stopped to stare at the balcony. "What was passed down to us from the Cathars was that Jesus taught pure gnosis. In those days most people could read and write to some extent, but as a rabbi and a scholar it stands to reason that he must have written much. But whatever he wrote, that's what it would contain, and if so, then Constantine would have also destroyed his writings. Unless of course, the Jesus Gospel was one of the books at the library at Alexandria the monks carried away to the desert, to Hafiz Mountain. And that's a very strong possibility, just from the fact that the document existed back then, it was very important, so there must have been copies in all libraries, and it was Christian monks who saved the books."

William assented, it all made sense. "Sire, I recall my teacher Jacob telling me about the Alexandria monks taking the books to the desert, but how do we know that it actually happened? That might be just a myth."

"That," interjected the rabbi, as he walked over to William. "We learned from the Arabs themselves. They told us that the extent and breadth of their civilization came from those books, and because Jews lived among the Arabs here and in Spain, we benefited as well. That there is an actual location where the books were taken has been known for centuries, but the specific name, Hafiz Mountain, was a secret obtained from the Cathars."

"So finding the prison cell leads to Hafiz Mountain and the Gospel," William said, "and we know where the prison cell is. That's where my uncle went, and that's where I will go."

"Thank you, Brother William," the grand master said.

William looked around the luxurious room. "I am most impressed that this group is made up of various faiths, but why would you, Sire" he said looking at the rabbi, "or you two, noble men" he said addressing the Sufis, "care so much about Jesus and his gospel?"

The rabbi turned and smiled at one of the Sufis who in turn bowed in response.

"Jesus did not endorse a religion, not even Judaism," said Rabbi Ben-Jashim. "If you study what survives of his teachings, his message was that we are all equal sons of God and need only go inside to realize that. That's pure gnosis, which makes religious dogma, with all its distinctions and rules, obsolete. The Jesus Gospel will make that very clear and unify all people with open hearts and minds of all faiths. "

"But the fanatics on all sides won't be unified."

"No," the rabbi responded. "Fanatics will remain fanatics no matter what. However, if the open hearted Muslims, Jews, and Christians proclaim their unity under the one God and the one way to know him, sectarian dogma would lose its power and by extension the power of the fanatics."

"Muslims view Jesus as a prophet," the grand master said, "and many Jews recognize him as well. Should his actual words be made public, it could unify all three religions."

Of course, thought William. The Gospel would be like a magic potion of peace. "Why do you think my uncle said he wouldn't be able to leave once he got there?"

"We don't know, son," the grand master said.

"You are the only one among us who can get to Hafiz Mountain," the rabbi said, as he produced a hand-drawn map from inside his tunic and handed it to William. "I made a map just like this one for your uncle. It shows Jerusalem and the location of Jesus' prison cell.

"The prison no longer exists; but we know it was part of the Antonia Fortress. The Romans razed the Jerusalem of Jesus' time to the ground twelve hundred years ago," the rabbi told him, "but the cell was underground and is still there."

Grand master Guillaime smiled. "Let us now plan your capture, Brother William."

"I can have the Sajuk attack one of the Christian villages," said the Druze Sheik Dun, from the back of the group. People parted to let him come in closer. "My riders can then capture you, William, as we did your uncle. Then you will be free to begin your journey."

"But the Sajuks are Turks." William said surprised. "They do your bidding, sheik?"

The Druze's lips compressed into a sardonic smile. "Ah, my friend, we in the

Brotherhood have learned to manage our little brothers, the fanatics."

The group discussed how to ensure that Hughes' squadron would be involved, and decided to make the attack big enough so the entire battle group would be engaged.

William shook his head in disbelief. "The attack will cost lives, how would you justify that?"

"The fanatics will fight no matter what, we are just staging one of those fights," replied the rabbi.

It was decided that a large band of Sajuks would attack one of the Christian villages not far from Atlit, in three months, on March 13. Without doubt that would necessitate both squadrons. During the battle William would be made prisoner. "Stay to your left flank, and I will be there waiting for you," Sheik Dun told him. "Look for the multi-colored star in the Druze banner."

The following day as William rode with his squadron back to Pilgrim Castle, his mind kept reviewing the meeting. Now he understood the enormity of what the Brotherhood expected of him. But what if he failed? They had placed so much faith in him, all because of his uncle. Maybe John did find Hafiz Mountain, but that was John, who clearly had attained some amazing spiritual state, could stop battles with his mere presence, make friends out of enemies, and have visions. Perhaps that's what it took. And now they were saying that he was like him and could follow in his footsteps. But how? After his staged capture and once released, how would he go about fending on his own? He didn't speak Arabic. Maybe Hughes could teach him some. William could see making his way to Jerusalem, but then what? *Where did uncle John go after visiting Jesus' prison cell?*

Late that afternoon, just past the ruins of Haifa, the squadron rode into a battle raging before them. Apparently Sajuks had attacked a caravan and Templars from Pilgrim had come to their rescue. Now the Templars and the caravan were both surrounded by a large band of Sajuks who were picking them off with their archers. The battle had been going on for a while: the ground was covered with the bodies of men and beasts.

Hughes had his Templars form a charge line, lances at the ready, Turcopoles behind them. He gave the order to charge head on, but at the last moment veer to the right, come around in an arc and surround the enemy's right flank, which appeared as their weakest formation. That would force the enemy to mobilize to protect their one flank and relieve the pressure on the defending Templars. As the squadron galloped down the road William's only thought was whether his brother was still alive.

As the squadron got close, some of the attackers tried to disperse, but Hughes signaled for the line to make a wider arc encircling them.

The fighting became fierce as the Sajuks tried to break free. At close quarters they dropped their bows and drew out their scimitars and lances. William knew that was it, they didn't stand a chance against the charging Templars. William concentrated on protecting Hughes, for the commander had been hit by an arrow on his right shoulder, had dropped his shield and now wielded his sword with his left hand. William saw three Sajuks. One charged at him to make way for the other two who aimed for Hughes. William looked back. His sergeant and squire were heavily engaged, as were the Turcopoles. Hughes' team was nowhere in sight.

William realized the one man charging at him was attempting to engage him long enough for the other two to finish off Hughes. William struck at the man with his lance, but the Turk maneuvered out of the way. William saw the two other Sajuks on either side of Hughes. William's horse appeared to be doing a dance all on its own, veering to one side, and then the other. On one such turn William used a brief opening on the man's left and struck him with the lance, then rushed over to Hughes, who was being attacked on both sides. William's lance unseated one attacker and then he went over to Hughes' left to face the other, but that had been all the help Hughes needed and the Turk was going down. At that moment Hughes' sergeant, squire and one Turcopole came roaring up.

The fighting subsided, and William saw only Templars standing. He went over to Hughes who had been wounded twice, an arrow protruded from his right shoulder and he had a deep bloody gash on his left side under his arm. William tried to help him, but the commander signaled that he was fine; his sergeant was tending to his wounds, and his squire and remaining Turcopole stood on either side, protecting him.

William circled around and found Templars in clear command of the place and Turcopoles guarding captives with their drawn bows. He spotted Maurice standing with Richard and two other Templars with the man in charge of the caravan. These were Jerusalem Jews probably on their way to Acre, and Maurice was yelling at the man in French, demanding he kneel before a cross the Hardcore had produced from under his hauberk.

William was relieved Richard was fine and tried to catch his eye, but his brother was intent in the conversation in front of him.

"If you don't kneel, I will kill you," Maurice said.

William dismounted and came to stand in between Maurice and the Jew. "We don't kill unarmed men, no matter what their religion," William heard himself say, as though his voice came from someone else.

[2]

Maurice felt anger boil as he glared at the insolent William. "You don't tell me what I can do. I am a commander and you are a knight. This man is a Jew, and Jews killed our Lord Jesus Christ. But if you are a true Christian why would I need to tell you that?" Soft Templars were worse than infidels, Maurice thought, for at least with the infidel you could tell who they were right away. He felt like driving his sword through William, through all the soft Templars. It was as though they didn't quite love Jesus enough, were not willing to go all the way for Him, the Son of God who suffered so much for them. Their existence was a blight on Christianity; with them around the Church would continue losing ground, for soft Templars lacked conviction, strength, endurance. You had to sacrifice everything for Jesus, your life, and your family! That was the only way.

Maurice decided he had to make the Jew kneel before the crucifix and acknowledge Jesus Christ as the Son of God and his savior, or slay him, for that was the true duty of every real Christian, what was necessary, and he had to use every opportunity the Lord placed before him to further His cause. Maurice had hoped he could have dealt with the Jews before Hughes and his men finished fighting, aware they would probably interfere, but now that William in all his arrogance was getting in the way, he would have to deal with him, for the good of his eternal soul, and of the men who now surrounded the two of them. It was important to set an example for them all.

"If you don't agree this man is the enemy of Christ, perhaps you would care to fight in his stead?" He watched for the soft Templar to back away... but to Maurice's surprise he didn't. Instead he drew his sword. Maurice was taken aback by the soft Templar's actions. Why would he risk so much over a Jew? Just the fact that he was facing him with a drawn sword was a crime punishable with imprisonment.

But then Maurice realized his words could have been taken as a challenge and the Templars standing around were witnesses.

"Very well, Brother Maurice. If you are willing to challenge me to a trial by combat, so be it," William said.

The resonance in his voice shook Maurice and he felt trapped. He felt the blood drain from his face. William stood in front of him willing to kill or to die, and it occurred to him William was possessed by the devil. He seemed bigger than Maurice remembered, solid, unmovable. And by contrast Maurice felt himself suddenly smaller and feeble and that was odd for he had never in his adult years felt diminished when facing another man. But he could sense there was no backing down; he could feel his men's gaze on him. They were far from the castle, the marshal and seneschal, and he had been the one who uttered the first words for the trial by combat to begin.

But then he had an idea. "No. As commander I cannot accept your challenge. But I can ask one of my men to fight you." Maurice turned to Richard. "Brother Richard, if you have truly devoted your life to Christ, you will fight your brother of the flesh to defend the honor of your brother in Christ."

Maurice turned to scan the faces of his men around him, most of whom had taken off their helmets. "This man, William, who calls himself a Templar monk like us, is defiling the cross on his chest. He is willing to shed a brother's blood to protect a Jew. He is worse than them!"

"I will not fight anyone but you, Brother Maurice," William said, "for it was you who challenged me. Perhaps you don't feel Christ will take your side? Are you afraid I am right and will win?"

Maurice stared at William. He was uttering those words with so much conviction… but what conviction? Where did he get it? William was a soft Templar; the Lord was not with him, so how could he have so much…strength? Maurice had faced the Muslims without fear, because dying for Christ had always been his ambition, and he couldn't understand why all of a sudden William made him tremble…it was not death, but something else, a sureness of his stance that seemed so solid, serene, as though William knew something Maurice didn't.

And he realized that William was right, Maurice was sure Christ was on William's side and he would win…but why? He again looked at his men. Richard was studying him closely, with a look Maurice had not seen before. The other men seemed disappointed.

At that moment Maurice knew that he could not lift his sword against William, but had no idea how to back down, because he had never done it.

"What are you men doing on foot?" Maurice heard Hughes' voice behind him.

Both Maurice and William looked at him. He was the senior officer, and now that they were a battle group, he was in charge.

"We were discussing what to do with the Jews, brother." Maurice said.

"Well, there is nothing to be done, is there? You let them proceed now that the Sajuks won't bother them anymore."

"Yes, brother. That's what I was about to say," Maurice said, and he knew no one in that group would say otherwise; but as he walked toward his horse he could feel his men's scornful looks, and when he looked at Richard, the man looked down at the ground, avoiding his gaze.

[3]

Hughes' workroom felt stuffy, and William opened his surcoat at the neck and rolled up his sleeves. He looked up from the letter he was writing. Hughes stood looking out the window, squinting against the bright afternoon sun.

Hughes turned around and met his gaze. "That was quite a victory for us, William. Maurice is not the same, the men in his squadron obey him because they have no choice, but backing away from a challenge is something he'll never live down."

William held his quill in one hand, erasing blade on the other. "That wasn't my intention, Brother Hughes. But I'm glad it happened." He looked down at the letter. "I don't know why Maurice did not fight me."

Hughes walked over to look over William's shoulder at the velum. Absent-mindedly he gently took the quill from William's hand, and proceeded to sharpen it with his knife. "The result, whether planned or not is excellent: Maurice keeps to himself when not in the field. The Hardcores are now mostly silent."

"I'm concerned about Maurice," William said as he waited for his quill. "During Matins I felt a strong disquiet. I turned around to find him staring at me with intense hatred. He seems to have found a new passion in life: me."

The following day their squadron fought a skirmish against Bedouins, and on the way back William discovered that his horse had been wounded. At first he noticed his charger slowing down, but then he saw that he was bleeding from the right shoulder. He got down, lifted up the horse's mail and discovered a deep gash.

That night after Compline, and after his meditation and visit with Hughes, he went to the stables to make sure that Brother Albert had properly treated the wound.

He stood next to the big beast in his stall, and petted his flank, thinking how much he depended on the horse, how the big beast seemed to know in which direction to turn even before William did. Many times the agile Percheron had veered in time for William to find an enemy thrusting at him with a lance, with just enough time to lift his shield. "What's your name, boy? What would you like to be called?" On a hunch William said "Black" and the destrier turned to face him, his eyes shining bright with intelligence. "Black it is, then."

William noticed other knights tending to their horses. Those were the ones who cared what happened to their animals. To the rest they were simply "equipment." He felt sad for the beasts, nobody had asked them whether they wanted to fight, but they did, and he wished that man could fight without them, in fact he wished the fanatics on both sides just killed each other off and be done with it.

Perhaps Armageddon would not be such a bad idea if the battle involved only the hardcores from both sides, without horses, and the rest could just watch. He imagined the scene, much like a tournament, with the Muslims on one side and the Christians on the other, and fair ladies from both sides cheering them on. They could break up into bands, those in favor of the virgin birth, those against it, those who thought Jesus was God, and those who didn't, those who believed in praying to images, and those who thought that was heresy. Those who believed in baptism and original sin, and those who didn't. Hooray for the believers, let them all kill each other in the name of God! To expedite the killing, they would be forbidden from wearing armor, and after the carnage the survivors would turn their faces skyward and praise God for their victory, while their fair ladies rushed at them excited by the carnage, trembling with passion, eager to procreate more idiots.

William looked around the enclosure, big enough for Black to roll around on the pile of hay in the middle. Next to the water trough and folded across the dividing half-wall lay a clean blanket, probably left by Albert.

He felt he was being watched, and turned his head to find Maurice standing some four paces behind him, leaning against the gate to Black's stall. "Brother Maurice, what pray tell, can I do for you?"

"Just keeping an eye on you, Brother William," he responded. "I know everything, everything, about you and Brother Hughes."

It was clear Maurice had followed him to his nightly meetings with Hughes. "Be clear, Maurice. What is it you mean? And what is it you want?"

"You two are engaged in secret rites, repugnant to God-fearing Christians. Do you want me to be clearer?"

William walked over to Maurice. They were both unarmed, and out of earshot from the other knights tending to their horses. William felt he could easily pummel the imbecile hardcore to oblivion.

"Brother Maurice," he told him, "Had you looked closer you would have seen us in prayer. But do you know what prayer is, real prayer, that is? Not the idiotic, repetitive, intonation to the evil god you worship, the god that reflects the brutal, stupid, small-minded, violent self you are."

Maurice did not respond, but stood staring at William in silence for what seemed a long time. He slanted his pale eyes, pursed thin lips, then turned and walked away.

William's own words now echoed in his mind. How was it possible the fanatics felt devotion? But he knew they did. How was it possible they contacted the same God? But in their case, God required that they kill unarmed people, the old, women, and children. Jacob and his family. How was it possible?

Three days later, in the late evening, while William sat with Hughes in meditation in the work chamber, Marshal Dimas burst into the room. At the sound, both William and Hughes, sitting on either side of the big table, turned to face him. Dimas had stopped short, and appeared dumbfounded. Behind him stood Maurice. For a time, the stern marshal simply looked, and he seemed to be studying them in the dim light from the one candle on the table.

"You two are praying," he said, his voice subdued, shifting his gaze from Hughes to William. "Yes, you two are praying." With this he turned and walked away, ushering Maurice out and gently closing the door behind him.

Hughes looked at William. "We have a convert." Then he closed his eyes again and continued meditating.

The following evening Dimas came in as they were finishing work and asked if he could join in their prayers. Hughes brought a third chair from the hallway, and the three sat in silence for some time.

Afterwards Dimas asked questions, and William was surprised on how openly Hughes talked about meditation…that it didn't differ from spoken prayer but it dwelled on the silence as a way to seek direct union with God. Dimas seemed to soak up all the information, apparently unconcerned about the heresy. He closed his eyes as though to experience what he had been told.

William studied the man—a Frenchman judging by his name of provenance, de Orleans— who up to then had remained distant, an efficient marshal who had to make all the tough decisions. He had brown hair starting to bald, a sparse beard, high forehead and pronounced cheekbones. Tall and thin, he gave the impression of a withdrawn ascetic. He was in charge of military strategy and decided where to allocate their two squadrons, which villages needed defending, when to deploy the battle group. He also decided when to pull back. He had a reputation as a very competent military man and administrator, but no one knew him personally.

As Dimas continued to meditate, his usual stern expression softened. When he opened his eyes, he smiled; the first time William had seen him do so.

Dimas, Hughes, and William met every evening, and Maurice, who had his workroom down the hall, made his presence known. They could see him standing by his doorway when they walked in, or silently making his way down the hall when they came out. They knew what they were doing was considered heresy by the Church. Claiming direct communion with God was the reason many people had been burned at the stake, but it was a risk they were willing to take.

Hughes sent a carrier pigeon with a letter requesting permission from the grand master to bring Dimas to Acre and make him a member. A day later they received an affirmative response. The Brotherhood had been watching Dimas for some time and knew he was a likely prospect.

A week later a delegation from the castle made a trip to Acre, under Dimas' command with the pretext of a parley with the Knights of St. John, also known as the Hospitallers.

William rode a spare mount for Black was in obvious pain. He was concerned about him, but knew how silly it would sound to others. After all, it was just a horse.

They met with the Hospitallers' Acre commander. Following the meeting, Hughes led Dimas and William to the hidden palace.

It was the same plush room, smelling of silk, strange oils and unknown subtle scents. The meeting this time was smaller, no more than thirty persons. The rabbi and the Druze sheik, among others were absent. William watched Dimas' face as he met the grand master, the Jews and the Saracen, and the marshal's reaction was much like his own, an indefinable feeling of belonging, apparent in his unabashed smile.

With Dimas on board, William's staged capture by the Druze would be made easier with his collaboration. However, the conversation was still about John and Hafiz Mountain, and the grand master wished William God speed as they said goodbye.

"Much depends on you, son. If I don't see you again, thank you." The words had a foreboding quality and William wondered whether Grand Master Guillaime de Beajeu was going to die.

[4]

Otto watched the sun rise from a window in his home's solarium. He rubbed his tired eyes and resumed pacing the room. The message from Cantor was clear: Flote had sent twelve Lombard Knights to Acre on a Florentine vessel, scheduled to arrive in ten days.

All Otto had to do was alert the Brotherhood in Acre. There was still time. The Lombards would be stopped and the truce with the Mameluks preserved. But then again, the French had already succeeded in killing all of the Scottish royals except for a little girl in Norway. But she was sure to die. The trap to lure the English into an endless war in Scotland was all but set. If the Lombards succeeded in Acre, the French Scheme would be fully operational.

Otto stopped by the window and stared at his cherished roses below. *So be it. Let the French go forth. I will defeat them, as God is my witness!*

CHAPTER V

[1]

Black seemed to improve, but was still limping, and Hughes told William they would have to put the destrier down. "I know you are fond of the animal, but we can only keep battle worthy horses."

William was aware how much it cost to keep each of the huge Percherons. The feed the local farms supplied was not enough and much of the hay was brought over by donkey-train from Acre each month, huge bales that originated from as far away as France.

He asked Hughes to give him another week; he found the thought of killing Black heart wrenching, and realized how much he cared for the horse. Black's injury had forced him to ride another Percheron and he didn't feel as safe in battle. And the big horse appeared to understand what the options were, for it was obvious that he was making an effort to walk without a limp whenever William exercised him.

"The ligaments of the shoulder have been severed," Brother Albert said as he rubbed a salve on Black's injury. "It will never heal properly." William stood to one side of the stall watching, and wondered whether Hughes was right and the best thing would be to end the horse's pain with a blow to the head.

He felt someone behind him, and turned around to find Hughes.

"I don't think any of Brother Albert's potions will do it," Hughes said. He then placed one hand on William's shoulder and whispered in his ear: "Too bad your uncle is not around. He could heal with his hands." The commander then walked away.

On hearing the words it occurred to William that he had to at least try and heal Black just as his uncle had done with his mother's little dog. After all, if the Brotherhood thought that he was like his uncle, wouldn't it make sense that he should have the gift of healing as well?

Once Albert had gone, William made Black lay down on his side, knelt beside him and placed his hands on his horse's injured shoulder. He began meditating and felt immense love for Black. At the awareness, William's hands grew warm and his palms tingled. Then his heart was joyful, and it told him that all was well, as he felt the warmth from his hands go into the wounded shoulder.

When William stood up, Black stood as well, firmly on all fours, shook his mane, then turned to look at him in the eyes.

That Saturday after Review and Chapter Meeting, William rode Black around the outer ward with Hughes watching. Black did not limp once the whole time, and seemed spirited and frisky, swishing his tail and snorting as he trotted by the smiling Hughes.

Back in his stall, William hugged Black's large head and rubbed his mane. "We did it, my friend. We did it."

Then he said a prayer of gratitude.

William continued fighting but he found succor in the thought that soon he would be captured and the constant killing would end.

The days dragged on slowly, as though time was refusing to pass to keep him from his liberation. Then, one morning, a whole month before his appointed day, a scout came with news of a large-scale attack on a village, and William thought the time had come for his capture, that things had been expedited for some reason.

The battle group rode out along with fifty crossbowmen, under Dimas' command. William felt that something bad was going to happen…his body was going to suffer; he could feel being pierced…the taste and feel of blood…but ultimately for a good outcome.

He bowed his head. *So be it.* Maybe he was supposed to be captured after being wounded. It made sense, as a Templar he had vowed to never surrender.

When they reached the village—two rows of huts surrounded by a stone goat enclosure—Dimas ordered the crossbowmen to attack first. They were to come within range and decimate the Sajuk, then break ranks and allow the Templars to charge. This infuriated the knights, who viewed warfare with arrows as cowardly, but they waited their turn. Each squadron was to ride in separate directions and come together, striking the enemy from two sides at once.

The Turks suffered a number of casualties from the arrows, but then formed a protective line and Turkish archers shot back.

It was time for the knights to do their job.

At the order, Hughes' men charged at full gallop, but not so for Maurice's, whose men rode slower and seemed to be making a wider arc. William was aware of their progress and realized that without them he and the rest of Hughes' men would be killed. William tapped Hughes' arm with his lance and pointed at Maurice, who rode as customary in front of his men setting the direction and pace.

Hughes understood right away, but it was too late and they made contact with the Sajuks. William fought as never before, and knew men all around him were falling, one after another. He felt an arrow hit him on the left side of his chest, and another on the right leg. He lost his lance, and fought with his sword. When his right arm was wounded, he dropped the shield and fought with his left.

Black seemed to know that William was wounded, for he kept veering and turning, and making impossible leaps. William felt weakened by the loss of blood as he spotted two Sajuks charging at him and knew he would not be able to defend himself, when out of the corner of his eye he saw Richard and a group of Templars charging head on. They flew past him and with relief William saw the ease with which they exterminated the enemy. When he turned to look for Hughes, he felt faint, slumped down on his horse and grabbed on to the mane to keep from falling.

He awoke and realized where he was when he recognized the doctor brother standing by his bed saying something. He made an effort to understand, and caught the words "You will be fine, brother knight." William tried to respond but found his mouth too dry; his tongue stuck to his palate and his breath felt like fire going down into his lungs.

He wanted to find out about the squadron, about Hughes and Albert but then the room and everything in it faded away.

He woke up with someone feeding him warm soup. He opened his eyes to find Richard looking at him with concern and holding a spoon in his hand.

William looked around. The long room was lined with two rows of beds, half of them occupied. Monks walked around with containers and cloths. In the far corner was the bed that Bridon had used.

"You worried me, Willy," Richard said. "My prayers have been answered for the doctor tells me you will not die.

"Six men died and seven were wounded in your squadron," Richard said as he scooped up another spoonful. "One of them was Brother Alphonse, the monk who brought us from Acre when we first arrived. Remember him? I sure do. But your sergeant is fine. He got wounded in the leg and tried to assist you, but there were too many of the enemy around him. Your commander was pinned down by his dead horse and got bruised ribs. Sorry to say your squire was killed.

"That horse of yours, Willy. It saved your life. It kept kicking and turning, knocking the enemy down, as though possessed. Between you and me, brother, I think that animal is an angel sent to look after you. He didn't get a scratch, and I personally saw two Turks trying their best to kill him."

Richard rested the spoon in the wooden bowl. "I'm sorry about what happened, all on account of Maurice, Willy. We were riding and your squadron was getting so far ahead, and then we figured out that Maurice was keeping us back. My friends just looked at me, and I knew what they were trying to tell me. Then I saw the Turks surrounding all of you, and that's when I galloped past Maurice and rode on ahead. And you know what, Willy? My entire squadron, except for two squires and Maurice, followed me.

Richard spooned some more of the thick soup. "Maurice brought charges of insubordination against us, but Marshal Dimas accused Maurice of cowardice, failure to follow orders, and willful endangerment of his fellow Templars.

"The seneschal held the trial two days ago, and Maurice was sentenced to two years in prison. After that he will be thrown out of the Order. It's only because of his previous record on the battlefield that he wasn't hanged.

William raised his hand. "How...how long have I been in bed?"

Richard held the spoon steady in midair. "Tomorrow would make it a week.

"Except for the two squires," continued Richard, "we were all found guilty of insubordination and sentenced to a month in prison, but since they are short of men, our sentences were commuted to daily penance for a year." He shrugged his shoulders and laughed. "We have to sleep on the floor, go barefoot when not in battle gear, and recite ten extra Paternosters for each office."

William studied his brother and realized how well things had worked out. He muttered a silent prayer of gratitude as Richard continued to feed him. William's only concern was to be well enough so he could go to his appointed capture.

It took him two more days before he could move about, and a week of exercise to regain his strength. He treated his pain and wounds with impatience, willing his body to heal.

On the fourth of March he went out on patrol, although still in pain, and began counting the days to March 13.

On March the 12th, William awoke unusually excited. *Tomorrow is the day.* He was going to find uncle John. He had no idea how that was going to happen, or even how he was supposed to survive. He had learned just a few words of Arabic from Hughes, and knew the Arabs could easily spot him as a "Frank," what they called all Christian knights. Perhaps Brother Dun, the Druze sheik who was supposed to capture him, would help him.

That day William made an effort to spend extra time with Richard, just in case they never met again. Ever since he had been wounded, he and Richard had spent much time together, often talking about home and wondering about their parents. It had been a year since they left, but it seemed much longer. England and home felt impossibly distant.

William last saw Richard making his way toward the armory after they said goodnight, and William fixed the image of his brother in his mind—how the sun lit up his dark hair, and the way his surcoat swayed as he walked with his usual long and forceful strides.

William, Dimas, and Hughes meditated as customary after Compline, when the castle was asleep. "God Speed William," Dimas said as they parted. Hughes patted William on the back, lost in thought.

Midmorning of the following day, a scout came with news of a Sajuk attack on a sizable Christian village on the road to Jerusalem.

The battle group mounted under Dimas' command. It was the first time in William's memory that he rode into combat with a light heart. With Maurice gone, a young monk, Brother Daniel, was now commander of the Hardcore squadron. The battle group arrived at the village, and as if in a dream William saw the two squadrons split up, just like in the last battle, except this time the two groups reached the enemy at the same moment. William fought pushing on to his left flank. Behind him, two Sajuks held Albert and the new squire back. William saw the riders in black and white headdress flying the multi-colored Druze star and spurred Black in their direction. Hughes, who had also been separated from his team, followed along, protecting him. The Druze quickly encircled both William and Hughes and escorted them away before the other Templars could rescue them.

William looked over at Hughes, expecting they would let him go, but they didn't, and kept riding at full gallop on over the next hill and through a jagged plain full of boulders.

After a fierce run for what seemed several leagues, they came to a stop, dismounted and shed their helmets.

William recognized the leader, Sheik Dun, the Druze he had met in Acre. His men stared at both Templars with curiosity, and came closer to inspect the Templars' big horses, which looked immense next to their Arabians.

"Brothers, welcome," Dun said, extending both arms in their direction. "Brother Hughes, I wasn't planning on you coming along."

"Neither was I," Hughes said. "Somehow I got carried away, or maybe it was riding a horse I'm not used to, but at any rate, here I am."

"Would you like to ride back?" Dun asked. "You can say you managed to escape us."

Hughes studied William thoughtfully then turned in the direction they had come from. He looked down at the ground, bit his lower lip and fixed his gaze back on William. "I will stay, if that meets with your approval, Brother William."

William was surprised and couldn't say anything for a moment, then quickly mumbled. "I'll be honored to have you come along, brother." Hughes was going with him on his search for his uncle, and he felt so relieved he wanted to hug his commander. "Two of us stand a better chance of making it."

"I believe that's correct," Dun said. "Especially because Hughes speaks Arabic. However, we still must prepare you for the journey. I was planning on having you spend two months at my village in Syria for some needed instruction.

"William, you need to speak some Arabic, dress and look like a native, or else you may get killed.

"But right now both you and Hughes need to replace your Templar chargers with Arabians." Dun lifted a hand and pointed to one of his men who came trailing two spirited white mounts.

William stroked Black's neck and watched as he was loaded with big sacks. By the time the Druze were done, Black looked like a common beast of burden.

"Your horses will still stand out because of their size, but amid the camels they are less noticeable," explained Dun.

Both he and Hughes shed their surcoats for Arab robes and headdress. Dun brought out scissors and clipped their bushy beards. He then stood a few paces away, inspected them and thought that from a distance they could pass.

William mounted the Arabian, and felt odd, ill at ease, his legs not accustomed to the smaller girth. He spurred his horse and it literally leaped forward, then eased into a trot. On impulse, William turned his head to check on Black, and found him standing his ground with nostrils flared, ready to do battle, while men, horses, and camels dispersed; but when the charger met William's gaze and recognized him, he calmed down, shook his mane and proceeded forward, swishing his tail. The four men in charge of the beasts of burden talked excitedly pointing at the big horse, while giving him wide berth.

That afternoon William and Hughes were looked at curiously by a band of Sajuk soldiers who stood by the side of the road and watched them ride by.

"You ride like Templars," Dun told them afterward, and the two watched the Druze and how they rode, how they sat on their saddles. It was a more relaxed way of riding, so William and Hughes emulated them, and found that it required more than they thought. "Stop thinking like Templars, think of yourselves as Arabs," Dun said.

The route to the Druze village took them through some of the most inhospitable territory William ever imagined, a barren landscape of rocks and sand. Dun knew where water was hidden in crevices on the bottom of wadis—dry riverbeds that only flowed during the rains. "Few people dare wander in this country," Dun told them, "and of those who do, few survive; you have to be born in the place to know its secrets."

The going was very rough, it seemed the rocks kept the heat in and everything felt hot and dry. Dun taught them to make their way slowly, to accept the desert and the heat, and to simply let the horses take one step after another.

After three days the desert gave way to less arid landscape, and then to fertile land, and finally they reached Dun's village deep in the Syrian wilderness.

The village was tucked in between two hills. All looked green and tranquil— sheep, goats, camels and horses grazing in the open valley, women, children and old men walking peacefully, apparently unconcerned about any possible threat.

What struck William most was how clean everything was. The floors of the houses were of smooth tile, the walls made of a mixture of sand and ground up burned limestone that when mixed with water and dried made for a hard surface. Dun called it "cement," a concoction they got from the Romans. William smiled to himself. Back home people had wondered for centuries about the rock-like substance evident in so many structures the Romans left behind.

Dun's house stood on a promontory all to itself above the village. There was no defensive wall and one entered by a hallway leading to a central courtyard—a garden of small trees and shrubs of various scents—that provided access to the rest of the house. The rooms had tall ceilings, with ornate ventilated panels up high, the cement molded into flowers and curlicues allowing for the passage of air but providing privacy. A covered walkway wrapped around the outside of the house, leading to two structures, the bathhouse on the east side and the kitchen on the opposite end. There were chairs around, but mostly people sat on large cushions arrayed on beautiful carpets.

They ate delicate foods wrapped in leaves and on flat breads, and drank aromatic water and curdled milk laced with honey and spices.

William and Hughes lodged with Dun's family and William felt relieved that women and men lived in separate wings of the house, for he would find it awkward otherwise.

The two Templars were asked to strip off their under garments—linen aketons they wore under the hauberks, and even their intimate *bries*—which servants carried outside with care, holding them at arm's length as though poisonous. They were invited to immerse in a tub in the bathhouse. "To kill off your lice and fleas," Dun told them. After that, they bathed in warm scented water and Dun instructed them to do it every evening. Normally Europeans bathed only on special holidays, but William and Hughes decided to go along, and their host mentioned how relieved they all were that the two no longer "smelled like Templars."

"Do Templars smell differently than other Christian knights?" William asked, half serious, sitting in the spacious pool, the clear water up to his neck, watching Hughes' amused expression.

"Well, no," Dun responded with a polite smile, "you all smell bad."

William and Hughes learned to eat, walk and dress like Arabs. Their beards were trimmed some more as was their hair. They oiled their skins, hair and beards, and were given brushes and scissors for upkeep. They were taught how to dress in robes and headdress and given new hauberks, swords, helmets and boots.

Dun studied them. "You could both be Arabs of Greek ancestry," Dun said as William compared his face in a hand-held mirror to his host's darker features. "There are many Arabs who look like you," the sheik said reassuringly, "The main thing is how you comport yourselves, the way you walk, talk, and particularly, your mannerisms." Dun demonstrated by calling a servant to his side, then a friend who sat nearby. The two men approached the sheik and stood two paces away. The servant with eyes downcast and slightly bowed, expectant; the friend, straight, his arms neatly folded in front. "Both you and Hughes are to become noble Druze. Don't speak directly to servants; pretend you are addressing the air. With your own kind," Dun said looking at his friend, "you are diffident but affectionate. Delicacy in manners is everything, even in anger." And the sheik proceeded to address his friend and seemed to hold an animated conversation. His fingers gently brushed a shoulder, a polite smile on his face as he gesticulated with slow and elegant hand gestures all the while making eye contact.

William was taught Arabic by a gentle old man who soon turned into a tyrant, demanding that William memorize an ever increasing number of sentences, and learn the written symbols. He walked to the old man's house early every morning, and by noon, almost dizzy from all the repetitions, he gratefully made his way back to Dun's house for dinner. But one day, he found he could hold a limited conversation, and was very happy, only to have his teacher increase the workload.

The old teacher informed William that Arabic was closely related to Aramaic, Jesus' mother tongue, and that made it more interesting.

Both he and Hughes joined group meditations, and for the first time in his life William was in a community of people for whom meditation was commonplace, although not everyone seemed to enjoy the silence, but rather spent much time in Gnostic rituals. The villagers performed a mass in a chapel with symbols of serpents, lions, and astrological signs and chanted words they felt had magical powers. They blessed what looked like a Eucharist, wine and bread, which they drank and ate, before entering a "bridal chamber" for a ritual to unite their masculine and feminine sides.

After the first "mass" William decided to avoid such things and looked for the times when people simply meditated.

William visited Black often in the village pasture, both for his own comfort and to reassure the charger that he hadn't been abandoned. William rode bareback reciting Arabic phrases to the horse, to the amusement of the villagers.

After the first two weeks passed by and the novelty of the place wore off, it dawned on William what he and Hughes had embarked on. He was grateful that Hughes had decided to come, but at the same time William felt guilty for dragging him along. Now they could both die, and possibly all in vain, pursuing someone else's dream. What if there was no Hafiz Mountain? What if his uncle was dead?

But after meditation, when William thought about it again, he felt reassured.

It was a huge relief not to be killing anymore, but otherwise William missed the life at Pilgrim Castle and the religious routine, for although every time he had knelt down to pray and wished he could meditate, the rigors of that life had a beauty all to itself, a feel that was familiar, an integral part of his being.

The village life was a quiet one, far from warfare, and William envied the existence of people who had never had an invasion or a war visit their doorstep. The village was so remote, and of such little consequence that no army had bothered them that anyone could recall. He wondered whether there were places like that in England, or the whole of Britain.

William started talking haltingly with villagers, and found that most had never set foot outside their mountains. Neither had their parents nor their parents before them. It was a life of predictable chores, and the overriding concern was the weather and not much more. Other than that, villagers were vexed with the usual human dramas of love and death and how to deal with the unexpected.

William's favorite person was Barak the baker, a simple man who had never met a foreigner before but came around to talking openly with his "new Frankish friend." He was short and portly, with a happy round face and easy laughter. He would sit with William in front of his bakery talking about his two wives who fought constantly, his three daughters whom he hoped to marry well; and in between he exhibited a basic wisdom. "I don't fret about the things I can't fix with my hands, that's God's job," Barak said one day when talking about a sick friend.

But Dun didn't think much of his friendship with Barak. "Associate with others in the village, please William," he pleaded. "You'll end up talking Arabic like a baker; that will never do."

And William expanded his horizons, and met the two village scholars, and the three merchants, and was invited to their homes for fancy meals, for everyone wanted to meet "the Franks." But not a day went by that he didn't stop to share a moment with Barak the baker.

William overhead discussions led by the two scholars about the difference between Gnosticism and the "people of the book," and the villagers spoke of their religious practice with as much vested emotion as the Hardcores back at Pilgrim Castle spoke about theirs.

When the two months drew to a close, Dun inspected William and Hughes as they sat on big cushions in his cool and comfortable sitting room that backed into the courtyard. The sheik listened to their Arabic. "Hughes, you could pass for someone from the East. William, at least you'll be able to communicate. If asked, tell them you were enslaved as a child by the Christians."

William realized he was not joking.

"People will believe that—for it does happen—and many former slaves have returned after years in Constantinople barely speaking their native tongue."

Hughes leaned forward. "So now what? Shall we leave for Jerusalem?" He faced William. "I don't quite understand how going to Jesus' prison cell will lead us to Hafiz Mountain, but that's what John did."

William felt apprehension tighten his chest. *Well, this is what I dreamed of doing for so long. Might as well get started.* He was about to speak when he noticed Dun's intense gaze.

"I'll come along as far as Jerusalem," Dun said.

William and Hughes studied their host.

"That will certainly help us, Dun," William said. "But are you sure?"

"I'm sure William. I won't be absent longer than a month, and it will ease my mind."

That same afternoon they started getting ready for their journey, packing what they needed. Dun left his younger brother in charge and went around making last-minute arrangements pertaining to the village.

Two days later, on the last day before their journey, William paid Black a last visit. "I won't see you for many months, Black. But I will return. You can't come with me, friend, because you are a big Frankish horse, and for now I need to become an Arab."

William walked away feeling the charger's eyes fixed on his back.

The following morning, with the sun creeping up behind the nearby grass-covered hills, William, flanked by Hughes and Dun, left en route to Jerusalem.

They rode three beautiful mounts of fine pedigree and trailed behind four pack-horses with water, food, salt, grain for the animals, a tent, and clothing. They met a Sajuk detail three days into their trip, but the Turks only bowed, got out of their way, and wished them a safe journey, "Allah willing."

After six days of crossing the rough desert, they came to the fertile depression of the Lake of Galilee. From there it would be another seven days to Jerusalem. They encountered a Mameluk band, but their headdress was enough for safe passage. They were also allowed to pass by the Teutonic Knights they found on the south shore, and the Hospitallers they ran across a day later. For William it was odd to be looked at so differently by his own kind, no longer addressed in familiar tones, but talked at with the simplistic French reserved for deaf idiots—a loud tone was invariably used: "Go careful, bandits road."

The going was now easy, the land bursting with greenery, pleasing to the senses after the harsh desert.

"What do you expect to find in Jesus' cell, William?" Dun asked two days after leaving the lake, as they walked their horses to a shade under some trees to rest through the noon hour.

"I don't quite know," William answered, "but John felt compelled to find Jesus' cell. It seems something very significant happened there that led him to Hafiz Mountain. Whatever it was, I hope to experience it."

Four days later they came within sight of Jerusalem. William had always wanted to see the city, knowing that few Europeans made it this far since Saladin had taken the place from the Christians a hundred years before. Every so often brave Christian pilgrims would make the journey, and some perished in the process, but to them it was worth it, just to set foot in the holiest of cities. The Mameluks in charge apparently had orders to allow pilgrims in.

The three noble Druze riders approached the huge ramparts and the two visible north towers of the city. William could see the archers along the wall and on the walkway above the Fish Gate, which according to Dun was the most traf-ficked, used mainly by merchants. Distinguished visitors used the main gate, on the other side of the city.

They crossed unchallenged through the gate, which consisted of two pillars with a walkway on top, with thick, wooden doors now wide open, and crowded with camels, horses, donkeys, carts, wagons, and pedestrians. William looked up to meet the gaze of one of the guards in the overhead walkway, who studied the riders curiously, perhaps wondering what the three noble Druze planned to do in his city.

On the surface, Jerusalem was much like Acre, with tall buildings, narrow streets of cobblestone full of shops, inns and vendors peddling fruit, food, trinkets and even captured Christian swords and armor. But oh, there was so much more, and one could feel it once inside its walls. This was where Jesus died, where the Prophet Mohammed was brought in his dream by the Archangel Gabriel so he could ascend to heaven, where thousands of devoted Jews, Muslims, and Christians over the many centuries—and for millennia before there were Christians and Muslims or even Jews—had given their lives fighting for their beliefs, defending their holy city. It definitely felt like a very important place, and William studied every stone, every structure, for some hidden meaning.

They found a stable and left their horses to be cared for. Then, guided by the map Rabbi Ben Jashim had given William, they meandered up a slope to the top of a hill. "This is the Temple Mount," William said, and then pointed to the remains of columns and a huge partial stone wall higher up. "On top is what remains of the Temple of Solomon." They circled around the rise until they came to the ruins of a large structure in between a new building and a cistern. According to the map, they were near the site of the old Antonia Fortress where Jesus had been tried and held prisoner. William led them to a rocky promontory.

They made sure no one could see them, then descended into a crevice. Heavy rocks had been piled to one side. They removed the stones and uncovered a narrow entry, possibly a vent hole, just big enough for a man to crawl through on his stomach. This they did, for a few paces and came to a tunnel that seemed to originate in the Temple grounds and led to the Antonia Fortress site.

Dun produced two torches from a sack. He struck a flint stone and lit the oil soaked rags. The tunnel appeared to have been built in recent times, and at the far end it ran into an ancient wall with a door. William got a hold of a torch and led them along the tunnel and though the door. They found themselves in a small room, about six feet square. Up on top was a small opening that led to the surface, and a sliver of light came through it.

The enclosure was dank and looked impossibly uncomfortable, but it had to be Jesus' cell because the feeling in the place was like nothing William had felt before. A powerful sense of joy and wholeness overtook him, and a smell of roses, ever so faint—a fragrance so subtle one was not quite sure it was there—filled the air.

They breathed deeply, trying to take in the aroma, and the sensation like an ever-so-delicate hand, gently caressing, soothing their weariness away.

William felt enveloped in a loving presence, and the heavenly scent became a part of him, and the joy reverberated through his body, accompanied by a booming sound, a roar that seemed to resonate with every part of his body.

He had no idea how long they spent in the cell, but at some point it became clear that it was over and they should leave. William could feel that his heart, his mind, his whole being, was different, but he couldn't quite tell how. He gently tapped Hughes and Dun on the shoulder, and they walked away, as if in a trance.

It was very odd to be among people: voices sounded harsh and loud, their presence, rough. They took a room at an inn, wanting to get away from strangers above all else.

In their chamber—long and narrow with a small window at the end—they sat on the first of four cots lined up against the wall, sharing the one candle on the floor.

Hughes stood and walked the length of the room to look out the window at the empty alley. After some time he let out a sigh. "That was most incredible. I felt such peace inside…such beauty. How did the cell retain Jesus' presence after so many centuries? Other prisoners must have used it."

Dun started to speak, then paused, as if to collect his thoughts. "Maybe because that's where Jesus achieved his final transformation."

"Or maybe," William said, "it's just a miracle."

"Whatever the case," Hughes said, turning to look at the two, "The Brotherhood is doing a good job at protecting it, otherwise the sacredness would not be there."

"What did you experience, Hughes?" William asked as he walked over to the second bunk and lay down.

"I don't quite know," Hughes said still staring out the window. "I've never experienced anything like that before. I am deeply touched, that I know. I feel kind toward everyone I see, and my heart aches for them as though they were dear to me. In this moment there's no way I would draw my sword, and would rather turn it on myself than hurt someone.

"What about you, William?"

William thought for a moment. "It was Jesus whom we felt. You are right, Hughes, we were all touched deep inside and made…holy."

"My mind has trouble understanding and accepting what happened," Dun said thoughtfully. "Were it not for the lingering joy, I would doubt I was ever in that cell."

"But as wonderful as our experience was," Hughes said, "the visit did not show us the way to Hafiz Mountain, John, or the Gospel. So now what do we do?"

William sat up on his bed. "We were going to see Rabbi Ben-Jashim tomorrow as a courtesy. Now I think we need him, he's obviously very knowledgeable."

That following morning William led the way to the rabbi's house guided by his map. They ended up in a street lined with trees and quiet two-story narrow houses, built shoulder-to-shoulder. They stopped by a metal door and knocked. A man went by in a slow- moving donkey cart calling out in Greek, selling oranges.

Rabbi Ben-Jashim answered his own door and led them to his second floor workroom.

They sat on hard wooden chairs next to a table on which a recently scraped vellum lay next to a bottle of ink and the knife used to erase the old writing. All around stood tall cabinets with books. A large window looked down into the street below where they could still hear the orange seller.

William described what happened in Jesus' cell to the rabbi. "We had a wonderful experience, but still don't know where to go next, brother."

The rabbi stroked his beard. "I don't know where John decided to go after he handed me his letter, but I have thought about it since he left, and…" At this the rabbi stood up and got a map from a shelf. "The most likely place to be Hafiz Mountain is the Orthodox Monastery of Saint Catherine on Mount Sinai," he told them as he laid the map on the table that showed the area between Jerusalem and Alexandria. The Sinai Peninsula was a huge triangular mass to the west of Jerusalem and southeast from Alexandria. The mountain was at the southern tip.

"You can see that the monks of Alexandria had to traverse a desert to get to Mount Sinai, but it was a relatively short distance and away from Christian hordes. And the mountain was then, and still is, a sacred site. As you are probably aware, it's where Moses received the Ten Commandments."

William, with Dun and Hughes looking over his shoulder, studied the map and thought Rabbi Ben-Jashim made a lot of sense. The monks would have had to go east from Alexandria across Egypt until they reached the Sinai, and then straight down the peninsula.

"The Monastery was built on the foothills of the mountain," continued the rabbi, "and has been around for many centuries and is known to contain early Christian documents."

That had to be it—their Hafiz Mountain. The other deserts where the monks from Alexandria could have gone were the huge Arabian Peninsula, and the large Libyan desert in Africa. Both of those places were remote and unknown, dangerous to traverse and with little signs of human habitation.

William looked up from the map to find Hughes' thoughtful stare. "Well, Hughes. That's our destination."

On their way to the stables they talked about the journey and Dun seemed to take it for granted that he was coming along. William decided not to remind him that he had planned to come only as far as Jerusalem.

From Jerusalem on it was desert, and the further west they went the dryer and hotter it became.

On the third day, in mid afternoon, they ran into a group of Berbers—nomads from Africa—armed men, probably looking for easy prey to attack. Suddenly, Bridon's image came into William's mind. Dun had stopped his horse and was about to turn around, when William grabbed him by the arm.

"Don't run, Dun. Hold steady. Tell them I have leprosy."

"What?"

William brought his headdress to cover his face and hid his hands inside his robe. "Tell them I'm a leper and that you are taking me home to die."

Hughes, who was by William's right flank, fell in behind, and the three approached the Berbers, who promptly surrounded them.

"The peace of Allah be with you," Dun said to the man who appeared to be their leader. "My cousin and I are taking my leper brother home to die."

The man in charge extended his arms sideways signaling his men back. His face had turned ashen and he sat erect on his saddle. "I just heard that the same fate has befallen on my own blessed mother," he said in a hushed tone. "Pass, brothers, pass in peace, and may Allah guide your way."

When William, Hughes, and Dun had put some distance from the Berbers, Hughes brought his horse beside William's. "That was amazing. How did you know that posing as a leper would get us through?"

"I don't know, Hughes, I don't know. It was just a gut feeling."

Dun turned to face them. "However you figured that, I'm glad it worked. Otherwise, by now we'd be either running our horses ragged or dead."

They entered the Sinai Peninsula and for six days made their way through the rocky hills coming across pools of brackish water. On the fourteenth day of their journey they came up the rise of a hill overlooking a wadi and a large pool of fresh water where other travelers had made camp. They had been rationing their water, and at the sight, William realized how very dry his mouth felt. The horses flared their nostrils and had to be kept on tight reins to keep them from running toward the pool.

Hughes was the first to spot a band of Egyptians coming from the north, apparently still unaware of the camped travelers or of the three men watching them from the hilltop.

"Judging by their horses and tents, the people resting at the wadi are Christians from Constantinople," commented Dun, "most likely en route to the Monastery of Saint Catherine, a pilgrimage site for Greek Orthodox Christians. The riders are bandits. Just look at the number of scimitars, lances, and bows they carry."

"What do we do?" Hughes asked. "They'll spot the Christians in another hour or so."

"Years ago," Dun said, "there were military orders around here safeguarding pilgrims, but the Mameluks drove them out. The monastery itself is safe. It's been protected by every Muslim army since the time of the Prophet Mohammed, who, according to legend, was once given refuge there."

The awareness of what was about to happen slowly dawned on William, for up to then they had stayed in a state of tranquility, and it was hard to think in terms of violence. He turned to Dun. "We have to protect the pilgrims. As Templar knights we have vowed to defend Christians at any cost."

"Well, in that case we are all going to get killed because I can't let you two fight alone. The bandits number around twenty and I don't think the pilgrims will help. I guess this is where our journey comes to an end."

"We have no choice, Dun," William said.

Hughes looked around at the surrounding hills. "Maybe we don't have to fight, William."

"What do you mean?"

"What if we were to go to that hill," Hughes said pointing to a rise that stood in between the bandits and the pilgrims, "and pretend to be Mameluks?"

After a pause Dun slapped his leg and laughed. "Of course, Hughes. Brilliant. The Mameluks patrol this area, and even if the bandits realize that there are just the three of us, they'll hesitate to attack for fear of retribution. But we need to change our headdress to white and appear military."

They spurred their horses through the rocks. Their hardy Arabians had gotten used to the terrain and trotted down the one hill and up the other, slipping and regaining their step as they went until they reached the other summit.

The Egyptians were temporarily out of sight, but would be coming around the bend at any time. Dun went to one of the packhorses and got out some white cloth. William and Hughes undid their headdresses and Dun showed them how to wrap the white cloth around their heads so it bunched on top.

Dun then sat upright on his horse. "Stand your horses on either side behind me. We'll look like an emir with his two bodyguards."

They heard the Egyptians approach—their horses making their way through the rocks, and their voices.

William said a prayer.

Dun waited until the bandits were right below him, some hundred yards away. "In the name of Sultan Qalawun," he shouted, "state your business in these parts."

"Allah be praised," was the reply, "we are but honest merchants."

"You are far from the merchant routes," Dun told them, "what brings you here?"

The reply came after a brief hesitation. "We lost our way, and are in dire need of water. We beg your permission to proceed on to the wadi."

Their ruse had worked; the bandits were addressing Dun with obvious deference.

"You may proceed to the water, but must leave your weapons behind. There are pilgrims at the wadi, and they are under our protection. Fill your water bags and leave."

The Egyptian bandits obeyed and meekly piled their weapons, then proceeded forward. If they were hiding anything, it could only be daggers. They made their way to the water where they were met by the surprised pilgrims, who had heard the exchange, and were now alternatively looking at the approaching Egyptians and staring at the hill trying to make out who was there.

The bandits came up to the pond in the dry riverbed, a generous wide pool of inviting clear water shaded by willowy palm trees. They watered their horses and crouched down by their thirsty animals to fill their water bags as they exchanged polite greetings with the Christians.

When it looked as though the Egyptians were done, Dun ordered them to leave, and this they did, protesting that they were tired and wanted to rest. Dun allowed them to pick up their scimitars, but nothing else. The rest of the weapons, which included lances and worst of all, bows, were left behind.

It had all been a miracle. The bandits were obeying as though a large army lay behind the hill, at the beck and call of Dun's slightest whim.

Once the bandits were safely out of view, William and Hughes followed Dun to the weapon pile. It took some time to break the bows and hide the lances in scattered places.

Next, they approached the pool and allowed the animals to drink. The pilgrims—eight men, four women and three children, spoke excitedly but kept their distance from the newcomers. But four men armed with swords and lances came out to greet William and the two others.

They were the pilgrims' escort, three Arabs led by a former Hospitaller knight named Andre of Berkeley, who was very surprised when two of the newcomers turned out to be Europeans.

Once reassured, the Greek-speaking pilgrims came forward, smiling, with cups of cool water in their hands. William thanked them in Greek.

The bear-like Andre, his beefy arms crossed over his chest, stared at William in awe, and searched his face. "John? Is that you?"

William felt his heart skip a beat. "How do you know John? I'm his nephew."

"Ah," Andre exclaimed with a deep sigh, and he appeared disappointed. "I had been hoping to meet John again. You see, twelve years ago I was roaming around these hills, wanting to stay. I had spent ten years protecting pilgrims from our castle not far from here, until the Mameluks ordered us out, but I felt my soul belonged in these mountains.

"To survive, I thought of becoming a bandit, and I did rob some Muslim travelers. Didn't hurt anyone, though, and that life did bother my conscience, but I saw no other way that I could stay around, that is until I met John.

"One day I was about to assault some merchants, and was lying in wait on top of a hill when a man dressed as an Arab approached me from behind and casually asked in French what I was doing. The stranger had been so quiet, I did not hear him come; so surprised, I answered: 'Trying to get something to eat.'

"'In a way the Lord would approve?' John asked me.

'Well, if the Lord were in my condition, I'm sure he would consider it,' I told him, and John laughed. I then explained that I hadn't had a full meal in a week, and had eaten nothing at all that day.

"'There are other ways,' John told me. He shared his food with me, and we talked. Then he led me to this same wadi and we waited for four days, until a group of pilgrims came by. He assured them that for a few coins I would agree to show them the way to Saint Catherine's Monastery and protect them as well.

"And that's how I met John."

William gave a side-glance to Hughes and Dun. "So John went with you to the monastery? Do you visit him there?"

"Oh no, my friend," Andre said as he took William by the arm and led him to a cushion under a palm tree, signaling for Hughes and Dun to sit on nearby pillows. "John told me he was on his way to Alexandria. I haven't seen him in all these years. I was hoping he was you. I need to talk to him again."

Andre waited until William, Hughes, and Dun were seated then he crouched in front of William. "Ever since that day I've been escorting pilgrims on this route by waiting for them to show up at the wadi, and each time I've stayed a little longer at the monastery where I'm always made to feel welcome by the monks."

The pilgrims came over to join Andre and the strangers. The men and women stood around and examined the Druze who spoke French and Greek, with curiosity. Their four children—three boys and a girl—squatted next to William, and unabashedly stared at him in rapt attention.

"If I didn't belong to the Roman Church," continued Andre, "I would consider joining the monks at Saint Catherine's, but they are of the Eastern Church, you know."

Andre went on to describe life at the monastery in great detail, his voice laden with longing.

"Maybe you should join them," William said.

"Ah, that would be betraying the Church," Andre said. "I really want to, it feels like my calling, but it means leaving the Roman Church, and if I do that, I'm sure to burn in hell."

"No," William said. "Please do. It's where you belong. It's Christ's Church as well…and John would approve."

"You think so? Oh, I have wanted to find him so I could ask him. I was hoping to see him on the way back to whatever place he was going, but he never made it back."

"Well, I can tell you that's what he wants you to do."

Andre studied his big hands full of scars. "I will then," he said softly. "This will be my last trip, because I will stay. Thank you, friend."

"By the way, Andre," William said, "did John tell you what he was going to do in Alexandria?"

Andre looked baffled. "I asked him, and one night he told me, 'I'm going to talk to someone who can tell me where to find old books. I asked him what he wanted old books for, but he said it was a complicated story."

Evening fell and the desert came alive as animals ventured out into the cooler air. William saw small hares and gerbils come to drink at the pond, as well as vivid blue lizards that darted from rock to rock. Birds also made an appearance: hawks circled overhead and larks fluttered excitedly among the rocks.

William and his two companions talked late into the night with Andre and the pilgrims, who belonged to the same extended family from Constantinople. "They are going to spend six months at the monastery," Andre said. "Then my men can escort them back to Alexandria where they can catch a ship home."

It had taken a while for the pilgrims to understand what had happened, that the three Druze had probably saved their lives, and they showed their gratitude with a lavish meal, and brought out the special supplies they had been saving for a celebration. They seemed pleased that the newcomers spoke their language well, "so unlike the Frank barbarians," said an outspoken, meticulously dressed matron. She talked about Constantinople, and of a comfortable life in a city of high culture, and described with disdain the rough manners and customs of the Franks and the Turks; how they didn't bathe and were perhaps but a step removed from the Mongols. "Our elders still talk of the years the crusaders occupied our beautiful city. They would drink water from latrines and defecate and urinate anywhere. The Saracen, on the other hand," concluded the woman with an ingratiating smile, "are like us, civilized."

William, Dun, and Hughes bid Andre and the pilgrims goodnight, then walked back to their campsite.

"Well, Saint Catherine's is not it," Hughes commented.

"Or at least not according to John," William said as he spread out his blanket by a palm tree, getting ready to meditate. "We were so sure about that monastery."

"But we are on John's trail, and that's a relief," Dun said. "It was just luck that we ran into Andre, otherwise we would have gone on to Saint Catherine's and been disappointed. Obviously John never even considered the place."

"From what he told Andre, he was going to Alexandria to consult with scholars."

"Scholars?' asked Hughes. "Is that what he meant by someone who could tell him about old books?"

"Yes," said William. "Alexandria is well known for its scholars. Once Andre said that, it made perfect sense to me."

"So are we going to question scholars until we find the one he consulted?"

"That's what I figured."

The following morning, William and Hughes filled their water bags, then all three wished Andre and the pilgrims a safe journey south, and made their way west toward Alexandria, John's next stop twelve years before.

They had to go north to where the Red Sea ended, then west again to the Nile and through the ancient city of Memphis, then northwest toward the coast.

They met a Mameluk patrol that gave them a passing cursory look. "Druze are well respected throughout the area you call Outremer," Dun said when the soldiers were out of earshot, "we are seen as above all the ideological strife between religions, including those brewing among the two main Muslim factions, Sunnis and Shiites."

"What do they fight about?" William asked.

Dun shrugged his shoulders. "Not all of them fight, but the fanatics among them do. Right after the Prophet Mohammed's death his followers argued about who should take over. They've not been able to agree for the past six hundred years."

In the weeks that followed, the three Druze noblemen were welcomed, given shelter and food by rich and poor alike in farms and villages. Their hosts vied for the honor to have them stay in their homes, and both William and Hughes discovered a gentility and graciousness they had not known before. It was good to be a noble Druze.

William found that he could simply nod in assent or avert his gaze when spoken to, and Dun answered on his behalf, explaining that "my cousin was kept as a slave in Constantinople for many years and forgot how to speak our language."

It took them nearly a month to reach the well-fortified Alexandria—a port city founded by Alexander the Great sixteen centuries before, William told Hughes. The city was a milieu of varied types of buildings and houses, reflecting the mismatch of cultures that had ruled: Greek, Roman, Egyptian, and Arab. The city had been the center of culture in the world for a long time with an influence even greater than Rome's; and its grand buildings still reflected that glory. William had never seen so many Greek and Roman temples, including the majestic lighthouse visible from anywhere. The wide and straight streets, flanked by columned covered walkways, were paved with smooth stones and there were fountains at nearly every corner. There were a few fountains in Europe left from Roman times, but people were just starting to learn how they worked; how the Romans managed to carry water in pipes over long distances and add the needed pressure. Dun said that every single house, even the most modest ones, had running water, so if a person wanted a drink all he had to do was approach an ever-flowing pipe; and to bathe, all he had to do was step into his own private bathhouse. William wondered what his mother would think of such things, and he recalled her sighs each time a servant brought in water from the well, splashing all the way up the stairs, or worse yet, spilling the contents of bed pans to be emptied in the cesspool. Not even the king of France had the luxury of running water or the sewage disposal that a lowly commoner had in Alexandria. London had open sewers, as did Paris, but most towns simply used their streets and relied on the rains to flush all manner of waste when the rains came. At the inn where they stayed, the bathhouse had a latrine connected to a huge pipe that dumped the city's waste into the ocean. Life was certainly easy.

After resting for the best part of a day, William felt an urge to begin making inquiries of scholars. Perhaps they could find someone who remembered talking to John. William led Hughes and Dun in a search of the various schools that gathered for the study and discussion of academic topics, a tradition that went back to ancient Greece. Getting around was easy, just about everyone spoke Greek.

They talked to experts on ancient documents and were led to Jews, Arabs, Greeks, Egyptians, and Berbers who shared a common thread: their interest in the books that had been housed at the long-vanished library of Roman times. Most had theories where the monks of the library would have taken their books, but no one knew for certain. Two remembered John, but not the exact conversation, nor where he might have gone next.

Then they met a Catholic priest. He was in a hurry to meet with his bishop, but he told them as he rushed down the street that he had once run across a "man of great knowledge of the library books" whose name he couldn't quite recall. Then he went inside the bishop's palace, but in a moment he poked his head out of a second-story window. "Go see Nikola." They could hardly make out the words.

"Where do we find him?" yelled William.

The priest pointed at his garments and held the crucifix dangling from his neck. Then he dashed back inside.

They decided that it was obvious that "Nikola" was a priest, and judging by the name he had to be Greek, so they went to the Greek quarter and started asking in every Orthodox church they found.

They began with the biggest churches. On their third attempt, an energetic and affable young priest told them where they could find a priest by that name who had a reputation for knowledge about the documents of the old Roman library. "But no one goes to see him anymore. He has forgotten much, and what he remembers doesn't make sense."

They found Father Nikola nodding off in a chair in front of a small-dilapidated church, tucked away in an ancient street.

Father Nikola, remembered John clearly, and kept staring at William, apparently not quite believing it wasn't him. "I'll tell you what I told my friend John the other day," he said in a raspy voice, his watery eyes coming to life. "The only place where the monks of the old library could have taken their books was the Tibesti Mountains in the Libyan wilderness, known in ancient times among the mystical underground as the best place to hide if you wanted to leave the world."

"Nowhere else makes sense;" the old priest said, smoothing his faded black vestments. "The Arabian Peninsula was too forlorn and far, and the library monks would have had to travel through Christian territory full of fanatics who would have lynched them if they knew what they were carrying. Going to the Sinai would make sense, but the only place there would be the Monastery of Saint Catherine, but that didn't exist back in 323, it was built a hundred years later."

They thanked the old Orthodox priest profusely and Dun gave him a generous number of gold coins for his church.

Dun led the way to the store of a scribe who specialized in copying maps. The one he chose showed the whole of the Libyan desert in great detail. On their way back to their inn, they ran across the Catholic priest as he stood in front of the bishop's palace talking with someone. William thanked him for the tip that led them to Father Nikola.

"Nikola? I don't know any such person," he said. "I told you to go to the church of St. Nicholas where we have an old parchment."

They walked away baffled, but thankful they had accidentally found the right man.

Hughes laughed out loud.

"What do you find amusing?" William asked.

"How we ended up finding Father Nikola and John's trail," he said. "If it hadn't been for the rabbi pointing us in the right direction for the wrong reason, we would never have found Andre of Berkeley, who led us to Alexandria. Then we misheard the Catholic priest and found Father Nikola, the only person who apparently knows where Hafiz Mountain is."

William smiled broadly. "There's no question in my mind that we are on some sort of magical journey and are guided and protected. On our own devices, we would be either dead by bandits, or scratching our heads at Saint Catherine's not knowing where to go next."

Back at the inn William unfolded their new map, and pointed out the Tibesti Mountains located far inland and to the west of Alexandria.

Next they talked to a scholar—who was known as an expert on the Libyan desert— at a nearby natural philosophy school and found that the Tibesti Mountains had plenty of water, the means to grow food, a welcoming people, and remote enough to discourage marauding armies.

"We must plan our trip very carefully," Dun said as they studied the map back at the inn. "We are about to set foot in a desert that's very different from the one in Syria or the Sinai. We'll run across massive sand dunes, some as big as mountains that move with the wind and can cover a village overnight. The map shows a few oases, but few and far between.

"We'll need to trade our horses for camels, animals much better suited to this desert. Their long legs and wide feet can negotiate the loose sand, and they can go without water for several days. They are not as nimble and fast as horses, but since we won't have to outrun anyone anymore, the camels will do just fine."

On a return visit to the scholar who knew about the Libyan desert, they learned that the old cities along the coast had fallen during the several wars, and Tunis, built near the ruins of Carthage, was the only booming port. Mahdia, south of Tunis, was mostly a pirate hideout.

In taverns and eateries, they found merchants and travelers who knew the area, but no one they talked to had actually visited the Tibesti Mountains, but they did tell them that there was little water on the way, except for the lake at the oasis of Siwa.

Two days later, William, riding alongside Hughes, tried his best to mimic Dun, who sat cross-legged on his camel. They made their way out of Alexandria just as the rainy season was starting. They trailed ten camels laden with provisions, and had left their horses in the care of their innkeeper, who assured Dun that he would look after his precious Arabians as well as he looked after his wives. Dun asked him to please make a distinction and not feed them as much.

The camels were cumbersome but steadfast, and their rocking gait took some getting used to. The freight camels carried grain, dried goat meat, nuts, and dates for the humans, water bags, and grass tied in tight bundles to feed their mounts. The three rode the banks of a wadi, not daring to go on the riverbed itself for fear of flash floods. That particular river seemed to lead them well away from the coast, the same route John must have taken. William saw no signs of other travelers, except for the skeleton of a horse they found on the second day.

The going was tedious, and in a non-changing landscape there was no way to determine whether they made any progress. It was even hotter than the Sinai, perhaps because the sand reflected the sun. They crossed dunes into rocky plains followed by more sand dunes. Each day they fell into a stupor that lasted until they made camp, only occasionally becoming alert enough to make sure they were still heading in the same direction. They stopped to set up their tent when the sun neared its zenith and the air seemed too hot to breathe. When the heat became bearable again, they would break camp and resume their trek until it was too dark to see. There were occasional water holes in the wadi, but these were not marked on their map and they filled up their bags to the top each chance they got.

When they made camp it seemed that they had camped in the same place the day before, and that each morning they were about to repeat an endless succession of sand and more sand, with no end in sight.

After two weeks they arrived at the oasis of Siwa, exhausted from the sun and the heat, and perennially thirsty from fear of depleting their water supply. They rode into the large fertile oasis with fruit trees, a handful of farms, a village and an incongruous lake, and decided to spend two days resting, feasting their eyes on water and greenery, and allowing their camels their fill of grass and water. Up on a hill sat the ruins of what they were told by a friendly date farmer was the oracle that Alexander the Great had come a long distance to consult sixteen hundred years before.

After the oasis, William, Hughes, and Dun trekked for four interminable weeks over mostly rocky terrain. They were running out of water and had ran out of grass for the camels when they finally saw the Tibesti mountains in the distance, a blue shimmering apparition. Three days later, hallucinating from thirst and walking beside their animals on the brink of collapse from hunger, they came across jagged rocks poking out of the sand, sentinels protecting the massive mountains behind them. That evening in the foothills they found a small trickle of water coming out of a rock, and right below it, grass growing in a hollow in between two hills. They stopped to rest and to say a prayer of gratitude.

As they climbed the mountains, the terrain became more hospitable, and shrubs started to appear, then more vegetation and grassy plains home to sheep and goats, then finally the signs of human life: a small village consisting of six stone huts, goats, a few crops, and four black men standing by, staring at them. William had seen black people in Alexandria, but unlike those, these wore little clothing. Dun lifted a hand, a universal sign of peace, and the natives immediately answered the same way.

"You lost?" asked the oldest one in halting Arabic.

"No, friend, we know where we are going. We come in peace," Dun responded.

"This…our land…we don't like strangers."

"I know, and we ask your permission to reach a place where we know people."

It occurred to William that they were acting as guards, discouraging unwanted visitors.

The black man nodded. "Tell me name of place."

"Hafiz Mountain."

At this the man signaled for them to pass. "The Tubu-Daza welcome you their land."

Hughes seemed curious. "Do you often meet travelers?"

"Last one…many months. They come… for Hafiz caves… no one else comes."

And William wondered why then they bothered to challenge strangers, but maybe that was the only way they could talk to someone from the outside. "Do you ever go outside these mountains?" he asked.

"Oh yes," the man said. "My father spoke of trip to Tunis when child. It's wonderful city next to sea," he said with an air of authority. "One day I will."

For a week they searched all over the mountain and its valleys and found small caves, but nothing that would house a colony. The landscape was pock marked with ancient craters and peaks of bare rock interspersed with valleys of grass, shrubs and trees. The recent rains were bringing the grasses back to life.

The three rode around the plains and the hills, inside dormant craters, and along cliffs. Dun questioned natives they ran across, but no one seemed to know what he was talking about. They tried for another five days, and started to doubt whether they were on the right mountain. After another four days they decided to go back and question the first Tabu Daza they had met.

They were crossing a valley next to a dormant crater, a place they had gone twice before, when Hughes spied a barely discernible trail cut into a cliff's sheer face. Excited, they approached the man-made steps and walked their camels behind them, carefully watching each step. After a switchback, they saw that the trail went into a crevice. They reached the crevice and saw the entrance to a cave.

Gingerly, the three made their way into the cave and their eyes adjusted to the dim light from a torch set on the wall a good twenty yards inside. It was then that William saw a smiling man in a white robe walking quickly towards them.

John.

CHAPTER VI

[1]

John's face was frank and open, with dark eyes that seemed to look right inside William. As John stood studying him, William tried to absorb every detail: a man of his own height and similar build, who stood very erect. He had dark brown hair down to his shoulders, just starting to gray, a wide, smooth forehead, clean-shaven; and a wonderful smile. His overall appearance was that of a youthful and strong man, and peaceful, very peaceful.

William was taken into his arms, a warm embrace that he could feel deep down.

John's presence was not of this world, it reminded William of Jesus' cell; there was a sense of wholeness and love, special and precious. But he was also human, still of flesh and blood; a reassuring presence close to William's heart, someone whose essence was somehow dear and familiar.

John slowly let go of William and wrapped his arms around Hughes. "Brother Hughes, I've missed your rascally ways!" He then embraced Dun. "So glad you came dear friend. These two would not have made it without you.

"But let's unburden your camels, then we can talk." With this John led them inside with their long line of animals through the wide torch-lit passageway.

William tried to understand what he was feeling. His mind was reeling with excitement, and he felt happy but also expectant, aware that this was only the beginning, that new and wonderful things would happen, because he had finally found John. But there was also the realization that what he was experiencing was finite and would have to end sometime; at some point he, Hughes and Dun would have to leave, and William wanted to fully absorb his uncle's presence, imprint it in his heart.

John led them through various tunnels, most of them man-made, evident from the smaller, uniform size and the chisel marks on the dark gray rock of walls and ceilings; the natural tunnels were irregular and meandered sometimes into impressive chambers, where voices echoed and the flow of water signaled an underground stream somewhere in the dark where the light from the torches could not reach.

There was a short climb, a sudden turn, and they stepped through an opening into blinding daylight. Before them was a valley shaped like a cooking pot, deep with sheer sides. The walls were about three hundred feet tall and almost perfectly smooth, as impassible as any fortress wall. But from where they stood, a gentle slope led down to the bottom of the fertile basin.

John helped them unburden the camels and set them loose. They watched the animals make their way down the trail, twitching their tails, heading for the five or so other camels, as well as goats and sheep that grazed in a pasture, separated by stone walls from the various crops and groves of fruit trees. A number of white-clad figures—apparently both men and women—were busy at work, their singing wafting over in a gentle breeze.

John studied William, Hughes, and Dun and smiled broadly. "Just like the visions I had long ago. Even before I left England, I could see this moment, except that back then I had no idea who the three visitors were. Now it has come to pass."

William could hardly believe that this was his uncle in the flesh. He turned around to look at Hughes, who seemed his quiet self, but William noted how he stole glances in John's direction and how his face glowed whenever John looked at him. Dun's usual sheik's reserve had melted away, and he stared at John with obvious fondness.

John took them through another maze of passageways into a large room that had a window on one end allowing light from the small valley. The cavern was lined with over a hundred wooden cabinets that extended from the floor all the way to the ceiling.

The feeling in the place was peaceful, a sweet serenity that seemed to come from everything.

"This is the original reading and transcribing room, built when Tiberius and his monks came a thousand years ago from Alexandria," explained John. "Tiberius had been a high official at the library and he couldn't abide the destruction of the books he loved, so he convinced a handful of his monks to help him save them. He knew that in the Tibesti mountains lived a colony of mystics, probably because he himself was a mystic and had thought of joining them. Tiberius and his monks made four trips to and from Alexandria in the space of a year, taking no rest in between, trying to save as much of the ancient knowledge as they possibly could."

John made a sweeping gesture of the room. "The cabinets contain books, some in parchment, some papyrus, some velum, some disintegrated and long copied, some newly copied, and some the original books the monks carried."

The room had three long rows of tables in the middle, with chairs, occupied at that moment by four men and two women who had been reading but were now quietly observing the newcomers.

John led William, Hughes, and Dun through the large room and into another tunnel, and then to his private chamber, a small cave with a bed, table with a lone candle, and a chair. Near his room were three small caves, about the same size. These were to be their quarters.

The peace was everywhere, like a silent melody.

William entered his assigned chamber, put down his belongings, lit the candle with the lamp in the hallway, then washed using a pitcher of water and a bowl he found on the table, and changed into clean clothes.

He sat on his bunk and looked at the rock walls, made smooth by someone's hard labor, perhaps long ago. He took a long deep breath. Hafiz Mountain was real; he had been led along with Hughes and Dun to this place, for a specific mission, to acquire the Jesus Gospel, which no doubt he would get to see very soon. And then they would travel back to Acre and hand it to the Brotherhood, and be able to say: we completed our mission; our job is done. William wished he didn't have to go back, but there was no other way, his destiny was to deliver the Gospel. Besides, he was a Templar, and only death could stop him from completing the mission he had been given.

Then what? He couldn't possibly remain a Templar and fight. Perhaps he could return and join his uncle here. William closed his eyes and felt the peace all around him. It was soothing, so soothing. And again William was reminded of Jesus' cell: he felt removed from the world, and knew that here he could reach his final transformation. That would be a wonderful reward, to return here and stay for the rest of his life. William smiled. *That would be grand.*

He heard Hughes and John's voices, blew out the candle and got up to join them.

John took them to a sitting room sumptuously furnished, Arab style, with carpets and large cushions on the floor and tapestries adorning the walls.

John sat on one of the big pillows and motioned for them to sit around him.

"For a long time I've felt you coming," he told them. "I knew you would arrive this morning, so after my meditation I waited close to the entrance. By midmorning I heard your voices as you climbed."

"The successful journey to Hafiz Mountain requires a personal transformation—a shedding of the world—which you achieved in Jesus' cell, as did I. After that, you were ready to come, guided by your higher self."

"Yes," Dun said, "that's what I thought."

"Otherwise getting here is fraught with difficulty and danger, and if you make it, you don't fit in, you may not even see the place for what it is."

"Yes, I understand," William said. "The cell transformed us…"

"Mainly it transformed you, William," Dun said.

"You were all changed," John said. "In the journey that led you here, each one of you had a role to fulfill. I started by calling William, but reached out to Hughes and Dun as well, asking your spirits to help. And you did. Thank you."

A man dressed like John came in bearing a tray with a jug and cups. He bowed as he served them what turned out to be cool water laced with an aromatic herb.

John went on to tell them that presently there were forty-seven monastics of both sexes at Hafiz Mountain.

"The first people who came here were Jews escaping the Mesopotamian invaders six hundred years before Jesus. There were families, comprising men, women, and children. From the very start the residents were spiritual seekers. Eventually it became a monastic order of sorts that welcomed people of all faiths. But it wasn't until the Alexandria monks arrived in 323 that it took on its present nature. We live communally with women, but practice celibacy to avoid family distractions."

William watched John as he spoke. Judging by his gaze and manners he was without doubt a deeply spiritual individual, but not much different than himself or Hughes, or Dun.

John must have felt William studying him, for he glanced at his nephew as he talked, and at that moment William felt a jolt in his heart, and then John's presence seemed to amplify and fill the room and William felt his own self expanding, commingling with his uncle's, into one deeply joyful essence; and he was held in the loving embrace for a powerful moment. Then William was himself again and he smelled that subtle aroma of roses, and saw a golden light coming from John, who went about explaining something as though nothing out of the ordinary had taken place.

William noticed that Dun and Hughes had not been affected in any way, and had continued listening. William smiled at his uncle, studying his every mannerism in awe. *So that's what a Christ looks like.*

John was saying that for the past thousand years the monastic order at Hafiz Mountain had included women. He explained that the order had been firmly established by Tiberius. "He and his dozen monks proceeded to copy the books and explore the means for dissemination. There were a number of monasteries out of reach of the fanatical Christian hordes, some as far away as Persia, and Tiberius sent monks to those places with copies. Tiberius himself headed toward the coast, where he visited several cities, former colonies of the old Phoenicians, Greeks, and Romans. He met with their leaders, told them what he carried and those who were interested received selected books. New libraries sprung up as a result, containing books written in Greek and Latin, which in turn were translated to various languages and dialects."

"But they didn't copy the Gospel as well?" asked Hughes. "I would think Tiberius and his monks would have disseminated it."

"No, no, Hughes," said John. "That would have been very dangerous. Remember that they had just witnessed Constantine declaring Jesus the physical son of God. He also picked four gospels out of over a hundred to become the New Testament, and called everything else heresy. Christianity suddenly became a powerful religion infused with fervent fanaticism. Tiberius knew that would be the case for centuries to come. He realized that the temporal books could survive once disseminated, but the Gospel and other Gnostic documents had to remain hidden.

"So Tiberius and his monks copied and distributed only the temporal knowledge. Eventually Tiberius was satisfied that they had planted the seeds for the knowledge to be transmitted to the minds he knew thirsted for it. As a result, the Arab, Persian, and Jewish cultures blossomed while Christendom descended into the darkness of ignorance.

"That's been the function of Hafiz Mountain through so many years, to safeguard and disseminate knowledge."

"But you didn't come here for that, did you John?" Hughes asked.

"Well, in a away I did. When I connected with the Christ consciousness and with the essence of Jesus in his cell—when His mind became my mind—I just knew that there was a Jesus Gospel."

Dun leaned forward as though ready to stand. "And did you find it here?"

"Yes, I did."

"Can we see it?" Hughes asked.

"Yes, of course. It's in the reading and transcribing room. Tomorrow, when you are rested, we can all look at the Gospel," John said.

John asked William about the family; and William told him, and about all the people John had touched: his mother, Sir Ian, the earl of Sheffield, even Andre of Berkeley. At their mention John smiled and wanted to know how each was faring. He seemed to have a special place in his heart for every one, but most of all, for William's mother. He wanted to know what she looked like of late, whether her hair was a light chestnut, and whether she still laughed until tears came to her eyes. "Does she still make those rag dolls for the poor?" At William's quizzical look, John said that it had been her favorite thing to do, and how she enjoyed making each doll special, knowing how much it would mean to the child who would play with it.

"No, she doesn't make dolls," William said. "And I've seldom heard her laugh." William wondered how much his mother had changed.

John told how much he had enjoyed talking with Lady Claire, her keen mind, sweet temperament, and good humor, and the long walks they took "exploring every corner of that valley." John seemed to be reliving those times with her, and a far-away look came into his eyes. Then he smiled broadly at William, studying him closely as though trying to discern Lady Claire in his features.

Still smiling, John stood and signaled with a flowing gesture for them to follow him. He led them on a tour of the colony, and they walked through the expanse of tunnels and caverns, with kitchens, dormitories, dispensaries, prayer and meditation rooms. In one room they walked in and found three Muslims prostrated in prayer, in another there were Christians kneeling. William asked about the prayers, about the adherence to ritual for people who communed directly with God.

"Prayer and ritual is what their hearts are used to, and it's what makes them ready for meditation." John explained that the Jesus Gospel was the foundation of the community, which called for going inside to find God, but for each seeker the route inside was unique. "They understand the function of prayer and ritual, and no one thinks of themselves as different from anyone else in the community."

John introduced his guests to colony members as they came across them, and many of them had a special way about them—a depth of being. They looked deep into the newcomers' eyes while talking; a steady, probing gaze, and William knew they were taking him, Hughes, and Dun, into their hearts, knowing and cherishing their presence.

William continually savored the deep peace that permeated Hafiz Mountain, and it occurred to him that this was the place he had been searching for all his life. It was the home he never realized he had.

That evening John took them to one of the group meditations. The entire community joined every morning and evening in an opportunity to "share our spirit," John said. And it was different than anything William had experienced before.

The colony members—all forty-seven plus the newcomers—sat in chairs and cushions set in rows in a large cavern called "The Chapel." Candles set in wall niches lit the ample space in a golden glow and incense wafted through the still, cool air. Silence spread through the room, quieting coughs and restless bodies, and a deep peace settled in. With each inhalation William took in the glorious calm, each exhalation expelled the last vestiges of the world. He felt himself grow ever so serene; his breathing became shallow, then stopped.

His spirit expanded, expanded into joy until William could hardly feel his body, it was as though it was just another chair. "The Knowing" was tangible; close by, his spirit told him. At that moment he also understood *Beauseant*; for there was no longer a William, no separation between his self, those around him, and Spirit, and he realized what harmony meant…this is God, he thought. Then his thoughts ceased and he was at once everything and everywhere, for what seemed like a brief flash; a total oneness.

That following morning after meditation and breakfast, John took them to look at the Jesus Gospel. They sat at one of the long tables, and then John walked to one of the cabinets, and brought over a wooden box, about two feet square. He opened it, and inside were parchment pages. He took them out and handed them to Hughes.

"My word, John!"

"Oh, not to worry. It's old, but one of three copies. On the bottom of each page is the name of the monk who did the transcribing. The Library monks were very careful tracking what and how documents were processed. The one you are looking at says that it's a copy made in the year 182 of a Greek document authored by Jesus-Son-of-Joseph."

William and Dun crowded around Hughes, looking over his shoulder at the pages.

"Jesus speaks as we thought," John said. "It's an instruction manual, describing the basic tenets of his teachings; a most beautiful document, a love letter to humanity."

William read the text aloud for Hughes' benefit who had difficulty reading Greek. Jesus spoke of love for the one father of us all, and the inner journey that each person must take to find Him. All around us is a reflection of God, and how we relate to the world is how we relate to ourselves, and ultimately to the Divine; a gloriously simple description of how the universe works. Within this perspective, forgiveness, loving our enemy, and focusing our entire selves on God made perfect sense. It was pure and simple Gnosis. John was right: it was a love letter to humanity, extolling them to find their common source, God, found in "The Knowing." What Jesus had attempted was heart wrenching in the face of man's constant unintended sabotage, simplicity perhaps beyond what man could understand, therefore the need for elaboration with dogma, intricate ritual, and rules. Even the Templars' beautiful concept of *Beauseant* was superfluous.

At Hughes' request, William re-read some sections. Then they sat in silence for quite some time. It was hard to believe that those were Jesus' actual words. You could feel his presence through his writing, not just the Christ in him, but also his human essence, and that was a powerful experience.

"How can current Christianity—killing in the name of Christ, calling other religions evil—derive from these beautiful teachings?" Hughes asked staring at the pages of the Gospel.

John nodded in agreement. "Out in the world the human mind cannot understand that state of oneness that is the focus of Jesus' teachings. So they did the best their minds could do, they made God an entity that is separate and distinct from them, and defined Him using an image of themselves. They imbued their religion with their pride and made it exclusive so it was the only true religion. The concept of Jesus being the only Son of God makes it so."

"Same for Islam," Dun said, "Mohammed is the only true Messenger of God. And of course both the Bible and the Koran are the 'Word of God.'"

"But they haven't changed, have they?" William said. "If we show them the Gospel, they still won't understand its message, cling to their dogmatic views and say that it's not real."

"Actually," Hughes said, "I hate to tell you this, but they will burn us at the stake for heresy. Ever since I joined the Brotherhood I wondered what would happen if someone found the Gospel and brought it to Christendom. Now that we are in actual possession of it we must face the fact that we can't take it with us. Not much has changed since Tiberius' time."

"You have a good point, Hughes," William said.

"I know what you are saying," John said, "and it makes perfect sense. But I also know that what the Caesarius Prophecy describes is real. I can sense it; and what my spirit sees is that the Gospel will stop the French king and eventually transform the world."

Hughes shook his head. "John, there are so many fanatics out there, from the pope on down…"

"Yes," John said. "But then, what about people like you and me, and Dun, and Ian, and the rest of the brothers? How many of us do you think there are in the world? Those are the ones we want to have the opportunity to read the Gospel and affirm that there's one God, and one religion."

"You mean that Islam derives from Christianity?" Dun said. "I know they have the same prophets, and that there are many similarities between the teachings, and it was the Archangel Gabriel who…"

"That's not what I meant, Dun," interrupted John. "All of those things are unimportant. What I meant to say is that above all the dogma is 'The Knowing,' that's why all the religions of the world are but one."

"Of course."

"I think that's the purpose of the Jesus Gospel at this time," continued John, "to show just that one fact. It's very essential that you take it with you. I can't tell you how important it is."

Hughes appeared to consider what John had said. "I trust you, John. Ultimately that's all I'm going by, your word. So yes, I agree to take it with us. But I still think we'll be burned at the stake."

William's gaze met Hughes'. "We'll take it with us, uncle. After all, we are Templars, and if we die for it, so be it."

"Yes, William," Hughes said. "So be it."

"Uncle John, why is it that you never returned with the Gospel?" William asked.

John gave him an apologetic smile, as he caressed the Gospel's box with his right hand. "Oh, I knew even before I came that it would be impossible. This place is meant for those who have lost all attachment to the world and are ready for their final transformation. We live surrounded by the love of the living Christ. I can't leave; I mean physically I can't. I'm like a fish, and Hafiz Mountain is my pond. I looked at what waited for me out in the world, and knew I wouldn't make it. I am willing to die, and a person like me would die quickly out there, but I didn't want to fail, this task is too important. I then realized that you, William, were meant to finish for me.

"Ten years ago I could feel you in the distance, William; a child growing up and unknowingly getting ready for this one task. Everything in your life, every lesson, every trauma, all the skills you learned, have been preparing you for this. You are the only one so uniquely qualified.

"Once you complete it, you'll be free."

William thought of Jacob, of his father and mother, his years as squire, then a Cistercian, the abbey and Jules. "I'll be more than glad to take over for you, uncle. But that means I should leave before I, too, become like you."

"That is the truth, William."

Hughes stirred in his chair. "I know about your transformation in Jesus' cell John," he said, "but how exactly was it that you were able to find the Gospel, when so many people failed?"

John smiled briefly. "Actually a few made it this far."

"You mean…"

"Yes, Hughes. I found evidence that three Templars made it to this place in the last two hundred years. There could have been more."

"But then why…"

"Why didn't they find the Gospel and take it with them?" interrupted John. "They came, looked around, asked people about the Gospel, but were told that there wasn't such a document, so they left to look elsewhere."

"You mean to say the people here lied about having the Jesus Gospel?" William asked, looking at a group studying documents some forty feet away.

John shook his head. "No, they didn't lie. They just didn't know it was here."

"How could they not know?"

"I asked myself the same question, and the answer is simple. There are so many documents, that not one person could possibly know all that's here."

Dun shook his head. "But surely it's so important, so precious…"

"No, actually, it became a commonplace document after a few years. You see, Tiberius and his monks lived it, and so has everyone who's ever come here since then," John said, his gaze panning the big cavern. "It's what has made this place Christ-centered —a God-state called by many different names in the various religions, but here we call it "Oneness." As a result, it has produced many Christ-like men and women, Christians, Jews, and Muslims.

"After some time, Jesus' teachings became an integral part of this place and the source unimportant. You see, Christ's teachings emphasize the God within, which dissolves the focus on anything external, including the physical source of the teachings. Evidently that's what Jesus intended, and that's exactly what happened.

"So the people here put the document away and forgot about it, because they didn't need it anymore. After a few centuries, when someone came asking about it, no one remembered the Jesus Gospel. The Templars seeking the document, like you three, assumed that if they had it, everyone would know."

"Then how did you figure it was here?" Hughes asked.

"I felt Jesus here just as vividly as in his cell, and the only way he could be here, was through the pure application of what he taught. So I started searching."

William looked at all the cabinets containing thousands of books, "It must have taken you years to find it."

"No, it didn't. Once I became familiar with their storage system, I just looked in the right place, and there it was. Three copies meticulously and lovingly stored away."

William shook his head in disbelief. Those Templars going through so much hardship and danger only to miss the document hidden in plain sight!

William, Hughes, and Dun decided they should stay for a month, no longer.

The place was heaven, and it would be hard to leave as it was, so the less time they stayed the better.

They were assigned duties the following day. Hughes was asked to work on a vegetable plot, Dun was to help with the care of the animals, and William was assigned to help an elderly monk.

William found that the colony was divided into two major complexes of caverns, one for the women and one for the men; they shared the valley, and the common areas such as the reading room, the chapel and the kitchens. Men and women took turns with the administration, and the present person in charge was a former Orthodox monk.

William learned that residents had found the secret to happiness: while going about their daily chores, they practiced seeing God in everything and everyone just as the Gospel taught; and that, William decided, he would learn by doing. He meant to use the month to the fullest.

The first day of work William was shown the chambers of the old monk he was to care for, a man in his eighties who turned out to be a former Teutonic knight named Helmut. He was a nice old man, made gentle and wise with the passing of the years, but William could tell that once he had been a formidable warrior; his frame at one point had been well muscled, and his eyes, now peaceful, still took a man's measure. Helmut told how he had been a monk in Germany, only to be sorely disappointed by the Church, and had sought salvation by dying in the Holy Land. "I fought hard for eight years but no one killed me, and one day after a long battle I got lost and ended up taking refuge with monks who fed me good bread, so of course I wanted to stay with them, you know what bread means to a German! After some time I made friends with a young monk who kept telling me about a place in the African desert where there was a secret mystical Christian colony, and that he was going to go there or die trying. I decided that I wanted to go with him; the pull was so strong, like an iron grip in my heart. Besides, the puny fellow needed someone to protect him. It took us over three years of very hard going, over hot deserts and fighting bandits, and we almost died of thirst and starvation. I had to carry the little fellow on my back for the last week of our journey because our camels died, but finally we made it.

"At first, life at Hafiz Mountain was very difficult, I didn't fit in, and couldn't understand how people could just sit for hours in meditation. I felt uncomfortable, thought everyone here was crazy and wanted to leave, but eventually I learned to enjoy the silence after prayer. Yeah, that's what done it for me. And that's how I learned to meditate. Then I found heaven.

"And now I'm one of the crazy ones," Helmut chuckled.

William took care of the old man as best he could, and found he had a lot of free time in between his duties and meditations, which he spent reading the huge collection from Alexandria. He had never imagined anything so vast, and was very grateful for Tiberius and his monks, but he also thought of Jacob, and how much he would have loved to read those books.

He spent what time he could with his uncle, mostly working outside in the garden pulling weeds, and getting to know him and enjoying his presence. His favorite occasions were when they didn't talk but were busy working in silence, and he felt John pouring love on everything that surrounded him, and that included William; who found himself in wakeful meditation, watching his hands doing things, being aware of his surroundings but in a state of sweet detachment.

William met the others like John—a woman named Sophia whose presence he discovered was like being with the most nurturing of mothers, and all he wanted to do was hug her. As if reading his thoughts, one day she put her arms around him. *If everyone had mothers who loved them like this, there wouldn't be any anger in the world.*

John pointed out that she had been named after the Gnostic's Divine Mother.

Then there was Zamur the Druze, a wise man with a joyful way about him, whom William expected to burst out in happy laughter at any moment.

All told, there were eight very evolved individuals including John. They didn't have to say anything, in fact they seldom spoke, it was their sheer presence that did the work for them. They were the silent teachers of Hafiz Mountain.

Besides the group meditations, people enjoyed reading a variety of books, but no one book was singled out. What they read was used as a point of reference, to know what was possible, and sometimes just as a means for inspiration. And that's how people looked at the Christ-like figures in their midst as well—a point of reference and a source of inspiration.

William observed Hughes from time to time, laboring away at whatever he had to do, carrying water in buckets for the plants, working for three hard days to pull out a stump, or cutting flowers for the many vases. Gone was the tough Templar commander, and in his place was a playful man with a contagious laughter. He seemed to enjoy the smallest of things with a look of delight in his face—a bird, a ray of sunshine in the early morning, or the singing of the nuns in the fields.

Dun appeared concerned at times, but eventually he did meditate deeply, and William saw the tension erase from his face, and instead, reflect a state of contentment.

If left here for some time, both would be completely transformed, William thought. *And so would I.*

One day it was over. They packed their things, retrieved their swords and hauberks that looked so foreign now, so out of place. John gave William one of the copies of the Jesus Gospel, carefully housed in its sturdy box and well padded with feather cushions inside so the pages would not rub or shake.

Once the three travelers were well outside the cave and in the valley below, they turned around for one last goodbye to the lone tall white figure standing at the entrance to Hafiz Mountain. They shouted *Beauseant* as they waved, and the mountain echoed back as though wishing them well.

His heart now heavy and forlorn, William knew that only death could keep him from coming back.

They found their return trip to Alexandria made easier by their knowledge of the lay of the land, where there was water and shade, how to cross the sand dunes and the easiest traverse of the rocky plains. There were still some hot and miserable days, but they knew where the next respite would come, and that seemed to make all the difference.

One day the wind blew so hard they had to stop and cover themselves with the big sturdy tent, for the sand had started to tear at their clothes. But when there was no wind, and the temperature pleasant, the landscape was beautiful to behold, the sand showed different hues, and it created shapes, long and majestic, that seemed to move ever so slowly if one kept watching them. One such time, in the early morning, with the sun barely in the horizon, it felt like an embrace by the sweet Sophia; the air just starting to warm up, soft and caressing against their skins. William noticed Hughes standing by his camel reins in hand, looking at the sunrise, his gaze slowly taking in the beauty all around. *Hughes has changed,* he realized, *but soon he'll be a Templar again.*

CHAPTER VII

[1]

Riding into Alexandria, William could tell that there was something wrong; he could feel a tension in the air, and people walked the streets in sullen silence. There were no children out playing, or old men sitting under trees passing the time of day.

Their now somber innkeeper told them that some Christian knights visiting Acre had broken the truce by massacring Muslims, and the sultan had vowed revenge in the Prophet's name. War had been declared against all Christians, and Mameluk armies were marching on Acre.

At a popular tavern in the Greek quarter, the air heavy with talk of war and the smell of strong liquor and anise tea, William, Hughes, and Dun heard from an Egyptian officer how the Templar Grand Master Guillaime de Beajeu had tried to broker a peace, and had met with the sultan. The sharp-looking officer in his distinctive white headdress and fully decked out with a new hauberk and scimitar, stood within a circle of listeners, describing how the two leaders had agreed that the handful of knights who had killed the Muslims in Acre would be punished, and in addition a token sum was to be paid for each of the dead. The grand master had returned to Acre with the peace proposal, only to be ridiculed by the local nobles who were sure that no army could ever take their city.

The young officer went on to describe in a somber voice full of emotion how Sultan Qalawun had gathered his troops, intent on destroying Acre, but no sooner had he started on his march, than he fell ill and died. The patrons of the tavern bowed their heads at the memory of the news. There was silence for some time and no one dared say a word or raise a glass.

According to the officer, the new sultan, Qalawun's son Al Ashraf—"May Allah grant him a long life"—was determined to not only raze Acre to the ground, but also push all the foreign armies into the sea. All Christian outposts were to be destroyed. "Allah willing." The main army was already on its way to Acre, and soldiers like him were busy recruiting additional troops and gathering supplies to follow in the next two weeks.

Those listening to the Egyptian officer—Christians, Jews, and Muslims, judging by their attires and accents—agreed that "the arrogant people of Acre should be punished, along with the rest of the Christian armies for allowing such cowardly acts," one Arab man said, and everyone gravely assented.

"They are all treacherous pigs, and the sultan should kill them all!" added a small, rotund Christian.

Those in the tavern continued their animated war talk, drinking the clear liquor and tea served in small cups. But it was obvious that for all the apparent unity of feeling, there was guardedness between those of different faiths, and William noticed Christians furtively scurrying out.

Once back at the inn, Hughes paced their room, "I should be there, I should be there with them," he repeated over and over again. Neither William nor Hughes knew whether Castle Pilgrim would still be standing when they arrived, or whether there would even be any Templars left in the Holy Land. William wondered aloud whether he would ever see Richard again. He knelt down to pray for the Templars, and all Christians, particularly for their grand master, whom he knew would die with his men in Acre. Hughes stopped his pacing and knelt next to William. After a moment, Dun joined as well.

Early the next morning William accompanied Dun to see their innkeeper—who by now was more like a friend—to claim back the horses. The man walked with them to the stables in the back, and Dun inspected his animals, running his hand along necks and rumps. The Arabians had lost some of their muscle tone, but looked healthy.

The innkeeper agreed to buy their camels, clearly a generous gesture since he offered a fair price. It was the quickest way to get rid of them, and he accepted one of them in exchange for the horses' upkeep.

William, along with Hughes and Dun, spent the rest of the day hurrying to get their gear and supplies in order, and left the moment they had finished. The coastal route was shorter, but if the Mameluks were mobilizing a huge army toward Acre, then it would be full of troops, so Hughes decided to return the way they came, detouring deep inland through Memphis on the Nile, and across the tip of the Red Sea into the Sinai.

William climbed on his horse, touched the Jesus Gospel safe in his saddlebag, and wondered whom he would deliver it to if Acre were to fall? He had envisioned handing it over to Grand Master Guillaime de Bejeau in Acre, in front of all the other brothers, a sweet triumphant moment, but that was not going to happen. *Well, one step at a time.* The first thing was to make it to Dun's village, and then to Pilgrim Castle, if it was still standing.

The sun was about to set as they left through the city's gates, and they pushed their horses as hard as they could. They made camp by a cool spring when it got dark, and started up again with first light. By midmorning they were crossing a large grassy plain with sporadic trees, when they saw a Mameluk detail, six riders who rushed over as soon as they spotted them. Dun explained to their commander that he and his two friends were Syrian Druze and as such, under the protection of the sultan. But the soldiers wanted the Arabians, their orders were to requisition all the mounts they could find, and Dun's horses were particularly fine. The Druze would have to surrender them, or be killed.

William surveyed the Mameluks who were fully armed with lances, shields, scimitars, and bows, and realized that a fight against them without shields would be suicidal, but letting go of their horses meant they would not get far and be easy prey to bandits, a death sentence at any rate. He detected sudden movement to his left. Hughes had drawn his sword and slashed the Mameluk commander's throat.

Hughes turned his horse around, grabbed Dun's reins and broke into a gallop. William followed.

The remaining five Mameluks hesitated a moment, then gave pursuit. William realized the soldiers would not use their bows for fear of injuring the horses. He looked at Hughes for direction, and caught his hand command to veer to the left flank while he took the right and directed Dun to stay in the center. They were going to separate their pursuers into three groups.

William did as directed and when he glanced back saw two men chasing him, one with a drawn scimitar, the second holding his lance at the ready. William allowed the one with the scimitar to catch up, drew his sword and in a brief exchange of three strokes was able to severely injure the man on the shoulder. He dropped his sword and allowed the second man to come from behind. Out of the corner of his eye, William saw the Mameluk thrust with his lance, and William caught the lance's shaft with his right hand, pulled it under his arm, crouched down, held the lance with all his might and brought his horse to a near stop, yanking the Mameluk off his mount. Armed with a lance, William charged the two men who were after Dun.

William lanced the man closest to him and rammed his horse against the other rider's who lost his balance; then he hit him on the side of his head with the lance's butt, and watched him tumble down. William turned his attention to Hughes, and found that the commander had killed his pursuer.

Dun was guarding the Mameluk William had wounded on the shoulder.

William stopped his horse to survey the scene. Two Mameluks—the one he had yanked off his horse and the one he had hit on the head were lying on the ground; one groaning, the other stunned and trying to stand.

Hughes approached Dun and talked to him. After a pause Hughes struck the Mameluk Dun was guarding with his sword, killing him, then rode to the two others and did the same.

That was inevitable, realized William. They couldn't let the men go and bring back others to hunt them down, and they couldn't take them along. Leaving them tied up to die of thirst or be mauled by wild beasts was not an option. It crossed William's mind that they had lost the magic, and were abruptly back in the world. Violence was now again a part of their lives.

Once the rush of battle had left him, William felt sick and wanted to vomit. But they were all fine; save for some cuts and bruises, they were all fine. And the Jesus Gospel was safe. Had the Mameluks taken their horses, they would have probably taken their saddlebags as well. William inspected the grassy plain around them. It was quiet and there was no one in sight.

Hughes removed the saddles and bridles of the soldiers' animals and let them loose. They would be found by another patrol that would probably assume the animals had gotten loose from a pasture.

They sat on the ground to calm down and gather their thoughts. Inside, William felt the heavy imprint of violence: a sick feeling in his gut, and heavy sadness in his heart.

He tried to meditate and it was as though he was now a different person, one who missed his old self but could do little to regain him. So he decided to pray, asking for help. He found himself reciting a Paternoster. He asked for forgiveness for having killed, and begged the souls of the dead men for understanding. But the harsh feeling remained.

"What now, Hughes?" William asked scanning the horizon.

"We can't stay out in the open," Hughes said. "We must hide."

Dun nodded. "Out here we are visible. In Alexandria we can blend into the population and wait for the Mameluk army to be gone."

"Except that would mean waiting about three months. By then Pilgrim might have been wiped out. William and I need to be there to fight with our brothers.

"Let's hurry and put some distance between ourselves and this place," added Hughes. "We want to avoid casting ourselves as the killers when the Mameluks find the bodies."

Hughes and William hid the dead Mameluks as best they could, along with their weapons. Then, the three spurred their horses toward Alexandria.

After a couple of hours Hughes decided they could slow down. He turned toward Dun. "Dun, can we find a ship to take us to Syria?"

Dun thought for a moment. "Good idea, Hughes. We have enough money to hire a big ship.

"Going by sea is our only alternative," added Dun. "The Mameluks don't have any ships of their own. They have relied on the Venetians and Genoese for their shipping, so we'll be safe.

"I know of a small bay south of Tortosa where we can land unnoticed. But having watched you two fight, perhaps that should not be a concern."

William sensed that Dun now thought of him and of Hughes differently. But why? What did he expect? He knew they were Templars, and that they killed. Perhaps it was Hughes' slaying of the prisoners, but there had been no other choice.

Maybe at some point they could talk about it, but for now they had to worry about getting back to Alexandria.

That evening they camped inside a small grove of trees. After Compline meditation that had turned into fervent praying for William, he and Dun gathered firewood to cook their soup of dried goat meat with lentils.

"You saved my life, William," Dun said, "that first man was about to kill me when you brought him down. I thank you. I'm not trained like you; I can't fight two men at once."

"I'm sorry we had to kill, Dun. It's never easy. Hughes and I are not killers."

"I know that," he said as he dropped an armload of firewood by their campsite. "I know you both did what had to be done. It's only that…it was savage and brutal."

William gathered a pile of dry grass and dropped kindling on top. "Yes, Dun, it was brutal. Especially after being in such a blessed state for so long. Now we have lost that state and are back to being who we were before visiting Jesus' cell."

"Does it have to be that way?" Dun sadly asked as he watched William strike the flint over the grass with his knife. "When I looked at you before, I saw a glimmer of the Christ. You were holy, William."

And William understood. He understood in the flesh why John couldn't go back. "Yes, Dun. It has to be this way. I'm terribly sorry."

The three arrived in Alexandria without incident. They went back to the inn and asked their friend the innkeeper about possible ships.

He didn't ask why. "There are a few at the harbor that would accommodate you with your horses," he said. "But be careful, some may be pirates."

Dun led the way to a massive stone embankment along the bay, lined with warehouses, and bisected by a long causeway that led to the lighthouse. It was the largest harbor William had ever seen. More than twenty ships were tied up and two were being unloaded. Skinny men—almost naked except for a cloth wrapped around their waists—with legs bowed from years of carrying heavy loads, scurried around with large hemp bags on their backs. The three wealthy Druze inspected four ships that were ready to sail, and talked with the shipmasters. Two were Arabs, one from Cyprus, and the fourth was Greek, but none inspired confidence.

William turned when he heard the sound of many hooves on pavement. Hughes stood frozen staring at a large Mameluk detail parading down the street fronting the bay. "Where are they stationed?" Hughes asked a man.

"Oh, those are the troops that guard the city," the man said. "They are out recruiting young men and requisitioning horses and camels for the war."

Hughes pulled William and Dun to one side. "We have no choice, we have to take our chances with one of those ships," he whispered. "Otherwise it's just a matter of time before the Mameluks spot our horses."

Dun hired the Cyprus ship, a large single sail dhow, about sixty feet long and twenty wide in the middle, with no bridge or any other structure, save for a space below deck where it was ballasted and things could be kept relatively dry. The sail was patched and dirty and some of the planks of the upper hull had rot along the joints. William guessed the ship would take in water, and he noticed two buckets hanging on a nail and guessed they were used for bailing.

William studied the crew and felt a lump in his throat. "I'm certain they plan to rob us and kills us," William said. "Look at the way they're inspecting our horses and looking us over."

Hughes nodded. Then the three of them watched as the boat master pulled his four men aside and gave them instructions. The five sailors talked to one another for quite a while.

"We can't stay," Hughes said. "This shipmaster is willing to set sail this afternoon. Let's take our chances. I'll much rather fight five sailors than the Mameluks."

They went back to the inn to retrieve their baggage and the packhorses.

In the early afternoon, William stood in between Hughes and Dun by the ship's bow as the crew secured the Arabians to keep them from moving. They hung a canvas to protect the animals from the sun and spread sawdust to keep the deck dry under the horses; then secured the water troughs and feed bags.

By mid afternoon the ship set sail. The wind blew hard from their left side and made the boat lean sharply to the right, and William was certain that they would capsize at any moment. He went to his saddlebag and felt for the Jesus

Gospel. If they sank, his thought was to cut his horse loose and swim alongside it to shore. Hopefully the tightly sealed box would protect the parchment from getting wet. The boat creaked and moaned with each wave, and it made the horses nervous. Added to it all was the certainty that the crew was just waiting for the right moment to attack; they watched the three Druze's every move. It was an eerie feeling, like cats circling around the mice they had caught, and it was just a matter of time before they pounced for the kill.

William was aware that the new concerns overlay the sick feeling in his heart since killing the soldiers. Things had changed so drastically, so radically. Before the killings, they had been living in bliss, now they were living a nightmare. He turned to look at Hughes, but the commander was intent on watching the crew. Dun, on the other hand, had squatted down by the horses, and appeared lost in sullen thought.

William went to stand by Dun, as if to keep an eye on the animals. Hughes approached and commented that the crewmen were not fighters. "They don't move fast, their bodies are accustomed to heavy labor, not fighting."

William observed the deeply sunburned men walking about, expertly tying ropes and hoisting big sacks. "They look healthy and strong."

"Let's wait until they attack." Hughes said, sweeping the flap of his headdress to one side as he looked at the horizon, to appear as though commenting on the weather. "We have to feign sleep to encourage them. They see us as rich, noble Syrians caught in the war, and willing to risk the sea to get home." He pointed to the lighthouse they were leaving behind and gesticulated as though talking about the impressive tall structure. "We should be easy prey. If we make it hard and take precautions, the crew could turn deadlier by planning their attack better. I want to disarm them, not kill them. After all, we need them to get to the bay south of Tortosa that Dun mentioned."

When night fell, the three settled down on the deck, wrapped in their blankets. After an hour or so, they lay very still and pretended to sleep.

Shortly after, the shipmaster and his men surrounded them. In the moonlight, William could see the knives and clubs in their hands through his half-closed eyes. When a man came close, William drew his sword from under the blanket and knocked the man's knife away, slashing his hand.

William saw the shipmaster lunging at him, raised his legs and tossed the man backward. Then he rolled to one side and stood as the shipmaster lunged again. William stopped him with a kick to the groin, then brought the hilt of his sword down on his head. William pointed his sword at the man with the wounded hand and looked around to find that Hughes had already knocked one man down on the ground and was pummeling a second one with his fists. Dun was struggling with the last one. William thought of disabling Dun's attacker by hitting him on the head, when he saw Hughes leap and do just that.

"It's over," Hughes said.

Hughes ordered the men to lay down, with Dun and William guarding them, as he went around the boat looking for weapons. He came back with a couple of clubs, hammers, saws and other tools, which he threw overboard. He also found a bow and a quiver with arrows, and decided to keep them.

The ship secured, Hughes made the five sailors stand. He then went around piercing each man's upper right leg with one of the knives. The sailors screamed at the stabbing and they bled, but it was the blood that came from muscles, not the gushing blood of arteries.

Hughes then went around applying bandages to their legs. "The wounds are not serious," he told them in halting Greek, "you can still get around the boat, but you won't be able to walk fast. It will keep you from attacking us again. Keep the wounds clean, and you will be fine; let them get dirty and you will die."

Then there were the pirates to look out for. The horses were clearly visible on deck, a valuable prize for many on that coast.

William watched as the now cowed shipmaster took his post by the rudder, then in a resigned tone ordered one man up front with a pole, and the other two to handle the sail. The fifth man functioned as relief, and Hughes tied him up until he was needed.

Hughes approached William and Dun. "We need to decide how to proceed. One of us will keep an eye on the crew. Another needs to stand by the horses and keep watch for approaching boats; anyone could be a pirate. One of us will rest. According to the other shipmasters we talked to this trip will take from twelve to twenty days, depending on the wind. If it blows from behind or the sides, we can sail on a straight line, if it becomes a head wind, we'll have to sail back and forth to make way." Hughes looked up and down the ship. "This is all new to us, and we have to rely on the shipmaster and his skills to get home. What if he purposely slows down to let a pirate catch us? How would we be able to tell? What if we are attacked? What do we do with the crew while we fight?"

Hughes didn't wait for an answer. He approached the shipmaster. "You know I will have to kill you and your men if a pirate boat catches up with us," he said with a shrug. "I'll have no choice, you understand. We can't fight both the pirates and you at the same time."

"No, no Sire, you won't have to do that. No pirate will ever come close."

Hughes then showed him Dun's bag of coins. "On the other hand, if you deliver us safely south of Tortosa, I'll pay you more than what we agreed."

The man responded with a nod and a weak smile.

They sailed with the coast always within sight. First there were cliffs, then a flat expanse of sand and rocks. Every so often there would be a cove or a bay with fishing villages.

On the second day William spotted some boats at a distance, but none came close. On the third day a long and narrow sloop with a big sail came fast out of a cove ahead, and William watched their shipmaster maneuver on a straight line toward it, then veer off at the last moment, passing it as the sloop tried to turn in their direction, but with no chance of catching up.

Obviously the shipmaster knew his trade, and would do his part to keep them safe. The man assured Hughes that his ship was as fast as any other afloat, and that he had been sailing all his life, and they had nothing to worry about. "We never intended to harm you and your two friends Sire," the shipmaster said, his heavily lined face skewed into a grimace. "We only meant to take your weapons away, for our own protection. After all, you never know who boards your ship.

"And I wish you hadn't thrown away my tools. Now how are we going to install the new mast I just bought?" And he pointed to a long timber, about thirty feet long that lay the length of the deck.

Hughes appeared mesmerized by the long timber.

"What are you thinking, Hughes?" William asked.

"What do you think, William? Should we be attacked, can we use the timber as a lance?

"Come, help me lift it."

William got one end, Hughes the other, and together they were able to move the spare mast.

"We'll have to use the momentum of the ship much like that of a horse," Hughes said, "and the contrasting movement of the other ship and the waves, to ram the pole into the attacker, but yes, it can be done.

"If attacked, William and I will be the lancers, and Dun can handle the bow."

As Dun picked up the bow and sat staring at it, Hughes went up to the shipmaster to explain. The man seemed to understand, and liked the idea. "But I paid good money for the replacement mast, and I'm not a rich man," he said while extending one hand around the ship, while he steered with the other. "Business has been poor for the past year, and only with the new war did I hope to make money taking rich people to safety."

"You mean killing and robbing them," Hughes said.

"No, no, Sire," he responded, "that was a most unfortunate misunderstanding. May Allah strike me down if I'm not telling the truth."

William fed the horses some grain and checked their ropes. The sun shone bright overhead with only a few clouds, and they were making good time with no threat on the horizon or from shore.

However, the sea and ship made him nervous, uneasy. It wasn't just the creaking of wood, or the precarious listing to the side, but also that there was no place to hide.

Dun came to stand by his side. "William, we are at a loss," he said with heaviness in his voice. "I feel we can die at any moment. But it's more than that, isn't it? I feel we have lost the magic that we had ever since Jerusalem, the peace inside and the knowledge that somehow we were made safe no matter what. Remember William how things always worked out for us, small miracles, one after the other?"

"Yes, I know," William said. "I've been thinking about it and I would like to regain that state, but now we must be ready to fight, and that's what's on my mind."

"I remember when we lost it," Dun said with a sad smile. "The moment we learned from the innkeeper in Alexandria that the Mameluks were going to attack Acre."

William did not answer.

"I don't want to live like this, William," continued Dun. "I'm sure that at this rate we will be attacked and one of us killed, or we'll drown. It's fear that attracts calamity. I don't want to die like this either. Please, dear friend, change. When you are in a holy state, we follow along and everything is different."

William studied Dun's subdued and troubled face. "I will try," he said and walked away to the place where he had laid down his blanket.

The following morning at daybreak William opened his eyes. He had meditated through most of the previous afternoon and through the night. He looked around and found that someone had rigged a blanket over his head, evidently to protect him from the sun. He felt a deep joy in his heart in place of the nagging hollow feeling of the past days, and knew that he had changed.

In the back of the ship, the shipmaster was steering. Hughes was asleep to one side. Dun sat next to the horses, awake, and smiled when their eyes met.

William stood and made his way to Dun.

"Thank you, William," Dun said.

"It's your turn, Brother Dun. I will keep an eye on the ship."

William watched Dun settle down where he had just meditated. As the sun rose and the clouds changed from pink to white, a breeze ushered the boat gently up the mostly empty coastline. All was well.

By mid-day, as Hughes came over to relieve him, William noticed the wind dying down and the sea becoming still. A few moments later the wind died entirely.

William, Hughes, and Dun stood around the shipmaster who eyed the limp sail.

"Now we are in real trouble," he said.

About an hour later William saw two rowboats coming out of a cove and making a straight line for them, the oars hitting the water in rapid succession.

"What do we do?" Dun asked.

"The best we can," Hughes answered. "Brother Dun, get your bow and arrows. William, help me tie up the crew." Hughes looked at William, who stared at the lead boat. Six men stood out front with bows at the ready.

"They are coming after us," the shipmaster said. "Those are villagers who every time the wind dies down, watch for boats sitting still on the water. I'm sure they are after your horses."

"William, we need to prepare fast," Hughes said. "Let's tie up the men."

"There's no need Hughes. We're going to be fine."

"Maybe they'll settle for our pack horses," Dun said. "Let's wait until they approach and I'll negotiate."

"Perhaps that's our only way out," Hughes said as he watched the villagers' two boats with ten men per boat, brandishing both bows and spears. "Dun, show your bow and arrows. William, let's draw our swords so they'll know that if they board us it will cost them a few lives."

The two rowboats slowed down, and in the still air William could hear the villagers' voices alternating with happy laughter. William kept observing the boats but inside he felt no concern, something was about to change, he could feel it.

The two boats parted way to come on either side of their much larger becalmed vessel. The villagers aimed their drawn bows up at the deck of the ship. Dun dropped his bow and arrows on the deck and cupped his hands around his mouth, ready to negotiate with the villagers, when the sails gave out a loud snap as a powerful gust of wind blew from behind and the ship lurched forward. No one was steering and the heavy vessel rammed the two smaller boats throwing them to the sides, like so much flotsam.

William watched the capsized boats and the figures scrambling to climb onto the hulls. The wind blew harder and the ship picked up speed and heaved in the now stormy sea.

Behind them, dark clouds had gathered and were moving fast toward them.

"What did you do, William?" Hughes asked.

"Nothing. But I knew that somehow we would be fine."

Dun pointed at the black clouds. "The wind often calms down right before a storm that size."

Hughes shook his head. "Whatever the natural explanation, it was still a miracle."

By late afternoon the storm was in full force, and with it came a pelting rain, but the wind pushed the ship, now steady and solid, along ever faster. There was no reason to be afraid anymore, the danger was long gone.

The shipmaster announced that should the wind shift to either side, they would have to seek shelter, for they rode low on the water and could capsize, but as long as it kept blowing from the back, he could handle it, in fact, they had more than doubled their speed from the previous days. The shipmaster appeared concerned, and was eyeing the storm, but inside William knew that all was well, and the wind and the sea were now with them.

The storm kept at it for the next three days, and by the third, on the seventh day of sailing, the ship reached the small cove south of Tortosa Dun had mentioned.

"The storm came from Allah to save us from the pirates," the shipmaster said, his voice laden with emotion.

The crew now eyed them with reverence, bowing to them, going about their business meekly. Gone were the furtive and angry looks, the mutterings under their breath.

As William, Hughes, and Dun unloaded the horses on the beach and got their gear ready, the once menacing Cypriot sailors stood on deck watching, and continued watching as the three men mounted their horses.

Dun rode alongside William, apparently simply glad to be in familiar territory, a three-day ride from his village. Hughes was concerned about encountering Turkish forces. "The Syrian Sajuks must be mobilizing as well," he said. "In the past four years they have taken over most of Cilician Armenia and have grown strong. They are probably on their way to Acre right now."

The following day they were coming up to a lone hill before a wide-open expanse, when William asked if they could stop. "Let's rest the horses," he said.

"But we just got started a while ago," replied Hughes, "they can't be tired."

"Hughes, let's please stop."

Hughes nodded and dismounted. They tied their horses by some trees. William and Dun walked slowly about, looking for dry grass and kindling to start a fire. Hughes decided to climb to the top of the hill and survey the area around them.

A while later Hughes came down from the hill in a hurry. "Good heavens, William, you just saved us! There's a huge column of Turks coming down the plain. One of their scouts almost spotted me."

The three backtracked to a rocky promontory where they hid their horses, then returned to the hill to keep an eye on the slow moving Turkish army. They were Sajuks under the command of Mameluk officers; thousands of men, infantry and cavalry, camels, donkey trains with supplies, and oxen carts loaded with the large timbers, baskets, and wheels of disassembled siege engines.

William slept fitfully that night, but by noon of the following day the Sajuks were nowhere in sight.

"Let's mount and go," Hughes said, "before another column comes through."

Dun saddled up but stood in place lost in thought. "William, the storm came to save us from the pirates and we have been free of danger ever since. It's no coincidence that we were far back and out of sight when the Sajuks marched through. You meditated long and I can tell you reached that place you were seeking. I know that's the reason we are alive; but can you tell me exactly what you did?"

"Yes, Dun," William said. "I vowed never to kill again."

"You vowed? But you are still a Templar" Hughes said. "You'll be slain on the first battle."

"I know, Hughes. But I realized that without the vow I couldn't reach that blessed state. So now I risk being slain. I think it's a worthy trade."

Hughes shook his head and appeared at a loss. He started to say something, but looked at William and was silent.

They spent two more days in the hardscrabble Syrian wilderness of small shrubs and the occasional tree before coming to the familiar green hills that marked Dun's lands.

First thing William did after arriving at Dun's village was to go see Black, who danced when he saw him, going around in small circles, hopping and kicking excitedly. William had never seen a horse do that before, but Black was a most peculiar animal.

William waited with Hughes for ten anxious days to grow their beards and hair to the unkempt length typical of Templars. They had not used the trimming scissors since leaving Alexandria, but that hadn't been enough.

They burned marks on their arms and legs to resemble the rubbing of ropes from being tied up, and practiced their story; that they had been kept prisoner in Syria, in a remote village held by a Sajuk warlord.

They spent their days riding their horses, for the animals had lost some of their training and had grown fat. It was a joy for William to be astride Black again, a familiar comfort he realized he had sorely missed.

One crisp morning with the sun about to rise behind the village hills, William and Hughes stood next to their horses taking a last look around before mounting. Dun had come to the stables to say goodbye. They had decided to use their own horses, but remain in Arab garb until they reached sight of Pilgrim Castle, and Hughes said it would be better if they traveled alone, rather than escorted by Dun and his men. There was no telling if there were Templar or Mameluk patrols around and two Druze who could quickly become Templar knights stood the best chance under all possible circumstances.

"A Mameluk or Sajuk patrol might get suspicious if they spot those big horses of yours," Dun said.

"We'll avoid Turks," Hughes said. "What I'm concerned about is whether Pilgrim Castle is still standing. If the Mameluks are attacking Acre, I'm sure they already laid siege to Pilgrim as well, because it's so close by."

"What would you do if Pilgrim is gone?" Dun asked.

Hughes slid a finger under his horse's cinch strap to see how tight it was. "I don't know, Dun."

"You are carrying a treasure you must safeguard above anything else. If Pilgrim Castle is under attack when you get there, please come back. You can't join the fight."

William and Hughes embraced Dun, mounted and then rode at a canter out of the village and through the hills in a southwesterly direction that would place them on the coast north of Pilgrim but south of Acre, right around the Haifa ruins. On their way, they ran across a group of Arab merchants who told them that Acre was under siege.

They came within sight of Pilgrim Castle four days later.

With great relief they noted the Templar *Beauseant* up on the north tower. They shed their Arab dress, donned their Templar surcoats and helmets and proceeded at a gallop toward home. Soon the sentries spotted them and as they came within fifty yards of the walls the castle's heavy gates opened up. When they walked their horses through the narrow passageway toward the outer ward, they became aware that many eyes watched their progress through the spy holes in the walls.

CHAPTER VIII

[1]

When William and Hughes reached the outer ward, men with drawn swords un-ceremoniously yanked off their helmets and surrounded them. The two watched as a number of Templars circled around them—Richard among them—without saying a word.

It took some time for a visibly aged Richard, tension mixed with surprise in his face, to hesitantly approach William and stand in front of him. "Willy? Is that really you?"

"Yes, Richard. It's me." William said as he studied his brother.

Richard embraced him hard. "I thought you were long dead," he said in an uncharacteristic broken voice, "I have been praying for your soul this past year."

William's sergeant, Brother Albert, silently took Black's reins and led him away. William was relieved; his sergeant would not question the wooden box, would not even think twice about it. He would keep it safe.

Richard and a number of his friends escorted the returned Templars to the infirmary for the doctor to look them over. They apologized for the rude wel-coming, but explained that they had become very suspicious of strangers, even those who appeared to be Templars. "All we need is for the Turks to send some Christian traitors disguised as Templars to betray us," said a man named Daniel. Then they all started asking anxious questions: where they had been all this time, how were they captured, who captured them, how did they get away, did they see the Mameluk army, and did they know that Acre was under siege?

Hughes cleared his throat. "We were captured because we were both wound-ed and unable to fight," he explained. He described a life of imprisonment at a Sajuk village, and how at the end they were simply let go when their captors learned of Acre's imminent fall.

It occurred to William that Pilgrim Castle was already under siege, although no enemy was in sight. The tension in the place was intense, ever present, and the men had the look of people who were already dead, but waiting for the final deed to take place.

After the infirmary, Richard led William and Hughes on a walk around the ramparts. William realized that Richard was relieved to see him alive, but didn't quite know how to show his emotions, instead he kept studying William and touching his arm and shoulder, as though to make sure he was real.

Richard pointed at the nearby town of Atlit, now deserted. Its inhabitants, all except for a handful of Christians who came to the castle, had fled to parts unknown at the news of the approaching Mameluk army. In a corner of the outer ward were a number of tents. "Those are refugees from Acre," explained Richard. "Women, children, and old men who for some reason didn't make it into the ships bound for Cyprus. Most traveled on foot, but some sailed on boats across the Bay of Acre and down the coast, and they're still coming. A woman and her two daughters made it in a rowboat this past week, exhausted and sunburned. Last time we counted, we had one hundred and eighty."

"Do you have current news from Acre?" Hughes asked.

"Yes," Richard said leading them back downstairs. "Carrier pigeons bring news almost every day. Last we heard the Templars there are under the command of the grand master himself, and they are sure to die."

A sergeant intercepted them at the bottom of the stairs. "Marshal Joseph wants to see Commander Hughes and Brother William."

William grabbed Richard by the arm. "What happened to Marshal Dimas?

"He's now our seneschal."

Later that afternoon, the two returned Templars were questioned by the marshal and the two commanders, mostly about the size of the Mameluk troops they reported seeing in Syria. At the end, the marshal congratulated them on surviving their ordeal.

That was it, thought William with relief as he walked out of the room with Hughes. "I'm going to find Black and retrieve the Gospel from the saddle bag."

Hughes nodded. "We can leave it with Dimas when we see him tonight. In the meantime, how will you hide it?"

"I'll just keep it in the saddle bag."

"Are you sure your sergeant has not touched it?"

"I'm certain of that."

But William walked briskly toward the stables, suddenly concerned. He was sure that Brother Albert would never look inside the saddlebag no matter how tempted, but others might.

William opened the gate to Black's stall, and his horse lifted his head from a pile of grain to look at him, and then went back to eating. Hanging from a peg was the saddlebag. William patted it and his heart sank: it was empty.

He turned to inspect the stall, but there was no sign of the box. He was ready to bolt out when his sergeant walked in.

"It's under the hay, Brother William," Albert said, matter-of-fact. "I'm sorry to have concerned you Sire, but I thought that would be the safest."

William went to the hay piled in a corner of the stall behind Black. He dug his hand about a foot and felt the hard wooden surface. William stood up and let out a sigh of relief. "Thank you Albert."

William approached the tall, skinny man. "Do you know what's inside the box?" William whispered.

"I'm hoping someday you'll give me permission to look, Sire," Albert answered in a hush. "All I know is that it's very precious, and that it was the reason for your absence, and that you and Commander Hughes risked your lives to get it."

William stood staring at Albert. "How do you know all that?"

Albert looked down at the ground. "Don't worry, Brother William. I have kept what I found out to myself," Albert said, "but the morning you were captured I saw happiness in your face that I had not seen before, and that told me you were aiming on going somewhere special that day. When the battle started and I saw the Druze up on a hill looking for someone, it occurred to me that that's whom you were meeting. Then I saw Commander Hughes by your side, and I knew he was going with you. That's when I charged two Sajuks with your squire just to keep him busy.

"Then you come back a year later with that box." Albert smiled. "Not terribly hard to figure out, Brother William. All a person has to do is know you well."

"And what do you think is in the box?"

"I don't know, Sire. All I know is that you are a man of God, and that's enough for me. That box is important to you, and I will keep it safe."

William felt a lump in his throat. He studied his sergeant's serene expression. "Thank you Albert, thank you."

William walked out of the stall. The Gospel was safe right where it was, better protected than he ever imagined.

That evening, Hughes and William met with Dimas in his chambers, and they told him about their journey. Under the light of two candles on Dimas' worktable, William undid the two leather straps that secured the lid of the Jesus Gospel box and placed the pages on the big table. The flickering light gave the parchment a soft, yellow hue.

"This is the fruit of our labors," Hughes said, as they watched an awed Dimas staring at the Gospel.

Over the next two hours Dimas read the Gospel, going over each and every word. In the dim light William could barely see the big room lined with cabinets. In the corner sat a big and heavy oak coffer containing Castle Pilgrim's monies: gold coins accrued from gifting, rents from Atlit and what their Templar master sent them every month.

When Dimas finished reading he seemed unable to speak for some time. "This is a worthy treasure to bring back after a year's journey, brothers," he said. There were worry lines around his eyes, and some gray in his beard and balding hair. His long face seemed worn out.

"I missed you two. I missed meditating with you and I often prayed that you were safe, but I can see how much you have changed, and unlike us who have grown in fear, you two have become saintly. This is the first time that I feel relief from the oppressive certainty that we are all going to die at the hands of the Mameluks. But it's not the dying that is so troubling. It's the waiting that's terrifying, as you will soon find out. It's torture the likes of which I never imagined. The sheer size of the Mameluk army—our scouts estimate more than fifty thousand—does away with any hope. We know we are going to die. Our duty is to protect the refugees to the very end, but if it weren't for them, I would've ordered my Templars to march into Acre and face their deaths, because the wait is making them crazy. Just two days ago we had to take two squires away in chains to the dungeon after they started screaming without stop with all their might. Three refugees have committed suicide, and we are watching the rest closely."

"How are we fixed for supplies, brother?" Hughes asked.

"We have enough for about four months without slaughtering the warhorses. But enough talk about war. Could we meditate?"

They sat down and meditated for quite some time, well past midnight, and when they got up to leave, William could tell that Dimas was much better. He beamed a smile as he bid them goodnight.

That following day William observed Dimas on his rounds of the castle and could sense the change in him as he inspected sentries, received reports from the infirmary about the sick, and talked to the two commanders and the scouts. Dimas gave assurances to those who approached him, and showed calm concern at the news of an unknown fever spreading through the civilians.

"You two need to plan your escape from the Holy Land and make the Gospel safe." Dimas told William and Hughes that evening in his chambers. He sat at his desk looking out the window at the moonlit inner ward.

He turned to William. "How well do you speak Arabic?"

"He can get by," replied Hughes.

"And I know you speak it very well, Brother Hughes. You two could pass for Arabs and make it safely north to Beirut.

"It's very important that the Gospel reaches Europe. Let's make sure it does."

As their seneschal, they would have to obey him, but William wished that he would not order them to leave. "Brother, I couldn't live with myself knowing that I left you and the others here to die."

"William, if you can come up with an alternative, I would like to hear it," Dimas said pursing his lips. "In the meantime, both you and Hughes get ready to leave."

William understood that in Dimas' mind there was no other choice. "Why don't we first try to come up with a way to save us all, and if that fails then Hughes and I will make our escape."

Dimas' hard gaze studied William. "Come up with a scheme that saves the Christians within our walls, and I will consider it. Otherwise, the moment Acre falls, you have to go, because we are next."

"Fine, brother," William said. "In the meantime, if I may suggest, why don't we try and live like monks. The men are suffering greatly, and it need not be so. Let's forget the war. "

"How do we do that, William?" he said in a tired, resigned tone.

"Remind them how to pray. Ever since the threat of war began, this castle has forgotten how to pray. The men go through the holy offices with their hearts full of fear and their minds going in circles."

Dimas seemed to ponder William's words. "You are right. I'll talk to them in the morning."

That following day after Matins, Dimas assembled everyone in the castle—refugees and Templars—in the outer ward. It was like a Saturday Review, except it was on a Wednesday, and the refugees stood in one big tumultuous clump beside the neat military formations.

"You are still alive," Seneschal Dimas de Orleans told the gathering, "and can choose to live each moment in the peace of the Lord rather than in fear. From this moment on, I beseech you to pray, continuously, with all your heart, with full devotion, stopping only to sleep and eat and cleanse. Forget the enemy. All we need are two sentries and one scout. But even while on duty, you can keep on praying."

Then Dimas led them in reciting two Paternosters, and they kept praying as they broke assembly and dispersed. Throughout the day William observed groups of Templars mingled with refugees, praying.

William sensed the feeling in the castle changing, and by the third day, the place was bearable. There was still fear and tension in the air, but it wasn't as foreboding and heavy. At times it even felt close to normal, like William remembered from before he left for Hafiz, a rigid but heartfelt devotion.

Life went on like that until one morning a few weeks later, they received a letter by carrier pigeon from Acre. The once daily messages had stopped, so everyone knew this was perhaps the last one. The urgent message requested assistance. The Turks were about to kill everyone. All the ships were gone, and an important emissary from King Edward had to be rescued. The letter said that if Seneschal Dimas sent a boat he would swim out to meet it.

Later that morning, William and Hughes were making their way up the stairs to the third floor and the seneschal's chambers when Dimas intercepted them.

"Brother Hughes, you heard about the letter from Acre?"

"Yes, brother."

"I want you to go rescue King Edward's official. You will take command of our two boats and sail to Acre immediately."

"But I'm not a boat master, brother."

"The boat master will assist you. What we need are your unique talents."

That afternoon William, along with Dimas and about a hundred Templars, stood watching from the ramparts as the two boats rowed out from under the castle, hoisted their sails and headed north along the coast toward Acre. In the hazy distance some thought they could see the smoke coming from the city. Hughes stood in one of the boats hanging on to the mast with one hand, scanning the horizon, and that was the image that William emblazoned on his mind as the boats disappeared from view.

[2]

Once he felt his boat being propelled by the wind, Hughes turned to inspect his men. He had picked all eight with care, with help from the boat master. All four Templars were experienced sailors and capable fighters. The four Turcopoles were the best long-distance shots in the castle. The boat master, who presently stood in the other boat's bow, was a personal friend. And they all would obey him without question.

The men were now putting away the oars, and assuming their sailing positions under the direction of the boat master who shouted his orders from the second boat. Hughes watched as one Templar in his boat manned the rudder, one the sail. The Turcopoles assumed their watch positions at either end. Hughes would rely on the boat master's expertise to maneuver the crafts, which according to him, could fit up to twenty-five refugees each.

The men—selected for their skills but also for their compact, light weight—

had come as unencumbered as possible; with hauberks, swords, and shields but no armor plates, lances, helmets or boots. The boats carried only water and packs of bandages. They would eat when they got back.

As rehearsed, Hughes lifted his right hand and made a fist, signaling the other boat to follow. He extended four fingers and watched the boat fall behind by four boat lengths.

The wind was strong and favorable as night fell, and shortly after dawn they were approaching Acre.

The city was burning. The Turks were busy torching, killing, and looting. Hughes could see small pockets of defenders holding out in various places: a barricaded house being stormed with a battering ram, a handful of men on a rooftop throwing rocks at the Turks below. But the fiercest battle raged in front of Templar House, as knights made forays into the Turkish line in waves trying to destroy two siege engines—mangonels by the looks of the shorter throwing arms—busy throwing missiles at the fortress. Hughes watched one of the mangonel's buckets being fitted with a single huge rock, and the throwing arm winched back. Then the arm shot forward, the engine shook and the projectile went on a straight line and smashed into the defensive wall, leaving a sizable gash.

Closer by, and aimed at the sea, stood a trebuchet, an engine made to throw missiles in an arc, at a higher range and far more accurate than the mangonels. Hughes guessed that it had been used on departing ships, by the looks of the debris floating about.

Wafting from the city came the sounds of war: screams, wood breaking in loud cracks, the roar of the flames, the clashing of metal and the thunder of the siege engines' missiles, punctuated by the ongoing background sound of the hundreds of Turkish drummers, banging away their steady foreboding cadence.

Hughes saw the trebuchet turning in his direction, and he gauged that his vessels would be within its range momentarily. He could now distinguish the sea wall of Templar House and a number of figures waving frantically on one of the towers facing the sea.

The trebuchet was getting ready to fire and Hughes lifted his left hand for the boats to maneuver to the left the moment he dropped his arm. He saw the machine's missile basket winched back, and the two cables on either side tightening up. Hughes counted to ten and dropped his arm; the boats changed course immediately and a moment later the basket shot forward and the missile whistled through the air. He heard a big splash about thirty feet to his right.

Hughes spotted a group of swimmers coming out of the tunnel under the sea wall. That was the secret escape route left by the Templars who built Templar House so long ago, and now was finally being put to good use. Hughes felt a lump in his throat: he would give anything to save Brother Guillaime and his men. But he swallowed hard and forced the thought out of his mind.

Apparently the Templars' was the last fortification left in the city, for most everything else was now burning. Hughes signaled for his two Turcopoles to aim for the trebuchet's crew and for the two other archers to protect the swimmers and ordered the boats to make a direct line for them. The trebuchet hadn't fired again, so either his Turcopoles were doing their job or the Turks had decided to concentrate on Templar House. By the time he reached the swimmers and the first set of hands grabbed the side of his boat, Hughes realized that he would have to make hard choices, for there were well over a hundred people in the water trying to get to the boats. He scanned the bobbing figures, and saw several capes, women's headdresses, and children's heads. Among them was what he was looking for: the fancy clothes of one of his Majesty's high officials. Hughes signaled for his boat to pick him up. Arrows were now raining all around, and he ordered the shields to be hoisted by the Templars with one hand, as they worked the oars with the other. Protected by his shield, Hughes checked his men: the Templars were rowing and the Turcopoles were busy shooting.

A Templar helped the fatigued but unhurt official and three women into the boat. By now dozens of hands were grabbing the boats' sides, and voices clamored for assistance. A few yards away a woman had given up and was drowning, to her left a wounded man was trying to swim, hanging on to a dead body. About twelve yards away Hughes saw a boy trailing a little girl behind. The water had now turned red with blood and he could see shark fins and thrashing all around. With the official safely on board, he grabbed hands and hoisted, then grabbed some more. The boat master, leading the second boat, signaled that Hughes' boat was overfull. Hughes looked at the side, and saw the water up to the second board. He ordered the boats to make way for open water, as more hands tried to hang on.

"Please, Templar, take my sister!" Hughes looked down to see the boy, gasping for air and holding on to the little girl's head with one arm. Hughes gazed around at his already overwhelmed boat. He looked down at the water and could tell that the boy—of around twelve or so—was about to drown: his one free arm was thrashing limply about, and both he and his sister were starting to go under. Hughes noticed a heavy-set woman sitting near him, one of the first people to come on board. Her bulk more than made up for both children. But did he have the right to decide who lived or died? Hughes looked at the boy's desperate face, his mouth gasping, his sister gagging with water. He grabbed the woman under her armpits. "Terribly sorry, my Lady." With this he lifted her to her feet—all two hundred or so pounds—while she stared at him, mouth agape, eyes opened wide, and he pushed her overboard, then quickly bent over the side and hoisted up the boy and his sister. He sat them down in the matron's place, trying to ignore the woman's screams along with the pleading and curses from the people thrashing in the water.

Hughes concentrated on disengaging hands off the side of the boat by stabbing them with his sword, as did the other Templars, until the boats were free. *This is much worse than combat.* For a brief moment he considered diving in to join the many who were sure to die. But his job was to take the king's official and whatever refugees he could safely to Pilgrim Castle.

Once underway, Hughes glanced at the boat master who signaled that the vessels were seaworthy. Should the weather turn nasty they would have to decide whether to get rid of weapons and hauberks or passengers.

All around arrows kept falling, and Hughes turned his attention to the oar closest to him. He dropped his shield and helped the Templars row. Hands went for his shield and someone held it up, other hands reached for the oar. They made slow progress until the sails were hoisted, filled with wind, and the boats lurched forward.

The arrows stopped hitting the shields, and were now falling short. They were safe. Hughes surveyed the boats. One Turcopole and a Templar had been wounded, and about twelve of the refugees were also bleeding. He got out bandages from the bag by his feet and went around washing wounds with seawater and applying bandages. On the other boat he saw one of his Templars doing the same.

Hughes signaled for the boat master to take over and he slumped down, exhausted.

[3]

William heard the sentry on the sea rampart announce the return of the boats. It was shortly after Matins, and the sun was still rising. He came out of the chapel and rushed to eagerly climb the parapet stairs with dozens of others. He watched the two vessels sailing back, and by the way they rode on the water, it was apparent they were full to capacity. William and a handful of other Templars followed Dimas through the iron trapdoor and the narrow stairs that led to the small quay where the craft usually brought supplies from anchored ships. They waited as the vessels rowed into the narrow opening carved out of the rock, and then watched as the refugees clambered out, some of them wounded, most of them women and children, save for three men, one of whom was of obvious high rank, judging by the deference everyone showed him, despite their evident exhaustion and the terror still written on their faces.

Hughes escorted the high official and introduced him to Dimas. His name was Lord Otto de Grandson, an advisor to King Edward and member of the Royal Council who had come at the king's behest to lead the fight in Acre; a man who looked somehow familiar to William.

"Templar House fell as we sailed away," Lord Otto told Dimas as he walked up the stairs. "It was the last bastion in the city."

"Should we send the boats back?" Dimas asked. "Are there more survivors?"

"No," Hughes said, "By now all the men have been killed and the young women and children made slaves."

There was a grim finality in his voice, and William could sense the pain Hughes was not expressing.

That evening Dimas called Hughes and William to his workroom, and when they walked in, were surprised to find Lord Otto de Grandson reading the Jesus Gospel. He stood up as they approached, and smiling, produced the small medallion from under his shirt that showed the familiar dove of a member of the Brotherhood.

Lord Otto de Grandson sat back down and studied the three Templars. "Grand master Guillaime loved and admired the three of you." Then he smiled at William. "Do you remember me, William?"

William studied the short and compact man. "Can't say for certain, my Lord, but you do look familiar."

"It doesn't matter, lad. But we met at Abissey when you were still a Cistercian monk."

William grimaced at the memory, and then he remembered the lord who had met with Sir Ian, the one who had apparently operated behind the scenes to get him out of the Cistercians and into the Templars. "I do remember you, my Lord, and I thank you for all your efforts on my behalf."

"The least I could do."

William found Lord Otto de Grandson friendly and down-to-earth. He was perhaps in his late thirties or early forties, with a clean-shaven round face, copper-colored hair and blue eyes. He told how closely he worked with the king, and that he had convinced Edward to let him come to the aid of Acre, but that had been an excuse to find out what had happened with the search for the Jesus Gospel. "You don't know the excitement you created in the Brotherhood," he told William, "during our meetings that was all people could talk about.

"Once in Acre, when I saw the desperate situation, my hope was to broker a peace with the Turks in the king's name, and when that failed to save our grand master, but Brother Guillaime told me his duty was to die along with his command."

Lord Otto de Grandson stared at the parchment sheets in front of him. "Had the king of Acre listened to him, they would all have been saved. Grand Master Guillaime had a spy in the sultan's court, and had provided ample warning of the attack, but very sadly, to no avail. The fools in charge of Acre wanted to fight. They thought their city was impregnable.

"You know that grand master could have escaped with his men anytime, through the secret tunnel that I used with the other refugees. It led from the basement of Templar House, under the city wall right to the sea. But grand master believed in his Templar oath to never retreat nor surrender."

Dimas had paced the room as he listened. "It's a miracle that Commander Hughes was able to save you, my Lord. I can't possibly let you die in this place. William and Hughes speak Arabic, and we have already talked of their leaving the castle dressed as Arabs. Now we must not only save the Jesus Gospel, but you as well."

"Brother Dimas," interjected Hughes. "It will take the Mameluks ten days at least to clean up their battle field, tend to their wounded, break up their siege engines and move them to within sight of our walls. I can come up with a plan that will save everyone in this castle. Please wait five days before ordering us to leave."

Dimas continued to pace, glanced at the Gospel and met Hughes' gaze. Then he said. "What's your plan?"

"I'm still working on it, please give me time."

"Three days, Hughes."

Lord Otto de Grandson stood up to leave. "Seneschal, I place myself under your command and will abide by your orders."

William walked out of the room with Hughes and was about to make a comment about the lord when he noticed that Hughes seemed lost in thought, and was mumbling something to himself.

"You know, William," Hughes said, "if only the Mameluks would choose to go north, then we would have a chance."

"Why do you think they would go north when we are within their reach?"

"Well, what I hope will happen is that they will consider doing away with the easier targets first. We are too well fortified and it will take them far longer to breach our defenses than Beirut, Sidon, or Tortosa, all for a far smaller tactical victory. If I were them, I would attack the weaker places first, conquer them, and then turn against us. By then we would be so demoralized, with absolutely no place to go, that we'll probably surrender without a fight."

William stared at Hughes in disbelief. "How could that possibly help us?"

"As long as they are close by, they must keep track of our movements," Hughes said thinking aloud. "Obviously they don't want a sizable number of Templars coming up from behind. I'm sure they have scouts watching us from afar. If they go north and we do away with their scouts, then leave, they won't know that we are gone for at least a couple of weeks. Long enough for us to hide."

"There are over six-hundred of us, including the two-hundred-plus civilians. How are we going to hide that many people?"

Hughes raised a hand and smiled knowingly. "Ah, William I like your questions because I have the answers.

"The Mameluks expect us to go north, our only possible escape route to the castles of Tortosa, Sidon, and Beirut, and they are presently blocking our way. In their minds we can't escape, because we have no place to go. But what if we were to go far inland—the route you and I took over here—and bypass their army? That desert is vast and empty; they'll never expect us to go there. If we are fast and smart, they won't find us."

That desert was a vivid memory in William's mind. It was a death trap for anyone who didn't know the lay of the land, but both he and Hughes did, at least a part of it, and maybe the part that counted.

"It's worth considering, Hughes. But if they find us?"

"Then we fight. Templars are at their best charging the enemy out in the open. Fighting from behind walls, we are only as good as common foot soldiers. We would probably all die, but at least we would have tried, and we would die fighting on our horses."

That following morning they told Dimas and Lord Otto of Hughes' plan. Dimas sat staring at the floor.

"If they go north, Hughes, if they go north! But that's asking for divine intervention. Most likely we'll be fighting them in a few days. You two are postponing the inevitable. Get your horses and gear ready. Now you have Lord Otto de Grandson to protect as well. You have two more days." Dimas reached inside a basket by his chair and handed Arab clothes to Lord Otto de Grandson. "Learn how to wear these, my Lord."

[4]

Otto carried his new attire to his chamber. He laid down the Arab garb that Dimas had given him on the only chair, and studied the robes and headgear with curiosity.

Four months before in London when he heard from the grand master that the Mameluks were preparing to attack Acre, Otto had dropped everything, took his leave from his king telling him he wanted to take up the Cross, and sailed on the next ship. He had hoped against hope that William and Hughes had the Gospel with them, and if that was the case, he couldn't afford to allow it to get lost in the confusion. If they didn't, or had not returned, he would have to consider his other option. But now here he was, and all was well. He had actually read the Gospel. It was real!

And Hughes and Dimas were definitely worth meeting.

So far they had not disappointed him. Hughes had been most impressive during the rescue. And that plan of his, it was good. Otto had been certain all along that Hughes would find a way out, and that Dimas would then carefully analyze his plan and then, together, they would shape the best possible escape.

It was just a matter of time before Hughes would convince Dimas of his plan.

As a last resort Otto could always surrender. The Turks would never execute a high official, for he would command a sizable ransom, but the rest they would kill, no question.

He was sorry that Grand Master Guillaime had perished. He was truly a great man. The new Templar grand master would have to be a well-known veteran, but he need not assume the Brotherhood's command as well, that could go to a charismatic new leader: William.

Yes, William would make a most wonderful Brotherhood grand master. And his election would be relatively easy to accomplish, with the Jesus Gospel under his arm, and the entire hullabaloo that went with it.

Then as William's lord, Otto would have the Brotherhood and the Templars under his control, all but guaranteeing the French king's defeat. After that—with England and King Edward safe—would come the rest of Otto's plan…securing his homeland so no imbecile despot, foreign or domestic, would ever rule over her again.

Otto knew that William was indispensable for his plans, and now he realized that he needed Dimas and Hughes as well. The three had a special bond between them, and would make an excellent team. But how to recruit them?

Tell them how indispensable they were to England and King Edward's future? No, that would be the wrong strategy; the three men owed their allegiance to the Templars only. Besides, Dimas was French, and Hughes sounded Scottish. Obviously Otto had to appeal to their loyalty to the Templars, and somehow the idea would have to come from one of them. Maybe if Otto were to explain what was really behind the Caesarius Prophecy, it would prompt them to readily volunteer. The three Templars were all very intelligent and would certainly understand. Surely they would want to help, for it was such a noble cause.

That would be perfect, the Gospel and all three of them, not just William. Otto went over to the chair, picked up the Arab clothes and tossed them into a corner. Good thought, but he would never have to wear them now; he was sure that Hughes' plan would work.

[5]

William sat in between Dimas and Lord Otto de Grandson as Hughes showed them the route to Dun's village. The afternoon sun came in brightly through the work chamber's window, and Lord Otto de Grandson, who sat next to Hughes on the opposite side of the table, squinted as he looked up. "You say there's water in those riverbeds, eh?"

"I can remember just about every water hole," Hughes said running his finger along one of the wadis. "But most importantly, I studied the terrain and learned to recognize where water is to be found."

Dimas seemed concerned. "I'm amazed..."

At that moment one of Castle Pilgrim's scouts came bursting out of breath into Dimas' chamber. "Seneschal, seneschal," he uttered as they all turned to look at the excited man. "The Mameluk army has started moving, but are going north, Brother Dimas, away from us."

William knew that everything had changed; Hughes' miracle had come about.

Dimas thanked the scout and absentmindedly stared at the map. "Hughes, you were apparently correct. Looks like the Turks are moving on Beirut next." He sounded resigned more than anything else.

"In that case let's move. We can leave tomorrow," Hughes said.

"No, not yet." Dimas looked up from the map. "Better wait until the Turks are well to the north and busy attacking Beirut before we make a move. We'll wait."

"But how long, Brother Dimas?" Hughes asked.

"As long as necessary, commander."

The refugees at Pilgrim were exuberant at the news. Some cried in apparent relief. A good many danced with joy. Others prayed fervently on their knees.

Three weeks went by with no news. Usually there would be an occasional traveler stopping at the castle, but no one came. Then, at the end of the third week, a carrier pigeon from Tortosa brought a message that Dimas read aloud to Otto, Hughes, and William in his workroom. "Beirut and Sidon have already fallen," Dimas read, trying to make out the miniscule writing. "My Seneschal Brother Pedro de Moncada ordered everyone else to leave before the Mameluks breached our defenses. I am writing this as he holds the enemy back single handedly, buying me time with his heroic sacrifice. I pray you make good use of this information."

Dimas folded the message looking at a visibly shaken Hughes. "It's signed by Brother Pedro's clerk."

Hughes averted his face to one side. "Thank you Dimas. Brother Pedro was a good friend. At least he died nobly."

Dimas sighed. "Nothing remains except for Ruad, the island fortress, and Pilgrim. The Mameluks don't have ships, so it makes sense that we'll be next."

"It's time," Hughes said. "Let's make good use of that letter, Brother Pedro's gift to us. The enemy is far to the north, it's now or never." He stared at Dimas, but the seneschal did not respond.

Hughes stabbed with his finger at the map on the table. "We can all go this way," he said, "go far inland and then through the Syrian desert well away from the coastal castles and the Mameluks. We'll go all the way up to Constantinople through Cilician Armenia and Anatolia. The danger would be from here to the Lake of Galilee where we could find Mameluk advance parties, but we could even avoid those if we move fast enough."

Hughes looked up from the vellum. "Right now at Pilgrim we have forty-eight knights, fifty-six sergeants, fifty-one squires and eighty-one Turcopoles; a strong enough force to deal with anyone other than the full-scale Turkish army. In addition there are close to a hundred non-combatant Templars, who could help. I wish we still had the crossbowmen, but they were needed in Acre. There are close to five hundred horses, camels, mules, and donkeys, not enough to carry everyone, but the non-combatants could double-up with a civilian on their horses.

"I estimate we can take enough provisions to last us three months, long enough to reach Constantinople."

Dimas looked at the map then paced the room, and looked at the map so more. "My primary duty is to protect the refugees," he said apparently thinking aloud, "and I would do that by taking them to safety. That wouldn't be retreating, that would be protecting the refugees."

Dimas was then silent for some time.

"Hughes, we will implement your plan. But we won't go as far north as Constantinople. That's too far and dangerous. Instead, we'll circle around the Mameluk army and come up far north on the Syrian coast. We'll find a port with ships to take us to Cyprus."

After studying the map, Dimas and Hughes concluded that the port city of Latakia was their best choice. It would have many ships at anchor, and the Mameluks stationed there were probably still near Tortosa, a good distance south.

The following morning Dimas told the assembled refugees and Templars in the outer ward what was going to happen, and his news was met with sighs of relief and then cheers. As the group disassembled there were now smiles on faces. It was as though they felt already safe, thought William, and he wondered how many would survive the journey.

Dimas ordered Hughes to secure the area around the castle, and then post scouts in a wide perimeter to have advance notice in case the enemy came within a day's march. Hughes left with six men and came back three days later, reporting that the scouts were in place, and they had found no trace of the enemy. The Turks either thought Pilgrim Castle unimportant, or that they had nowhere to go.

It took them two weeks to prepare, mainly packing supplies and the training of the Templar noncombatants and civilians on what to do if attacked, and how to travel through the desert. Every able-bodied person—including the prisoners in the castle's dungeon—was assigned a role while on the road and a task if the column came under attack.

William could tell that the terrible stress they had lived under was now mostly gone, they were doing something, and they were going to escape; and the castle took on an air of busy anticipation as people worked late each night, packing and talking about what to do during the trip. Templars went around making sure the civilians only took with them what they needed.

On the night of August 13, Hughes and five knights fanned out to bring back the scouts, and the following morning Hughes told Dimas the Turks were still nowhere in sight. Figuring that things could be no more auspicious, they left that same day.

The Templars and refugees marched in a military formation, led by Dimas and followed by sixteen squadrons of twenty persons, each under the command of a Templar knight. They headed toward the Lake of Galilee. Dimas sent four scouts on ahead to look out for danger.

William was in charge of a squadron near the rear consisting of Brother Albert, his squire, ten non-combatant Templars, mostly the cooks, and ten civilians from Acre. Each civilian shared a horse with one of the cooks, whom William had armed with swords and shields. In case of attack, William's command was to fall in a center formation along with the fifteen other squadrons and protect the civilians. The battle group would do the rest.

William worried about leaving the Gospel unattended in his saddlebag each evening when the column made camp, but he noticed Brother Albert's watchful eye whenever he unsaddled Black.

"Not to worry, Brother William," Albert commented on the third night. "Your saddle bag will be safe as long as both Black and I are around."

"Thank you Albert. I know you will take good care of it."

Albert smiled. "It's Black who watches over it. I'm just around to protect innocent trespassers. That horse understands more than you imagine. He's figured out that box means a lot to you, and he won't let anyone but you and me near it."

William rubbed Black's nose. "I thank you both, then, for all you do for me."

"It's an honor, Sire," Albert said.

William walked away feeling sad that he couldn't share the Gospel with Albert. He would probably be horrified by anything that went against Church dogma.

Otto de Grandson rode in front with Dimas, but on occasion he would seek out Hughes and go along with him on his constant rounds of the long column, or fall in beside William. Invariably Lord Otto would ask William questions about John and Hafiz Mountain. William was a bit concerned about this, for people started talking about the "high and mighty lord" who seemed to have befriended him. He let it be known that Otto de Grandson was a relative of his, and the odd stares subsided. Then he thought about his lie and was worried that he would be caught. Otto's name of provenance was de Grandson, and William had never heard of such a place.

Next time Lord Otto came to see him, William asked where he was from.

"I'm from a forest canton up in the Alps, William."

"How did you end up in England?"

"My father came to serve King Edward's father, Henry III, when I was a child. I grew up alongside Edward. I'm a year older. We became good friends, like brothers, and I've served him ever since."

William was surprised. That meant Lord Otto was fifty-three years old! He certainly didn't look it. "What is a forest canton?"

"They are beautiful areas, of trees, lakes and snowy mountains, still wild. We come under the Holy Roman Empire, and the Duchy of Austria has been trying to claim us for many years. You see, the duke of that province wants a route to Italy, right through our region."

"Do you all speak French, or did you learn it in the English court?"

"Some of us speak French, others Italian, and German. We are a mixed bunch, but hope to become a federation some day."

"You mean, independent of the Holy Roman Empire, and not a kingdom or a duchy?"

"Exactly, William. Not ruled by any one person, but by a group of men representing the various cantons and city states."

"That's what the Athenians of old talked about, right?"

Lord Otto studied William with a smile. "Along those lines, my friend."

"And where does your name—'big sound'—derive from?"

"A river that runs near my hometown of Grandson. In the summer, when the snow melts in the mountains, it rumbles down to Lake Neuchatel."

"Your are fond of the place, eh?"

"Ah, my friend. It's heaven on earth!"

"And your family rules it?"

"We have large lands and a castle. But there are other barons as well."

All villages and towns they ran across were deserted, their citizens long gone to seek refuge in fortified towns. On the fifth day of marching, as the Pilgrim Castle refugees approached the depression of the Lake of Galilee, two scouts came back with a group of eight Templar knights and four Hospitallers, most of them wounded, all tired and hungry, as were their horses. The twelve men had been hiding in the area for the past two weeks, not knowing where to turn. They reported that a band of Mameluks controlled the lake. The men had watched helplessly as the Mameluks slaughtered a group of wounded knights who had arrived at the lake two days before.

The exhausted Templar and Hospitallers told how they had made their escape from Acre as it fell, and how the Turks killed all who surrendered, so they had gotten together and fought their way out, and were about to be slaughtered when a squadron of the Knights of Lazarus came to their rescue. "I've never seen people fight like that," said one of the Templars, "like mad dogs. They all died fighting to the last man so we could make our get-away."

William thought of Bridon, and wondered whether he had been in that squadron.

The rescued men looked at Dimas and Lord Otto de Grandson with desperation, probably expecting to be punished for failing to fight to the end at Acre, and William guessed that was the reason they didn't come to Pilgrim.

"You men did everything you could," Dimas told them, "I'm glad you made it out."

At Dimas' words, the men relaxed. One of them, an English knight in his early twenties held his face and sobbed gently. Dimas went over and placed his hand on the young man's back. He then sent out two scouts to pinpoint the Mameluks' location.

The scouts came back that afternoon, saying that there were two encampments consisting of thirty soldiers each, mostly archers, well protected behind stone walls on the west side of the lake, not far from an abandoned fishing village. Dimas decided to draw them out, and ordered a detachment of ten knights to ride toward the encamped Mameluks. The Turcopoles were to follow behind out of sight, as was one of the squadrons. He placed Hughes in command of the operation, for he was the most experienced.

"Hughes," ordered Dimas, "find out what the enemy is doing at the lake, so far from their main army; something must have drawn them to the place. If they are an advance party there will be other detachments nearby, but if they were sent to guard the lake, chances are they are on their own. Unless I find the answers to those questions I will have to order us to return to the safety of our castle."

By nightfall Hughes and his men came back, along with six Hospitaller knights they had found in chains after they killed the Mameluks. They also brought the Mameluks' horses.

The Hospitallers said there were more refugees hiding in the canyons on the other side of the lake.

Hughes reported there were no more Turks in the area. William noted Hughes' hard expression as he talked and could only guess at the means he had used to extract the information from the Mameluks. *We are getting farther and farther away from Hafiz Mountain,* thought William with sadness.

Seneschal Dimas ordered the formation to proceed to the lake, where they made camp and let their animals graze in the fertile valley. The refugees spread out blankets under trees and stretched out to relieve bodies unused to riding, while the cooks got fires going. Children waded into the calm waters of the lake, and a cool breeze blew across its surface.

William took the opportunity to check on Richard, to see how he was faring.

Richard seemed more thoughtful than usual, and he asked William to walk with him. "Willy, I don't know what you and Commander Hughes did for a year, but you were not anyone's prisoners. You came back changed, and what I can see and feel in you is different. When I'm near you I can feel the goodness in you as though you were some sort of saint. I know that's heresy, and I don't understand. So please, don't tell me what really happened, and I won't ask."

They continued walking and Richard told how much he missed home, and talked about the old times when they were children and had played in the creek in back of their house.

On his way to his squadron's campsite, William took a different route. He looked into people's faces to get a sense of how they were doing. He was studying a child when he felt someone's hard gaze. William turned around to find Maurice sitting on the ground, shackled along with two other men. He no longer wore a white surcoat, but was dressed in what looked like the remnants of a squire's surcoat.

William approached him. "Brother Maurice…"

"I can see you survived your imprisonment, Brother William."

"Yes, I did. Thanks for your concern."

"There's no concern. Let me say this so you'll remember: I will kill you someday."

William could feel the man's hatred, heavy and dark. William stared at him with sorrow and walked away.

That afternoon the scouts found the refugees the Hospitallers had talked about. They were six young girls—aged ten to fifteen— and six Templar knights. The worn-out knights told how they had escaped at the end of the fighting in Acre, and a week later had spotted a caravan of captured women and girls being led by a group of Mameluks on the road to Damascus. They had struck the soldiers and liberated as many of the captives as they could, who were en route to be sold as slaves. But the surviving Mameluks apparently reported the attack to their army, because a Mameluk battle group came after them. The six Templars and the young girls hid in the hills of Galilee, and the Turks camped by the lake to wait them out, knowing they would not venture into the Syrian desert that lay beyond the mountains. The knights and the girls were all on the verge of collapsing from hunger when the scouts found them.

That evening Dimas gathered his squadron commanders. "I would prefer to stay at this camp to allow the new refugees to be treated and rest before resuming our journey, but I have decided against it. It's just a matter of time before the Mameluk forces that would normally be at Latakia return. Each passing day makes it more likely, and we must try and get there before they do."

They were about to enter the Syrian desert, an area feared by many in the group, particularly the knights who had heard so much about the place over the years; to them it was a death trap, but they had no choice, they were under Seneschal Dimas' command and they would obey. The civilians voiced their concern and tried repeatedly to talk Dimas into finding another route. Some even begged to surrender to a Saracen unit that would protect them from the Turks, but Dimas refused to bend.

A group of refugees told Dimas they didn't want to go into the desert, and would rather venture on their own. A total of eighteen women stayed in the campsite as the rest of the column made their way.

The Castle Pilgrim column climbed the rough and steep mountains that led to a high plateau, and from there they descended into the desert, where they meandered along the many wadis and canyons.

Scouts trained by Hughes reconnoitered for water ahead of the column, and they always found some, but the problem was the unpredictable amount found at each location. Pools would be emptied after supplying but a handful of beasts and people, and then refill slowly. Dimas decreed that the animals would get watered first, and the riders last, and he ordered that a Templar be posted at each water site to enforce this. When people protested, he reminded them that without the horses they would die, but as riders, they could stand to go thirsty for quite some time.

The sixteen groups lined up into a single file, with horses ten yards apart. Eventually the line stretched for well over three leagues, encompassing five or more water holes at any given time.

Templars periodically monitored the horses, to check if they were still perspiring, and gave water to animals close to collapse. Dehydrated riders were tied down to their mounts to keep them from falling when they fainted.

In William's group, there were five elderly refugees, two men and three women, and although the constant riding was hard on everyone, for them it was torture.

"The good news," Dimas said when he next saw William "is that thanks to both you and Hughes we have found enough drinkable water."

But little else, for the area was a big wasteland.

William rode at the head of his squadron and Albert brought the rear, watching for stragglers. In the evenings, Albert reported to William any problems requiring attention: a weakening horse, a sick civilian, or dissension among the refugees because of fatigue or low morale.

After their business was done, William and Albert lingered in conversation, and William found a dimension to his sergeant he had not thought was there. One time Albert talked about his love for God that drew him into becoming a monk. "I wouldn't think of doing anything else with my life, Brother William. God pulls me to Him with so much love, that sometimes it's hard to bear." William tried to detect a note of fanaticism in his words, but found only devotion, and in the days when things were the hardest, William found inspiration in Albert's company.

As the days wore on, William felt the pain of the refugees as though it were his own, and he made a mental note of every death, and every night with Albert, he said a prayer for those who suffered a loss, and for those he knew were about to die.

While on the road, the Templars observed only Matins and Compline together; the other offices were left up to each person as the column made its way during the grueling days.

After Compline, William meditated with Dimas, Lord Otto, and Hughes. They would talk afterward and got to know Otto. He proved to be a forceful but generous man with a great intellect and was knowledgeable not just about war and politics, but commanded an impressive general knowledge.

But the group's conversations were often about the Brotherhood and affairs in Europe. Otto told them about recent events in England. He was very concerned for King Edward, whom he obviously loved and respected and talked about the missions he had gone with him in France and lately Wales.

"He's a good man, Edward Long Shanks," Otto said. "But of late he's fallen into a trap, I'm afraid."

"Who is after him?" Dimas asked.

"It's all about the Caesarius Prophecy."

"What does the Prophecy have to do with King Edward?" asked Hughes.

"When I first heard of the Prophecy, things made so much sense to me. It confirmed something so big and horrible it has kept me awake many nights, a threat to the world as we know it, not just the Templars."

A full moon lit the desert around them in a silvery glow. Otto scooped up pebbles off the ground and began throwing them, one at the time, at a boulder some distance away. "A few years ago, as you might have heard, the entire Scottish royal family died. First, it was the youngest prince in '81, then in '83, the daughter who had married the king of Norway. The third to die was the oldest son, in '84. At this point the Scottish king, Alexander III, had only one remaining heir—his granddaughter, the seven-year old princess of Norway. He remarried hoping to produce new heirs, but he died in an accident on the very night he was to meet his new betrothed. That was in '86. Nine months ago, this past November, his young granddaughter was sent to Scotland on an English ship, but before it landed, the little girl died mysteriously. Those deaths were very convenient for Edward, who then began his maneuvering to take Scotland for his own."

"How would he do that?" William asked, who felt like he was suddenly privy to the high-powered and exciting world of kings and bishops.

"By declaring himself overlord, William. The Scots were in disarray and had set up a panel of guardians," continued Otto, bouncing the pebbles in his hand. "They asked Edward to oversee their process in selecting their new king, but just as I was leaving England, Edward was planning to declare himself overlord, and as such the one who decides the line of succession. That's what the French are counting on, for the Scots will never abide by it and are sure to rebel."

"Too bad things are going that way," Hughes said. "I know King Alexander would have fought the French alongside Edward."

"You are right, Hughes," Otto said." Alexander was married to Edward's sister. A Scottish-English alliance is the last thing the French want, and Edward is playing right into the French king's plans by antagonizing the Scots."

"So Edward will select a Scottish king he can control?" William asked.

"Someone he can defeat. Edward and his chief advisor, Bishop Anthony Bek, decided to select John Balliol as the new Scottish king, because he's the

GRIGOR FEDAN

weakest of the three pretenders to the throne. The other two are John Hastings and Robert de Bruce who would not be as easy to manage and eventually defeat. Once Balliol is crowned, Edward and Bishop Anthony plan on applying pressure and humiliating him until he rebels, and then Edward will march into Scotland and take over the kingdom. They know that Balliol is no military leader, and are counting on an easy victory."

"Sounds like a wicked plan, but that's what kings do, right?" Dimas said, who had been listening attentively.

"Yes, that's the way things are done sometimes," Otto said throwing a pebble at a big rock but missing. "However, I'm sure it wasn't King Edward's idea, and that the plot is far more diabolical than it sounds. It's obvious that the Scottish royals were all murdered, those were not accidental deaths, but I know Edward is not capable of such thing; they were his kin, after all, and those were his nephews with whom he had a close relationship. But once they died, he was talked into taking advantage of the situation."

"By whom?" Dimas asked.

"Bishop Anthony Bek," Otto said. But Anthony alone is not capable of such complicated machinations."

"Who is?"

"The kings of France. And since '85, the most vicious one, Philip the IV," Otto said. "I have had a spy in the French court dating back to his father, Philip III, and since then I have known of the French plans to foment a Scottish war with the English, not just to keep them from joining forces, but also to weaken King Edward. I can't share the information with Edward, because he'll tell Bishop Anthony, who's in contact with the French, and it will get back to King Philip. He'd deny it, accuse me of sedition, and I would probably end up in prison."

William felt drawn by the intrigue. "What does King Philip stand to gain?"

"As you know," Otto said aiming another pebble at the rock, "Edward is not just king of England; he's also the duke of Aquitaine, a duchy that has been in his family for well over a hundred years, but it's a part of France, and the French king is overlord. French monarchs have felt it a matter of national honor to take back Aquitaine, ever since Eleanor Duchess of Aquitaine got her marriage to King Louis VII of France annulled by the pope in 1152 and married King Henry II of England, effectively bestowing a large portion of France to the English.

"Once Edward is facing a full-blown Scottish rebellion, Philip will declare war on Edward and use Aquitaine as the reason."

"The problem is, I know that Philip won't stop there; that he has a grander plan on his mind. He wants to be the next Charlemagne."

"You mean take over the Holy Roman Empire?" William asked.

"Exactly," replied Otto. "The current title is hollow, and in the hands of the Germans. All Philip needs is for the pope to name him emperor, and enough money to pay for a large army, and he will have most kings falling in behind him.

"Then, as a powerful Holy Roman emperor, he will retake the Holy Land and this time do away with all non-Christians. He will do the same in Europe. I assure you that he will have much support for he will be playing into the fanatics' dream of a Christian-only world."

William stood up. The story was now very disturbing. It was time to make a fire and he started gathering sticks and dry grass while he listened.

Dimas studied Otto. "So this is where you see the Caesarius Prophecy fitting in? Philip needs a lot of money and at the same time do away with any potential threats, such as the Templars, a formidable force, not interested in power, not to be bought. By doing away with them he gets their money as well."

Otto smiled at Dimas with apparent satisfaction. "Yes, the treasure of the Templars would be more than enough, for the Order has more than England and France put together."

William dumped an armload of grass and kindling on the ground in the middle of the group. "I've heard so much about the Templar treasury. Where did it come from?"

"Mostly from the gifting of nobles joining the Order for the past two hundred years," Dimas said." Add to that a number of grateful kings and dukes who have given generously."

"Don't forget that the Templars have managed the treasuries of several kingdoms—including France—for a fee," said Otto, studying the remaining pebbles in his hand, "and that they issue letters of credit to merchants all over Europe, all of which produce a sizable income."

"Then there are the properties the Order owns all over Europe," added Hughes. "In Scotland alone they have eight hundred farms, mills and other income-producing properties."

Dimas chuckled. "And that's what Philip wants."

"But the pope would surely stop the French king," William said as he reached under his surcoat for the pouch where he kept a flint stone.

"Yes, William," Otto said. "A reasonable pope would stop him, by declaring a crusade against the French king. That's part of the reason why Philip plans to name his own pope. He would have to wait until the elderly Boniface VIII dies. Philip is grooming one of his bishops, Bertrand de Got, to be the next pope. I have heard rumors from Rome that the French are passing large amounts of money around, and that can only be to ensure the cardinals' vote for Bertrand de

Got when the time comes."

"Don't you have to be a cardinal to be elected pope?" Hughes asked.

"Ordinarily, yes. But Phillip is circumventing that small detail. Legally, all you have to be is a Catholic."

"How likely is it for a king to set up a pope of his choosing?" asked William.

"Very likely," answered Otto. "At least for the French. Only ten years ago, King Philip's father, Philip III, and his uncle, Charles of Anjou, set up the Pope Martin IV, also a Frenchman, who was totally beholden to the French crown. They didn't accomplish much with their ploy, but I think it set the stage for the current plan."

William crouched down over the kindling and used his knife to strike against the flint and made sparks fly. "How will Philip get rid of the Templars? They are so powerful and spread out through many countries."

Otto threw another pebble hard against a boulder, and it bounced up in the air. "The pope can order a crusade against the Order for heresy, just as another pope ordered one against the Cathars not that long ago."

Dimas stood up and stretched. Then he shook his head as he crossed his arms over his chest. "I beg your pardon, Brother Otto, but the whole thing sounds too farfetched. First, Philip needs to neutralize Edward, then elect his pope, then do away with the Templars, then…"

"Yes, it sounds outlandish," Otto said, "except that we know about the Caesarius Prophecy. Let's take a logical trajectory that will tell us whether Caesarius was right," continued Otto as he threw another pebble, missing the boulder. "For one thing, all Christian armies are presently being pushed out of the Holy Land, just as the Prophecy predicted, right?"

Dimas nodded. "Unfortunately, yes. Go on, my Lord."

Otto took careful aim and this time bounced a pebble off the boulder. "We will know that Philip and his father were behind the murders of the Scottish royals if Philip declares war on Edward the moment the Scots rebel, as they inevitably will. That will be our second validation, agreed?"

Dimas picked a stick from the ground. "Possibly. But it's conceivable that Philip would attack just because the opportunity presented itself."

"Well, let's make certain that we are on the right track and look for a third sign, Otto said. "If after Pope Boniface VIII dies, Bertrand de Got is elected pope, that would confirm that we have uncovered a plot, right?"

"Yes, without doubt," Dimas said.

"In which case, I would suggest that the moment we hear that Philip has declared war on England, we start planning for the protection of the Templars, their treasure and most importantly, the Jesus Gospel," said Otto.

"Why the Jesus Gospel?" William asked watching the flames flicker.

"If the Templars are destroyed and their treasure taken, the power of the Brotherhood goes with them," Otto said absorbed in the sputtering flames. "With no secret society protecting it, news of the Gospel would likely reach Philip who would need to destroy it. Just like the Roman Emperor Constantine a thousand years ago, he would realize that the Gospel, that is 'The Knowing,' does away with Church authority."

"And like Constantine, Philip needs the Church for the source of his power," added William sitting back down next to Hughes who seemed frozen in place, staring at the flames.

"This scheme sounds so involved, "Dimas said. "It took years to devise …obviously preceding the current French king or even his father, right?"

"Yes, Otto said. "I think it was originally thought up during the reign of Saint Louis, Philip's grandfather, who went on crusade and was defeated so badly by the Turks. He realized that the only way to conquer the Holy Land once and for all required the power of a Holy Roman emperor."

"I still don't understand why Philip wants to wage war against King Edward," William said. "I think you said that Aquitaine was not the only reason…"

"Because Edward is the second most powerful king in Europe after Philip," Dimas answered, "so if Philip conquers England, he'll not only have the English resources at his disposal, but would also have done away with a potential threat, and proven his military might…that would be enough to make him a most powerful emperor."

"But England has but a quarter of France's people. Why is it a threat?" William asked.

"You are right, by itself England is no match against the French," Otto said. "But if you were to add both Aquitaine and Scotland; that is, should Edward win over the barons in both, then the two are close. Philip is certain that the Aquitaine barons are primarily Frenchmen, and that the Scottish will end up hating Edward."

They sat in silence; the only sounds Otto's pebbles bouncing off the boulder, the flames starting to crackle, and the faint murmur of voices from the camp.

After some time Hughes turned to look at Otto. "Brother Otto, how can we be of service?"

Otto studied Hughes, apparently stunned by his bluntness. "Yes, thank you, Hughes. I believe Philip can be stopped, and only the Brotherhood can do it. I also believe that the Caesarius Prophecy was meant as the signpost to alert us to Philip's evil. After all, the struggle would be much bigger than just protecting the

Templars, don't you agree?"

Hughes nodded. "Yes, brother. What can we do to help?"

"We need to keep an eye on events and be in a position to act; a small secret group at liberty to do whatever is required with the full support of the Brotherhood at large," Otto said, counting the remaining pebbles in his hand, as though they were precious. "Because I am close to King Edward, I can ask him to assign me to work against the French when the war starts. You can work with me. I know that the three of you are capable fighters and strategists, and because you are brothers I can trust you as I trust no one.

"I need you."

Dimas smiled, perhaps embarrassed by the praise. "There is nothing I could wish for more, than to apply what I have learned here in Outremer for a good cause. It would also mean that I would work with Hughes and William. I was concerned that once we reached Cyprus we would all be assigned to different places and waste our talents managing farms."

"We need to get to Cyprus first," Hughes said. "I just hope we make it."

Otto stared at Hughes as though he had said the unthinkable. "Have faith, commander. I trust we'll be in England soon."

"If we get to Cyprus, don't you think the Templars will try to retake the Holy Land?" Hughes asked.

"No, I don't," Dimas said. "The French king is right in that respect; it would require someone with the power of the Holy Roman Empire of Charlemagne's time. The kings of Europe have known about the Turkish threat for years, but have been unable to unite and do anything about it."

"For that you have also to blame King Philip," Otto said. "It's part of his plan, to lose the Holy Land. He needs to have the Templars in Christian kingdoms."

Dimas thought for a moment. "That's wicked. Of course, if we are still here, there is no way he could imprison us, but with the Holy Land lost, he knows we'll be where the pope can order to have us imprisoned. So he's sabotaged efforts for a crusade.

"Brother Otto, I would love to fight him on that account alone."

Otto looked around at William and Hughes, then back at Dimas. "If I understand you, it sounds as though you have decided to join me?"

"Yes brother, I will support you with everything I have," Dimas said, "and I would hope that both William and Hughes will agree as well."

William didn't hesitate. "I agree, whatever Brother Otto requires, I will be there to serve."

"Yes, of course. It will be an honor," Hughes said. "Provided we get out of this place alive."

Otto thanked them, and shook each man's hand effusively, apparently deeply touched.

Hughes bid everyone goodnight, stood and started back to camp, and William decided to walk with him.

"What do you think, William?" Hughes said when they were alone. "Quite impressive how the Prophecy is playing out, eh?"

William had felt uneasiness when Otto was speaking and was questioning everything he had heard. However, uncle John had seemed convinced that the Prophecy was real, so perhaps his uneasiness was unwarranted. "What Otto said sheds much light into the Prophecy, Hughes," William said in a quiet voice, not quite believing his own words, "we are certainly fortunate that he confided in us."

"One thing, though," Hughes said, "you have to tell me about the Holy Roman Empire and Charlemagne. I don't know about those things."

"Glad to tell you what I know, Hughes. Charlemagne was a king of the Franks, a Germanic people who invaded Gaul when the Romans left, and gave France its name. The Roman Empire lasted about a thousand years, and was the biggest in European history—covering most of Europe, North Africa, and the Holy Land, but in the fifth century it broke apart. In the year 800 Charlemagne decided to revive it, but he called it 'holy' because he saw himself as the defender of the Christian Church. He had the pope crown him emperor—and decreed that from then on only the pope could bestow the crown—and proceeded to conquer Europe. Even Constantinople named him overlord, and in those days that included the Holy Land.

"After a couple of centuries the Empire lost territory and authority, and now it's a rather insignificant title bestowed on German kings. But Philip can make the case that the title belongs to the French kings. That's what gives Philip's claim validity."

Hughes seemed impressed. "Sounds like we'll have quite a fight on our hands."

Yes, quite a fight, thought William. And he wondered whether he'd ever see Hafiz Mountain again.

It took the Pilgrim Castle column twenty-seven days to reach Latakia. They lost thirty-two refugees, seven horses, and three donkeys. Had they spent another week on the trail, William was certain that at least another fifty refugees would have died. Most were semi-conscious, and for the last three days all rode tied to their saddles.

Dimas chose to make camp in a valley surrounded by vineyards and orchards, with plenty of water and grass, but still safely out of sight, about a league from the city. It was such a relief to have left the desert and people and animals drank water with abandon from two creeks. The refugees, used to the harsh desert that spoke to them of death, now gazed at the green hills in wonder, perhaps not quite believing what they were seeing.

When night came, Dimas and his battle group made their silent way to Latakia, leaving Hughes in command of the refugees, telling him that he would send a scout with orders to either approach the city, or escape.

William accompanied Dimas and his men.

Dimas had been right about Latakia. The Mameluks had left only twenty soldiers to guard the city and they seemed lax because one of the Templar knights simply climbed the unguarded wall, then snuck around and opened the gate for the rest to come in. Dimas and his men overtook the sleeping soldiers in the barracks and put them in chains. He left four men to guard them.

Past midnight Dimas sent a scout to tell Hughes that all was well.

In the harbor they found a wide assortment of ships, mostly fishing vessels, but among them, four sturdy cargo ships. Dimas wanted to sail as soon as possible, and leave little to chance. He estimated that with the ships in hand, it would take two trips to ferry everyone across to Cyprus. With a coffer full of gold coins by his feet, he had no trouble enlisting the boat masters he wanted.

William found Latakia a beautiful port city surrounded by gentle hills full of vineyards, and evidently a very old place with some ancient buildings that dated back to the time of Alexander the Great, sixteen centuries before.

The Pilgrim Castle refugees assembled on the quay, and the Templars started loading all the civilians on the four cargo ships and twelve of the larger fishing vessels that Dimas had hired. The operation was witnessed by a number of curious inhabitants of Latakia who seemed to take turns watching the Templars but made no contact. The refugees from Pilgrim walked in a daze, perhaps too exhausted to realize what was happening, that they were almost completely out of danger. They did what they were told, slowly and clumsily. The Templars and Hospitallers, on the other hand, seemed energized, and worked frantically without rest. They were able to load all the refugees and forty non-combatant Templars in half a day.

Dimas sent the ships with Hughes, with instructions to make camp on the first beach he found in Cyprus. Dimas, Otto, William and the remaining Templars and Hospitallers watched as the fleet sailed away, and spent the next five days praying and hoping the Turks were still busy somewhere. But nothing happened, and they loaded again and this time managed to fit everybody and every horse, except for the Turcopoles, whom Dimas dismissed, paying them a hand-some reward for their services.

William realized Dimas had apparently waited until that moment to dismiss the Turcopoles not because he needed them, but rather because he feared they would turn against the Templars to ingratiate themselves with the Mameluks. Other local Christians had been known to do just that.

Dimas sent for the four men he had left guarding the local garrison. Then everyone boarded the four cargo ships. When they were finally sailing, and safely away from shore, the men seemed to collapse all at once right where they stood. William watched them place their weapons by their sides, take off their surcoats and hauberks, and lay down on the deck. Otto unceremoniously stretched out beside William, let out a sigh and went to sleep. Only Dimas remained standing, still vigilant.

The flotilla landed near Famagusta on the eastern shore of Cyprus and found the beach where Hughes had assembled the camp.

Dimas observed the final disembarkation, and William could tell how re-lieved the seneschal was and watched him leave immediately with Otto to meet with the Cyprus Templar master to discuss the disposition of his men and civil-ians still under his command.

William learned the island was now teeming with Templars from all over the Holy Land. Everyone who could escape came to Cyprus. Fortunately the Tem-plars had been long established in the place and had even ruled it at one point.

It took the Templars from Pilgrim Castle a week to be assigned to a post, but mostly because Dimas refused to have his command dispersed throughout the three Templar forts in the island. Finally, they were all sent to Lemasol, a two-day ride away on the south shore.

Otto was invited to stay with the king of Cyprus. The Hospitallers, who had an even stronger presence on the island than the Templars, pledged to take in all the refugees from Pilgrim Castle.

As Dimas and his men were leaving the beach on their horses, the refugees came to say goodbye. Dimas was approached by a delegation of four women who came to kiss his hand.

"Thank you, noble Templars," said a middle-aged woman who had emerged as their leader during the journey. As Dimas and his men rode through the crowd, the refugees waved goodbye, a good many with tears in their eyes.

Cyprus was a quiet and peaceful island, with long beaches and a warm, blue-green sea. The towns were small and without protective walls. White houses had perched on hillsides for centuries, as the people went about their quiet lives. The

Templars walked around unarmed and unprotected by armor. They spent their days in prayer, and Lemasol Castle was now their cloister.

Otto had promised that he would be in touch as soon as possible, and two days after they settled in Lemasol, a Templar messenger came from Famagusta to summon Dimas, Hughes, and William to meet with Otto at a palace in the city.

A week later, William, accompanied by Dimas and Hughes, entered what looked like a manor house in Famagusta with the Gospel box under one arm. William realized that he was looking at what remained of the Brotherhood in that part of the world. Sitting around were a good many Templars, but also a few Hospitallers, as well as several local officials and noble men of Greek ancestry. There were also several Orthodox and Roman Catholic priests, several monks, and rabbis. The mood was subdued. *These are defeated people*, William thought.

William recognized several from the meetings in Acre.

The group looked at the Gospel in awe as they filed past it on the table where William had spread the parchment pages. As they read the Greek words and recited them silently, tears flowed freely. And William understood: that now they hadn't lost everything in the Holy Land, for they had their long-sought after treasure.

The meeting started with a somber note, an acknowledgement of the many of their brothers who had perished.

Then Otto stood and gazed at the congregants. "My mission is to safeguard the Gospel. Your mission is to let the other groups of the Brotherhood know that we have it, and that we are taking it to London." He announced that Dimas, Hughes, and William would be coming with him, and he asked the local Templar master to make the necessary arrangements with Temple House in London to attach the three to his service. "Our work will be most sensitive and secret, and will have to do with the Caesarius Prophecy."

At Otto's words, the assembly murmured among themselves. Then the Cyprus Templar master vowed that he would do as he had been told.

Evidently there was little else to talk about, no other decisions to be made, no plans.

"Very well, my brothers," Otto said standing up. "My three Templar brothers and I set sail for Marseilles within a month. Let's us all fulfill our respective duties. *Beauseant*."

William decided to spend time with Richard for that next month. William was worried about him, he seemed subdued, as though a heavy conflict was taking place inside him.

One morning they walked barefoot along a deserted beach by the water's edge. A few puffy clouds floated overhead. Small birds ran on ahead of them, and out at sea, four fishing boats made their way south.

Richard talked about home, and how he wished he could go, and William realized that perhaps his brother no longer wanted to be a Templar. But they both knew monastic vows were not to be broken. It was clear that Richard had been disillusioned by Maurice, his comments told William as much, and that had been a big let down for him about monastic life in general.

William rode to Famagusta the following day and asked Otto if he could arrange for his brother Richard to get leave from the Templars and come with them to England so he could go home. It was highly unusual, but they were the only two sons, and his father was getting on in years.

Otto summoned the Templar master that very moment, and when the man arrived, directed him to release Richard from his vows.

"But vows once taken cannot be undone!" replied the master.

"Talk to whomever you need to, and find a way!" commanded Otto.

Four days later, William accompanied Richard to Famagusta, where the Templar master told them that Richard's primary duty was to his father, and therefore the Templars had decided to assign him to work with his family. "We encourage you to keep your vows, but of course, we cannot force you to do so, and you are free of any obligations to the Order." The Templar master added that there was to be no appeal, the decision was final.

Richard was at first surprised, perhaps upset by the news, but then appeared delighted as he rode back with William. "I don't understand, though, am I a monk, or am I free to wed?"

William couldn't disclose Otto's explanation, a legalistic play of words that amounted to the circumventing of Canon Law. The Templars couldn't outright release Richard from his vows, but agreed to no longer consider him a monk.

"You are free to wed."

"I am to be Sir Richard again then, I am to go home!"

"You missed home, eh, Richard?" William asked.

"I put it out of my mind, so as to not hurt inside. But I want to see mother, and by God, I would love to see Elizabeth."

"But I thought you decided she was a fallen woman…"

"Ah, those things matter none, not after so much fighting, so much dying. I just want her back. I pray that she hasn't married or become a nun…but if she has, I can't blame her. My heart aches for all she went through."

The day before setting sail, William went to see his sergeant to say goodbye and found him brushing Black and talking to him in a gentle voice.

"Brother William, I'm just getting Black ready for the ship. He's got that saddlebag by him. Now remember, Sire, he won't let anyone near it, and it can be dangerous. What if a sailor without knowing touches it; why, he'll be dealing with a demon of a horse, two-thousand pounds of hard muscle protecting that one bag."

William stood watching how the brush made Black's velvety hair shine...a most beautiful animal. "Have you heard where you might be posted next, Albert?"

Albert continued brushing and did not answer right away. "If it were up to me, Sire, I would ask to go with you."

William felt guilty for not thinking of his sergeant earlier, perhaps having been too preoccupied with Richard and the journey back to England. "Albert, I would be honored to have you come with us."

Albert's eyes became moist. Then he smiled. "Thank you, Brother William."

PART TWO

CHAPTER IX

[1]

They sailed the length of the Mediterranean in rough winter waters under an angry sky, and their galley had to seek refuge for two days in a fishing village in the Kingdom of Sicily, before finally arriving at the busy port of Marseilles after three more endless weeks. Then it was another ten cold days of quick-paced riding across France to reach the English Channel and England, stopping every night at a Templar property, either a farm or a castle, where they were received with great courtesy by the local commanders due to Otto's rank. On one occasion they had to outrun a company of brigands—renegade knights operating as bandits. Another time they found the road blocked by one such group, and doubled back to a Templar post to seek assistance. "There's no sense in risking our lives, let's play it safe," was Otto's reasoning.

The long days of riding were a mixed blessing; it was very cold, even with the sun shining, colder than William remembered, but there was time to reflect. He reviewed what Otto had said about the Caesarius Prophecy, and what it meant: they had to stop the French king at all costs. That night around the fire in the desert seemed so long ago, but the words still resonated in William's mind. He was certain that what he, Hughes, and Dimas had committed to do was the right thing, but still there was a nagging doubt of something missing, something wrong, and he couldn't figure out what it was. But anyway, it was not his responsibility, he was not in charge, his duty was to follow orders. His own responsibility was to the Jesus Gospel, nestled safely in Black's saddlebag.

When the weather offered a reprieve, they talked; so unlike the customary silence that William, Hughes, and Dimas were used to as Templars, but Otto enjoyed a good conversation, and he was very inquisitive. Dimas was the only one who bemoaned the loss of the Holy Land. Otto apparently had accepted what he viewed as the inevitable, and Hughes never looked back. William real-

ized that he would rather not be part of an occupying force, for he didn't believe
that Christians had any right to the Holy Land, and he said so, and both Otto
and Hughes agreed. All the while Richard listened intently, but offered no opinion, and answered questions politely, but with few words. Sergeant Albert trailed
behind lost in prayer at the head of the four cross-bowmen and the two servants
they had picked up at Marseilles' Templar House.

One day they crossed the Channel and two days later arrived in London on
a fog-shrouded Tuesday afternoon.

London Templar House was a large modern compound built in the last hundred years, fronting on the Thames just outside the west end of the city walls.
It was famous for Temple Church, a round-dome edifice, a replica of the Church
of the Holy Sepulcher in Jerusalem. To one side of the Temple was the rectangular Chancel, and further inside the massive perimeter walls were the refectory,
dormitories, stables, smithy shops, infirmary, kitchens, warehouses, armory, and
training grounds. The Templar in charge was a preceptor, an administrator with
broader responsibilities than a seneschal of a castle in the Holy Land because in
Europe the Templars' operations were not so much warfare as managing farms,
large estates, and banking.

On the other end of the city walls, was the imposing Tower of London. Up
the river from the city, about half a league from Templar House at the end of
the fancy avenue called the Strand, lined with imposing fortified manors, stood
Westminster Palace.

It had been three years since William and Richard had come to London
Templar House as anonymous novices. Now they were back as veterans from
Outremer.

While Albert took care of their personal possessions and horses, and Richard
ambled about, the Templar master of England, Brother Guillaime de la More,
who was also preceptor of London Templar House and a member of the Brotherhood, escorted Otto, William, Dimas, and Hughes to the huge underground
vault in the Chancel where gold and large sums of money were kept and where
the Jesus Gospel would find a home. "This is the same process we follow when
a king or a bishop asks us to safeguard something for them," the soft-spoken
Brother Guillaime said smiling at William. "I thank you for the honor of allowing us to store the Gospel."

William caressed the wooden box lying safely in a metal coffer of its own,
and wondered whether he would be able to fulfill his responsibility to the Gospel
in the face of the threat from the French. In ten years, would it have reached fame
as an instrument for change, or would it still sit in that same vault, unknown?

Brother Guillaime, deferential and in obvious awe, showed the three arriving

Templars their chambers. William stood admiring his spartan but private and quiet cell, while Brother Guillaime explained that William was now a commander, therefore had private quarters, and that he could come and go as he pleased. "The Cyprus master sent word of your arrival, and we prepared accordingly."

The following day Otto showed Hughes, Dimas, and William Westminster Palace. It was a huge, solidly built but utilitarian stone building on the Thames surrounded by gardens and a forest preserve to one side where the king enjoyed hunting boar and deer. A wall went around the palace grounds, and outside it, a sizable moat connected at both ends with the river, making the castle a veritable island. Otto took the three Templars to his chambers on the second floor where they would work. It consisted of an antechamber for clerks and a large room containing four worktables and lined with cabinets full of books, documents and maps, and four comfortable chairs for reading or talking in one corner. The smell of parchment and ink filled the air, and a somber light came from three fortress style windows, tall and narrow, that looked past the inner moat to the gardens and the front gate. "My clerks used to occupy the antechamber, but I want you to work with me in the big room, so we can all work as one," Otto said.

Otto suggested that William accompany Richard home. After all, it was close to Christmas. "Visit your parents, William, spend a fortnight and rest, then make haste and come back. We need you."

The following morning at daybreak, William and Richard rode out of Templar House and into the city through the Strand Street Gate, past the Monastery of St. Paul and on to Watling Street where they turned right toward the only way across the river Thames, London Bridge. Stores along the normally busy thoroughfare were still shuttered, and they ran across farmers delivering produce, wagons full of barrels with live fish, and cows, goats, and pigs being herded to the butcher shops. In a few hours storekeepers would open their stores and customers would fill the street slowing down traffic for the day.

A freezing drizzle fell steadily and William was thankful for their newly acquired heavy woolen aketons under their hauberks to protect against the cold. Riding under their oil tarps it wasn't too bad, still cold, but at least they kept dry.

At midday William decided to stop at a Franciscan monastery just to get out of the miserable weather. They sipped hot cider and dined on rabbit stew with a handful of other travelers. Richard looked around at the tradesmen and merchants stealing glances in their direction, and smiled. "We are home Willy! No more fighting for me. I'll marry Elizabeth and eventually inherit father's lands. I plan on expanding the fief's cattle and becoming rich. I can do it." Richard went on talking about his new life, and William halfway listened, thinking instead what he himself had embarked upon, and half-wondered how his brother had changed.

The drizzle stopped the following day in late afternoon as they went past the Jewish village. William stopped with Richard at the meadow with the big oak where travelers had made a cozy fire. Everyone stood around the flames warming themselves and the two brothers met up with one of their father's neighbors who looked at them as though they had come back from the dead. "You two are back!" He was a man about their own age and from a family with means, but he had not been accepted as page at the earl's household because of a sickly constitution. He eyed their surcoats, horses, and weapons with apparent envy and wanted to know how they had survived the Turks. When it became apparent that neither William nor Richard seemed eager to talk about their experiences, he wished them well and left.

A league from home—the weather-now merely crisp—they encountered a boy riding bareback. On seeing them, he took off at a fierce gallop ahead of them. A while later, when they rode up to their family's manor, all the neighbors and most of the village were there to meet them, lining the path to their house, bundled up against the cold air, whispering and glancing at them.

At the front door, their mother looked them up and down. "My boys, my boys," was all she managed to say as tears ran freely down her cheeks. Their father stood to one side, proudly taking note of their darkened skins and surcoats. Everyone knew about the fall of Acre— it was all people had talked about at the monastery where they had stopped. William expected that neighbors would be parading through the house for the next few days wanting to hear all about the loss of the Holy Land.

That evening Richard donned his clothes from before and shaved his beard. He came down to the great hall, smart looking in his tunic with the family colors, sporting his second-son medallion, hose and pointed shoes.

Their father was clearly pleased with the development, and then stared at William's surcoat and his commander's mantle. "William, why can Richard leave the Templars but not you?"

William started to explain that he felt a strong vocation, but stopped when he noticed that his father was not listening.

The following day, as William strolled about the house, he found his mother sitting alone in the solarium, sifting through a box of colorful fabrics she would use to decorate the house for Christmas. He yearned to tell her all about John, but knew he couldn't.

"Mother," he said, "I have news about uncle John." At this she turned her face slightly in his direction, but kept her gaze on the red and green kersey cloth in her hands. "He's a prisoner in an isolated Saracen fort. He's well treated for he was made a teacher." Lady Claire pursed her lips and her hands kept caressing the fabric. "Please keep this a secret," William said, "for I heard it from a fellow Templar who has connections with the Arabs, and if found out he could get in trouble."

She put the red and green cloth aside and dug for another fabric. "Tell me how he looks, please. Is he well? Has he aged?" She spoke without looking up.

William was momentarily taken aback and knew there was no need to try and pretend. "He looks very well. He's healthy, and fit. I suppose he's aged, but to me he looked grand, wise and gentle."

William noticed his mother paying close attention as she absent-mindedly turned a cloth every which way. "He remembers you well, spoke at length about you, asked whether your hair was still chestnut, whether you still laughed until tears came to your eyes, and told me how you used to make dolls for the children of the poor."

His mother was silent, apparently lost in thought.

"When did you see him, Willy?"

"About a year ago. Please mother, I can't tell you more."

There was a long pause. "So he remembers, does he?"

"Yes, he does, mother. He clearly cherishes those memories. He told me how you two used to take long walks all around the valley."

His mother gave William a wistful look.

"Why don't you laugh like that anymore, mother?"

Lady Claire ran her fingers along a satin cloth, and then she sighed. "Those were very special times, Willy. We all change." She went back to sifting through her box, and William decided that some things were best not talked about.

William and Richard visited the castle and paid their respects to the earl of Sheffield. As they stood before the earl, William saw him brimming with joy at seeing him, far more joyful than his own father had been.

"William, so glad you made it back. And Richard."

The earl—sitting in his customary high chair in his reception chamber with all the flags and shields lining the walls—seemed different, as though shrunk in stature. William noticed a tension in his voice when he talked about Farwell. "My son is a powerful man now, and has taken over many of my responsibilities."

Orland was but a shadow of his old self, thought William, a sickly old man. William walked away with a heavy feeling, certain that something was amiss.

Everyone they met at the castle looked at them in awe, and wanted to hear what it was like in the last weeks in the Holy Land.

The brothers saw how much they themselves had changed when reflected in the eyes of the people they talked to. In turn William and Richard found their former friends and acquaintances bland and superficial, their speech unnecessarily elaborate and boring—it was now in vogue to imitate a Parisian accent—and their studied mannerisms, childish. "I wonder if we were like that back then," mused Richard. William noticed that people appeared shocked by their frank words and manners.

William and Richard watched knights practice in the armory, sparring with swords, and realized how easily they could take them; their mistakes were so obvious. Richard shook his head and announced that he would become a rich man in the next tournament. "It's a good thing Templars are not allowed to tourney," he said. "Good for me."

William was glad not to have run into Farwell. The brothers were told by one of his friends that he was "very busy these days," and had to travel much, even in the winter.

As the day wore on, William and Richard concluded that no one knew about Elizabeth. The last time anyone had seen her was at her sister's wedding, and even then, she had hardly been noticed, apparently she'd come in and out as briefly as she could.

On the way back home they made a detour to Elizabeth's house. They met her father, Sir Leonard, in the great hall of his modest manor. He appeared aloof. At Richard's request to see Elizabeth, Sir Leonard hesitated, and then told him that his daughter was gone.

"Where is she?" William asked. "Please, Sire, Richard cares for her, and we can help if she's in trouble."

Sir Leonard studied William's surcoat. He eyed the bench behind him and plopped down in it. "One night we had words," he said, lifting a hand to smooth his remaining gray hair. "She left that same night with nothing but what she wore, and the following morning when her mother asked me to look for her I found no trace anywhere. I rode for three days and no one had seen her, either she was good at hiding from travelers, or the very night swallowed her." He glanced up the stairs. "My wife will not forgive me. It's been close to three years, and she has spoken nary a word to me." He paused and looked at his hands. "I beg you to leave, gentle lads, for I have things to do."

William took Richard by the arm and pulled him away.

"What do you think happened to her?" Richard asked, as they rode back home.

"She's smart," William said. "I'm certain she hid from travelers to avoid trouble, and probably made it to a convent."

"I'm going to look for her," Richard said. "Father has plans for me, and I will need to find her before I get too busy."

To his mother's consternation, William felt he couldn't stay home another two weeks until Christmas. He felt guilty, but his days now belonged to Lord Otto de Grandson.

The months passed slowly as William tried to settle into his new surroundings, a place so immense, Otto had told him, that people at one end of the palace could be complete strangers to those who worked on the other side.

That following spring Otto took Hughes and Dimas with him to Scotland. William was left to fend on his own for a few months.

Mid-morning of an unusually hot summer day, Westminster Palace felt stuffy; people seemed to mill about busy doing nothing, just chattering and staying out of the sun.

William found an enclosure off a landing of the main stairs. It was perfect for a short meditation, out of the way, a small sitting space with two facing stone benches. On the other side of the alcove and framed by sturdy columns, was a large opening looking out into a courtyard with trees and shrubs two stories below. William could escape all the courtiers, clerks and knights at the palace, if only for a moment, a silent and golden moment. He closed his eyes and breathed deeply to calm his mind and shut out his surroundings.

He felt the silence and sweet feeling in his heart as he was being transformed. He sat for what seemed a short time, but then heard the horologe in the main hall chime the fourteenth hour. It was time to get back to work. He opened his eyes and stood up. As he turned he was surprised to find a young redheaded skinny girl of about twelve standing by the entrance, looking at him with curiosity.

"What in God's name were you doing, Templar?" The tone was brash, as someone used to authority. *Probably the daughter of some palace official.*

"I was praying."

"That didn't look like prayer to me. If you were praying why were you not on your knees?" asked the girl as she played with her red tresses that were wrapped in careful crespinettes with gold ribbons.

"My knees get tired from all that kneeling. Besides, my sword gets in the way. I'm certain God does not mind."

The girl came up to examine him closely and William noticed the expensive silk of her red overdress. "Your skin is dark from the sun. Did you just arrive from Outremer? I've never seen you before."

She seemed smart, thought William, but he didn't have time to entertain some spoiled highborn. "Yes, I did," he said as he started to make his way past her.

"Templar! I'm not done with you! You leave when I tell you!"

William stopped. She was staring at him with a fiery look, her mouth set and arms folded. "Fine, my Lady, what do you require of me?"

"Oh, nothing. Now go."

William left hurriedly. He would have to watch his step even with little girls, you never knew who you were talking to, and Otto could not protect him all the time. He never imagined that life at the king's court would be such a tense affair.

William avoided making eye contact with passers by. Some were courtiers waiting to engage anyone in empty conversation or play their silly courtly games; others were officials who would invariably have some urgent matter for him to do, write a letter or deliver a message to someone. They would leave him alone when he told them that he worked for Lord Otto de Grandson, but it was a constant chore, avoiding people, and it was all for naught, just a matter of prestige for them; having a Templar commander at their disposal. Finally William reached his worktable, and resumed reading the tally of supplies used at Sommereaux for the month of May to try and determine the number of soldiers at the French castle.

But he had trouble concentrating, and found himself again thinking of Hafiz Mountain, a bittersweet memory. He realized that it was like thinking of heaven, and at times he had to push the memory out of his mind for fear that he would drop everything and simply start running toward the place. Once King Philip had been stopped and the Brotherhood and the Templars made safe, he could think about it again. At this, William felt the familiar uneasiness about the Caesarius Prophecy, but he decided to dismiss the disquiet. He would follow orders without question; that was his duty.

The following morning before he started work and while staring at the ledgers in front of him, he wondered how Richard was faring on his search for Elizabeth. Perhaps he could go home for Michaelmas. William was about to reach for one of the ledgers when two young girls burst into the room, giggling as they hid behind a cabinet; they were followed by two young men who searched the room, throwing books on the floor. Once they found the girls, the four laughingly cavorted on the thrown documents, ignoring William, who felt as though he was just one more piece of furniture.

William didn't dare say anything, not knowing who they were, obviously highborns. The whole place was like a big party most of the time, people laughing, running, telling jokes, or in corners whispering their inane plots, while clerks tried to do the king's work. Unfortunately, crown prince Edward was their leader; another Farwell as far as William could tell. It was only when the king was about, or Otto was in the room that things quieted down, and the highborns behaved themselves. William wished he could have gone with Otto to Scotland. Anything was better than life in that wretched palace.

However, the drudgery of his work was beginning to pay off and two months later, a week past Michaelmas, William was able to get an idea of the size of French troops at key castles. The French were obviously building up their defenses and getting ready for something. Their navy had many new ships as well, judging by the type of supplies going to major ports. William sat looking at the figures he had compiled and knew the importance of his findings, but he had to wait for Otto. No one else knew what Otto's Templar clerk was up to, not even the king or Lord Walter Langton, the keeper of the wardrobe. From time to time a clerk from the wardrobe would peek in and engage William in trivial conversation all the while glancing at the documents on his table.

One day William was busy with a recently arrived logs of expenses, when the Keeper of the Wardrobe, Lord Langton, walked in. "What type of work are you doing, Templar?" he demanded.

William looked up at the slight man of ruddy complexion whom he had previously only seen from afar.

Otto had prepared William for just such a visit, telling him that the wardrobe was the most powerful department in the realm, and jealousy and suspicion among departments was part of life. William stood up with hands behind his back. "I am preparing for a trip to France with my Lord Otto de Grandson, Sire."

Apparently satisfied, Lord Langton left and William let out a sigh of relief. The last thing Otto wanted was for anything to get back to Bishop Bek, who would surely warn the French. Liaisons at the palace were murky, Otto had warned William, and there was no telling who reported to whom.

His work done, and with Otto, Hughes, and Dimas nowhere in sight, William had to keep the appearance of being busy. The king forbade locked doors, and since William knew inquisitive clerks would come in unannounced, he decided to spread a multitude of documents about to confuse them. He grabbed thick codices as big as small coffers; some dealt with the Italian Lombard bankers, others with the Vatican. For good measure he brought down a huge volume on the Kingdom of Sicily.

Yearning for a familiar face, William made his way to the stables where he found Brother Albert working in silence among the horses. Brother Albert was busy with Dimas' spare horse, scraping a hoof. He sat on a low stool, with the horse's leg on his lap, working away and mumbling a prayer. The horses liked him and seemed to do whatever he demanded of them, even holding still in awkward positions for long periods of time. William watched him for a moment then went over to pet Black who had poked his head over his stall.

"How are things with you, Albert?" William asked as he felt his charger's lips search his hand for a treat.

"Ah, Brother William," Albert said looking up, his angular face wet with perspiration. "Didn't hear you come in, Sire. I'm fine, life here is easy taking care of the horses. I have plenty of time for prayer."

That had been Otto's condition for allowing Albert to come along, that he take care of their eight destriers, which Albert kept in great shape.

"The three other horses will soon be back, tired and in need of care. I want these spares to be in good order for the lord and our two brothers."

William watched Albert's bony hands expertly rounding off the hoof with a file. "Is the work to your liking Albert? What you are doing is groom's work. Should I request other duties for you?"

"No need, Sire. I love horses."

They talked about Westminster Palace and how different it was from Pilgrim Castle. Like most English-born Templar sergeants Albert spoke a mixture of English and French, and it always sounded quaint to William's ears.

Albert gave some short file thrusts. "I never knew another post besides Pilgrim Castle, brother. Seven years I spent there, my whole Templar career until now." Albert let the hoof drop. Dimas' spare horse stayed put swishing its tail, apparently waiting further pampering. "Now that I no longer have to fight," Albert said, "my spirit wants nothing but prayer. I find myself entering a silence that begins at Matins, and it seems that I no longer pray with words, Sire, but my soul enters a blissful state and I want to be very still and not say anything."

William realized that Albert was talking about meditation. "Yes, Albert, I do the same. We call it meditation. In fact, Jesus' teachings were all about meditation, and how we don't need anything else. That's what he meant when he said 'the kingdom of God is within you.'"

Albert looked up at William with a thoughtful look. "I always figured there was much the Church was not telling us. I suppose they would call this what we are saying heresy."

"I'm afraid so. If a Dominican Inquisitor overhead us, we both would be brought before trial."

Albert scooted over with his stool and took up the horse's other hoof. "That's a crying shame. The silence is so beautiful. I suppose, Sire, what you had in that wooden box had something to do with it, eh?"

William didn't respond and continued rubbing Black's nose.

Albert understood the rebuke and began talking about the other sergeants in the king's service and how they kept asking him questions about Outremer. He mentioned Templar House and how busy it was, the constant comings and goings of earls, bishops and merchants depositing and withdrawing money. "I never knew the Templars did so many things besides fighting."

The following morning William sat at his worktable staring at his bogus documents and planning his escape to his meditation spot when he heard someone walk in.

"So this is where you work, Templar." William recognized the redheaded girl. She stood inspecting the room.

"You found me, my Lady." He thought of a quick way to get rid of her without giving offense, but then noticed that she had been crying. Her eyes were red and her manner seemed tense.

"These are Lord Otto de Grandson's work chambers, are they not?" she asked. "Then you must be an important man."

"I do what I'm told, my Lady."

The nosy girl stood in front of William's worktable and seemed to study him with interest. "You are not like the rest—you don't want power. I can tell by just looking at you. What's your name, Templar?"

"William, my Lady."

"Mine is Mary. You are lucky, William, being a man. I wish I were a man, then I would not be offered in marriage to some clod by my father. If I were a man, I would be just like you, a glorious Templar." She went over and inspected his scabbard hanging by the door. "Did you kill many Turks with this sword, William?"

"I did what I had to do, Mary." William studied her expressive eyes, small upturned nose, and firm chin. Even downcast, she gave the impression of a strong will and pent-up energy looking for an outlet.

Mary hoisted herself up on one end of William's table, and sat swinging her feet. She turned her head toward William. "You don't sound proud of killing the enemies of our Lord."

"I did my duty before God."

"Ah, that's better, William. Be proud of what you did." Then she became thoughtful, her piercing blue eyes riveted on William's. "What would you do if you were in my place, William? What if you were in my place and your father was about to marry you off? Would you do your duty?"

William pushed his chair back away from the table and stretched his legs. "I'm not a good one to give advice on that account, Mary, for I disappointed my father. I am the eldest son, but I decided to enter the monastery. After he tried everything, my father realized that my mind was made up, and he finally let me

go. But it was a difficult and painful thing for both of us. At one point he threatened to have me thrown in prison for disobeying him. Had it not been for my
loving mother's intercession, that's where I would be right now."

Mary slid off the table and walked around the room pensive, ran her fingers
along some books, and then left the chamber. William concluded that she was
probably the daughter of an earl, and had just heard of her marriage prospects.
Good luck, he thought. Life was not easy and everyone had their role to play. She
was young, obviously smart and learned, and judging by her attitude, headstrong
and independent, a certain recipe for misery. God help her.

The following morning after reviewing a few letters addressed to the bishop
of Lyon by one of the French king's clerks regarding that city's annexation, William thought it was enough busy-work for the day and decided to go to his new
hideaway behind the elm in the courtyard. On his way out he found the two
young girls and men who had burst into his room. One of the young men looked
him up and down as he approached.

"Oh, the mighty Templar!" The young man of eighteen or so took two steps
to block William's path, and placed his fists on his hips. "I can defeat you, Templar. I am a champion at tournaments. Last spring I defeated two well known
knights at the Canterbury Tournament."

"Good for you Sire. I am certain you are the better knight. I can tell by the
way you carry yourself that you are well practiced with lance and sword." William gazed at the spoiled youth with flabby muscles, the type who never made it
past the first week of Templar training.

"You can tell, eh?" the youngster said as he crossed his arms over his chest.
"Well, today I will prove it." Then, addressing his friends: "Let's take this Templar
to the main ward and see how well he fights."

"I would oblige you, Sire, but I have important business on behalf of Lord
Otto de Grandson."

"Otto is still in Scotland with Bishop Bek. You will come with us, Templar."
With this the young man took him by one arm, and his friend took the other.

William didn't know what to do. It was almost impossible to spar with inex-
perienced men without hurting them or being hurt, but he dared not resist. The
two couples—with much laughter and horseplay—headed down the hallway
with William between them feeling small; a mere toy to be played with.

"Cecil and Andrew, let go of the Templar this very moment!" a firm female
voice said behind them.

They all turned around to find Mary standing by a column, glaring, her arms
crossed on her chest.

"William is my friend, and you will leave him be from now on!" She sounded exasperated, as though talking to small children rather than youths five years her senior.

The two couples reacted immediately, quickly releasing William. "Yes, your Highness," said the young man who had challenged William. "We beg your pardon, your Highness. We did not mean to upset you, please forgive us."

The four youngsters meekly walked away backward, bowing the whole way. William stood looking at Mary. "Are you…"

"Yes, yes. I'm Princess Mary. Now for goodness' sake, act yourself. I need a friend." With this she took his arm and escorted him to the alcove off the main stairs where they had first met.

They sat on opposite stone benches.

"I've thought about what you told me, about becoming a nun, William."

William felt his face go pale. "Your Highness, I never meant to say…"

"You gave me the idea, William. But don't fret, no one will ever know. And call me Mary when we are alone, please."

But William was worried. If the king even remotely suspected that he had suggested she become a nun instead of marrying, he could end up in prison. Outside the alcove he heard a multitude of running steps, probably courtiers playing, and for a moment was afraid that one of them would peek in, but they continued down the stairs.

The animated girl wanted to know what it was like to live in a cloister. William looked at the restless expression on her face so different from the peace of the devout and knew she didn't feel any real calling. She would be just like Jules and his friends, using the monastery to lead a comfortable life and escape the perils of the world, in her case, an unwanted marriage. "But your father won't allow it. He's counting on you for some needed alliance."

"Let that be my concern, William. Tell me what I can expect at the convent. Will I be made to pray from morning till dusk? I mean I've heard the tales…"

He gazed at her shoes. They were of good leather, carefully stitched, but not as fine as those Jacob made for his mother so long ago.

"Look, William. I know what you're thinking, that I don't deserve to be a nun, is that right? That somehow your precious world would be soiled by the likes of me, is that right?"

He detected anger in her voice and looked at her freckled face, now streaked with tears.

"It's not for me to judge, Mary." Her eyes were now even bluer. She began sobbing and instinctively he sat next to her and placed his arm around her shoulders. She nestled her head in his chest, and let go of pent-up emotions.

He felt her pain and her fear, and the trace of long hours worrying about her fate. He began stroking her loose red hair under a toque that barely covered the top of her head, and found his fingers getting tangled in a myriad of wild curls.

At this she laughed softly, still sobbing. "Careful, you may never find your hand again.

"Please help me, William." Her voice was soft and pleading, "I would rather die than be sold like a cow at market. Tell me what to do."

Curious how the girl had taken to him. She hardly knew him, but was relying on him for perhaps the greatest crisis of her life. Of course she couldn't talk to her father about it, and William knew that her mother had passed away the previous year. He sensed that the girl was facing the world alone and somehow had latched onto him in desperation.

"I don't want to marry, I want to be on my own," she whispered. "I swear that I will kill myself. I don't care that it's a sin, I will make it look like an accident so I can be buried in consecrated ground."

William realized that she had thought things thoroughly, and given her temperament, would probably carry out her plans; so after all, the best possible route for her was to join a convent. Why not? If anyone deserved a safe haven, it was this fiery girl. He would loath to see her spirit broken, or even worse, dead at her own hands.

Someone was going up the stairs with slow, measured steps, and William waited until they were gone. "I will help you, Mary." William heard his own words and the conviction behind them, and knew he would.

"There are many a noble who have found refuge in the Church," William told her in a low voice. "It's possible for the well-to-do to lead quite a comfortable life, but you would have to make an endowment first."

"An endowment? My father has promised me a money fief, is that it?"

"Yes. You would turn over some of your income to the convent or abbey, and the mother superior would rely on you for influencing people to gift additional funds."

"I love reading. Would I be able to read?"

William smiled. "Yes, you would be able to do anything you want, as long as you don't interfere with life at the convent. You can even bring along your ladies-in-waiting and your servants, and travel as you wish." William was describing how Jules and his friends lived at his former Cistercian abbey. Although they didn't have their own servants, they did have younger monks waiting on them. He assumed a princess would fare much better.

Mary was calmer now, and she smiled. "Ah, William. That would be heaven. I would read for the rest of my life and not have to worry about men."

"I take it you don't care for men?"

"No, it's not that. I do fancy men. What I detest is the thought that I would be given to a total stranger, who would immediately take me to his bed until he tires of me and then goes off to seduce other women. That's what happened to my sister."

"But it's not what happened to your mother. I understand your father was loyal to her until she died."

"Yes, he was." At this Mary looked down and new tears came to her eyes.

"You could lead a happy life in the right convent," William tried to sound reassuring. "But it's important to make sure you have a secure income after your father dies. A money fief would guarantee it. The wardrobe department would send you periodic amounts for the rest of your life."

It was well known in the court that the king had a soft spot for his daughters—Otto mentioned it several times, so the money fief was certain to be generous. "There are several convents and abbeys nearby that you could enter, Mary. But it's a question of whether your father would let you."

Mary's eyes sparkled with glee. "No problem. I know how to deal with my dear ogre. Your job, my friend, is to find me the right convent. You know what I need." With this, she suddenly stood up, planted a kiss on William's cheek, and ran out of the alcove.

William rubbed his cheek and walked to a place where he could watch her skipping along, slapping columns and an unsuspecting guard's helmet as she went. The horologe in the main hall chimed the eleventh hour, and William thought that was symbolic. The girl would get her way, no doubt, but he also got the premonition—distinct and certain—that she would do something important for him, perhaps even save his life. He felt a distinct pang of danger in his heart, followed by a sense of relief imbued with her essence.

Still thinking about her he made his way to the work chamber and when he approached his table, he saw a sealed document. The back was addressed to Knight Templar William Montfort, in the service of His Majesty King Edward. The parchment had a wax seal with an emblem of some sort. Whoever sent it belonged to a notable family and had access to the royal post, the only way besides the Church and the guilds that letters made their way.

William opened it. It was signed by Sir Maurice Beauchamp, and made reference to Pilgrim Castle. "You will not escape me, William. I know where you are."

He now had Maurice to add to his list of concerns, starting with an angry king who could send him to prison for meddling in his daughter's life. He also worried about Elizabeth's whereabouts. Then there was the Gospel, which he had done nothing about. And of course, the overriding unease about King Philip and what he might do to the Templars…and Otto's honesty. At this last thought, William felt his heart sink. He knew that was something he had kept hidden deep down, something he had dared not think about. But the words had come out. Yes, he was sure Otto was being deceitful and that it had to do with the Caesarius Prophecy.

But surely King Philip was an evil man, and the work he, Hughes, and Dimas were doing with Otto was of the outmost urgency. William reminded himself that whatever he felt, it was not his duty to question. His was to do what he was told.

Otto, Dimas, and Hughes arrived two days later, weary from a long trip and dreary work. They rested for the afternoon, and early the next day William rode along with Dimas and Hughes the short distance from Templar House to Otto's manor, so they could ride with him down the Strand to the palace.

They found Otto waiting for them astride a handsome white Boulonnais. As they rode along the beautifully paved and ample road, shaded by giant oaks, and with fortified manors on either side, William told Otto about Mary.

Otto thought it was a very interesting development, a new resource. "There's a convent not far from here where she'll do well. I know the mother superior." Otto said, his mind seemingly on something else. "But we have more pressing business to attend to."

Once in their workroom, William handed Otto his report on key French castles, which Otto scanned as he talked. "We have to prepare for a Royal Council meeting followed by a Parliament in the early spring, all having to do with Scotland. At the same time we have to keep an eye on the French." At this Otto read a number of the pages William had given him. "This is good, William, very good."

Otto walked over to a map of Europe on the wall facing him. "We also have to attend the Brotherhood meeting to be held over Christmas near Paris. This trip has to be done in secret, and I'm trying to convince King Edward to send us on a mission to Aquitaine…Paris is on the way. There's always work to be done with the barons of the duchy to keep them in line."

All the while Hughes had not said anything, but sat in his chair busy with something, and it occurred to William that it had been quite a long time since they talked, beyond a simple greeting. In fact, he couldn't remember having a meaningful conversation with his former commander since leaving Pilgrim Castle. Dimas was different—William had never been close to his former seneschal, but even he seemed friendlier now than Hughes.

A week later, Mary informed William in passing that she had told her father of her plans to become a nun, and that it had been her grandmother's idea. "The old lady is sometimes forgetful. Yesterday I thanked her for her advice, and she was pleased for something she didn't remember saying. Father is afraid of her, so I'm certain he will eventually agree so as not to antagonize her, but for now he is furious."

William walked away shaking his head. *She would have made a grand monarch, so unlike her brother Edward...a dandy devoted to courtly games.*

[2]

On a cold gray morning four days after Christmas, in the grand salon of a well-appointed palace twelve leagues to the north of Paris, Otto de Grandson surveyed the gathering of the Brotherhood and was satisfied that all who counted were there. The huge room—occupying the entire west side of the large rectangular structure, with the interior wall completely mirrored and the other three exterior ones mostly all windows—had been cleared of furnishings, except for benches, arranged in concentric circles on the wood parquet floor. The host—a prominent French bishop—sat in the center of the front row, chatting amiably with a Spanish noble. By the tall windows, looking out into the frigid garden, Otto saw a cardinal from Rome. Milling about were several bishops of all nationalities, dukes from the Holy Roman Empire, a Florentine prince, Arab sheiks and Jewish scholars from Spain. Most notable was that the entire Templar top leadership was present; the new Grand Master Jacques de Molay, his Visitor Hughes de Piraud, the overseer of the Templar Rule, and all the Masters.

Otto recognized a few people from the year he spent in Toledo when he was twenty-four, an eager student. His teacher had been a Muslim and he had befriended several Jews. It had been such a revelation to speak openly about anything without fear. It was only in the Brotherhood's meetings that he could relive those golden days of freedom.

He saw many familiar faces, and among them, a simply dressed Sir Ian, the elegant Lord Ralph Hengham and several other Britons. William and Sir Ian embraced fondly, and Ralph treated William as a long-lost son. Bishop Gregor, whom William had never met, but who played such a critical role in his life, quietly watched William from a distance.

Everyone assumed that the new Templar Grand Master Brother Jacques would succeed the late Guillaime de Beajeau as head of the brethren, because for the past two hundred years the brothers had taken it for granted that the leader of the Templars was the best qualified to take charge of the Brotherhood as well.

But Otto knew things would be different this time.

The large gathering of the Brotherhood—close to three hundred—chose their seats. Ralph Hengham and Jacques de Molay sat in front of the group.

Otto decided to stand by the mirrored wall to observe the proceedings, but close enough to the front so he could talk when needed. As planned, following the customary chorus of *Beauseant* and introductions, Ralph brought the conversation to the Jesus Gospel.

Ralph—after stealing a glance at his image in the mirrored wall—described at length how William, Hughes, and the Druze Sheik Dun had found John at Hafiz Mountain, and had taken possession of the Gospel. It was a well-known story by now, but most members were anxious to hear the official version. In the telling Otto saw William and Hughes through the group's eyes: two heroic figures who had undertaken hardship and great risk for the Brotherhood. William, who was after all John's nephew and proved to be much like him, was endowed with great spiritual stature and wisdom. Hughes was the clever and bold protector without whom the mission would have been doomed to failure.

Ralph finished his story and the group sat murmuring for a time. Then the Cardinal stood up. "It was the Gospel that brought us to this juncture, we must recall that it was the search for it that prompted the formation of the Templars two centuries ago. I'm just glad that the Caesarius Prophecy provided the impetus that moved us to find this most holy of gospels."

The participants talked for quite a while about what the Prophecy meant, but, "could not fathom how the French king could possibly go about the destruction of the Order," as one of the French bishops put it. "The Templars are so powerful," added a sheik, "can you even imagine their destruction?"

"True, true," mentioned a young Venetian merchant. "But the Holy Land has been lost, no? And right when Caesarius predicted."

The time was right, thought Otto, and he stepped to the front and told them about King Philip and of his plans to become Holy Roman emperor to conquer Europe and the Holy Land. Otto explained the French king's role in Scotland, how it would unfold, his ambitious plans to elect a French pope that would do his bidding, just as his father and uncle had done, and how that would lead to Philip becoming emperor and the destruction of the Templars by orders from the new pope to usurp their money and to neutralize the threat they posed to his ambitions.

Otto observed with satisfaction the grave impact his words had on the members, who talked eagerly among themselves and he heard several mention how unbelievable King Philip's plan sounded.

Otto waited for the excitement to die down. "The real purpose of the Caesarius Prophecy," he said, "without a doubt, is to alert us to the danger the French king poses to the world. You can't imagine how shocked I was when I learned about the Prophecy…it fit the secret information I had collected over the years through my spies so well. It was truly amazing."

"It all makes perfect sense," Pierre de Grez, the powerful French royal clerk said.

The confirmation couldn't have come from a better source, noted Otto.

Pierre de Grez smoothed his red velvet heincellin robe as he stood. He was a dapper man of middle age, very distinguished with his graying hair showing under a flamboyant torus. "A person can tell what Philip is up to next, his next grand move, by the propaganda his people—myself included—put out. It happened when he went after the Italian bankers, the Lombards, and took over their holdings, and when he did the same to the Jews. It happens every time he gets rid of a powerful bishop.

"Now Philip's people are spreading negative talk about the pope, and about the Templars. The Order is being portrayed as greedy, arrogant, and given to heretical and sinful practices. The pope is likewise heretical and evil. Talk in Paris is circulating about Philip becoming *Rex Bellator*—the king in charge of all military orders, what could only be a prelude for him being proclaimed the rightful Holy Roman emperor."

Pierre de Grez stared at his signet ring. He seemed troubled. "There is little doubt the Prophecy is underway, and little doubt that Philip has grand ambitions, and destroying the Templars and taking their money is just a stepping-stone.

"But the power of the Gospel will give us the strength to fight him," de Grez concluded.

"Thank you, Brother Pierre," Otto said. "You know brothers, Philip really hates the Templars; it's not just business, it's personal. In his youth, Philip joined the Templars but could not endure the first week of training. The experience embittered him and since then he has nurtured hatred against the Order."

"But that can't be the only reason he's coming after us," Brother Jacques said.

"No, of course not," replied Otto. "But it certainly infused the French scheme he inherited from his father with a great deal of passion."

That led to the next item for which Otto had prepared carefully with Ralph and Jacques de Molay.

Ralph asked Brother Jacques to address the gathering. When Jacques stood, people started applauding, expecting that Ralph would proceed to ask for a show of hands confirming the veteran Templar as the new Brotherhood grand master.

Jacques stood for a moment surveying the congregation. His long white beard and hair, imposing stature, and the white, knee-length mantle of command gave him the appearance of a warrior god from a heroic tale.

"*Beauseant*, my brothers," he said in his booming voice. "We stand at a cru-cible in our history. The steps that we take in the next few years will shape the future of mankind: whether it slips into dogmatic evil or rises to the all-encom-passing wisdom, love and compassion of the Christ.

"It's up to us, my brothers.

"Evil is crafty. It cloaks itself in the mantle of religion and pretends to stand for Jesus, while destroying everything our beloved Lord stands for. That's what we are facing.

"The challenge requires abilities not found in ordinary men." Brother Jacques ran his gaze across the room. "I'm talking about our new grand master, a person who can lend us his wisdom and supernatural vision to lead us in the next peril-ous years."

Otto detected the disquiet growing in the brethren. A rumble of whispering and nervous shifting of bodies in benches went through the gathering. It was obvious that Brother Jacques was not talking about himself.

"That person is not me. For one thing, I'm too old, am getting tired and set in my ways. Our new grand master needs the unbounded energy and flexibility only found in the young. We need someone who has proven his mettle the old-fashioned way: by rising to a tremendous challenge, something that would have defeated the rest of us. Brothers, I present to you such a man: Brother Knight Templar Commander William Montfort.

"Brother William, please step forward."

Otto could see William's expression of utter shock. After a few moments William got to his feet and slowly approached the open area in the front where Jacques de Molay stood.

"Brother William," de Molay asked, "do you accept the position of grand master of the Brotherhood?"

William's gaze was fixed on the floor. Then the congregation applauded, and the applause grew louder and louder until William was forced to look at the at-tendees, and he scanned the room, resting his eyes on each face as though asking each person in turn. Finally his gaze met Brother Jacques' eyes. The room became silent.

"I can't say no, brother grand master," he said in a hoarse whisper, "I can't disobey you. I would rather die."

Otto joined in the ovation. Things had gone according to plan. Of course William had to accept. After all he was a Templar, and would never dream of declining a request from his superior officer. That part of the plan had been bril-liant, thought Otto with satisfaction as he continued applauding.

William waited for silence to return. "But Sire, I beg of you, let this group decide after observing my actions for some time. All they know so far is that I was part of a team that reached Hafiz Mountain, found my uncle and retrieved the Jesus Gospel. My two companions deserve as much of the credit."

Grand Master Jacques placed a hand on William's shoulder. "Yes, but John chose you as the only one who could find him, because you had what it took to follow in his footsteps, because you led the way to Hafiz Mountain, because it was through your spiritual essence that the three of you survived. We are asking that you take another similar trek, this time taking us all to safety."

The applause became louder and louder as those in attendance stood up, excitement and hope reflected on their smiling faces. Then they slowly left, and only William remained standing with Brother Jacques in the big and now mostly empty room. Otto watched them from afar.

"Are you certain brother grand master that you chose the right man?" William asked as he looked into the older man's wizened face.

"Son, I've seldom been so sure of anything in my life."

The following day was devoted to strategy. William sat in a chair in the middle of the big room flanked by a clerk to his right, and Ralph Hengham to his left. A dozen or so brothers lined up in front of William to make requests for Brotherhood involvement, and the brethren got ready to listen, ask questions, and discuss options. But the final decision was always the grand master's, and this time, Otto could only guess, the brothers wanted to test their new grand master's wisdom.

Participants shivered bundled in blankets. Only the Templars seemed impervious to the cold in their white surcoats.

Jacques de Molay sat in the front row, still and straight, proudly observing William.

The group heard from Muslim brothers in the Sultanate of Granada, the last corner of Spain that remained under Muslim control. They were in danger of being overrun at any time by fanatical Christians dead set on ridding the last vestiges in Spain of the "enemies of Christ." Of course, Granada was also in danger from the fanatical Al Mohad Sultanate of North Africa, focused on ridding Islam of Muslims who appeared tolerant of other religions.

One Arab brother—dressed in fine Parisian clothes—told how life was evolving under the Turks in the Holy Land. "The Knowing" was in danger of being eradicated, along with scientific knowledge. The only haven for open-minded Muslims was Granada.

"We have to preserve Granada, at any cost," Ralph said. "Eventually it will succumb to the fanatics, but as long as it remains, its knowledge will be of tremendous benefit to the world. William, what can we do to protect Granada?"

"Those closest to the problem are sure to have the answers," William answered. Otto watched as William asked questions of Muslims and Christians from all over Spain. He seemed to distill the information into a cohesive answer: the fanatical forces were unstoppable. "Granada will eventually fall, but we can help her survive for another hundred years, long enough to safeguard her knowledge. But we must act now." William then dropped the topic, and asked for other business.

Several French petitioners filed past, all asking protection from Philip's officials who were avidly collecting not only taxes, but requisitioning their property.

During a lull in the proceedings, the Cardinal stood and walked over to the center of the room. "I know that Philip is a great concern. But what about the Jesus Gospel? We have been waiting for two hundred years for it, and now does it just sit in storage? How are you planning to disseminate this most precious of teachings, Brother William?"

"That's a most delicate matter, Brother Massimo, and one that I cannot answer at this moment. What I can tell you is that I am working in the company of very learned men, and with their assistance I will explore whatever avenues open before me. I pray for divine guidance."

The members murmured among themselves. They had wanted to hear a more concrete answer. So far, William had not shown to be particularly wise nor resolute. Otto thought it time to bring out his own project. "Brother William," Otto said as he walked toward the center of the room. "I have a matter of great concern that will benefit us all. It's about the land of my birth."

"The forest canton in the Alps?"

"Yes. I have good news. A few months ago, after long prodding from me and two other worthy brothers, three cantons decided to unite and form a federation."

The group burst into polite applause.

"Thank you," Otto said. "It's most promising. But the cantons need urgent help. As you know, the duke of Austria wants to incorporate the region so he can have access to Italy."

"And you want Templars to help?" interjected William.

"Yes, Brother William. I think if we gain our independence, we could be a place of refuge to the Brotherhood should the need arise."

At this, the brethren enlivened, as Otto knew they would. It was a good, positive prospect. William led the discussion on how to proceed. Some argued for a show of force, "let's awe the Austrians with a sound defeat!" said a priest. "We have the thousands of Templars we could send over. Wouldn't that make Philip shudder?" Several liked the idea, but William shook his head.

"Let us send thirty seasoned Templars to help organize and train an army in your region, Brother Otto. It's best if we remain as low profile as possible, and that locals learn how to defend themselves. Later, we can send more as the need arises."

That was the right answer, firm and decisive. The membership signaled their approval with brief clapping. Otto sighed with relief.

"Brother William, how shall we stop King Philip?" a French bishop asked, and the members fell silent. Otto braced himself. *He better have a good answer.*

"Knowledge is a powerful means to combat fanaticism." William said and then turned to the Cardinal. "Brother Massimo, would you spearhead the effort to make sure the knowledge in Granada reaches the right places?" Then he addressed Ralph. "My Lord, please take the task of keeping Granada alive long enough for our purposes. Brother Hughes," William said to his friend who stood off to one side hidden from view. "Your mission will be to protect the Brotherhood from King Philip.

"Those three steps will help against Philip. But more directly, I will be working closely with Lord Otto de Grandson," he told the congregants, "along with Brothers Dimas and Hughes, to plan operations against Philip." William paused. "I pray you'll be ready to act should I request your assistance."

An ovation rang out.

Brilliant, thought Otto.

The meeting took one more day, mostly for the socializing people required on these occasions. Otto introduced William to the Templar master of Rome, an affable man in his forties with an easy smile, and by the looks of his ample belly, a lover of food. When the Italian left, Otto whispered: "Don't be fooled, William. He's one of the most politically adept men we have. The pope thinks the world of him, as do most cardinals and at least three kings." Next they met a Lombard banker, one of the men whose money the French king had confiscated and who talked about Philip with disgust. "A bloated pretty-boy who wants total power. Say the word, brother grand master, and I'll gather such an army in Italy you won't believe!" Ralph then came over with an Austrian count who was in favor of a Helvetic Federation in the Alps. "Enough with despots, grand master." He then offered to become a spy in the Austrian duke's court. After he left, Otto pulled William by the arm and said, "The count's brother is one of my better spies, and as you can tell, has been able to keep it secret from his closest relatives."

[3]

Early in the spring William accompanied Otto to a meeting of the Royal Council. The select number of men sat around a table in a second-floor salon of Westminster Palace called "The Painted Room," sumptuously decorated with plush furniture and big frescoes. Bishop Anthony Bek—his plump figure decked out in black silk church finery—sat to the right of his king, talking to no one but whispering constantly in Edward's ear. William stood on the sidelines against the wall, taking notes along with the other ten clerks. The proceedings were informal, and the king—dressed casually in tunic and hose—alternatively shouted when frustrated, joked when he heard what pleased him, and turned repeatedly to Bek for approval and counsel.

William had been told by Otto that the main purpose of the meeting was not so much to advise Edward—whose mind seemed to be well made up about Scotland—but to influence the royal counselors to muster support for the crown.

As William listened and took notes, he watched the drama in that room. There was much posturing and positioning for power. Otto was one of the few quiet ones; he answered questions and made remarks when necessary. Observing him, it occurred to William that now their roles were different. Otto was his subordinate. He, William, was now in charge. He was the grand master of the Brotherhood. The Brethren had placed their trust on his shoulders to do what was right. William let out a sigh. He would have to confront Otto and find out the truth about the Caesarius Prophecy. Eventually they would all have to fight the French king and perhaps die in the process. If so, he had to make sure it was for the right cause; the cause they had all embraced.

The royal counselors talked about the upcoming meeting of Parliament to be held in London, and who should attend. The major thrust was to identify the barons who were against performing their feudal duty to Edward in Scotland because they opposed his claim of suzerainty over the Scottish king. The strategy was to neutralize their influence by identifying their enemies and making sure that they attended instead. The king's sheriffs were busy rounding up barons, powerful merchants, and bishops to represent all shires.

Bishop Anthony Bek stated what he expected from Parliament: agree that Edward was in fact overlord of Scotland and had exercised his rights justly in selecting John Balliol as king. Parliament would also be informed of the other two claimants to the Scottish throne, Robert de Bruce and John Hastings—potential rebels—and be made to understand that Edward had every right to enforce his rights, by force if necessary, which opened the door to raising a war tax.

The meeting of Parliament started in late spring in London at Westminster Palace and ended in Canterbury in July, with a loyal earl presiding. Three members of the Royal Council—Otto, Ralph and a bishop—attended as witnesses. The great hall at Westminster was filled to capacity and although people grumbled about the expense and time spent meeting, no one dared not show up. The Scotland case took time to discuss and more time to convince a number of attendees that it was indeed necessary, but eventually there was consensus in support of Edward's plan.

Following the discussion on Scotland, the archbishop of York brought a claim against Bishop Bek on his ecclesiastical authority. The presiding earl influenced Parliament to decide in Bek's favor—alternatively cajoling, and menacing—and imposed a heavy fine on the archbishop for his audacity, leaving a dangling threat of prison. That was a bizarre meddling in Church matters, thought William, but also a mighty statement of Bek's stature.

At Westminster, all departments concentrated on Scotland, the one and only topic on everyone's lips. But William continued gathering information on France, and he came to suspect that Otto's greatest spy was a man called Cantor de Milly, a powerful clerk King Philip had entrusted with his daughter Isabella's welfare, who was now in the enviable position of writing and reading all the correspondence between father and daughter, but most importantly, he had access anywhere in the French court. He was one of those invisible figures everyone trusted and no one questioned. A lot of information in Otto's files bore Cantor's initials as the source.

Otto unwittingly confirmed the man's role as a spy when William reminded him of his promise to find a convent for Princess Mary. "Ah, yes, another one of those beloved princesses who work themselves into such key positions of influence with their fathers," Otto said as he stood and pulled out a note from a cabinet with the name of a convent not far from London and the name of the mother superior. "Tell your princess that it has all been arranged," Otto said as he handed William the parchment. "All she has to do is show up with her ladies-in-waiting and servants. One day, we can probably use your friendship with her."

One day she will save our lives, William wanted to say, because he felt it deep down.

After his conversation with Otto, William was left with a nagging feeling, and realized it had to do with Cantor de Milly. The man had provided Otto with crucial information over the years; nearly everything that Otto knew about King Philip and his ministers had come from him. William resolved to find out what he could about the man. He went to see Brother Guillaime de la More, Templar master of England and preceptor of London Templar House.

Brother Guillaime contacted his counterpart in Paris, asking about Cantor de Milly.

Two weeks later William had the information. It was mostly what he suspected: Cantor had worked directly under King Philip for many years, carrying out his orders faithfully and skillfully. In return he had been rewarded with a comfortable job, looking after Princess Isabella. In all appearances he was a very loyal servant of the crown. But the Brotherhood discovered that Cantor's family had been massacred during the crusade against the Cathars carried out by Philip's father on orders from the pope. Somehow the very young Cantor had been spared and adopted by a family in Gascony.

Sitting in his cell at Templar House late in the evening, William filled in the missing pieces. He felt deep inside that Cantor embellished the French threat when reporting to Otto. The threat was real, but all he had to do was exaggerate a little, and invent a detail or two.

How about the part about Philip wanting to destroy the Templars? That one detail was critical if indeed Cantor planned to pit the Order against his king. That would play into Otto's own dream of achieving independence for his homeland. Perhaps Cantor had spies of his own and knew all about Otto and the Brotherhood; or maybe Otto simply told Cantor all about himself.

William put his concern aside and meditated. When he stood up, he revisited his thoughts about the Caesarius Prophecy, and felt clear about his suspicions. Cantor and Otto had invented the part about the attack on the Templars, and very likely the part where Philip would massacre all Jews and Muslims. If the French Scheme was reduced to nothing more than a struggle for supremacy between the kings of England and France, and preventing Philip from becoming emperor to protect a few forest cantons, then the Brotherhood had no business meddling in.

William decided to confront Otto the following morning. But first he had to confirm his findings, and for that he decided all he had to do was to accuse rather than question and go by Otto's reaction. If his suspicions proved correct, he would have no alternative but to tell him that the Brotherhood would no longer help him and that he, Hughes, and Dimas would leave his employ.

The following morning when William walked into the workroom and saw Otto already hard at work, William found the thought of confronting him daunting. So he sat at his table to wait for the right moment, and then Hughes and Dimas walked in, and it was too late. He had to find him alone.

By the end of the day, when the bells were ringing for Vespers, William approached Otto and asked him to come to his cell that night after Compline.

Otto smiled. "You are summoning me, William?" he asked with a hint of sarcasm.

"I suppose I am Otto. I am summoning you as your grand master."

By the time Otto knocked on his cell door, William had meditated and his heart and mind were calm. He knew what to do. He let Otto in and let him sit on the bunk. William pulled over the one chair to sit facing him.

"Otto, I found out the truth about the Caesarius Prophecy. I know that you fabricated it with information provided by Cantor de Milly. I intend to withdraw the Brotherhood's support."

Otto sprung to his feet. "What William? How…how did you find out?" his expression went from surprise to alarm. "You will no longer work for me?"

"Yes, and I will also have to expel you from the Brotherhood."

Otto's face grew pale. "William! You can't!" He began pacing the room, in slow, measured steps. "Fine. I did fabricate the Caesarius Prophecy. But there was no other way. Had I revealed the French Scheme to the Brotherhood, they wouldn't have believed me! And as Edward's advisor, they would have suspected my motives! It was my only choice! I approached Ian, who was much respected in the Brotherhood, and was one of your uncle's friends. I knew people would trust him. I told him I had discovered the Prophecy and that it confirmed what my spies were telling me, and that I needed him to tell the Brotherhood about it. He immediately understood that without the Gospel the Templars would not fight. It worked, William, it worked! Thanks to the Prophecy, we found the Jesus Gospel, and are presently poised to stop King Philip."

"Frankly, I don't see the harm!"

"Except that Philip has no plans to attack the Templars, does he? Or the part about slaughtering the Muslims and Jews; that's all false, isn't it?"

Otto stood looking at William wide-eyed. "No, no, no. Everything is true, Cantor told me…"

"Did you verify it through your other spies? That's what you taught me when I came to work for you: 'confirm everything!'"

Otto resumed his pacing. "No, there was no one else with the kind of access Cantor had…I assure you…"

As Otto talked about Cantor's and his own motives and honesty, William felt gladness enter his heart, a sudden feeling that seemed to come from nowhere, and it was as though someone was trying to tell him something. William closed his eyes to tune out everything else, and the words formed in his mind: "Everything Otto said was true, but he doesn't know it. It wasn't Otto, or Cantor who came up with the Prophecy…"

And William understood; it all made perfect sense.

Otto was speaking and William paid attention.

"…on our way to Latakia."

William rose to his feet, and then took a deep breath. "Yes, I remember,

Otto. We agreed that we would verify the veracity of the Prophecy by two sign-posts."

"Yes, William. Allow me that. Please! If Philip declares war on Edward the moment the Scots rebel, and if he maneuvers Bishop Bertrand de Got to be elected pope."

William nodded slowly, still trying to decipher what he felt. "Fine Otto, I can do that. I'll wait for those two events. But lying to the Brotherhood, spe-cifically to such good men as Sir Ian and our late Grand Master Guillaime de Beajeu; that is something you will have to atone for. That speaks for your lack of trust. They would have believed you without your lying."

Otto was lost in thought. Then his eyes grew moist. "You are right," he said softly, "and I'm terribly sorry. Please forgive me, grand master."

"You will need to find forgiveness in your own heart."

That summer Mary entered the convent, but was back at court two months later, now wearing a habit. It was clear what her rank had accomplished; normally she would have gone through three years as a novice. But here she was, looking the same, behaving much the same, except that now she was at ease, and it seemed, carefree.

In late fall, William received a letter from Richard in the familiar scribble of the local priest. "I would not trouble you, brother, but I think I have found Elizabeth and I need your help." William had no idea what his brother meant, whether he had located her after searching for more than a year and she needed convincing to return to him, or whether she was now some rich man's indentured servant; but at any rate Richard was asking for help, and William would go. He asked Otto to give him leave. To his surprise, Hughes asked to come along.

Otto told him to wait over the winter and see if King Edward had anything major planned for the spring. If there was nothing in the offing, William and Hughes could go.

That would be the first time since Pilgrim Castle that William would have Hughes' company for a significant period, and he hoped that the journey would be their chance to renew their friendship.

In the intervening months, William meditated, and tried to encourage Hughes, Dimas, and Otto to do the same, but they seemed to always have some reason why they couldn't.

Nothing of consequence happened at court, and in the spring, a week past Easter Sunday, William and Hughes left to help Richard find Elizabeth. The weather was perfect, sunny and cool. Invariably travelers gave the two Templars the right-of-way in deference to their surcoats with the red cross on their chests, and inn-keepers provided them with the food and shelter reserved for bishops. Knights examined their weapons as they went by, as though trying to extract their fighting secrets.

They rode along for the first day hardly exchanging a word. On the second day, after they had watered their horses at midmorning from a farmer's pond, Hughes seemed to hesitate before mounting. "William, if you are concerned about disseminating the Jesus Gospel, and what the Church might do, I would gladly do it for you. Once our fight with Philip is over with, I wouldn't know what to do with myself anyway, so what better task than having me spread copies of the Gospel far and wide. I just think that if the Dominicans burn me at the stake for it, it would be a most worthy way to end my life."

So that's what he had in mind. "Very well, my friend, after we defeat Philip, we'll talk about it again."

William climbed on Black and started for the road. "Hughes, I've noticed we don't talk like we used to. It seems as though you have tried to avoid me."

"Well, we are talking now," Hughes said now riding beside him.

"You appear troubled, as though carrying a burden."

Hughes' expression took on a renewed coldness. "If I knew we would be discussing me I would not have come."

They came across an open gate in the stone fence bordering the road and went through it. "Hughes, please, tell me what's ailing you."

Hughes shook his head in frustration. "William, do you recall when I was asked to sail to Acre and rescue Otto?"

"Yes. Few could have done it."

Hughes gazed ahead, absentmindedly taking stock of two riders coming their way. "I'm not asking for praise, William. Do you then recall when at the Lake of Galilee, I was ordered by Dimas to take on a Mameluk position and find out from them what they were doing so far away from their army?"

William felt uneasy. "Yes, Hughes. You came back with valuable information that allowed us to proceed."

"And on both of those instances I had to do unspeakable things that would turn your heart in disgust. It certainly disgusted me, but it had to be done."

"If I could have taken your place either time, I would have."

"That's not what I wanted. I know I was the best qualified. We all have our jobs, I guess, but I think mine is destroying me."

"What we are given in life is meant to make us grow, Hughes. Try and find the lesson in it, and you will find the conditions changing."

"How do I do that?"

"Through meditation."

Hughes spurred his horse and rode in silence. William followed. After some time Hughes turned to look at William. "Thank you."

At midday William decided to stop for dinner.

They found an abbey not far from the road.

They sat facing each other at the long refectory table, with the other diners a respectful distance away. The Franciscan monks had brought them roasted duck with parsley and leeks.

"William, do you trust our lord?" Hughes asked.

"Otto? Why, yes, he's a brother." William said in between bites, as his gaze took in the other travelers, four wealthy merchants who seemed engrossed in their own conversation.

"I think he's probably using us."

"Oh, of course he is. It's his job. He believes in his cause, stopping King Philip, and he is using us for that end."

Hughes wiped his greasy hands on his now empty trencher. "And that doesn't trouble you?"

"No, why should it? I wish for the same. In fact, that's your mission, Hughes, to protect the Brotherhood. He's doing your work."

Hughes dropped the trencher on the reeds on the floor and watched as a dog came to eat the greasy bread. "Yes, that's true. Still I'm not entirely comfortable with Otto's ways. He's always scheming."

"If there's anything I've learned, brother," William said, "it's that when we set events in motion for a higher purpose, players will come along to do their part. Some will be aware of their role, others not. Maybe that's the case with Otto."

"I believe he's placing King Edward above the Brotherhood."

"Then at some point we must part company. But also recognize that thanks to him we are in a position to watch events unfold. Otherwise we would be cloistered somewhere or working away in some Templar farm, not aware of what's happening."

Richard, a visibly aged Sir Lawrence, and Lady Claire, looking much the same, greeted William and Hughes in the great hall.

Hughes undid his hood and looked at the long table and cupboards, at the garden outside the window with Lady Claire's flowers. "This reminds me of my home."

"And where is home, Hughes?" Lady Claire asked.

"In the north of Scotland, my Lady. A place called Elgin."

Richard took the two out for a stroll in the grounds around the house and told William and Hughes about Clancy, a knight who had been a good friend of Richard's since childhood. "He's now serving Farwell, although Clancy doesn't much care for him and is still loyal to his father Orland. According to Clancy, Farwell found Elizabeth, and has vowed to kill her because she's spreading vicious lies about him."

They walked into the apple orchard and William inspected the new leaves, fresh and bright. "Did Clancy say where Elizabeth is?"

"No, only that Farwell had located her and is planning on silencing her, and others who are with her."

"How can Elizabeth be spreading vicious lies about him? Who is she talking to?" mused William.

They discussed what to do as they strolled among the trees. They could follow Farwell, but once he went after her, it might be too late to save her. The best thing would be to find Elizabeth before Farwell had a chance to harm her.

"What other information did Clancy give you? Hughes asked.

"That she might be attached to a weaver's guild. That much he overhead from some of Farwell's friends. Also, that a man who came to the castle to tell Farwell of Elizabeth's whereabouts wore a weaver's tunic."

"If she's attached to a weaver's guild, she should be easy to spot. After all, there are not many working ladies about," William said.

"I did ask around," Richard said, "but the weavers I talked to were suspicious and wouldn't talk to me. It seems they are protecting her."

Hughes studied Richard. "If they are protecting her, they won't talk to any of us, because we are gentry."

"Of course," William said. "Elizabeth probably won some allies within the working class, and convinced them to keep her hidden." The guild people had a natural animosity toward the gentry, although they were considered above most peasants and close to the merchant class. It was not the first time someone from the gentry had sought refuge there, the working class had absorbed many an impoverished knight's family. Even rich peasants had been known to marry a distressed knight's daughter. It was a love-hate relationship, their lot made better by someone joining them from higher up. Elizabeth could well be married by now, William realized, but hesitated to say it aloud.

"Richard, what news do you have on Farwell?" William asked.

Richard led them out of the orchard. "Clancy said that Farwell has virtually taken over his father's possessions, that Orland is his son's prisoner. Talk is that Farwell found the means to slowly poison him and that's why Orland is looking sickly. But so far Farwell has not meddled in the earldom's affairs. However, if what people say is true, Orland won't live much longer and Farwell will soon become earl, and everyone frets what that would mean. I heard that during past tournaments Farwell set up a band of thugs to attack winning knights during melees to intimidate them, and then Farwell or one of his friends would challenge them and win easily. It's gotten to the point people refuse to attend, and no tournament was held last year," Richard said, and he spat on the ground.

"What does father have to say about it all?"

"Father, along with other powerful knights has not been touched," Richard said walking toward a pond. "I guess Farwell does not dare antagonize them. But they all know it's a matter of time, and they are thinking of banding together once Orland dies. They hope they can keep Farwell at bay, but he is gathering an impressive gang around him. I guess I'll have to face him some day."

William nodded. "You won't have to do it alone, Richard."

The following morning, William, Richard, and Hughes rode to the village to talk to a local weaver, but beyond the obligatory salutation and bowing, the man ignored them and continued repairing a spinning wheel. When pressed by Richard, the weaver claimed not to know anything about Elizabeth.

Richard led them to the village tavern, a hut with bare-dirt floors covered with reeds, where they found a group of masons drinking ale and playing dice. Both Richard and William knew two of the men; they had worked on their father's house doing repairs, and had built a nearby bridge in his lands.

William decided on a direct approach and walked up to the men. The masons stood up and bowed to William. They seemed friendly.

"We are trying to find Mistress Elizabeth, Sir Leonard's oldest daughter," William said. "She left about three years ago and her family has not seen nor heard from her since. We have heard that she might be with a group of weavers. Can you men help us find her?" William looked in their eyes earnestly.

"We know the lady you speak about," said the older of the masons. "But we don't know her whereabouts, only that she disappeared."

"Yes," said a man in his twenties with blond hair. "But we know a weaver fellow," he said, turning to the older man. "You know, Edgar Weaver of Salisbury who lives out by the creek. Maybe he can point you gentle sirs in the right direction," he concluded. The other masons nodded their heads.

The two masons who had volunteered, the young blond man and the older one took one last sip of ale, bid goodbye and escorted the three gentry to Edgar's place; four huts with a stone fence around it and a dozen sheep grazing about.

Beyond standing up and paying his respects to the gentry, Edgar seemed reticent when the young mason asked him about Elizabeth. He sat back down and resumed working a spool of recently spun wool.

Hughes became suddenly quite animated. "You know of a Templar sergeant from Salisbury named Simon?" he asked the weaver who kept picking dirt from the wool.

Edgar seemed to be thinking.

"Well, the fellow saved my life," continued Hughes. "I just wish I could find his kin to tell them about him. We fought together in Outremer for seven years. One day we got caught in the tail end of a fierce battle against the Turks and were surrounded."

William noticed that Edgar had stopped working and was paying close attention.

"Sergeant Simon of Salisbury insisted on staying behind with two Turcopoles to provide cover as I retreated with four other knights, three sergeants and two squires." Hughes sighed and shook his head sadly. "I never saw him again."

"We were all just Templars on the battlefield." Hughes concluded in a hoarse voice, apparently overcome with emotion. "Simon was like a brother to me."

The weaver was obviously moved. "I knew one fellow you might be talking about. He went to the Templars when he was but a small lad." Edgar talked at length about the man's family and who they were.

Hughes thanked Edgar with moist eyes, then reached under his surcoat and produced a small medallion. "Kindly give them this, please. It belonged to Sergeant Simon. I've carried it for the past five years hoping to hand it over to his family. I meant to make it to Salisbury, but haven't had a chance. I'm just lucky we ran into you."

Edgar took the gold image about the size of a schilling and looked at it.

Hughes turned to leave when Edgar grabbed him by the sleeve. "You know, Sire, now that I think about it, I may be able to help you find the Mistress Elizabeth.

"She's joined a roving group of actors, who're also weavers," Edgar told them, pocketing the gold medallion. "I don't recall their names, although I did meet them once. The summer of three years ago they camped in the meadow not far from her house, and gave some performances. John Weaver from across the creek told me that Mistress Elizabeth came everyday, and became their friend. I figured that when she ran from home, she must have walked to the meadow and was taken in by the actors.

"Last year, when I went to a guild meeting, I heard about her next. Word within our brothers is that she is writing plays for the actors, and she's good. Problem is, she wrote one about the earl's son, Sir Farwell; how he took her by force, and how he's fixed tournaments so he and his friends always win, and that he stole nuns for his pleasure.

"The play is well liked," Edgar told them, "but word has gotten to Sir Farwell, and he's very angry. Grooms from the castle heard him rant and rave. They told Andrew Weaver who has a place near the castle, so that word would reach Elizabeth, but we don't know whether she's aware."

Edgar thought that Elizabeth's troupe would probably perform in Dunbury during the fair around the Feast of St. George, because that was one of the better-attended fairs of the entire region.

Richard thanked Edgar and the masons, and provided them with a coin each so they could drink an ale to Sergeant Simon of Salisbury's memory.

When they were back on their horses William turned to Hughes. "We are lucky indeed that you knew that sergeant, Hughes."

Richard seemed ecstatic. "I don't know how to thank you, commander."

Hughes chuckled. "I have used that story about three times over the years; it's never failed me. And I always carry at least one spare medallion of the Virgin with me."

St. George's day was almost a month away, and they decided to spend the time helping Richard with his work. If they were to run into Farwell in the process, they would decide how to deal with him.

For the next few days Richard took on the most pressing jobs. William found out that their father was only marginally involved, and when Richard didn't work, things didn't get done. Hughes seemed to enjoy learning all about the apple cider business, raw wool, and timber processing. Merchants, guildsmen, and peasants of the fief appeared amused by the nosy Templar who asked so many questions. After a few days they were emboldened to ask him questions of their own, and he entertained them with tales of furious battles, exotic Saracen maidens, and the many wondrous things he had seen in Outremer. "There are cities so rich, even the servants have servants," he told them. "Not only does everyone have enough to eat, they have delicacies that play with your senses, and feed not just your stomach, but your mouth, and your mind. Once you taste them, you never forget them." He told them how easy and comfortable life was for the average Arab. "Beautiful houses of smooth, colorful stone floors, water running from pipes everywhere, lush gardens in the middle of homes, with ripe, strange fruit ready for the taking." His rapt audience listened how their doctors could cure anything, and everyone could read and write and were taught so many wondrous things. "Many a Christian captive, after seeing all that, and being treated so well, has refused to leave."

That was a part of Hughes William had not seen before. He was a storyteller, a good one, and he used his stories to bond with his listeners. Merchants, guildsmen, and peasants alike greeted him warmly, and children ran up to gawk at him in wonder.

A week before Saint George's Day, the three got ready to travel to Dun-bury's Fair. They decided to go dressed as merchants. "We can pull it off," Hughes said, " if we carry only our swords and dress plainly. People may spot our big horses, but assume we are wealthy merchants with knightly aspirations."

Three days before the fair was to start, they rode toward Dunbury, and spoke in English rather than the gentry's French, doing their best to roughen up their speech and use the slang they had learned from their sergeants. Richard, who had spent a fair amount of time at the tavern, could speak low English well, but for Hughes and William it took some practice. William had dug around his clothes at home and had come up with two tunics and hose for both himself and Hughes. They wore Richard's hats, bourrelets tipped to one side, the type that successful merchants liked to wear.

After two leagues they caught up with a traveling troupe of actors; three men and two women in a covered wagon pulled by two mules. The man driving told William that they were on their way to Dunbury to perform at the fair.

They chatted amiably with the troupe, and William noted how relatively easy they were taken in without their knightly apparel. The troupe was headed by Anthony, an energetic and jovial man, who invited the three merchants to dinner.

The actors were members of the weaver's guild, which was a common ar-rangement. They could make good income performing during the summer, but in the off-season they had to earn a living by making cloth.

"Do you know of a play we heard so much about," William said casually, "it's about an earl's son who steals nuns for pleasure?"

"Yes, I've heard of such a play," Anthony said.

"And the earl's son took a fair young lady by force."

"Yes, that's the one. You have to ask for old Sidney's group. That play is all the talk at the fairs, how clever it is."

When the troupe stopped to rest for dinner, one of the men pulled out a bow and arrow, set up a target some twenty yards away, and started shooting with incredible precision. William looked at Hughes, and knew what he was thinking. The man could shoot as well or better than the best of the Saracen. It turned out that it was part of his act and it brought him good money.

William, along with his brother and Hughes settled at an inn in town, but made their way back to the actors' wagon to help them set up for the fair, to be held in a pasture right outside of town. Afterward, William and Anthony ambled around the fair grounds, while Hughes and Richard stayed behind. Wil-liam watched how Anthony made small talk with the people he knew, which were many. They were setting up stalls to sell everything under the sun—clothing, shoes, gloves, knives, tools, glassware, wine, toys and trinkets, earthenware, tinworks, foods of all sorts and treats; interspersed with game stalls with darts, dice, and horse shoes. Then there were the games William knew were there but wanted to ignore, those involving the killing of animals with clubs, arrows, rocks, and head-butting; of which there were many judging by the hundreds of dogs, cats, and pigs in cages. There were also dogfights, cockfights, bears against dogs, wolves against dogs, dogs against foxes…all the savage idiocy people had enjoyed from the beginning of time.

The sound of many voices and hammering was everywhere and the air carried the smell of cooking. William ambled through the theater groups busy rehearsing, and caught the usual religious themes interspersed with the violent and sadistic themes that were in such demand.

William asked Anthony to see if he could spot old Sidney's troupe, and Anthony guided him to a group in a corner of the grounds. The skits were all satire of the upper classes, and a crowd stood by laughing. William watched an impersonation of a drunken earl, a lecherous bishop, and ladies who cheated on their foolish husbands.

In all of the plays, the hero was a good-natured workingman who got the best of the gentry through his cunning. The interesting thing was, how accurately the troupe mimicked the gentry's speech and mannerisms.

In one performance, a perverted young nobleman went around stealing nuns for fun. He was a pathetic cowardly knight who dressed as a dandy and only won tournaments by cheating. Likewise, his only love conquests were by force. Besides the nuns, he also raped a fair young lady who was then rescued by a handsome merchant from a life of misery. The story made William wince, it was too close to Elizabeth's own, and he was sure that was the play Edgar Weaver had told them about.

In between rehearsals William approached one of the actors—a man dressed as an earl, with an imitation hauppelande "Do you fellows know Old Sidney?" the fake earl stole a glance to one of the other actors and didn't say anything. When William tried to approach a man dressed as a knight, he scurried away into their wagon. Anthony too seemed to grow uneasy, said he had work to do, and hurried off.

William decided to stay in the make-do theater, consisting of an enclosure of cloth hung from strings and benches made with planks facing a stage and the actors' wagon to one side. Hiding as best he could in the crowd, William made it a point to watch that particular troupe rehearse all their skits that following day, and when they came to the one about the fair lady, he was sure that it had to do with Elizabeth. However, he hesitated to tell Richard, for fear that his brother would charge around tearing through the place trying to find her. It was very likely that she was married, and there was no telling how Richard would deal with that.

William went looking for Hughes and found him helping an actor set up a set, hammer in hand, nails sticking out of his mouth.

William took him aside and told him what he had found.

"We'll just have to watch the troupe's performances this coming week," Hughes said. "And maybe we'll spot Elizabeth. If we do, and if she's married, we'll talk her into hiding from Farwell and leave her be, and not tell Richard until we get back to your father's home."

"I agree. Where is he?"

"Well, fortunately for us," Hughes said, "Richard is hard at work trying to find Elizabeth by walking around the fair. He said that it was best if we split up." With this Hughes went back to work, deftly sinking a nail with two blows.

William and Hughes watched the performances the first day of the fair, from morning through the night, all ten of them, and came to realize that the life of an actor was not an easy one. The skit about Farwell was indeed one of the most popular, and people booed the evil nobleman, and cheered when the stalwart but poor merchant rescued the distressed lady, not caring that she had been raped for he loved her.

That evening William saw Elizabeth. He recognized her at once, even though she wore a hooded cape. She stood out just by her height. Most gentry were taller than the common folks for they grew up eating better. It was also the way she walked, clearly a lady.

She went behind a curtained enclosure where the actors changed costumes, and William stood casually near the rear. He heard her read lines to the actors. Apparently they were illiterate and had to memorize the words as she read them. It was her voice. William debated whether to approach her, but then thought how guarded the actors had been. They were all obviously scared of tall strangers who might be knights. What if she didn't recognize him, and took him for one of Farwell's men? When William heard her say that she was about to leave, he quickly dashed off into the crowd.

The following morning William sat down with Hughes on a rear bench, searching the crowd for Elizabeth. Instead, William spotted four knights not far from where he was sitting. One of them was Farwell.

As the week wore on, William watched as Farwell and his friends darted in and out of the theatre, clearly keeping an eye on the actors. On the last day of the fair, Farwell and his friends changed clothes.

That following morning, William sat with Richard eating breakfast at the inn where they were staying. This was a good time to tell Richard about Elizabeth, now that the fairgrounds were mostly empty; but he had to wait for Hughes to show up in case he needed help restraining his brother.

When Hughes finally sat beside his brother, William leaned forward. "Richard, Hughes and I found Elizabeth."

Richard dropped the chicken leg he was about to eat. "What? Where?"

William told his brother all he had learned about her and the troupe. He also told him that Farwell was planning on killing Elizabeth and the actors. Richard stood up in a hurry, but Hughes got a firm grip on his arm and sat him back down.

Richard looked at Hughes quizzically. "We'll just take Elizabeth and be gone. We can easily fend off Farwell and his gang if they come after us." He then tried to pull his arm away from Hughes and seemed surprised that he couldn't.

"No," Hughes told him, tightening his grip and making Richard wince. "That would save Elizabeth, but not the actors. I'm certain Farwell plans to attack the troupe somewhere on the road. The clothes he and his friends bought are too rough for merchants. They want to look like highwaymen, in case someone witnesses the attack."

Richard relaxed. "You are right; I was thinking only of Elizabeth."

Hughes' plan was to follow the troupe a short distance behind, and no matter if the actors spotted them, they would simply be more alert. However, when Farwell and his men attacked, the three of them would have to act fast to avoid any of the actors getting killed. Warning the troupe would not work; they were too suspicious of gentry-looking people. Contacting Elizabeth was risky, for there was no telling how she would react, or her possible husband. It would be best to follow the wagon as close as possible and avoid being spotted by Farwell and his men.

"I kept an eye on the troupe through the night, and watched them leave a while ago," Hughes said. "We best hurry and follow them."

They caught up with the actor's slow-moving heavy wagon while still within sight of the town and stayed a short distance behind. Hughes walked beside his horse, and William and Richard rode by his side; three merchants apparently nursing a sick horse.

They walked for a good part of the morning past several places where bandits might hide, but nothing happened.

Shortly after noon, the troupe reached a thickly wooded area, where the road dipped and then went up a steep incline. William got a feeling that this was it; he could feel Farwell's presence. "Hughes, I think Farwell may be lying in wait here."

Hughes looked at the woods, at the approaching hill, and mounted.

The wagon made it out of the dip and was climbing up the hill, the old horse pulling hard, when the actors decided to climb out and push. William assumed that Elizabeth was the one driving, because all the men were pushing in back.

Four hooded men on horseback emerged from the trees, yelling and swinging swords. At the sight of the bandits, the actors let go of the wagon and started climbing back in. The wagon began sliding back down the hill with some of the actors clinging to the sides.

"Left Richard, right William!" Hughes ordered.

William drew his sword and spurred Black toward the rider on the right of the wagon, who turned to face him. The man raised his sword to block what he thought would be William's downward swing to his head, but instead, William slashed his arm, causing a deep and disabling wound. The man's sword dropped to the ground and he turned his horse and ran.

William turned to see two men attack Richard: Farwell, who faced him with sword in hand, while another attacked him from the right. Richard leaned his torso over his horse's neck avoiding a wild slash from the attacker on his right, then swung his sword in a wide arc that cut Farwell's stomach and went on to puncture the other man's leg.

William rushed to help his brother, but both Farwell and his friend sped off.

Hughes had gone over to look after the wagon, now standing still at the bottom of the hill.

"Where's the fourth man, Hughes?" William yelled.

"All four have escaped, William. The man Richard wounded in the stomach is as good as dead, the other three will live," Hughes said as he inspected the old horse and the wagon. The actors stood gaping at their defenders while Elizabeth sat with reins in hand studying Richard.

Richard dismounted, and walked over to Elizabeth, who appeared stunned and pale. "Elizabeth, it's me, Richard. I've come for you."

It took some time for Elizabeth to respond, and when she finally spoke she could only say, "Thank you," in a trembling voice.

But Elizabeth didn't want to come. Richard sat next to her in the wagon for quite a time talking. William overhead him telling her how much he missed her, and how he thought about her all those years. The actors stood a discreet distance away, while Hughes attended to the old horse.

"I've never taken up with a man," William heard Elizabeth tell Richard, "and have not thought of marrying. The actors are now my people, and I want to remain with them."

"But Elizabeth, I love you!" Richard blurted out.

Elizabeth cried for some time. "Ah, Richard. I so dreamed of you saying that. But it's too late, my Richard. I love you too, dearly, with all my heart; but I realize that we don't have a future together. I belong with these actors who have accepted me as their own, and I write for them, and I'm good at that, and it helps them. If we marry, in due time what Farwell did to me will come to haunt you, and you will despise me. Why embark on such a painful path? Find someone who's unsoiled. Many a lady would be honored to be your wife."

That afternoon after saying goodbye to the actors and Elizabeth, the three rode back together toward William's family's home. A dejected Richard rode in silence.

"What would you counsel me, William?" Richard asked after some time. "I can't think of my life without her," he said, his gaze lost on the road ahead.

William thought for a moment. It was such a tragedy for those two to be apart; they clearly belonged together, he could feel it deep inside. "If you want her, you have a lot of work ahead of you. But I think you can win her, because you love her dearly, and because she feels the same for you."

Richard's face brightened. "What should I do?"

"Woo her. Convince her that nothing will stand between you two."

Richard seemed to ponder and then he smiled, his mood lifting as if by magic. "I will, by God, I will!" and with this he turned his horse around and went after the actors' wagon, his charger's hooves kicking up dust in a furious gallop.

William watched him go. "I meant woo her over time, patiently...but never mind," he said to himself as Hughes shook his head.

"What now, William?" Hughes asked. "Our work is done. Shall we head back to London?"

"No, not yet. The man Richard wounded was Farwell, and I care for his father. I want to go to Sheffield Castle and do what's required."

Hughes studied the blood on the ground. "With a stomach wound like that Farwell has at most two days left to live."

William sighed as he examined the trail of dark blood. "I will talk to the earl. It's my duty, Hughes. Face the father and tell him I killed his son instead of Richard. There's no telling how the earl will react at losing his only heir. Besides it being a justified killing, I am protected by Otto."

They arrived at Sheffield Castle the following day. William had taken his time to allow Farwell to be seen by a doctor and for Orland to absorb the new developments.

William led Hughes up the stairs of the now somber castle to Farwell's chambers and found the earl of Sheffield sitting on one of the spare beds watching in silence the scene in front of him: the bloodied and bandaged Farwell moaning in his bed, his mother the Countess Lorena kneeling by her son, praying and crying, a doctor going about his business, and a priest standing by, also praying, supposedly after having administered the last rites.

William crouched down next to Orland. "I am sorry, my Lord," he said in a whisper. "I didn't mean to hurt Farwell, but he was dressed as a bandit and he attacked a group of unarmed actors, and I had to defend them. Elizabeth, Sir Leonard's daughter, was among them."

The earl turned to look at William with gentle eyes. He opened his mouth as though it pained him to do so. "That son of mine was a bad seed, an evil man," he said and he paused for a time, as though confused. "You did me a great service," the earl continued, his voice gathering certainty, "and I am glad to be rid of him, for my sake and my people's."

Orland observed William a while. "I always wished you were my son. William...take Farwell's place."

"I will do as you wish, my Lord. What is it that you require of me?"

"I will name you my heir. Mind this place, and take care of my wife and me until we die. I am no longer well; not in my mind, nor my heart."

William looked at the frail man, and at Farwell, groaning and glaring at his father with hatred. "As you wish, my Lord." William didn't know what his words meant exactly; he only wanted to fill a void he felt in the earl's heart. He then kissed him on both cheeks. The earl embraced him in return.

Later that afternoon, William rode with Hughes back to his family's house to bid goodbye to his parents. "What are you planning on doing with your new possessions?" asked Hughes.

"I can't become the earl, you know that, Hughes. I'm not related to Orland, but I didn't want to contradict him. For now I will go along and see what happens. I will ask Richard to move into the castle and be my surrogate. I'm certain we will hear from Orland's kin, and I will face them when the time comes. Orland has aged well beyond his years, but with Farwell gone and someone taking care of things for him, I'm certain he'll recover some of his health. Maybe Farwell was poisoning him, after all."

"What do you hope to achieve?"

"I want to make sure the people of Sheffield have a just and honorable earl to rule over them."

"Are you sure Richard will not stray?"

"Left to his own devices he might. But with me watching, he'll do what's right."

CHAPTER X

[1]

William returned to London with Hughes and found that little had changed, except that another hate-filled letter from Maurice was waiting for him on his worktable. Otto and Dimas, who had been conferring about something, stopped to watch his reaction. William read the folded parchment and then tossed it on the floor.

Hughes bent down and picked up the letter. "That won't solve the problem. Why don't we deal with him, rather than fretting about what he might do?"

"Hughes is right," Dimas said.

"We know Maurice has means," Otto said, "because his letters can reach us. His family must be powerful."

"He knows where I am, let him come," William said, and he buried himself in a new report.

He put Maurice out of his mind; but King Philip was a constant topic of fervent conversation at the work chamber, to the point that William could feel the evil monarch's presence everywhere, everyday, in that room. Life would try and engage him through fear. He decided to meditate for an entire day to keep balanced. *I'm no longer a monk if I allow the world to overtake me.*

A few days later as he sat in the workroom with Otto and the others, King Edward walked in. This was the first time William had seen him up close. He was a tall and powerfully built man, with an imperial air about him, a booming voice and crass manners: after clearing his throat he spat on the floor, and thought nothing of scratching his crotch as he talked. "The French want to discuss Aquitaine," Edward told Otto. "I just got a threatening letter from that pretty-boy Philip. He says he is willing to go to war if we fail to agree. I want my brother Edmund to head the negotiations. You brief and assist him, Otto."

"But your Majesty," Otto said, "your brother is not an experienced diplomat, and this matter is much too delicate…"

Edward shot Otto a furious glance. "From now on you and your Templar clerks will work for Edmund!"

After Edward left, they stood looking at each other.

"That's it," Dimas said. "That's Philip's first move toward war against Edward."

"I'm afraid so," replied Otto. "Let's see what happens."

Hughes seemed to be enjoying himself. "At least we are getting ready. But I wager Edward won't see it coming until it's too late."

Otto studied Hughes. "You are right, Hughes, but that's the whole point, the reason we are working in secret, isn't it?""

"The situation in Scotland is still peaceful," William said, " so why is Philip being aggressive now?

"Perhaps he's growing impatient," ventured Otto, "decided he couldn't wait for Scotland to rebel and wants to implement the French Scheme another way."

Over the following six months, Otto, along with William, Hughes, and Dimas accompanied Edmund to Paris as he met three times with King Philip's Prime Minister, Pierre Flote, and the royal counselors Engerrand de Marigny and Guillaime de Nogaret.

Edmund stayed at the palace, and Otto and his Templars at the imposing Paris Templar House. William had a chance to look over the most important city in Europe, and certainly the most modern. University students from all over Europe crowded the left bank of the Seine to attend the preeminent university, and were famous, as their counterparts in Oxford, for violent rioting after heated polemics, in the course of which they were known to attack each other with fists, clubs, and swords. In the center of the city was the island, the *Isle de la Cite*, the oldest section, with the royal palace and the newly built—a bit over a hundred years old—Cathedral of Notre Dame. The right bank was the domain of the merchants and the guilds. Shops dominated the area. Giant signs, same as in London, illustrated wares: a glove, a shoe, or a tooth for a tooth puller. And just like London and every major city and town in France, Britain, Germany, and Flanders, the Provost of Merchants—as powerful as any baron—ruled Paris. The city was starting to use plumbing thanks to the university scholars who had deciphered the Romans' engineering books found in Spain in the past two decades. New fountains were being built as well as public baths, many baths, and town criers stood in street corners trying to induce passersby to use them. William realized how much he missed daily bathing, back when he was a noble Druze. But what caught his attention were the many books, fine, sturdy codices for sale; produced using a writing material made from old rags rather than parchment and vellum, which made the books cheap and easy to make. Because of the many documents being translated from Arabic in the past few years, the monks who did the copying had been overwhelmed and Paris now had guilds dedicated to copying. Books were ridiculously inexpensive, and almost anyone could now afford them. All the titles that Otto had talked about were available; works by Ramon Lull, the celebrated philosopher and alchemist, the Dominicans Albertus Magnus, and the famous Roger Bacon, the new Aristotelian philosopher. William bought one by the adventurer Marco Polo, which had just come out.

Prince Edmund and his entourage met with the French ministers at the fortress of the Louvre, an imposing block of a building surrounded by a moat and a thick wall. On one occasion while they negotiated, Philip made a grand entrance, with footmen and a coterie of attendants who preceded and followed him, pulling a chair, pouring water, smoothing his clothes, gently fanning him. The French king appeared a quiet man, with fine features: a thin and perfect nose, gently curved eyebrows, blond wavy hair, and blue eyes. Had he lost some weight, he would be handsome, but his face looked bloated and he had the appearance of a petulant chubby boy.

There was something disquieting about Flote, Marigny, and Nogaret. They treated their king with deference, but didn't consult him. It was as though they knew well in advance what needed to be said and done, and it didn't matter who among them said it.

Later that day while on the road to England, Otto, riding next to William, appeared lost in thought. Dimas and Hughes were right behind leading Otto's Templar detachment. They were following Edmund's coach, surrounded by his guards.

"Perhaps it's the French ministers we should be watching, and not their king," Dimas said.

Hughes nodded. "Doesn't seem as though Philip is the one in charge."

"I'm not certain who's in charge," replied Otto. "Philip's letters signal a very clever and sinister mind."

William felt their gaze, silently asking his opinion.

"There's great darkness all around those men," he replied. "Who is in charge probably doesn't matter since they all work as one."

"Did you notice how the king kept staring at our surcoats?" Hughes asked. "He could hardly contain his hatred."

Otto gazed at William's red cross over his chest. "Had I known that Philip was going to show up, I would have asked you three to shed your surcoats."

There were two more meetings with the French ministers and Edmund, but as before, there seemed to be an impasse. The French categorically wanted King Edward to relinquish Aquitaine, but Edward was adamant that he was the rightful duke.

"Could you warn Edward of Philip's plans now, Brother Otto?" William asked. They had spent most of the morning discussing Philip in their work chamber and had come down to the great hall for dinner. Otto asked the servants for a side table off in a corner to be out of earshot of others. "After all," William continued, "he knows the French are preparing for war and with everything going on, he'll believe you."

Otto stared at the oyster and shad stew in his bowl. "No, William. You forget about Bishop Bek and his secret allegiance to Philip. I'm sure he'll have me thrown in prison."

Hughes held his forefinger in midair to hush them as a courtier walked by. "What do you think is Bek's motivation?" he whispered, "I remember you saying that he's not a traitor."

Otto shrugged his shoulders. "My guess is that he thinks he can use the French to distract Edward so he can have a free hand in Scotland to gift lands to his friends. He sees a war with France as a most convenient event."

Like Otto, Dimas had not touched his food, but played idly with his knife. "What do we do?"

Otto stood up to leave. "Let's get ready for war."

Back in their workroom William observed Otto, Hughes, and Dimas. As far as they were concerned the Caesarius Prophecy had mapped out the future, and it was unfolding before their eyes. Otto paced the room while he talked with his characteristic measured steps, as though he were marching, while Hughes sat staring into space, listening. Dimas followed Otto's every word…they were all intensely engrossed—maybe even savoring—the drama they knew was about to take place. In William's heart, and in his mind when he sat with the thought, stopping the French king was a dark, foreboding, and insurmountable proposition. When he talked about it with Otto, Hughes, and Dimas, they all spoke about small pieces: containment in Scotland, avoiding an invasion, defending Aquitaine, but no one actually knew how to stop him. Would that mean killing him? His successor would just carry on with the French Scheme. Defeating the French? Would that mean invading and conquering France? Those were big concepts, too big and nebulous to be considered. And then, how was he, William, supposed to protect the Templars when Philip made his move against them? Hide them? William sighed. Perhaps the small steps were all they could think about.

"Let's create a distraction for the French," Hughes said suddenly. "Brother

Otto, who do you know who is powerful and has threatened to make war on Philip?"

Otto continued pacing. "The County of Flanders. Count Guy de Dampierre has resented Philip's attempts at claiming suzerainty over him, trying to collect taxes in Flemish towns, demanding feudal duty," Otto said as he paced. "Flanders would gladly make war, the only problem is they don't have the means, no army. Guy has just a few weak and rebellious barons."

"Can we help stir things up a bit?" Hughes asked. "We can start by approaching our Flemish brothers, and ask them to recruit for us until we have a sizable army. I'm sure Count Guy would then be glad to tell Philip where he can go."

"You may have something there, Hughes," Otto said as he stopped pacing. "William, could we count on the Brotherhood in Flanders? If the French had to fight the Flemish, it would prevent them from waging an all-out war against King Edward and invading us. Maybe we can also distract the French in Aquitaine."

"Good plan," William said, noting how captivated his friends seemed. Like children being absorbed into a new adventure, oblivious of anything else.

Otto instructed Hughes to investigate the prospects in Flanders. Dimas was to do the same in Aquitaine.

They came back a month later after consulting with local Brotherhood masters. In Flanders the barons were definitely hard to motivate; however, Hughes said that a significant number of brethren were well-off merchants, former workingmen who had made their fortunes with wool and fabrics and were well connected with all the guilds, a potentially huge source of manpower for an army. The guildsmen were willing to fight because most were ethnic Dutch and they feared being dominated by the French. Aquitaine was very different, the gentry were willing to fight, they didn't consider themselves part of France, and viewed their allegiance to England as a means to maintain their independence from "the big government" embodied by King Philip. However, they were not well trained nor organized.

On a warm morning when Otto was busy with his Templars trying to define a plan of action, one of Edmund's clerks came to summon them. They found a distraught Edmund pacing his work chamber. "Philip sent a letter to my brother declaring war. The reason he gave was Aquitaine, and he demanded that Edward immediately surrender the province. What do we do Otto? My brother says it's all my fault, and has threatened to have me thrown in prison."

Otto stood by the door, calm and reassuring. "Don't worry, your Highness, Philip is still building up an army and training crews for his ships. They will want to buy time. My guess is that they will call for another meeting, and that would be your opportunity to bluff them. Tell them King Edward is ready for war. I assure you they'll back down."

William and his two Templar brothers followed Otto back to their chamber, down the two flights of stairs and along the many corridors, and ran across groups of officials and knights feverishly discussing the new war.

Hughes seemed puzzled. "Otto, you don't believe what you just told Edmund, that Philip will back down, do you?"

Otto seemed lost in thought. "No, but a bluff would stall the French. Let's hope Edmund follows my advice. Let's go to my home where we can talk uninterrupted."

A servant opened the door of Otto's manor as they came up the front steps. William heard the sound of small feet scurrying off and a female voice warning that their father was home. For a man his age, Otto led quite a full life. They climbed the marble stairs to the second floor solarium.

"My thought," Otto said, arranging four chairs in a circle, "is that Philip thinks he can successfully invade England. Thanks to our spies we know that Philip is amassing an impressive army and has built new warships. That can only mean that he's planning on invading us soon."

"How many ships does he have?" Dimas asked, fixing his gaze on William.

"Around fifty, most of them galleys suitable for troops," William answered.

"So they can also bring siege engines," added Hughes.

Otto sat down. "Yes, I believe they can bring siege engines."

"If Philip invades, London is not ready," Hughes said. "The wall around the city is crumbling, people have built up against it; it's a mess."

"Edward has ordered repairs to the city's walls, and is trying to raise an army," replied Otto. "But at this point, should the French land on our coasts we don't stand a chance."

"So we make our move in Flanders and Aquitaine?" Dimas asked.

Suddenly things made sense to William; like pieces of a puzzle that had magically come together. "We could certainly help Edward with the French in both places," he said, feeling upbeat, "But I think we might as well get some recognition. Perhaps we could have Grand Master Jacques meet with King Edward and agree to a pact: in exchange for the Templars gathering support for Edward in Aquitaine and stirring up trouble in Flanders, King Edward agrees to protect the Templars against Philip."

"You are not thinking of revealing the Brotherhood to Edward, are you?" Otto asked.

"No, not at all," William said, excited that he was now dealing with not just small pieces, but the bigger picture. "As far as he's concerned it will be the Templars aiding him. Makes sense that he would want to protect those who are helping him."

Otto seemed incredulous. "But we would have to reveal the Caesarius Prophecy and the particulars that confirm it."

"Not necessarily. Grand Master Jacques can tell Edward the Templars have uncovered the information we possess about the French Scheme and not mention the Prophecy."

Hughes leaned forward in his chair and looked at Otto. "How much time do we have before Philip invades?"

"I would say that we have six months before hostilities start," answered Otto. Then he seemed to get excited. "Let's get going with Flanders and Aquitaine, but in the meantime let's bring Brother Jacques to London."

"Yes, and let's call a meeting of the Brotherhood," William said. "They need to know what's happening."

William asked Brother Guillaime de la More to arrange the Brotherhood meeting, while he sent letters to the Templar Masters in Flanders and Aquitaine mapping out the new strategy, and dispatched Dimas to Cyprus, the new headquarters of the Order. He told him to bring Grand Master Jacques back with him.

Otto decided to arrange a meeting between Brother Jacques and Edward as soon as possible. But the timing had to be right, otherwise Edward would dismiss it as unimportant. Grand Master Jacques would have to stay at the Templar House in London and wait for the opportune moment.

"The whole city is afraid of war," Dimas commented one morning when he walked into the work chamber. "This morning I rode down Old Fish Street and noticed a group of merchants talking in a corner. As I went by they asked me if I knew when the French would attack. It's starting to feel like Pilgrim Castle during the Mameluk siege of Acre."

A few days later Otto received orders from King Edward to accompany Prince Edmund for further talks with the French to try and negotiate a peace.

He decided to take Hughes and William with him, but asked them to wear Household Knights' uniforms.

The meeting was held in a grand salon of the royal palace in the Isle de la Cite with shiny wood parquet floors and windows that looked into a courtyard. Flote kept saying how embarrassing it was for a foreign king to own a province of France. "Our national honor is at stake, the people clamor for justice, and King Philip can't take the pressure anymore. His Majesty wants peace, you have to know that, but he has to please his people."

"Tsk, tsk," Marigny said as he rocked his head from side to side.

Edmund appeared at a loss, and had started saying something about how everyone wanted to avoid war, when Nogaret stepped in. "Let's arrange a secret pact between the two kings that will make everyone happy. After all, they are family," he said as he smoothed his moustache, and his dark eyes studied those present. "We'll have King Edward sign an agreement surrendering his rights to Aquitaine, but after it's publicized and accepted by our *Parlament*, our beloved King Philip will bequeath the province back to Edward, showing his magnanimity. This way our national honor will be upheld, and everyone will be happy, with no need for war."

Flote and his colleague Marigny, applauded. "It's brilliant," exclaimed Marigny.

Edmund didn't hesitate. "I'm certain King Edward will heartily agree!"

Edmund seemed very pleased with himself on the way back to England. "Philip just wanted to save face," Edmund told Otto and his Templar clerks as they rode together, "and once his honor is satisfied, things will be back to normal.

"You must agree that was quite a masterful stroke of diplomacy. Otto, we don't need to fret about an invasion anymore!"

Otto seemed to hesitate, as though he had trouble coming up with the right response. "I trust you are right, your Highness."

Later that day, while Edmund rode in his coach, Otto—riding with William and Hughes at the head of his Templar escort—seemed troubled. "You realize that Flote, Nogaret, and Marigny just pulled a fast one. Once they have Aquitaine, the French will stay. That's their idea of sport, making fools out of Edmund and Edward."

The day after their arrival at Westminster, Edmund summoned Otto and his two Templars to his chambers. Edmund smiled broadly looking regal in a sumptuous robe. "My brother just loved Nogaret's clever proposal." Edmund walked slowly to stand by a large portrait of his famous ancestor, King William the Conqueror, who invaded England with his Norman warriors two hundred and fifty years before. "I'm certain my brother will reward me with rich lands as a reward, just as he did for you, Otto."

A week later Otto's assessment of Philip's mindset was confirmed when he received a copy of a letter from Philip to his daughter Isabella. It was from the previous month, and in it the French king expressed his frustration at Balliol's "timidity," and concluded that the French would have to proceed without the Scots. He said he couldn't wait to fulfill his God-given destiny.

There was no question that Balliol was timid. Otto had told William how the Scottish king put up with a lot of abuse from the English. Over the previous two years, King Edward and Bishop Bek had imposed humiliating conditions on the Scottish king. Bek was now hearing claims made by Scottish barons and invariably ruling against Balliol. Bek demanded that the poor man appear before the English Parliament to answer accusations of malfeasance. Each time Balliol complied, the humiliations worsened. In the previous month, Bishop Bek had levied heavy fines on the Scottish king for made-up infractions.

One rainy afternoon William sat at his worktable staring out the window at the garden below and feeling terribly sorry for King John Balliol. On the other side of the room, Hughes and Otto talked heatedly about the prospects in Flanders and Aquitaine, and William had the sensation that they were being sucked in by a powerful whirlpool into a dark and evil void of strife and difficulty. But there was nothing he could do about it. It was too late.

In the midst of Otto's preparations for war and the English court's jubilation at Edmund's "brilliant" truce agreement with the French, William received a letter from Richard that a cousin of the earl of Sheffield's, named Francis, had brought suit to establish himself as the rightful heir to succeed Farwell. The hearing was to take place before a king's justice in a month's time.

William decided to visit the claimant, and determine whether he would make a good earl. William asked Otto for a week's leave, and rode to the man's lands, a day's ride west of Sheffield.

He arrived at midmorning at what turned out to be a knight's fief, not much different than his father's. William rode up to the manor entrance and announced himself.

A servant showed William to a sitting room. That was not a good sign. Francis was trying to assert his superiority by making him wait. Now it was a question of how long.

Several hours passed, and finally the servant came to escort William to Francis' chambers. He followed the footman to a room set up as a receiving chamber, much like that of an earl's, with banners of his apparent vassals on the walls. At a glance William could tell some of the vassals were not Francis' for he recognized several neighbors. A blond man of non-descript features sat in a big chair in the middle of the room. On either side of him stood two young men in knightly garb. William came up and was made to stand in front of the blond man.

"You will bow before our lord," said one of the young men.

William decided to bow, even though the man was neither his overlord nor superior, but it was worth the gesture if he could talk and find out more about him.

"This is our Lord Francis de Velford," the knight said. "State your name and position."

"I am William Montfort, a Templar monk, currently acting on behalf of Earl Orland of Sheffield."

"This house does not recognize your position as such," Francis said. "I, Sir Francis of Velford will soon take over the earldom and there will be hell to pay for all the infractions so far committed by yourself and your brother." Francis then studied his hands, and his ring.

"Be aware," the young man by his side announced, "that my Lord proposes to govern with an iron hand. Your days of lax rule are over!"

William felt a weight in his heart. Why did people have to behave so badly? "You will never rule over my friends and family," he said and walked out.

Back in London, William decided to ask for help and went to see his fellow brother, Lord Ralph Hengham, who was considered one of the top lawyers in the realm and had been the king's chief justice for many years. King Edward had dismissed him from his post when he refused to levy a heavy fine on an impoverished man. That was to be expected of a brother.

Lord Hengham received him personally in his London house, in his luxurious and comfortable sitting room, richly paneled in yellow cedar. On hearing his case, Lord Hengham smiled. "Leave the matter to me, Grand Master William, and come back in a week."

This William did, and was surprised to find a king's justice in the sitting room. He was not the one who would hear the case but was acquainted with the justice who would. Lord Hengham came to the point. "I've asked my friend Simmons —and he smiled at the justice—to look into both bloodlines; yours' and Francis'. Simmons feels that the earl of Sheffield's cousin has a strong case, and Justice Arnold may rule in his favor. However, Francis is a cousin twice removed, and the closest relative with the strongest case is the earl of Sheffield's niece, a girl of fifteen. But since she is unmarried, Justice Arnold will have to decide on the male heir, that is, Francis."

William was about to speak when Lord Hengham raised his hand. "The good news is that according to Simmons' research, both you and your brother Richard are qualified to marry the earl of Sheffield's nice, and should either one of you wed the girl, Arnold would have to rule in her favor."

William nodded. "I'm a monk, I can't marry. So I suppose my brother must."

"No, you are a monk and are to be celibate," Lord Hengham said, exchanging knowing glances with the justice, who sat in silence in a big chair to one side. "There are many Templars who were married but took leave of their wives, left a competent surrogate to administer their lands, and became celibate monks. You can do the same."

That was an interesting scenario, the product of a keen legal mind. "Need I consummate the marriage?"

"No, the law doesn't require proof of consummation."

William realized that it was the best possible solution. He was loath to make Richard forego Elizabeth, and also concerned how Richard would behave should he become the earl. "Very well my Lord. I will marry the girl."

Lord Hengham gave him a wry smile. "The problem is—and this I found out through a powerful friend—that the girl has been absconded to a manor house in Shrewsbury by Francis. But not to worry, I've already made plans. Please give me another week, Brother William."

The following week Lord Hengham told William how a dozen Templars stormed the manor house where Orland's niece had been imprisoned, had found Francis's two knights and twenty Norman mercenaries, had a brief fight, wounded four men, left everyone tied up, and then simply walked out with the girl.

A few days later William faced a priest in Lord Hengham's private chapel. Beside him stood a shy girl named Alphonsina, a frail and scant figure, not yet a woman, of light brown hair and eyes, dressed in her family's colors. Her thin lips trembled, and at the end, tears came to her downcast eyes.

Following the ceremony, as he escorted his new wife to the garden outside, William addressed the girl. "I am sorry if we had to steal you away."

Alphonsina wiped a tear with her hand and looked sideways at him. "I don't mind. I was treated poorly in that house, and you seem like a nice man," she said in a shy voice.

"Do you know what will happen to you?"

"I was told by Lord Hengham that you will not be my real husband."

"That's right, my Lady. I am a monk and am prevented by my vows from consummating the marriage."

"What does that mean?"

"I can't go to bed with you and make babies."

"Oh, I don't mind."

William smiled. Life was getting simpler. "You can move into Sheffield Castle where you will lead a comfortable life. My brother Richard will look after you and you can do what you please."

"Can I bring my friend along? I've been lonely for her."

William bent down to kiss her on the cheek. "Yes, bring whomever you want." He felt bad for the girl, but then again, there had been no other choice. Hopefully the justice would rule in his favor, otherwise the wedding would have been for naught and he would have a wife to support.

Ten days later, William—dressed in his family's colors—sat next to Richard in a hearing room in Dunbury. Two seats down was Francis, dressed in regal finery, escorted by his two knights. All three men glanced surreptitiously at William while whispering.

Francis' solicitor made an impassioned case, about how family ties had to be respected, "and Sir William Montford, disregarding the law of the land, stole a young girl, the earl of Sheffield's niece, with the sole intent of usurping Sir Francis Velford's rights by wedding her against her will."

"Is this true?" the justice asked.

A friend of Ralph's, a brash young solicitor, called Alphonsina to testify. The girl went up to the front and approached the justice.

"Were you wed against your will?" William's solicitor asked.

"No, Sire, I am fond of my husband," she answered in her small voice. "But those men there," and she pointed to Francis and his two knights, "they are the ones who stole me from my father's house, beat me, and kept me tied up in a dark room with nary anything to eat."

There was a communal gasp in the room.

That was news to William. He turned to look at Francis and caught Richard's menacing glare directed at Francis and his two knights.

"You bastards," Richard said, loud enough for everyone to hear, and that prompted an appreciative mumbling from those in the room.

Francis laughed nervously. "Never fear," he said to one his knights, "we will prevail."

The justice shot a glance at Francis, and ruled in William's favor.

William stood to shake hands with his solicitor. When he turned to look for his brother, found him gone. So were Francis and his knights. Then William heard a commotion outside, and rushed out to find Richard holding Francis by the tunic while he slapped him. The two young knights lay on the ground with bloodied faces, groaning, and attempting to get up as a group of women pummeled and kicked them. A laughing and cheering crowd had formed to watch the spectacle.

"Try hitting a defenseless girl again, you pig," Richard shouted while Francis tried to protect himself.

William disengaged the shaken Francis from his brother. "Richard, that's not necessary." Then he ushered the vengeful women away and helped the two knights to their feet.

Francis bent down to pick up his hat, and then hurried away.

William approached his brother shaking his head. "Richard, such manners!"

"Oh, Willy. You are way too nice."

After his wedding, William was able to put his mind at ease regarding his family's welfare. He thought about taking time out to concentrate on the Jesus Gospel. The problem, he realized, was that it remained the secret of the few, and there were so many people who would readily embrace "The Knowing" if they only learned about it. He needed to find an equally secretive and powerful organization to the Brotherhood, people who were not afraid of the Church and were seekers of a higher truth. But who and how? That was a good question. Obviously if members of the Brotherhood knew of any such group they would have come forward long ago. William decided that he would pray for a solution.

Two months later, after the trees had lost their leaves and the air was turning increasingly cold, William sat talking with Mary in their alcove off the main stairs. London and the palace felt at ease, relaxed; the fear of an invasion now a nightmare that had been pushed away. Courtiers chatted in Westminster's hallways and people in the city went about their usual business: stores were full of merchandise, ships and wagons with goods came and went, and defensive repairs were put on hold.

Mary wore her black habit with ease, as though already a nun for many years. Her freckles had faded away, and she had become a woman, young and fresh, with intelligent blue eyes that studied William's every expression. He knew that it would be easy to feel attracted to her. *This is a challenge, but one I must meet well, for my sake as well as hers.* Lately he had started to look for her, anxious to hear her voice or catch a glimpse of her tall figure making her elegant way down the hallway with gliding strides, as though dancing rather than walking. He vowed to stop, and make sure she remained a dear friend, a sister, and nothing else.

By now people didn't question the propriety of their being alone. That is, no one dared say anything openly. Because of his friendship with Mary, the highborns now kept their distance. In fact, people in the palace made the most respectful and polite remarks to William, and treated him as part of the royal family, even bowing and curtsying to him.

When together, William and Mary spoke in English. "It's about time the gentry spoke the people's language," she had announced one day. "Just because some Norman brute invaded two-hundred and fifty years ago, doesn't mean we have to keep speaking French forever."

That day William could tell from the expression on her face that she was worked up over something. "I convinced my father," Mary said in a forceful voice, "to enact a law making it a crime to steal nuns. William, I can't fathom how people allow that!" her face flushed in anger. "That's a most appalling practice. This past month, three nuns I know were stolen as they rode from my abbey into town. The thieves left a fourth nun, the least attractive of the four, who ran to tell the abbess what had happened.

"The three nuns made it back a week later, telling a horrible story of debauchery."

William was about to tell her about Farwell, when they heard someone in the great hall downstairs shouting the news that French troops had invaded Aquitaine. The voice reverberated up the staircase, and both William and Mary hurried to the banister so they could hear. "The French have reinforced their forces in castles along the border. They have invaded his Majesty's duchy!"

It's war. "Mary, Philip just made a fool out of your father. Their agreement was for token French forces to occupy a few castles until Philip gave Aquitaine back. Now he's not giving it back."

"Oh, no!" Mary said. "Poor uncle Edmund. Father is going to be furious."

"Poor us, Mary. A lot of people are going to die." It was as Otto had predicted, the French ministers had duped Edmund and King Edward. William got up, bowed to Mary and went to find Otto.

When William walked into the workroom he found King Edward pacing the floor, and Otto, Hughes, and Dimas standing meekly by as the king fumed. "You should have prevented this disaster! Why do you think I sent you along? You are the diplomat, my brother is just a horse's ass."

Otto remained silent as the tirade went on for some time.

"I don't even have the troops to protect London. Get me out of this war!!" Edward ordered as he stormed out of the room.

Grand Master Jacques and Dimas had arrived the previous month. The time was perfect to propose the Templars to Edward. Otto waited until that afternoon to make it seem as though he worked on his idea long and hard, then went to see Edward with the plan to meet with Grand Master Jacques, who just happened to be in London. On hearing the reasons for the meeting—Otto later told his Templars—Edward became jubilant, and complimented his counselor for "acting sure and fast."

Two days later, the day before their scheduled meeting with the king, Otto decided to review their strategy. It was a typical foggy day outside, not too cold, just uncomfortable. William sat next to Brother Jacques and across a table from Dimas, Hughes, and Otto, in the Templar master's work chamber, a second-story room with a wide view of the Thames through a paned window.

"Let's make sure that we attribute all of our information to the Templars," Otto said as he concluded his remarks.

"Doesn't Edward know that you have spies, Otto?" William asked.

"Just the official ones, not my real spies. I realized early on that I couldn't compromise their identities. Bishop Bek would want to know who they were and either use them himself or worse yet, notify King Philip to ingratiate himself."

Brother Jacques looked incredulous. "So you pay for all those spies out of your own purse?"

"No, Brother. My spies want nothing more than to stop the French Scheme, I don't pay them anything.

"But I make use of my 'official' spies as well—people known to Edward and Bek and I assume to Philip also—who send me periodic reports. When I think it convenient I embellish these reports with my own information."

"I can see why you are such a valued member of the Brotherhood," Brother Jacques said.

"Let's talk about the meeting," William said. "Let's have Otto sit next to Edward. Dimas and Hughes will sit across the table on either side of Brother Jacques. I will stand behind them as befits the lowest ranking Templar. If anything comes up I can whisper instructions to Dimas, who will then relay them to Grand Master Jacques."

The following morning, sitting at the head of a large oak table in Otto's sumptuous receiving room in his immaculate manor, King Edward appeared dumbfounded as Grand Master Jacques told him of the intelligence that showed how Philip had meddled in Scotland, was determined to take over Aquitaine, conquer England, have Bishop Bertrand de Got elected pope, then destroy the Templars and gain possession of their treasury. "With the power and money from his conquests Philip will then have his new pope crown him Holy Roman emperor," Grand Master Jacques said. "He will rule the world!"

After a pause to let Edward mull over the information, Brother Jacques continued. "We need to stop Philip at any cost, your Majesty. We can't allow him his first steps, to conquer England and destroy the Templars. So it's only logical that the Order and the English kingdom help each other."

Brother Jacques answered repeated questions from Edward. Aquitaine was indeed just an excuse for war, and yes, Philip's agents had killed the Scottish royals and broken the truce in Outremer…yes, Bertrand de Got could become pope…and yes, as pope he would have the authority to order a crusade against the Templars, bestow their treasury on France and crown Philip emperor…that was the plan.

Edward took a deep breath. "It's incredible, but it makes sense. Philip has always liked to play courtly games. This is just another one, his biggest one."

Edward walked around the table a couple of times then sat down again. He slammed his fist on the table. "By God's blood, let's stop him!"

Brother Jacques nodded. "But we must keep our agreement secret, your Majesty. The French have many spies, and if word gets out that we are on your side, Philip will immediately speed up his plan, and capture and kill all Templars within France."

"I'll make him eat his own testicles!" Edward said. He then told how the Templars had helped his father, Henry III. When some rebellious earls had come after him, Henry had sought refuge at London Templar House. He needed money to hire troops, but was broke. The Templar master couldn't lend him money openly and break the Order's neutrality, so instead he counseled the king and his son to steal ten thousand pounds from the Templar treasury, "and he gave us a mallet to break the lock," Edward said with a laugh. The money saved King Henry and since then Edward felt a great debt to the Order. "This agreement only solidifies our bond."

Brother Jacques studied Edward. "That's a great story, your Majesty. The Knights Templar have always stood on the side of fairness. I wouldn't want to be a Templar otherwise.

"Your Majesty, for this one struggle against the French, how shall we join forces?"

"Tell me your side of the bargain, and we shall see."

Jacques brought his hands together on top of the table and entwined his fingers in a solid bond. "I will send Templar knights in disguise to Flanders and Aquitaine to build up a local resistance against the French. We will recruit, organize, and lead local militias. My knights will lay down their lives to safeguard England's freedom. In exchange, will you vow to protect my Order from the French king?"

King Edward, his eyes moist, placed his two hands on top of Jacques'. "For as long as I shall live, that pretty-boy will not touch a single Templar. I swear by almighty God who watches over us."

The two men stood, embraced and kissed each other on both cheeks. The agreement was sealed.

Edward vowed to keep the agreement a secret, even from his top advisers, including Bishop Bek. No one outside that room would ever know that the meeting took place.

As the Templars and Otto were about to take their leave from the King, Edward looked William in the eyes. "You are the Templar commander my Mary has told me about, are you not?"

William felt unsure how to answer, but decided to face whatever was coming. "Yes, your Majesty. I have befriended Princess Mary. We share a love for books and have become good friends." He had emphasized the "friends" and hoped the king understood.

"And I'm certain you find her challenging at times, eh?" King Edward said with a laugh.

William was relieved; there was no accusation of impropriety, but only curiosity in the king's part. "Princess Mary has a strong will and a keen mind. I am certain she will challenge many in her lifetime."

"Oh, lad, that girl is a tempest!" Edward walked over to William and placed his hands on his shoulders. "I can tell that you care for my Mary and place her welfare above yours. For that I am grateful."

Following the meeting, Grand Master Jacques walked with his brothers to Templar House along the Strand. All of them were due to leave the following day for the Brotherhood meeting to be held in an abbey in Brittany. They talked as they strolled past the sumptuous houses of Edward's key advisors and officials toward the Templar compound. The sun was beginning to break through the fog. It was going to be a beautiful fall day after all.

"Brother William," Brother Jacques said, "your current plan is to use Brotherhood members in both Flanders and Aquitaine to recruit local barons to fight the French, right?"

"We have very influential members in both places," William answered.

Brother Jacques thought for a moment. "Who will take charge of the Templars I'll be dispatching to Flanders and Aquitaine?"

"Brother Hughes will be responsible for Flanders and Brother Dimas for Aquitaine," William said. "They will organize the local barons and take charge of whatever Templars you send us, Brother Jacques."

"We won't use the local Templar *commanderies*?" Hughes asked.

"I will personally approve of the Templars for you to lead, Brother Hughes," Grand Master Jacques said. "In some cases these will come from the local commands, but most will come from as far away as Greece."

"The natives would be far more useful," Hughes said.

"Of course," Brother Jacques said. "But let's not discount anything at this point. This type of secret war is new to all of us. By the way, both you and Dimas need to be of higher rank. From now on please wear a master's mantle."

The Brotherhood meeting was an exciting one. The eight hundred or so participants crowded together in a huge storage cellar in an imposing Cistercian abbey. It was well protected by a huge wall, encircling a farm and many buildings.

William told them the progress they were making, and about the upcoming secret wars in Flanders and Aquitaine. The brethren were jubilant: They were going to actually stop King Philip; there was no doubt in their minds. They vowed to do whatever their grand master asked of them.

At the end of the meeting, during a break in between the socializing, Brother Jacques casually walked up to William, who had just sat down after making the rounds of the room.

"Brother William, will you walk with me?"

"Certainly, grand master."

Brother Jacques laughed. "Are we going to call each other grand master all along? Come, indulge an old man, and let's have a quiet talk."

The weather was cool, and they walked amid the abbey's pear orchards. Monks crouched among the trees spreading manure from wheelbarrows. Brother Jacques watched them with curiosity. "You have a hard decision coming up, dear Brother William, perhaps the hardest you'll ever make in your life."

William felt the grave silence that followed Brother Jacques' words. "I'm sure there'll be many, but you are referring to something specific, aren't you, grand master?"

"Yes, son. I have thought long and hard about King Philip, and, besides my blood, he wants to destroy our Order, no matter what. My counsel is that you let him."

Brother Jacques filled in William's stunned silence: "You have an option, utterly defeat the French king and take over his kingdom, which is next to impossible, but if you don't, he or his descendants will hunt us down wherever we go." Brother Jacques stopped and turned to face William. "Instead, sacrifice some of us, to satisfy the French king. Then he'll leave the rest alone, and the Brotherhood and the Templars can go on, in secret." Brother Jacques resumed his walk, staring down at the ground. "That's the counsel of an old, tired warrior."

Heaviness in the pit of his stomach told William that Brother Jacques was right, and he was talking about the unthinkable, big picture. Chances were that the French king could not be stopped, and William knew that the Prophecy was right; Philip would attack the Order. What he had not wanted to admit was that the attack would be successful. It was inevitable; the Prophecy was real, and Brother Jacques had verbalized what he had been afraid to say to himself; the French were too powerful, they could reach anywhere and do anything they wanted. There was no place to hide.

William observed the majestic man of white hair and beard walking beside him, and he understood what Brother Jacques was asking of him, to make the right decision, no matter how difficult, when the situation arose. But that was still in the future, and perhaps a miracle would happen. "I will do what needs to be done, Grand Master Jacques. I swear."

"Thank you William. May God guide your steps, son."

That following spring war started with the French navy striking the English ports of Plymouth, Portsmouth, and Weymouth. Several English ships were burned with some loss of life, but the English naval forces regrouped in defensive positions against the superior enemy. The priority was to fend off a possible invasion, but so far King Philip's attacks were mostly a form of harassment.

London and the palace once again buzzed with nervous talk of a French invasion, but Edward appeared at ease. He ordered repairs in the city walls to resume, and tasked Parliament with raising taxes for an army.

The following month Edward sent knights and foot soldiers into Aquitaine, a relatively small force. Obviously he was counting on his secret arrangement with the Templars, and Otto guessed that he wanted to concentrate his resources on Scotland.

William felt the pressure mounting. The wait was starting to take its toll on him, he felt angry and out-of-sorts. He remembered how haggard Dimas looked when he first saw him at Pilgrim Castle on his return from Hafiz Mountain and the effect that meditation had. There was nothing William could do for Westminster and London, but he could help himself, and he went into seclusion for two days in his cell at Templar House.

His meditation at first was like trying to swim in heavy mud, but by the afternoon of his first day, William felt peace. He sat still, and let the feeling turn into bliss. By the end of the day he knew he had been transformed once again. The second day he spent in total enjoyment of Spirit, and could have gone on for many days, but he had work to do. With serene mind and peaceful heart he thought of the Prophecy, and wondered how and when Philip would go after the Templars. First, Philip needed a pope he could command, someone who could declare a crusade against the Order. That hadn't happened yet.

When Hughes came back from Flanders his face and eyes were like those of another person, ruthless and hard; but he was also excited, clearly enjoying his task. William watched him as he described how he had been able to enlist Count Guy of Flanders to fight the French, as well as a handful of barons, but mostly he had recruited guildsmen, lots of them. Hughes was totally immersed in his work; now nothing else mattered. "Brother Jacques sent me a hundred and twenty Templars, all excellent fighters. We are now busy training and organizing the guildsmen, and will soon be ready to kill French soldiers."

Happy with how successful Hughes had been at recruiting, Otto asked, "Did you happen to know a Flemish sergeant who saved your life in Outremer?"

"Why yes, my Lord. I am only astounded you know about it. That was quite a battle and a heroic deed that touched me deeply."

Otto laughed, but to William, Hughes' words sounded grotesque.

Dimas remained in Aquitaine. He sent a message by courier reporting his progress in recruiting local barons who resented Philip, of which there were many. Grand Master Jacques had provided him three hundred and forty Templars.

Otto was sure that the barons of Aquitaine would fight against the French, judging by Dimas' accounts. In Flanders the barons were not particularly loyal to Count Guy, and would just as soon fight against him. Otto believed there was nothing to prevent Flanders from being overrun by a French army.

"Leave it up to me, Brother Otto," Hughes said, sitting at his table strewn with maps. "I have faith in the men of the guilds. They'll come through for us."

Otto walked over to Hughes' table, curiously scanning his maps. "But how would they fight the French cavalry? The guildsmen can only fight on foot, for they are common men without horses, and we both know how ineffectual infantry is against the powerful onslaught of horsemen."

"I've given that some thought," Hughes said, spreading his arms wide on the table. "The Scots use foot soldiers chained together to keep them in formation. They are effective against cavalry, to some degree. The big flaw is the use of chains instead of discipline, and the use of lances, too short and light against horses. In Outremer, the Saracen often used long, sharpened poles against our chargers. My plan calls for heavy pikes, twelve feet in length, that can be butted into the ground and used against a horse, or swung forward to demolish shielded infantry."

Otto rubbed his chin. "I pray it works, Hughes, I pray it works."

William studied Hughes' hard expression. He was now so different from the Hughes he remembered at Hafiz Mountain, the one with an easy smile and a blissful look in his eyes. *He's lost in the whirlpool, the French Scheme has sucked him in.*

A month later, Balliol rebelled against the English. Almost immediately, Philip vowed his support for the Scots.

Bishop Bek paraded around the palace in sword and hauberk, followed by Dominican friars also dressed for war. Their posturing looked ridiculous to William's practiced military eye.

Edward took on the task of rounding up an army, pressing his earls to fulfill their feudal duty by providing armed men or the equivalent in money. The wardrobe department tallied monies needed for the campaign in Scotland, and Edward approached his Lombard bankers for a loan.

"Perhaps we made a mistake, Otto," William said, watching from the work chamber window as Edward and Bek exited the palace grounds on their horses followed by a number of troops. "Edward is clearly counting on us to fight the French and keep them from invading. I was hoping he would abandon his conquest of Scotland, but look at him!"

"You are right. We should have fought the French without telling him. But then again, we need him to protect the Templars against Philip. So in a way, we are letting him have Scotland in exchange for the Templars."

William received a letter from Richard, this time written by one of the earl's clerks, stating that the sheriff had come by asking for the earl of Sheffield's obligation to the king. He wrote Richard to vouch ten lances—knights along with squires, pages, and grooms; and fifty foot soldiers. "But please write me back with news from home, Richard."

Richard responded with a second letter saying that he was now residing at the earl's castle and Elizabeth was back, and he had convinced her to live at the castle, to help him. She still refused to marry him, saying she would want some time to see how people reacted to her, including her own family. Alphonsina had moved into the castle along with two of her friends. Richard said the girls were playful, polite, and kept to themselves. He had purged the castle of troublesome people, "so no one would bother the girls." The earl spent his time peacefully tending his garden, receiving visits from old friends, and was by all accounts, miraculously recovering his health. The Countess Lorena was still mourning Farwell and told Richard that "my son was a good and honest knight, but a little wild, as befits young men."

William's concern was the extent of the earldom's enterprises—wool and lumber mills and extensive farms and forests, which seemed well beyond Richard's ability to administer.

William decided to go home for a visit before the war with France and Scotland became all-consuming. On this trip he decided to ride his beloved Black for one last time, and leave him in the earl's pastures. The horse was getting on in years and not as strong and nimble as he used to be, and the shoulder wound he suffered in Outremer seemed to bother him from time to time.

William rode alone, savoring Black's company and letting him set his own pace. It was a bittersweet trip, and William realized how much he would miss his peculiar horse.

When he got home, William found that his father was ailing from a bad humor in his legs and could hardly walk for the pain. Lady Claire was unchanged in appearance, and as her husband declined, she seemed to enliven.

The actors had settled in the village of Sheffield and William offered to build a theatre for them on the earl's behalf, which pleased Elizabeth. "That's an answer to my prayers, William!" she said. William had found her in Orland's former work chamber, which she had taken over and made soft and feminine. Gone were the earl's hunting trophies on the walls, and instead there were now paintings of pastoral scenes and vases with flowers. She had been going over the castle's finances and had found irregularities on how one of the clerks made entries. She sat hard at work, with a cat on her lap. Elizabeth had adopted a number of wounded and forlorn animals; a colt Richard had wanted to put down because of a deformed leg, three cats she had found lost and hungry, and a big mongrel dog that wandered into the castle grounds one day, looking for her, according to Richard.

William had noticed that Elizabeth had a way with Richard. She kept him on track with a gentle, playful way: "Now you're getting huffy, big oaf. That won't get you far."

Curiously, people didn't seem to react against Elizabeth the way she thought they would, and William thought it was perhaps because Richard had used his authority to set the tone, but found that to be only a partial answer. The comments he heard from Clancy and the other gentry was that they saw her as their savior because it was through her that they had gotten rid of Farwell. According to Elizabeth, there were at least two matrons who said unpleasant things about her behind her back, but it didn't seem to bother her.

As he watched Elizabeth at work, it occurred to William that Richard had enlisted her help in his own way; simply assuming that she would do the things he was not good at. She knew all the details of the earldom: how many feet of lumber had been sold, how much meat, how much grain the farms were expected to produce, and cajoled Richard to make better deals. "Now, Richard, I'm certain that Arnold of Dover could charge less for those fabrics next time, if you only press him. Offer him twelve pounds for the whole lot next year."

Elizabeth continued writing at her table, caressing the cat with one hand, and as he waited for her to finish, he studied the now beautiful woman, so unlike the girl he knew before. She refused to pluck her hairline or powder her skin white, and looked natural, but better yet, mature. "Elizabeth," he asked her, "would you assist Richard with his letters? I'm not comfortable his using earl Sheffield's clerks, for some things are best kept in the family, don't you agree?"

Elizabeth looked up with a crinkle of laughter in her eyes. "I'm not yet family William, but yes, I'll be glad to help." She then gave him a big smile. "Are you going back to London today?"

"After I leave Black in the pastures and pick a new horse."

"Mind if I come along? I know all the horses."

They walked in silence, William holding the reins in his hand, Black behind him and occasionally prodding his shoulder with his nose. William smiled when he felt the horse's breath on his neck. Elizabeth thought it was "all very sweet," but seemed to understand that leaving Black behind was a difficult thing for

William.

He let Black out into a pasture, and after a brisk little gallop, the horse turned around and looked at him, which made Elizabeth laugh. "That horse is almost human," she said.

William was certain the charger understood why they had to part ways.

"I'll look after Black for you, William," Elizabeth told him on their way to the nearby stables.

He chose a new horse, a white, four-year old spirited gelding. As he climbed on the unfamiliar animal he realized how much he would miss that feeling of total trust he had with Black. *And affection.*

They visited Alphonsina. She lived with her two friends in a cottage tucked away in a corner of the castle's gardens. The girls had been busy planting a new flowerbed, and when they saw William and Elizabeth, they curtsied to William, then happily embraced Elizabeth and dragged her down to sit with them on the grass. William went to stand by a tree, and watched as Elizabeth engaged Alphonsina and her friends in a conversation about flowers, about birds, then the weather, and finally men. William found that he enjoyed the sound of their voices, their soft mannerisms, but mostly how easily they seemed to have slipped into a comfortable rapport and forget completely about him.

Afterward, he and Elizabeth rode along the garden toward the castle's keep, when they heard Richard's voice.

"Willy! Elizabeth! Wait for me."

They turned to see him running on foot toward them, and got down from their horses. Evidently he had been helping masons cut stones, for he had dust all over his clothes.

"Brother, you are wise," he said, out of breath. "Perhaps you could counsel me. This stubborn woman won't marry me; although she's told me she loves me, and enjoys my company above anyone else's. Now, what do you make of that?"

"The problem, Richard," Elizabeth said with a grin, "is that you haven't asked me properly."

Richard wiped dust from his face. "And how would that be?"

"I read this romantic tale once where the knight drops to one knee, takes the lady's hand, and begs her to marry him."

Richard had started to bend down when she laughingly grabbed a clump of his hair and held him still. "Before doing that, he climbed up to her balcony, in the moonlight."

"Climb up to your balcony? But your chamber doesn't have a balcony," he said as she kept him bent over.

Elizabeth hung on to Richard's hair as though that was the only way she could keep his attention. "I know of a grand chamber that has one. It's on the third floor."

"I suppose I can climb up there," Richard said with a foolish grin, looking up at her.

"Oh, and before climbing, he sang her a beautiful song…one that goes…"

William got up on his horse and rode away to leave the two to their foolishness. But it was good to see how well they got along.

Two weeks later he received a letter from Elizabeth with the happy news: the wedding was set for the early spring, "with the new blossoms, two weeks before Easter."

Elizabeth and Richard's wedding took place on a placid Sunday morning after mass. It was a big, happy affair. Lady Claire made sure that neighboring earls were invited, and of course the entire earl of Sheffield's clan, including Francis.

William met relatives from far away, people he didn't know existed, cousins many times removed: old ladies professing to have been present at his birth, then a group that were rumored to be the disgraced descendants of a former earl his father had never mentioned, and some who came from far corners in France. They all wanted to know what life was like at Westminster.

The little village church could not possibly hold everyone, so the ceremony was held in Sheffield Castle's ample gardens, near the fountain where Richard and Elizabeth used to rendezvous when they were young.

Both Richard and Elizabeth were dressed in their respective families' heraldic colors. Richard appeared nervous and giddy, she, self-assured and at ease, taking in the details, beaming at the crowd. When the priest blessed their union, the smiling Richard placed a ring on Elizabeth's finger making her his wife, from hence forth, the Lady Elizabeth.

Orland sat in front with his wife the countess, in between Richard's parents and Elizabeth's, and surrounded—at Elizabeth's insistence—by the eight actors in her troupe, who after the ceremony entertained the guests with a series of skits about the lives of the gentry. Surprisingly, the highborns and knights laughed heartily seeing themselves parodied and would shout, "That's just like you, Henry!" and "Look! That's what Max has been up to!"

But Sir Maxwell didn't find it amusing, and sat livid, staring straight ahead.

Alphonsina, along with her friends, laughed merrily. She seemed to be growing surer of herself, her manner less shy and more playful.

In the perimeter, at a respectful distance, enjoying the performances and watching the pageantry, stood the villagers and peasants. At Elizabeth's instructions they were given food and refreshments.

It was interesting how Elizabeth was affecting life at the earldom. Obviously because of her, relations between the social classes were less rigid; she had set the tone and people followed along. It wasn't just that she fraternized with the actors, but seemed equally at ease with merchants and their wives, some of whom had been invited to the wedding and mingled with the gentry. Perhaps better yet, courtly games had all but disappeared because she did not approve.

William relished the thought that for the present the earldom was in good hands. Eventually there might rise another tyrant, but for now all was well.

There were skirmishes in Aquitaine. French troops attacked a number of rebel castles and to most everyone's surprise, were beaten back. Dimas had decided on fighting out in the open using the tactics the Templars had perfected in Outremer: no frontal assaults, but focusing on the enemy's flanks, and when forced on a frontal assault, going for the middle of the formation to splinter defenses. Dimas reported that his Templars were successful at training the local knights, and they were becoming a well-disciplined and skilled army.

Both Dimas and Hughes had decided on using the harassing tactics the Saracen had used so effectively against them in Outremer: strike, run, and make the enemy pursue a small force into a trap. It worked again and again, both in Aquitaine and Flanders. The strategy was to decimate the enemy's forces and create in them a feeling of hopelessness.

But the most significant thrust against the French was in Flanders. Hughes' guildsmen were good at harassing French garrisons and managed to kill a good number of Frenchmen. When pursued, the Flemish would disappear into the countryside, only to attack again when least expected. Emboldened, that summer the Flemish Count Guy declared war on France, and they sent an envoy to ask King Edward for help, who decided to send some soldiers as "a gesture."

William prayed for Hughes and his Templars. They had to succeed, Flanders was proving more important than Aquitaine because Philip seemed more interested in acquiring the county than in taking back the duchy, perhaps because Flanders promised much greater wealth with its large textile industry.

Hughes spoke highly of his guildsmen. "They are highly motivated, and already organized, with a strong central leadership," he told Otto during a visit.

"Your harassing tactics are brilliant, Hughes, but one day you must have a battle," Otto said. "What can infantry do against Philip's well-trained cavalry?"

"A lot, brother, a lot. They are deadly with their pikes, and so far are good at draining Philip's resources; but you are correct, eventually we must have a battle and will need help.

"What about the English?" Hughes asked, "I understand that Edward just marched into Scotland, eh?"

"Yes, Hughes. He's set on pacifying it."

"Is there a chance that he'll give it up and help us in Flanders and Aquitaine?"

"I'm afraid not."

A week later, with just William in the workroom, Otto looked up from a report he had been reading. "Well, William, I don't know whether you'll like the news, but King Edward found almost no resistance in Scotland. Balliol, as Edward and Bek had gauged him, is no fighter. Balliol's barons deserted him, and he found himself with only a handful of men, hopelessly staring at the English siege engines and powerful army."

"Did Balliol give himself up?" William asked.

"Yes. He decided to throw himself at the mercy of the English king. But Edward was not satisfied with his surrender. In a ceremony in Edinburgh, Balliol was stripped of his coat of arms, and sent in chains to the Tower of London."

"Poor Balliol," William said. "So Philip couldn't help the Scots."

"No, William. I guess that's a mark of Hughes and Dimas' success."

And William felt terrible remorse. He was party to the invasion of a peaceful kingdom and the overthrow of a just and righteous king by a greedy, evil aggressor: Edward. It occurred to William that Edward was equally as wicked as Philip. If they traded places, Edward would be just as likely to be vying for the Holy Roman Empire's crown and planning much the same things as Philip.

During the following year, the Brotherhood's secret wars against the French in Flanders and Aquitaine gained momentum, and the French apparently decided that they couldn't afford to keep going on both fronts. King Philip proposed a peace plan to Edward and a truce in Aquitaine was put in place until negotiations could be completed.

"My father is so happy that he gets to keep his precious duchy," Mary told William during one of their meetings in the courtyard. William noticed her long and graceful hands, and the now familiar way in which she cupped them on her lap. "My brother will marry Isabella, Philip's daughter, and their first male offspring will be the sole heir to Aquitaine. And you know, William, what made my father the happiest?" She raised her left hand plaintively with palm upturned. "To cement the peace, he gets to marry Philip's sister. He told me he misses being married." Her hand folded gently, like a graceful flower, and her full lips parted in a quizzical smile.

Edward took advantage of the truce in Aquitaine and marched again into Scotland, this time in an attempt to capture or kill the fierce William Wallace, a lowly knight who had emerged out of nowhere to lead the rebels. "I'm sure the French are behind this new rebellion as well," Otto told William. "Once they detect that Edward is deeply entangled, they'll jump at the chance."

And that was the case. Edward got bogged by Wallace and Philip broke the truce with renewed attacks in Aquitaine. Otto asked Hughes to harass the French as much as he could in Flanders. "But be careful, Hughes, don't push them too hard. If Philip decides to send a real army to deal with the Flemish once and for all, we are doomed."

"William Montfort?" asked a young knight of the Household Guard as he stood in the doorway to the workroom. Hughes had been busy describing in gory detail his success in Flanders, and William welcomed the interruption.

William looked up from his work. "Yes?"

"Sire, you don't know me, but I've heard much about you. I've come to warn you of a possible danger." He told William about a knight, recently come to the household, apparently under the auspices of Edward's seneschal. There was nothing particular about him, except that he was heard making inquiries about William.

"And what is this knights' name?" William asked.

"Maurice, Sire. Maurice Beauchamp. Word is that he's made quite a name in tournaments."

The young knight told William and Hughes, who stood listening nearby, that the man seemed sinister, and his questions went beyond innocent curiosity. He had asked about William's habits: when he rode, when he came and left work, when and where he went to mass. He had been seen questioning several grooms.

William thanked the young man and asked him to keep him abreast of what Maurice did.

"It appears Maurice is very determined," William told Hughes after the knight left

"William, we can't afford for anything to happen to you. I'll take care of Maurice."

"No, no."

Hughes smiled. "I don't mean killing him. He's here within our grasp."

"You mean sequestering him off to the island prison? No, Hughes, that wouldn't be right. We would be as bad as any other tyrant, abusing the Brotherhood's power. This is a personal matter between him and me."

Hughes shrugged his shoulders. "Just trying to help. But please remember who you are; you are beholden to a lot of people. Your welfare is no longer just your affair."

William decided to take a look at this Maurice Beauchamp. He went to the stables to talk to Brother Albert, who confirmed the story. "Yes, Sire, that indeed is the Maurice we both knew at Pilgrim Castle. I asked a young knight to go warn you, for it wouldn't be proper for me to be seen up there."

On his way back, William took a detour around to the Household Knights' barracks. He asked a sergeant about Maurice.

"Sir Maurice is a senior knight, and is busy training, Sire."

"How long has he been here?"

"Half a year, Sire. He's a great fighter, and our knights look up to him."

While circling the training grounds, William saw Maurice teaching combat riding to a group of young knights. It was him all right—clean-shaven, but the same Maurice without a doubt.

There was nothing to be done. Even if William could have him expelled from the guard, it was best to have Maurice where he could watch him. A man that determined to kill him would do anything, and at least as a member of the Household Guard his whereabouts were predictable.

When told, Hughes' response was to turn to William with a sarcastic smile. "Maurice will kill you, William. Then what will happen to the Brotherhood? Who do you propose will take over the Jesus Gospel? And all for what? Because you think of yourself as saintly. At least let me deal with him! I'm not saintly!"

"Hughes, I can take care myself. Don't fret about me."

That afternoon William became aware that three Templar knights followed him.

Early the next day William approached Hughes at his worktable. "Hughes, would you please dismiss my escort? I know it's your doing."

Hughes briefly looked up from a list he had been preparing. "Ah, William. Fine."

But the next morning when he left Templar House William discovered that the three burly men were still there. And Hughes, Otto told him, had just left for Flanders. William tried to order the men to leave him be, but when he approached they scurried away. It was like chasing shadows. He had to admit, they were very good.

After dinner when he got back to the workroom, William could tell by Otto's ashen face that there was bad news. The large army that Philip had been busy assembling was now ready to move against Flanders under the personal command of Philip's prime minister, Pierre Flote.

Otto called Hughes to return home immediately.

Five days later, in Otto's second floor solarium, William, Otto, and Hughes sat down to discuss how to stop the mighty French army.

Hughes seemed at ease and unconcerned. "Not to worry, Otto. I am currently working on setting a trap for the French."

"I admire your confidence, Hughes, but you realize what will happen if you fail?"

"Yes, that's very clear. Philip will massacre at will in Flanders to show what happens to those who dare confront him."

"Of course, Hughes. Making an example of Flanders will mean that the barons in Aquitaine will surrender immediately for fear of the same."

William saw Hughes' apparent façade come apart. "I get it, I get it! After that he will invade your precious England."

Otto ignored Hughes' outburst. "And the rest of Europe."

For the several hours that Otto and Hughes talked, William sat and listened, knowing that all he could counsel would be to minimize the killing, and that was the last thing they wanted to hear. And it was obvious that Otto and Hughes knew that as well, for they didn't ask for William's opinion and appeared to be avoiding his gaze.

"Is Edward sending any soldiers to Flanders?" Hughes asked Otto.

"A handful of ships."

"Oh, those will come in handy in stopping Philip's cavalry!"

"Edward must focus his attention on Scotland," Otto seemed apologetic. "William Wallace has become a real threat."

They went on to discuss tactical matters, mostly how to maintain an open line of communication with couriers.

After the meeting, William asked Hughes to dismiss the three Templars following him.

"Hughes, you have so much on your mind right now, but the three are so unnecessary when they could be utilized elsewhere."

William saw a shadow of concern cross Hughes' tired face. "William, please, put up with them. Do it for the rest of us, if not for you."

With everything the man was dealing with, William decided not to argue.

The following morning William saw Hughes leave from Templar House, a full pack on his horse signifying that he was on his way to Flanders. Next to him rode a man carrying a long bow and wearing a weavers' tunic, and he seemed somehow familiar. It wasn't until that evening after Compline when William was making his way to his bedchamber, that he realized the man with Hughes was none other than the highly skilled archer they had seen with Anthony's actors six years before when they went searching for Elizabeth. It had been the unusually long bow that had tipped him off. That, and the weaver's tunic.

That night William prayed for Hughes. A big battle was coming, one where their futures were at stake. William knew that they were on the side of the lesser evil, King Edward; that Philip was indeed a monster who, if allowed, would slaughter perhaps hundreds of thousands of innocent lives in his quest for empire. But there was also another battle underway; a quiet one, under the surface, and that one was for Hughes' soul. If lost, he would continue on his course of ever-increasing brutality, and become another monster. William prayed that something would happen to cause him to reverse direction and become the Hughes who once upon a time stood blissfully listening to the nuns of Hafiz Mountain singing in the distance, the one who meditated and was gentle and kind.

A feeling of reassuring joy told William his prayer would be fulfilled.

[2]

Hughes arrived at the busy port city of Antwerp just across the border from Flanders. He was met by one of the weaver guild's leaders, Fredrk, who informed him about the enemy: Fredrk had no idea where the French would strike first. Their army was still in France.

"What about Kortrijkt?" Hughes asked.

"Oh, it's now occupied by the guilds."

"Good. Pass along the order that next time the guildsmen decide to attack French speaking citizens in that town, let them; but allow some to escape."

Fredrk arranged for an escort for Hughes and his companion. "Things are dangerous for anyone who doesn't speak Dutch," Fredrk told Hughes, "all foreigners are considered French, and mobs are in a killing frenzy. Where would you like to go, Sire?"

"Kortrijkt."

Hughes, escorted by two members of the potters' guild, was led along with Arthur, his archer, to a hay wagon. But first, Hughes had to change clothes. "Things are dangerous for Knights Templar and gentry as well," Fredrk said apologetically as he handed Hughes a merchant's tunic and black hat.

Hughes sat with Arthur in the back of the wagon. The two potters took their places in front, one driving the team, the other clutching a crossbow. Arthur settled down beside Hughes in the back of the cart, cuddling his bow.

The wagon made its way for two grueling weeks, stopping on the way in three villages were Hughes met with Templars in charge of local militia. When they arrived outside Kortrijkt, Hughes decided to reconnoiter.

He met with Brother Arnaud, a Templar seneschal, dressed in a tanner's tunic. Brother Arnauld told Hughes that Dutch-speaking guildsmen had slaughtered French-speaking citizens of the town three days before. "Were those really your orders, Master Hughes, to allow for such a thing?"

RIGOR FEDAN

"Yes, those were my orders, but also to let some escape. Was that the case?"

"Yes, more than a dozen escaped and made their way to France."

"Good."

Arnauld appeared upset. "Why did you want people to get slaughtered?"

Hughes knew that Arnauld was French, and a member of the Brotherhood. He owed him an explanation. "Look, the Dutch speakers have been at odds with the French-speakers for many years and have attacked them before. I just made good use of one such incident."

"But why allow it in the first place, what do you gain by it?"

"To anger Philip. He will order his army to seek revenge on the town."

"And that's good?"

Hughes reached for the man's shoulder. "Yes, Brother. That's how we set our trap."

"Then why let some escape?"

"So word of the slaughter reaches the French king quickly."

"And when the French army comes, then what?"

"We fight them. On the grounds outside the town."

"We fight out in the open?"

"Yes. Wait and see. It'll be a grand battle."

Hughes, along with Arthur, moved to a small village of French-speaking guildsmen to await the French. They lived with the town's priest, and walked up and down the small lanes among the thatched roofed houses, waiting, and waiting. Finally one day Arnaud came with news, and as usual, Hughes led him under a tree far from any house, and spoke in Greek to safeguard against possible spies.

"Your wish has been fulfilled, Master Hughes. The French army is headed our way."

Hughes smiled. "Our trap is working! Are your men ready, brother?"

Brother Arnaud described the eight thousand foot soldiers at his disposal, guild people—mostly Dutch, whom he and his Templars had trained over the past year. "They will be assisted by a hundred and fifty Templars, a hundred Flemish knights, and another sixty assorted horsemen. Everyone is well disciplined, Brother Master Hughes. You'll be proud."

The following day Hughes walked the ranks of the infantry with Arnaud. The bored Arthur trailed behind them. Hughes had to admit, the men looked good, they carried themselves well, and seemed to handle their long pikes with familiarity. The pikes had been fashioned with heavy ax blades at the end to cut through infantry's shields, and long hooks on the back to pull down riders.

Hughes scanned the large open field that lay in front of the town where the battle was to take place. He surveyed with satisfaction how it was broken up by creeks and canyons, ill suited for a cavalry charge, and where the pike men would have the best advantage.

Arnauld pointed to Arthur. "I meant to ask you before, who is the English-man?"

"I came to stop Pierre Flote. Arthur is an expert marksman."

Seneschal Arnauld seemed perplexed. "How are you planning on doing that? Flote will be well protected and in the rear, along with the Army's commander, Count Robert d'Artois."

"I was going to mention that next. I need for you to imbed us deep inside the territory the French will occupy."

The next day Arnaud took them to a farm and Hughes and Arthur spent a week living with the farmer's family, dressed in plain peasant's clothing, and watched the French army come through. The farm was on a clearing a league east of Kortrijkt. On the second day of occupation the French "requisitioned" the farmer's pigs and chickens, and on the third, they took all the wheat he had just harvested from his fields.

Arthur became a mess. He couldn't sleep, and hid most of the time in the loft, concerned that the French would kill him. On the fourth day, two French officers came to take the farmer's daughter, and there was nothing Hughes could do but stand by and let them, but he etched the face of one of the French knights in his mind, a young man of light complexion and long blond hair, sporting a two-headed dragon on his coat of arms.

On the fifth day, the battle started when the French marched toward the Flemish infantry lines with their cavalry, about four thousand of them, followed by five-thousand foot soldiers. Making up the cavalry's vanguard was the pride of French knighthood, over a thousand men with flowing capes, beautiful mounts, and gold spurs. Hughes noted that a good number of them were fully armored from head to toe. That was the new lightweight plate made in Milan where they had perfected thin but very strong steel. He had heard that a full suit of armor weighed no more than forty pounds, and the plates fit together so well that a person could move with ease. Those knights didn't bother with shields, and prob-ably felt invincible.

They would just have to see about that when they faced the Flemish pike men.

Hughes watched the French make their progress toward the Flemish lines as he made his own way with Arthur behind the French lines, silently walking through the forest. When he could see the tips of the French command flags within fifty yards, he stopped and looked around. They were at the edge of a grove of trees. He stood by a tall and ancient oak.

"Let's climb, Arthur," he whispered as he undid his heavy sword belt and hid it at the base of the tree.

Arthur stood looking at him. "You never said anything about climbing a tree behind enemy lines. You said I would have an easy shot from a church steeple."

Hughes patted the tree. "This is the best I can do. Now climb."

Hughes ended up having to climb first so he could let down a rope for Arthur to tie around his waist and have Hughes help him up. Hughes found a large branch where they had a good view of the French high command on top a small hill, their flags all around them, their aides and buglers by their side. Behind them was a coach from which servants brought food and refreshments. Hughes could distinguish Flote and Count Robert in the middle, conferring, as they watched their cavalry make it in and out of a canyon. "Arthur, I want both of those men dead," Hughes said as he pointed at Flote and Count Robert.

"You only mentioned one. That will be double my fee." Then he demurred. "Five times, or I don't shoot."

Hughes pulled a long knife from his belt. "We'll talk about your fee once we are done. For now, either they die, or you die."

From where they stood on the big branch, Hughes could clearly see his two targets. They sat on their horses, well protected by archers and foot soldiers with shields facing the battle, but as he suspected, no protection to the rear, where he happened to be with Arthur. Hughes cut a few dangling branches, then sat Arthur down with a clear line of sight to his targets in front of him. He then positioned himself behind Arthur, braced the branch with his legs and held on to Arthur's belt. "You are now very safe, Arthur. I won't let you fall. Ready your bow and wait for my order to shoot."

Arthur flexed his fingers, laid four arrows on his lap and tested his bowstring. In the field in front of them, the French knights clashed with the pike men. As Hughes expected, Flemish knights came out of the forest to harass the French cavalry, like wolves circling sheep, he remembered telling the Templar commanders. With great satisfaction he watched the French cavalry retreat in disarray as the pike men made their inexorable and methodical advance. The French decided to use their bowmen and crossbowmen to save their knights. The Flemish bowmen responded with their own arrows against the French archers.

With arrows flying all around, Hughes ordered: "Now." Arthur pulled his bow taut and shot, then shot again. The man was good, no question; both arrows found their targets, as both Count Robert and Flote slumped down to the ground with arrows through their necks. *What an amazing feat.* Such a well-honed talent that so far had been wasted shooting apples at fairs. Hughes watched as officers gathered around the fallen bodies and made a canopy of shields over them, but soon they were overwhelmed and had to beat a hasty retreat.

Hughes and Arthur stayed hidden in their tree for the remainder of the battle, as the Flemish pike men swept through the battlefield, mowing down everything in their path, assisted by the archers, crossbowmen, and the ever-harassing Flemish cavalry.

The battle over, Hughes helped Arthur climb down from the tree. He paid him double his fee, forty pounds, and told him he never wanted to see him again. The man had talent, but Hughes felt disgusted by his extortion attempt.

"But how do I get home?"

"That's your problem," Hughes said as he picked up his sword and turned away to look for a French knight, the one with the double-headed dragon on his coat of arms.

Hughes carefully skirted the forest around the battlefield, avoiding the Dutch guildsmen in case they confused him for a Frenchman, and aimed for the place where he saw the French knights being cut down. As he got closer, he drew his sword, not knowing who might confront him, a pike man or a fleeing Frenchman.

Hughes came to a clearing and looked. Riderless horses stood about, and on the ground, moaning French knights tried to stand, only to be cut down by pike men. The guildsmen were not following even remotely the rules of chivalry, it appeared as though they were venting centuries of anger toward the gentry on those now defenseless youths, most of whom Hughes guessed would be in their twenties.

Hughes felt a heavy burden in his chest and a lump in his throat. That particular carnage was too much for his eyes, and he wondered what he had created. The pike men doing the slaughtering had been trained using tactics he developed, with a weapon he had devised.

It was more than he could take. Hughes rushed into the battlefield not caring about getting killed, but trying to save at least one of those young men. As he ran, Hughes discovered that he was crying, as though those were his kin being slaughtered, and he wondered what had come over him.

On a small rise between two hollows, Hughes found three knights. One was dazed and attempting to stand, two lay on the ground but were beginning to move. Nearby stood a number of chargers, their fancy saddles and mantles now a pathetic sight. Hughes reached for a nearby horse's reins, grabbed the man about to stand, bent over, placed a shoulder on his stomach and threw him on top of the horse. He walked with the horse to the two prostrate youths and hoisted one up by the sword belt until he could get his shoulder under him, and again threw him on top of the horse. He did the same with the other young man; then mounted behind them and scurried away to the safety of the trees. He had no idea what to do with his captives, but first things first. He would find a safe place to hide and tend to their wounds.

[3]

William read a report from Hughes and a Templar seneschal, describing the battle outside Kortrijkt, how the French army went to punish the town for the slaughter of French citizens, and the ensuing encounter where Philip's army was soundly defeated.

He skipped over the killing of Flote, the fact merely registered, what stood out for him was the killing of civilians. William could tell that it had been the means to draw the French army, and figured it must have been Hughes' idea; the trap he had mentioned to Otto.

William stepped outside the workroom, and walked the hallway, back and forth, thinking about Hughes and how he was now a cold-blooded killer; like so many out there who practiced as children torturing and killing small animals for fun at fairs and then thought nothing of butchering whole villages of peasants when they grew up. But Hughes was a brother; he was supposed to be different. What happened to the Hughes from Hafiz Mountain?

"A worried William? Is that what my eyes are seeing?" He heard Mary's voice behind him.

"Why aren't you in your convent, young lady?" he said as she planted a kiss on his cheek.

"Someone must keep an eye on you, my dear William. Otherwise you'll wear out the hallways walking your worries away."

Mary took William by the hand and led him to their customary place, the alcove off the stairs. She kept a hold of his hand after they sat down. Her touch was soft, cool, and nurturing.

"What ails you, William?"

"War."

"But you are a knight. And you understand that this is a just war and my father will win on all fronts. God is with him, is He not?"

Her eyes were dancing before William, trying to decipher his mood, his thoughts. "Ah, Mary, my Mary. It's not that simple." How could he tell her about what really bothered him? The pain he felt at every violent death particularly of innocent civilians, and more so when a dear friend was responsible for the slaughter.

"Your father could win over the French," William said, "but everyone has to do their duty, fight for him."

Mary looked surprised. "These are very trying times, William. Isn't everyone helping as much as they can?"

William shook his head. "I can now confide in you. I've always been suspicious of Bishop Bek. He recently gave your father terrible advice regarding Robert de Bruce. Your father humiliated de Bruce to the point where he's on the verge of joining the Scottish rebels."

"What did my father do?"

"He set up a ruling council in Scotland of loyal barons, but on Bek's counsel decided not to include Robert de Bruce."

"Oh, William. I never liked that pig Bek! I think he's a devious man."

"Mary, would you help us help your father?"

Mary looked at him with wide, trusting eyes. "Yes, William, whatever you want."

"Please try and talk your father into including Robert de Bruce in the government, and after that, distancing himself from Bek. That would be the best service you could possibly provide." William realized that Edward and Bek were probably positioning Robert de Bruce on a similar path to Balliol's, a strategy that apparently called for the annihilation of all rightful heirs to the Scottish throne. What he was asking Mary to attempt was perhaps hopeless, but he had to try and stop such evil.

Mary told him she would talk to her father right away. Then her eyes grew moist. "William, could we be more than friends?" At this she blushed.

William took her hands. "Mary, we have both taken vows of celibacy."

"But those are just words, William. Don't you want to express your love for me? I know you love me."

"Mary, those are not just words."

"But why is celibacy so important?"

"It's not. What's important is the vow. That's how we grow strong, by keeping our word no matter what. And that's what takes us to God; our characters tempered like steel."

She stood, kissed him again on the cheek and rushed off.

William walked away feeling sad. That evening he would pray for Hughes, and Mary as well.

"Maurice was promoted to bannerette, brother," Albert told William later that day in the stables. The sergeant was sitting on his low stool cleaning and arranging his tools: pincers, hammers, scrapers, punches, knives, and files he used on the horses' hoofs.

"That's interesting, Albert. I know the man is an excellent fighter."

"Please be careful brother. He surely plans to do you harm, perhaps kill you.

Otherwise why is he here?"

William mounted his horse. He knew that Maurice followed a strict code of chivalry; his reputation on the battlefield was proof. That one time when he withheld his men from aiding Hughes' squadron had been an aberration, an isolated impulse he probably had regretted ever since. His plan would have to involve a challenge, rather than lurking in the shadows with dagger in hand. Besides, Hughes' Templar escort would be a deterrent for even the most deranged man.

William turned to look behind him and saw three figures dart behind a wall. Perhaps he would have to get rid of them for Maurice to make his move.

When William entered the workroom the following morning, he found Hughes, who had arrived just moments before from Flanders, in animated conversation with Otto.

"That was quite a deed, Hughes," Otto was saying.

'Thank you, Brother Otto, I thought I would cut off the snake's head and see what happened."

"I meant the battle. Your men defeated the French. That was a monumental victory. It's all people around here can talk about, how infantry managed to defeat cavalry and save England in the process...but yes, killing Flote was a brilliant move."

William studied Hughes and found him cold, perhaps even cruel. "I can't rejoice," William said, "when I think of all the women, children and old men slaughtered by the guilds just so you could set a trap, Hughes."

Hughes turned to look at William for what seemed like a long time. "I don't have the luxury of sitting here reading reports," Hughes said in a slow and measured tone. "I am out there making decisions as I go along. In this case, I traded the lives of the few for that of the many. Had we not trapped the French army and defeated it, they would have slaughtered the guildsmen, all of them, and by now that same army would be assembling in Normandy ready to invade England.

"Eleven years ago when Brother Dimas sent me to Acre to rescue Brother Otto I traded lives then too. I threw an old matron overboard so I could make room for a young boy and his sister. Was that any different?"

"There are other ways, Hughes."

"How William? If you come up with an alternative, please let me know."

There was a sharp edge to Hughes voice and William realized that his former commander thought his work so important and the outcomes so crucial, that nothing else mattered. But it was sad, so sad thought William. The Hughes he had once known was gone. "Have you had a chance to meditate, Hughes?"

"I've hardly had time to sleep much less meditate. That's a luxury I would like to have."

In the days that followed William read reports and heard talk from visitors from abroad. The battle in which Hughes killed Flote was a big setback for the French, and it became known as the Battle of The Golden Spurs. Happily, the end result was that the French were willing to sign a final peace with England.

"However, that doesn't mean the French are giving up on their scheme," Otto said. Dimas was back and all four of them rode to the palace along the tree-lined Strand on an early winter morning. "Peace in Aquitaine means they want to concentrate everything they have in subduing the Flemish. Once accomplished, Philip will, without doubt, renew his war against Edward."

"The French are leaving Aquitaine, all right," Dimas said. "But I'm betting Otto is right. Engerrand de Marigny replaced Flote as King Philip's prime minister, and he's all about war."

"Keep up the recruitment and training of your guild infantry, Hughes," Otto said. "I think we've just discovered a formidable weapon."

William went home to bury his father the day after he received news of his death. When William arrived, he found his mother, brother, and Elizabeth sitting by the coffin in the great hall. Neighbors, vassals, fellow knights and some important knights were filing past, paying their respects.

William stood by the coffin looking at the familiar face. Sir Lawrence's features looked peaceful, the eyes that had held reproach for so long, now closed.

That evening Richard pulled him aside. "Willy, I think mother is not well, perhaps she's been affected by father's death more than she lets on." He told how the day after their father's passing, she ordered her servants to scour the village collecting rags. "Now she's got her chamber full of rags, where she spends most of her time."

"Not to worry, Richard, I think that's good news."

When he opened his mother's door, he found her happily making dolls, and when she looked up to greet him, there was a big grin on her face.

Time was passing quickly. It had already been six years since Richard and Elizabeth's wedding. He studied Richard's face and saw how much he had aged. But there were joyful changes that time also brought: Richard and Elizabeth now had two boys presently chasing each other with wooden swords.

Elizabeth was a steadying element in Richard's life and a capable administrator, a taskmaster both feared and respected throughout the earldom. When it came to troublemakers, she dealt with them forcefully, and a few ended up in chains. One baron, who tried to take over his neighbor's lands by first slaughtering his peasants, was still in the dungeon after two years. She had made a few enemies, but most people had nothing but praise for her.

Alphonsina told him how Elizabeth had become like a loving older sister to her.

William studied his wife as she chatted with her friends. They were gossiping about a particularly handsome knight. Alphonsina was happy, he guessed, she was cared for and had no one to abuse her. Her life would be uneventful with her two companions. They would carry on just as they were for many years to come.

William visited a now slow-moving Black and walked with him, musing aloud, certain the horse understood him. He sat on a log and watched Black rub his rump on a tree trunk. William thought how perfect things would be if horses lived as long as people, and women like Alphonsina could marry whom they pleased. He walked over to his horse feeling forlorn; he sensed that he would never see him again. He wrapped his arms around the big neck, placed his cheek against his and said goodbye to his friend.

Three months later, Otto, William, Hughes, and Dimas escorted King Edward to the signing ceremony for the formal peace treaty with France at a castle halfway between Paris and London. During a celebratory banquet—an impossibly long table decked out with stuffed geese arranged so they looked to be flying—Edward sat across from Philip, and they exchanged pleasantries, until Philip's gaze fell on Dimas' surcoat, who stood along with the other two Templars behind Edward. With obvious hatred Philip muttered to the English king: "Why do you keep those heretical pigs around?"

Edward stared at Philip for a moment then shouted, "You touch a single Templar and I'll personally cut off your pretty head and feed it to my dogs!"

Everyone gasped at the outburst, and for a moment it appeared that the peace would never be signed, but Engerrand de Marigny appeased the two kings, assuring Edward his wishes would be respected. Then he had them kiss each other's cheeks.

The following day the treaty was signed.

Almost immediately after the signing, Otto's spies reported that the French were now concentrating their efforts on two fronts: Marigny on Flanders, while Nogaret's sole task was to get rid of Pope Celestine V.

Nogaret disseminated vicious lies calling the pope a heretic, accusing him of terrible sins against God and nature, an usurper to the papal throne who threw his predecessor in prison.

"I wouldn't be surprised if Nogaret personally tries to murder Pope Clement," Otto told William one morning riding to the palace. "He's an impatient man, and he, Philip and Marigny need desperately to have Bertrand de Got elected pope.

"Please have the Brotherhood keep an eye on Pope Clement, William," Otto asked. "Maybe have two or three Templars around him at all times."

Two months later, Otto and William received a report from two Templar knights who had been assigned by the Italian Templar master to protect the pope. They said that Clement had been attacked by a party of mercenaries led by Nogaret and two Italian cardinals at his palace at Anagni in Italy. The Templars had rallied citizens from the town who rushed to save Clement and succeeded in driving the attackers away. However, the Templars suspected that they had actually arrived too late, for the pope's health started declining, perhaps the result of poisoning.

A month later church bells in London rang mournfully. The pope was dead.

William and Otto realized they had to act fast. William sent Dimas to Cyprus for funds, then to Italy to contact the two cardinals who were in the Brotherhood. Their job was to use the Templar funds to buy as many cardinals' votes as possible to prevent the election of Bertrand de Got as pope.

That night, after meditating, William prayed for them all. He was certain that Philip was nearing his goal. He would have Bertrand de Got as pope. He would then be ready to destroy the Templars, just as the Caesarius Prophecy predicted. The Templars would be imprisoned on orders from the new pope, and William had to make sure that he could fulfill what he had promised Brother Jacques. He would let some be sacrificed so the Order could be saved. William felt a heavy load descend on his chest. *The time has come.* He recalled Hughes' words about letting the few die so the many would live. *I will be doing the same.* But he had no other recourse.

William forced himself not to dwell on the dark and awful thought, but on saving the Order. But how was he supposed to do that?"

William sat with his thoughts, and he suddenly remembered how distraught he had been at Balliol's capture. How he wished he could have done something! And it occurred to him that he could. He was, after all, in charge of all the Templars. Why not use them for a good cause? Then he felt a jolt to his heart, and knew he was on to something. Of course! Wouldn't Scotland make a wonderful place for the Brotherhood and the Templars? All he had to do was help make it safe. He stood up and walked around his small room, excited at the notion.

That following day William asked Otto to call Hughes back from Flanders. He told him that they needed to plan the next steps in their fight against Philip.

Dimas was due to return from Rome any day.

A week later, William studied Hughes and Dimas as they walked into the workroom. Dimas' face was even thinner, his forehead heavily furrowed, the intensity of his countenance heavier. Hughes' once graying hair was now almost completely white as was his beard, but his eyebrows and moustache remained black. There were heavy creases going down his cheeks, making him look even tougher. William realized that he saw Otto almost every day, and in his eyes the man had not aged; but now he noticed Otto's face a little heavier, his jowls more pronounced, and it dawned on William that Otto was in his mid sixties.

A heavy mist veiled London as Otto took his Templars for a walk along the twisting, narrow streets of the city, cobbled over the years with a variety of stones. The ones laid down by the Romans were large, perfectly square, and painstakingly fitted together; the rest, the ones used in later years, were smaller, roughly cut, and haphazardly placed. The houses were typical of the working class, white washed wattle and daub construction, narrow, two-story, and easy to burn because of the straw roofs.

"As things now stand," Otto said as he paced slowly along a lane, "for Philip to mount a full offensive against the Templars, he would need an edict from the pope. So far the cardinals have not selected a new pope, and there is no telling if the French will succeed, but we have to contemplate the worst possibility—that Bertrand de Got will be elected. In that case only Edward stands in the way of Philip's ambitions and the destruction of the Templars. If Edward dies before Philip, then we'll be in trouble.

"Philip is twenty years younger, so the odds are not in our favor," Otto added.

William thought it time to unveil his plan. "I agree we must think of the future," he said. "But the only way to guarantee the Templars' and the Brotherhood's survival is to have a kingdom of our own."

"You mean gather all the Templars from all over and invade a kingdom?" Dimas asked. "The new pope, whoever he is would declare a crusade against us, and both Philip and Edward would join and come after us."

"We don't need to invade and rule," William said. "We can instead help a kingdom in secret ward off an unjust invasion and then help build it with our administrative, military and financial skills. We can become indispensable, and in return have a permanent sanctuary."

"Well, we've been working with the forest cantons in the Alps, and they are forming a federation," Otto said. "I always thought it could become a haven for us...surrounded by mountains and easy to defend."

"Yes, Otto," William said, "but we need a place right away, and the cantons are still trying to unite."

A servant in a nearby house opened a window to empty a bedchamber into the street, and the three moved out of the way. "You are looking for a kingdom that we can secretly rule and that would welcome us right away?" asked Hughes.

"But which? And how?" Dimas asked.

"Which kingdom do you have in mind?" asked an incredulous Otto.

"Scotland."

William watched Otto's reaction. He appeared stunned. Otto was not the only one who seemed dumbfounded. Dimas and Hughes looked at William as though he had lost his grip on reality.

"Right now the place is in chaos, and Edward will have to keep sending armies to pacify it," Hughes said. "He just returned from his recent Scottish campaign. Do you know what happened, Otto?"

"He failed to capture William Wallace and his allies, but left Bishop Bek behind to set up a government comprised of Scottish nobles."

"But not including Robert de Bruce," added William.

Otto shook his head. "That's correct."

"So Scotland will continue being a troublesome possession for Edward," Hughes said.

"Exactly," William said. "Just think of the difference that one thousand well-placed Templars would make. We just did it in Flanders and Aquitaine, why not do the same in Scotland, only for our own benefit?"

"You mean, fight Edward?" asked an incredulous Otto. "That's not just breaking our agreement with him, that's treason."

William shook his head. "No, brother. That would be neither breaking our agreement with him, nor treason. In the first place, we are foremost members of the Brotherhood and owe our allegiance to our fellow brothers. As Templars we owe our allegiance to Christ and by extension, the pope, and no one else. We agreed to help Edward in Flanders and Aquitaine in exchange for his protection against Philip. We fulfilled our bargain.

"But that has nothing to do with Scotland, where King Edward is the unjust aggressor. Had he acted with honor and integrity with the task asked of him at the beginning by the Scottish barons to help them select a new king, there would not be a war in Scotland. Instead he was overcome with greed for power and in this one instance, became evil. It's our sworn duty as members of the Brotherhood to fight such evil, just as it is our duty to fight Philip in his equally evil actions. Even if you have sworn fealty to Edward, it does not apply when it involves evil."

Otto pulled on William's arm. "But William, he's my king!"

"You have to decide in what aspects of your life Edward is your king," William said as he prompted the group to continue on their walk down a side street that appeared deserted.

"Tell me your plan," Otto asked.

"I can't tell you until you have made your choice."

Otto took two brisk steps and stood in William's path. "You don't trust me?"

William could see the hurt in his eyes. "I love you Brother Otto. But in this one instance I think your loyalty to Edward stands in the way of your duty as a brother."

Without another word Otto turned his back and walked away toward the river.

Dimas eyed William with his characteristic intensity. "What now, William?"

"Let's give him until morning. I'm sure he will make his decision sometime tonight."

Hughes turned to look at Otto's departing figure. "And if he decides against us?"

"He's an honorable man. We can always negotiate with honorable men."

"But if he decides against us, do we leave him?" Hughes asked.

"If we have no other option, yes."

Late that night as William sat in his cell at Templar House in meditation, he heard a knock on his door. It was Otto. William let him in, and noticed the tension in his face.

William sat on his bunk and offered Otto the only chair.

"You asked me to make a decision, and I have," Otto said. "I can't help you as long as Edward is alive, but I won't stand in your way either. You can remain in my service and do what you need to do, just don't involve me. If Edward dies, everything will change. I will not swear fealty to his son." Otto studied William. "Is this agreeable to you?"

"Yes. I think that's a good compromise. We'll continue working for you everywhere except in Scotland. There we won't help you. And you will turn a blind eye to our work with Robert de Bruce."

"You think de Bruce will rebel?"

"I'm certain. He's the rightful heir to the Scottish throne. I want to help him, and he can help us."

There was relief in Otto's face. "Fine William, we have a pact. But it must remain a secret between the two of us. No one else can know."

William got to his feet and placed a hand on each of Otto's shoulders as he looked in his eyes. "It's our secret pact."

"But we'll continue working against Philip, right?"

"Of course, Otto. The man must be stopped. But he will destroy the Order, and we must let him."

"What do you mean?"

"We'll sacrifice some Templars to make Philip think he destroyed the Order. A few of my brothers will be imprisoned, probably tortured, and some may die, so the rest of us can go on." At the words, William felt a lump in his throat and heaviness in his chest.

Otto appeared stunned. "Are you sure that's necessary?"

"Sadly, yes. It's something that Grand Master Jacques foresaw eight years ago. We'll be much more effective in keeping "The Knowing" alive if we become invisible, that is, if we work in secret. Otherwise we'll always be a target for someone like Philip."

Otto was silent for some time. "So the Order will be no more. But what about the other Templar functions, like the letters of credit?"

"That must end."

Otto sat back down on the chair. "In that case, William, I need to ask a special favor of you. The Templars we sent into my homeland to help us fight the Austrians have performed splendidly, thanks in great part to the tactics developed by Hughes. But I need more."

"What would you like me to do?"

"The moment Philip destroys the Order there'll be a great void that will hurt many merchants who have relied on the Templars for their letters of credit. That's the only way that they can travel safely from fair to fair, with only a piece of paper in their pockets they can redeem at any Templar *commanderie* rather than coffers full of gold for bandits to seize."

"And you want us to continue doing this work from the Alps."

"Yes. Just think of it, William. In the process we'll be building a second haven for the Templars and the Brotherhood. Please give it some thought."

"I will, I promise I will."

In the morning, the bells rang from the many abbeys, convents, monasteries and churches throughout London. A town crier in a street corner shouted the news: The College of Cardinals had elected a new pope.

William stood by the window in the workroom at the palace along with Hughes and Dimas, watching people rushing down the street in celebration.

Otto walked calmly into the room with a big smile on his face. "We won. Bertrand de Got is not the new pope, it's an Italian cardinal, and he is now known as Benedict XI."

William had a bad feeling; it was as though he could almost see the new pope lying dead. "Otto, we must protect him with everything we've got."

The spy reports Otto received in the following weeks portrayed Philip's intense anger and frustration.

Eight months later, on July 7, 1304, the church bells rang again, a mournful peel. The new pope was dead, and it was clear that Nogaret had killed him. The French minister had stormed the papal palace in Rome with a large armed guard and virtually kidnapped the new pope in his chambers for a few hours. When Nogaret left, the pope was dying of apparent poisoning. The attack had been so blatant it was as though Nogaret felt safe from punishment or wanted it known that the French were so powerful they could get away with anything. Caught by surprise, Otto and William again sent Dimas to Rome, but this time Philip had prepared well, and the two cardinal brothers reported that none of the other cardinals would even talk to them.

Months passed by, winter came and went and St. Peter's throne remained empty. One spring morning Otto and his three Templars were busy planning further work in Flanders when they heard the news from a town crier walking the palace grounds: Bertrand de Got had been elected pope as Clement V. After a moment, Otto stood, gave William a meaningful glance, and walked out.

Dimas and Hughes came to where William sat.

"We now need to speed up our plan for Scotland," William said in a whisper, in case someone went by outside their workroom.

"Why did Otto walk out?" Dimas asked.

"So he wouldn't hear. For now it's easier on his conscience to stay out."

Hughes frowned. "What do you want us to do, William?"

"Hughes, go to Scotland and find Robert de Bruce. Tell him of our plans, see if he accepts."

Hughes leaned on William's table. "Oh, I'm certain he will. I already sounded him out a couple of months back through a relative of mine."

William studied Hughes. "That's great news. Thank you. In that case, let's contact Grand Master Jacques and ask him to send a thousand men to Scotland as secretly as possible and as soon as the de Bruce brothers are ready."

"I suppose that's my job," Dimas said.

"Yes. But you have another message I want you to deliver. We must let King Philip destroy the Templars."

"What?" exclaimed Hughes.

Dimas stood in silent shock.

Hughes pulled William by the arm. "You are not serious, are you?"

"There is no alternative, brothers. To save the Order we must give Philip the appearance that he destroyed it. For that, a few of our Templar brothers will be imprisoned, accused of heresy, and who knows what else. Some may die at the hands of the French. But I hope and pray that most of those rounded up by the French will survive.

"There's no other way, believe me. Philip will pursue us, to the ends of the earth if necessary. His hatred is that intense."

Hughes started breathing hard, as though he couldn't get enough air. "What about Grand Master Jacques, what's his opinion? After all, it's his command you are talking about."

"He's the one who first mentioned the plan to me eight years ago. I was just as shocked as you are now, but I have come to terms with it."

They discussed alternatives for what seemed hours. Finally, William detected a look of resignation coming over Hughes. Dimas seemed withdrawn.

As he was about to leave, Hughes turned around. "What about Maurice? Let's send him to Flanders, out of the way. It might even get him killed."

"No," William said. "Let him do what he needs to do. I can defend myself. Besides, you have those three Templars following me everywhere. By now they know me better than I know myself. Hughes, I'm no longer asking you, I'm ordering you to dismiss my escort."

Hughes nodded.

Dimas cleared his throat. "William, let's be practical," he said in his curt voice, "we can't afford any distractions. Why don't we offer Maurice the chance to be reinstated in the Templars? Maybe then he'll leave you alone. I recall that during his trial he hardly reacted when told that he would be imprisoned for two years, but almost broke down when he learned that he would be dismissed from the Order."

As a Frenchman, Pope Clement V refused to live in Rome, and moved St. Peter's throne to Avignon. One of his first decrees was to threaten excommunication to anyone who opposed King Philip in Flanders.

French intellectuals in Paris intensified their propaganda against the Templars, with accusations of an opulent lifestyle and suspected heresies. There was nothing in any report to indicate that Philip knew of the Templars' involvement in his recent wars, but there was evidence of his growing hatred against the Order, and Otto concluded that he knew.

Early on a Sunday morning, after a stroll through London's streets, William was making his way back to Temple Church for mass, when he heard quick steps coming down an alleyway. He turned to see a young woman fleeing from a man.

"Oh, a Knight Templar. Thank God. Please, Sire, protect me!"

William drew his sword and faced the man pursuing her, who stopped but a few paces away. On seeing William's sword the man turned around and fled.

"Was he trying to hurt you?" William asked.

"He's trying to take me by force," she said in between sobs, "for I would not consent to marry him." She was young, perhaps twenty, and very pretty. She spoke in cultured Provencal French, and gave the appearance of a noble woman of means.

William thought what to do. He looked around. The woman's attacker was nowhere in sight. It was important to be seen in church. He had already missed a few masses, and he knew people would talk. But he had to make the young woman safe. He escorted her through the narrow winding streets to a nearby inn where he got her a room and instructed the innkeeper to not let anyone know where she was. William told the young woman that he would soon return, and to wait for him, that no one could harm her now.

After mass William went back to the inn. He sent a servant to fetch the young woman at her room, but was told that she was too distressed and would not come. She asked for him, the servant said, "and is in direst need."

There was something that didn't seem right, something about the young woman that didn't ring true. What would a noble woman be doing alone in the streets of London? She was too well dressed, too prim and proper for a woman in distress. And something about it all rang false. Odd for a man to be openly chasing his prospective bride through the streets because she refused to wed him… Then William laughed. Now things started to make sense. Her story was close enough to Princess Mary's. A few courtiers had spread the gossip about William's role in Mary's life. If Maurice wanted to set a trap, what better way than to identify a sensibility of his, and lure him with another young woman being forced into a brutal marriage? William had just recently started going for walks through London before mass on Sundays, something predictable enough to lend itself for a trap. And the young woman showed up two weeks after Hughes dismissed the Templar escort. It all made sense.

If this was what Maurice had planned, William decided to follow along and get the whole thing over with. He prayed for a harmonious outcome, for both himself and Maurice.

William went to see the innkeeper. Who were his current guests? Was there perhaps a member of the Church?

The man glanced at William's surcoat and commander's mantle. "Well, Sire, we have several distinguished members of the Church, but the only one about is a priest."

A servant escorted William to the priest's room. He knocked on the door and a young man answered. "Father, would you give me but a few moments of your time?"

The priest stood inspecting William. "What do you require of me, Sire?"

"Just to be a witness."

The young man assented. He was traveling on important matters of the Church, but surely he could spare a few moments for a Knight Templar.

William led the priest to the inn's courtyard. They could see the young woman's room on the second floor; she was brushing her hair and apparently humming a tune. William asked the priest to keep careful watch on everything that went on in the room. If he stood on higher ground at the far end of the courtyard he would be able to see most of the woman's chamber. "Just stand about," William told him, "and pretend to be in silent contemplation while admiring the garden."

William explained that he would knock on the woman's door and be invited in by her, and that after some time, a man, possibly a bannerette in the king's Household Guard would burst in.

The priest looked at William with surprise, but then nodded his assent.

William walked to the young woman's room and knocked softly. He heard muffled sobs inside, and slow steps approaching.

Her eyes were red, but her hair was in place, and she appeared soft and vulnerable. "Oh, you finally came!" She opened the door to let him in, then peered outside into the hallway, nervously looking in both directions. She closed the door, and broke into tears and loud sobs. "My life is ruined. I don't know where to turn. I can't go home and be married off to that horrid man!" With this she collapsed on the bed, her hands about her face.

How clever, William thought. Things had been carefully planned. He guessed he was now supposed to come over to the bed, sit beside the woman, who would promptly put her arms around him and drag him down.

Instead, William went to stand by a cabinet, a place where he was most visible to the priest, whom he could see in the courtyard. He discovered that he felt strangely calm, as though he were just playing a game whose outcome had been prearranged. He knew he was not going to die that day, and surely he was not going to kill; his vow was more important than life. A few moments passed, and the woman continued crying.

Then the door flew open and two Household Guards burst into the room.

The two men looked at the bed, and then looked around the room until they spotted William.

Maurice made as if to move in his direction, then saw William's crossed arms, and checked himself.

"Maurice, nice to see you after all these years!" William said. He then addressed the woman. "My Lady, I suppose you know Bannerette Maurice?"

"She's my cousin," Maurice said curtly.

The woman stood up and smoothed her clothes. William waved at the priest through the window and signaled for him to come.

William waited until the priest came to stand beside Maurice and his friend. "Your trap didn't work, Maurice. After rescuing your cousin, I was supposed to try and comfort her, at which time you and your friend would have burst into this room, just in time to save her honor, and cast me as a despoiler of young women. Is that right?"

Maurice glared at William. "You can't bring any charges against me, nothing happened."

"Those were to be my words, Maurice. You tried to trap me with a woman and have me expelled from the Templars. I suppose since she's your cousin, you would also have challenged me to a trial by combat to avenge her honor, am I right?"

Maurice stared at the floor in silence. His friend stood beside him appearing uncomfortable. The priest looked both shocked and ill at ease. The woman was busy in front of the mirror.

"Thank you father for your help," William said bowing to the priest. "Perhaps you would be so kind and escort the young woman out along with His Majesty's Knight, so I can have a private talk with the Bannerette Maurice?"

The priest was the last to leave. William faced Maurice who continued staring at the floorboards.

"I will kill you one day, William, for what you did to me. It took me some time to realize why you protected those Jews, a Christian such as yourself. It was all meant to humiliate me in front of my men because you were jealous that your own brother was one of my followers. Then you managed to have me thrown in prison and expelled from the Templars!"

"I won't discuss what you did to me, or I did to you. The point is, I accept your challenge. Tomorrow at dawn, I will fight you in a trial by combat to decide who is right. Meet me in the castle's inner ward after Matins. We'll each bring a witness who will testify to a fair and just match. Let's fight with swords."

Maurice stood up. There was a new look in his face. He was jubilant.

"In fact, let's get it over with right now," William said as he drew his weapon. "Maurice, draw you sword."

"You will fight me here?"

"Yes." William stood in combat stance, his legs apart and sword held firmly with both hands in front. Then he slowly opened his arms wide, exposing his torso. "You can kill me now, go ahead. I will not resist."

Maurice stood staring at him, incredulous. "You want me to kill you?"

"Yes, Maurice. I vowed never to kill again, so go ahead and slay me."

Maurice gazed at William, trying to read him. "Why would you vow that? You are a knight."

"That's my affair. But it's the truth."

Maurice's eyes shifted from side to side. "Then this won't be trial by combat, this would be…"

"Murder? What do you care? You would achieve your dream. I would be dead by your hands. I'm certain that your friend, who just left with your cousin, would vouch that this was a fair duel. If you slay me now, most likely you won't stand accused of murder."

Maurice drew his sword and stood in front of William, who stared at him, unblinking and calm.

They stood for a time and Maurice started to breathe hard, then his body began to tremble. He opened his hand and his sword tumbled down onto the floor. He turned around and sat down on the bed, grasping his face with both hands.

William sheathed his sword and studied the man who shook like a leaf. "Killing me would not be as easy as you thought, eh?"

Maurice seemed to regain his composure, and looked up. "You robbed me of my only dream, to die for Christ! Now if I were to be slain in battle I would be dying for King Edward instead. You took from me my most sacred desire!

"The only thing left for me was to salvage my honor by killing you in just combat. Now you are cowardly taking that away as well.

"Have you no shame?"

Dimas had been right, this was a real Hardcore, but one without his Templar surcoat. He would give anything to wear the red cross again, and die a glorious death.

William looked out the window. The courtyard below was empty, the few shrubs looked serene; silent witnesses to man's constant folly. "Maurice, I can make you a Templar again, and you can die a glorious death."

"You?"

"Yes," William turned around to face him. "You will be a Templar and will get to die the way you always dreamed."

Maurice stared into William's eyes. He stood and slowly picked up his sword. Then without a word, he walked out.

The following day, as William sat with Otto in the workroom, Maurice walked in.

"Will you swear to it?" Maurice asked without preamble.

William nodded. "I swear by the Holy Mother that you will be a Templar again within a fortnight."

A week later, William heard from Albert that a French Templar had come for Maurice. They left together on route to one of the most important *commanderies*: Paris.

William let out a grateful sigh. He could now focus on the French Scheme and saving his Order.

Hughes was in Scotland, but kept in regular contact via couriers who could reach William with an important message within a week's time. Dimas had recently returned from Cyprus: Brother Jacques could have close to a thousand Templars ready to land in Scotland within a month's notice. Now it was just a matter of staying ahead of whatever Philip was planning, and figuring out a way to minimize the damage to the Templars when he did decide to strike.

Otto kept a respectful distance, and it was becoming awkward to share a workspace, but he did share information. One morning he placed a letter on William's table and walked out. After a quick glance, William turned to Dimas. "William Wallace was captured as he visited his mistress and was brutally executed by the English."

Dimas sighed. "That was to be expected, William. Now the fight belongs to Robert de Bruce if he wants to pick it up."

"I'm sure he will. He must. It's just a matter of time. But let's hope we can help him before he too is trapped and killed by King Edward. I can't tell you how disgusted I feel over what the English—my own people—have done to the Scots. I would be thrilled to right that wrong."

All the de Bruce brothers had to do was ask Hughes to send Templars to help them train and organize their fighters. William waited impatiently for that one letter from Hughes.

But the de Bruce brothers were silent and William could do nothing but wait.

William now talked with Otto about Flanders and Aquitaine, but never about Scotland, and William found the distance building between them painful; but he knew that Otto had to remain loyal to his king and tread on his own path of honor.

Spring turned to summer and into fall in the endless wait. The tension was taking its toll and William had difficulty sleeping and meditating. He prayed for detachment, but couldn't help but worry.

William asked Templar Master Brother Guillaime de la More for a work chamber for both he and Dimas, and was given a room with an ample view of the river. From then on both he and Dimas spent most of their days at Templar House, and came in twice a week to their old workroom at the palace mostly for appearances' sake.

One cold February morning, William received a letter from Hughes: Robert de Bruce had declared war against the English and proclaimed himself king of Scotland.

"I thought they would ask for our Templars first," a frustrated William exclaimed to Dimas. "What is Robert de Bruce thinking? Edward's troops will slaughter him. Why didn't Hughes stop him?"

In the following months the new Scottish king suffered continuous defeats at the hands of the English, and a nervous William could do nothing about it. If Scotland fell to the English, the Brotherhood and the Templars would have no place to go. At present Otto's home in the Alps offered no safety, particularly if Philip became emperor.

Finally a letter arrived from Hughes: "Send as many men as you can, right away."

Eight hundred and forty Templar veteran combat men secretly made their way into Scotland by first arriving at London, Plymouth, and Dover over a two week period and riding overland by various routes in groups of twenty so as not to attract attention.

Just as in Flanders and Aquitaine, they were ordered to shed their Templar surcoats, and try and blend in as best they could. They were sent to work in small groups within Scottish commands, made up of the various clans, with instructions to train and organize and fight only when absolutely necessary. The last thing the Brotherhood needed was for a Templar to be captured and questioned. Fortunately, French was the universal language of the nobility even in remote areas of Scotland, so the newcomers were at least able to communicate. Hughes wrote William that eighty Templars from Scottish castles had been added to his troops, and he used these men as guides for some of the foreigners who came from as far away as Cyprus.

Scarcely three months after the new Templars arrived, Robert de Bruce's losses came to an abrupt stop.

William sent notice to Grand Master Jacques de Molay to select the Templars who would move to Scotland and those who would be left behind on the day that Philip and the pope moved against the Order. A number of high-ranking brothers would have to be left behind to "manage" the inquisition. That meant providing leadership and support to the imprisoned men. The Templar brothers would confess to many heresies and crimes, that was inevitable under torture. Brother Jacques and William decided to let the men come up with whatever they had to, there was no sense in trying to prepare them, that would be far more dangerous for news of any rehearsed confessions would just lead to more strenuous torture. The Templar grand master sent William the list, and Brother Jacques de Molay's name figured first among those to be caught in Philip's raid. Brother Guillaime de la More, master of England, was also to stay behind.

William examined the list with great sadness. It was tantamount to agreeing to have those men burned at the stake. But Jacques de Molay assured William that the French king would be satisfied with killing the Templars' top leadership. That was no consolation.

Part of the treasury from each *commanderie* was also to be left behind, just enough to keep the French and the pope guessing whether they got it all.

William focused on preparing a fleet large enough to move some twelve thousand Templars. This constituted about two-thirds of the Order. William had wanted to save more, but Brother Jacques was adamant that they needed enough men to make it appear as though Philip caught them all. The French king could always look for a buried treasure, but at least he wouldn't be hunting down Templars all over the world. "Besides," Jacques wrote William, "a good many are ill suited for your venture. Don't fret, William, even Philip is not into torturing and killing old men, and that's mostly who will be left."

William tried to contact Brother Roger de Flor, the shipmaster formerly from Acre, who at last report was working in the Mediterranean and Adriatic seas. Sadly, he had been murdered, but his second-in-command agreed to help. Brother Diego moved his seven ships from Cyprus and Italy to ports in Spain, and took it upon himself to plan the exodus to Scotland. In a period of two weeks he met with key Templar shipmasters in English, Irish, French, Italian, Greek, and Spanish ports. In a letter to William, he suggested using a variety of departure points and for the mass move to take place over several months, "a trickle flow" to avoid detection.

After a month, Brother Diego had thirty galleys standing by if needed, but suggested they start using two galleys right away from the ports of La Rochelle, Marseilles, London, and Venice to ferry a hundred Templars and their horses once a month.

William agreed. "A hundred Templars a month will not be noticed, particularly if they all come from different *commanderies*," he told Dimas in their new workroom in Templar House. "I wish I could move them all at once, but there are so many things to consider."

Dimas stared at William. "Surely, if we move everyone, all twelve-thousand at once and too soon, then if the English invade Scotland and win, we could all be executed for treason. There is no question that the English will invade; it's just a matter of when."

Dimas' normally intense but quiet manner took on a restlessness that William had not seen since Pilgrim Castle, sixteen years before; and just as before he began pacing the room.

"If we wait too long Philip and the pope could catch us all," Dimas said as he walked up and down their work chamber. "However, as long as Edward is alive, we are safe from the French…unless the English king discovers our plans to assist Robert de Bruce, or unless Philip decides to challenge Edward's vow to protect us."

William watched Dimas' nervous pacing. "Yes, we need to exercise care."

"Have you noticed how sick Edward looks of late?"

"Yes, Dimas. I have. Mary asked her father to look into Bishop Bek's affairs, and he found that the bishop had appropriated royal possessions at will in his bishopric, and has ruled the place as a virtual king for many years. She says that right at that time her father started looking sickly, and she's certain that Bek is poisoning him."

Dimas seemed frantic. "If Edward dies now, I'm sure Philip will attack the Templars. Maybe it's the French who are poisoning Edward. Maybe Philip is anxious to move against the Order."

William sent an urgent message to Hughes. Robert de Bruce had to win. They needed a safe haven fast. He told Brother Diego to start ferrying two hundred Templars a month. Templar masters, seneschals and preceptors on the list were notified to ready their men.

William realized that in all probability he would do well by the Order and the Brotherhood, but not by the Jesus Gospel. *We never did anything with it, the whirlpool sucked us in and we lost our real aim.* The Gospel and "The Knowing" would remain the secret of the few. William closed his eyes and visualized Jesus and when he felt his sweet presence, apologized for failing him. Maybe one day when the Brotherhood was well established and safe, someone else would complete his mission.

Hughes now had over three thousand Templars under his command in Scotland, and it showed. That following spring Robert de Bruce had an amazing string of victories; he was no longer on the defensive, but was marching throughout his kingdom virtually unopposed, conquering a number of castles long held by the English. In response, King Edward raised a war tax, borrowed money and started amassing an impressive force to be led by his son, Edward the prince of Wales.

William asked Brother Diego to speed up the exodus.

A week-and a half later, on July 7th, 1307, a distraught Otto walked into William's and Dimas' workroom in the Chancel at Templar House. "King Edward just passed away," he announced with a blank expression.

"Now there's nothing stopping Philip from attacking the Templars," Dimas said.

A sense of dread settled on London, and on the entire realm. Not a single person William encountered thought that Edward's son would be a good king, and England mourned their "Edward Long Shanks." Most people had only known life under Edward. He had ruled forever.

Bishop Anthony Bek presided over the funeral service.

The day after the king's funeral, William and Dimas walked with Otto in the palace gardens. "Pope Benedict XI also died on a July the seventh," noted Otto, "three years ago. Do you think that's a coincidence, or are the French trying to send us a message?"

"If it's a message," Dimas said, studying the unusually quiet palace, "they are saying that they know of our existence."

"You are right." Otto said, his voice suddenly hoarse. "If they have spies in our court—which they must—they would know that Edward has been unconcerned about Flanders and Aquitaine, yet they have been soundly beaten in both. They can tell that someone organized effective resistance against them. Of course they are certain it can only be the Templars."

William wrote Brother Diego to increase the voyages. He wanted to move all twelve thousand at once but Scotland was still dangerous. The prince of Wales, who would soon become Edward II, kept enlarging his army to settle the Scottish matter once and for all. A clear victory would establish the new king's reputation and silence his critics who viewed him as a weakling.

On the morning of September 28, Mary surprised William and Dimas by walking into their workroom at Templar House. Brother Guillaime showed her in, and left. She was the only nun in the realm with access anywhere she pleased, even a men's cloister. William noticed that she appeared agitated. "My brother told me some disturbing news this morning at breakfast. He received a most important visitor yesterday afternoon, a French cardinal who tried to convince him to arrest all Templars in England. The Cardinal said that the pope will issue an order next month to all kings but it would look better if the kings did it on their own initiative," she said in a hushed voice.

"Please, don't get caught." With this she kissed William on the cheek and walked out.

William and Dimas sat in silence looking at each other.

"Oh my!" was all Dimas could say.

William realized that Mary had just saved their lives.

"I wonder why Otto's spies didn't get wind of the news," Dimas asked.

"I don't know, Dimas, but I'm glad Mary did."

William rode down the Strand to Westminster to inform Otto. He too needed to plan his escape or else would have to swear fealty to a new king, an arrogant young man he couldn't stand. The previous month, in one of his first actions after his father's death, the prince of Wales had placed the Keeper of the Wardrobe, Lord Walter Langton, in chains, without due process. That was the type of royal arbitrary action Otto despised.

There was little time for debate and no other options. The evacuation of all listed Templar personnel was to take place immediately. When he returned from the palace, William asked Templar Master Brother Guillaime de la More for couriers.

"How many do you need, Brother William?" he asked with a grand smile.

"Thirty men you would trust without reservation."

"That won't be hard. I place my faith on all my men without question."

The following day, thirty Templar riders went in all directions, some to farms in England, others to Spain and some as far as Italy and Greece. William knew that in a week's time all who had to know would be informed of the pope's intentions, and that they needed to evacuate as soon as possible. Brother Diego was told to make every galley at his disposal available, even if he had to use "extraordinary measures" to secure extra vessels.

Almost immediately, dozens of ships started sailing from ports in Europe and Cyprus, and they were to continue until the last man on the evacuation list was out of harm's way. William and Dimas were to leave on the last vessel out of London, scheduled for October 11.

William now could only pray that Scotland would be a safe haven, and that when the English invaded, the Templars would keep it so. Robert de Bruce now had to win. The Templars would help de Bruce defend his realm, and what better way than to infuse his army with the best fighting force in the world? The recent victories in Scotland were testimony to that effect, and that was with only three thousand Templars.

As planned, the Templar galleys, their big red cross gone from their mainsails, now flew a variety of flags for the entire world to see—merchant ships from Venice, Spain, Cyprus, and Sicily, taking cargoes of wool, spices, cloth, grain and wine to destinations unknown. On board were passengers, all clean-shaven and well dressed; apparently nobles, merchants, and knights on business, along with their horses.

William went to see Mary at her abbey the day before he sailed for Scotland. He rode up with an escort of well over a hundred Templars, who promptly surrounded the abbey and set up crossbowmen in key places. All the nuns watched from windows and doors as the Templars secured their convent.

When William knocked on the front door, Mary herself answered. "William, for God's sake, what is taking place?"

"Sorry to concern you Mary, but my brothers insisted on guarding me."

"Heavens, man. With that escort not even the devil himself could take you." Mary eyed the Templars. "They are guarding you as though you were a king. Why William? Who are you, really?"

"I came to say goodbye, dear Mary."

William watched tears form in her eyes, and then she flung herself into his arms. He held her and she cried freely. "I'm becoming a real nun, William," she said. "I want to be like you, so now I'm praying and keeping company with my sisters. It has become my life."

He felt her grief at his departure. "I'm so glad to hear it." She buried her face in his chest and sobbed gently. "Thank you dear Mary, thank you for your affection," and at that moment, with sadness flooding through him, William realized how much he loved her.

On his return trip to London William stopped to say farewell to Otto. He led his massive escort through the city past Templar House where Dimas joined him, then down the Strand to Otto's house.

A servant led William and Dimas to Otto's solarium where only a select few were ever invited. The big house felt unusually still.

Otto stood up from a reading chair as they walked in, a sad smile on his lips. "So this is goodbye, eh?" Otto sounded subdued.

"It is, brother," William said as he embraced him.

Otto's eyes switched from William to Dimas. "We did well, didn't we?"

"We performed splendidly, brother," William said.

Otto walked over to a low table and came back with a parchment. "Please remember our pact, William," Otto whispered as he handed him the folded document. "This is for Hughes. All my spies. That's my parting gift."

"What will you do now, Otto?" Dimas asked.

Otto sighed, suddenly looking old and tired. "I can't stay here, Brother Dimas. I don't wish to pledge allegiance to England's new king. I'll move to my family's home on the western shore of Lake Neuchatel. I have a grand castle waiting for me, and with the years left in me I'll work hard at building a Helvetic Federation out of the forest cantons and a handful of city-states."

William embraced Otto once again. "Thank you dear brother for everything you've done," then William whispered in his ear. "Your heart has always been true. Nothing else matters."

William noticed a sad, but quizzical look in Otto's eyes. "You are…a most singular man, Grand Master William. Thank you, with all my heart, thank you."

That afternoon William withdrew the Jesus Gospel from the treasure room at Templar House. He kissed the box and felt guilty for the years it had sat abandoned in that vault. As he walked toward the stables he said a prayer so that once in Scotland he would find a way to spread its message.

William found Albert, sitting on his stool by the horses.

"Albert," William said softly.

The sergeant turned toward William with a smile.

"I have a favor to ask of you," and William showed him the wooden box.

"Ah, the mystery," Albert said with excitement.

"Yes, Albert. It contains the words of Jesus as he wrote them, and he speaks of that which you already know." William heard his own words and was surprised. It was as though his heart had already decided to let Albert in on the secret.

William sat cross-legged on the ground next to Albert, who remained on the low stool. William undid the leather straps and opened the box. He took out the first page and translated the Greek into the mixture of English and French his sergeant spoke. William took the second page, and the third. Albert stayed frozen in place, a faraway look in his eyes, absorbing every word.

About two hours later, William was done. He placed the loose parchment pages back in the box and turned to look at Albert. "That's the secret, Albert, one that I ask you to protect for me as you did once before. I think we can best protect it by not calling attention to it, and that's why I'm asking you to carry it in my stead. We don't have Black with us this time, but I'm certain you will guard it as well as he did."

"With my life, Sire, with my life. Where are we going?"

"To Scotland, my friend. We leave tomorrow. Please don't tell anyone."

"That's at least a fortnight's ride."

"We're going by ship, Albert. There are people watching us and if they spot us sailing away, they'll never suspect we are going to Scotland."

On the morning of October 11, William's ship sailed down the Thames, and three days later anchored by St. Mary, one of the Isles of Scilly, at the entrance to the Irish Sea, where William's ship met the last nine Templar vessels from the continent.

William's galley assumed the lead. On its bow stood Dimas, anxiously scanning the horizon for Philip's navy. William turned to look at the blissful Albert, hugging the Gospel's box, sitting on a coffer containing London's Templar House gold. Most of the Templar Treasure—from all over Europe and Cyprus—had already been transported to Scotland, except for Albert's comfortable bench.

As his ship lurched in the rough seas, William knew he would never see his family, Otto, or Mary ever again. Not in this life, anyway.

CHAPTER XI

[1]

On a Saturday morning, cold, crisp, and clear, William stood on the quay watching his ship unload along with the nine others that had escorted him. He was dressed plainly with hauberk, tunic and hose, as was most everyone else filing out of the ships. The only way he could tell those were Templars was by the familiar way they marched, moving as one in cloistral silence.

A cold wind blew in gusts from the ocean, and most shielded their faces in hoods or with blankets over their heads. William held his tunic's hood around his face with one hand. Everyone that could be saved was now safe, and the Templar treasure as well. William took a look around. The quay was in between two villages, on a secluded bay with nothing but rough coast and windswept hills all around, with not a single tree to be seen, but grass and shrubs.

Anyone watching would probably assume that Robert de Bruce was receiving reinforcements from abroad. That was fine.

William took a long last look at the ships. The distinguishing Templar flag, the beloved black and white *Beauseant*, was gone. There was nothing to tell the world that these were Templar vessels. He felt a pang of sadness knowing that from then on there would not be a Templar fleet and the flag that so many had lived and died for was no more. But he also felt immensely relieved. The work of so many years had paid off, and at least for the present, the Order was safe. But other Templars would be paying a heavy price for it, perhaps even burning at the stake. *God bless them all*, William intoned silently as the image of Grand Master Jacques came to his mind.

Templars filed past, including some nuns—wearing simple, homemade cloaks—then the prisoners from the secret island. Unfortunately they had to bring them, all twelve of them. That was the Templars' burden, ten men and two women who if let out in the world would find a way to do damage. When the

Templar sergeant in charge of them walked past, William asked him about Jules. "Oh, yes, I remember the noble-born Cistercian friar! He died crying without stop for the last year of his life; that's what we believed killed him, a heart full of regret."

That's hell, realized William, and he said a prayer for his soul.

Templars continued to pour out of the ships and William noted that about a third were non-combatants, but those who were, looked fit. Combat Templars in Scotland now numbered over eight thousand. That would make Robert de Bruce very happy.

William saw Hughes approach, bareheaded, his neck-length gray hair tussled by the wind, but otherwise impervious to the cold. "Good journey?" he asked as he came near.

"It was uneventful. No French warships."

"Look at them William," Hughes said pointing at a group of Templars coming out of a ship from Spain. "Grand Master Jacques sent us the best, but not just the warriors, some of these people are administrators, financiers and lawyers. Everything we need to set up a kingdom."

"We are in great shape! The fight in Flanders was a great military experience," Hughes mused aloud. "The use of pike men is now being used by the Scots—the improved version, not the clansmen's idea of chaining men together and giving them spears.

"There is no way the English can possibly win," Hughes concluded.

"Everybody in Europe is talking about your pike men, Hughes. Some are calling it the beginning of the end of the knightly class."

Brother Albert came towards them hugging the wooden box to his chest, brimming with happiness. William had kept an eye on Albert during the trip and knew that the man had clutched that box the entire way.

Albert bowed to Hughes, and then handed the box to William. "Oh, people should know about what Jesus wrote, Brother William!"

"Yes, Albert, that's what I've been trying to do ever since we left Cyprus. But we can't just make copies and let people read them, we could all end up being burned at the stake for heresy."

"I hope you find the way, Sire."

William settled down with Hughes, Dimas, and Albert in Galloway—the very southwestern tip of Scotland—in a castle provided by Edward, brother of Robert de Bruce. It was a rudimentary place on top of a hill built with crude but strong walls. Most everyone slept in the great hall with a fire burning in the only fireplace that was also used for cooking. The fuel available was peat moss for special occasions, and dried cow dung the rest of the time, which gave off a pungent smell that took some time getting used to. Planks cantilevered out of windows over the moat were used for latrines, but most people used chamber pots because of the cold. William was allotted his own work chamber, a drafty room on the third floor where he also slept. Hughes and Dimas shared a chamber on the second floor but opted to sleep in the great hall.

The important thing was that messengers could reach them with the news and reports they needed.

Albert assumed his usual role with the horses. Hughes and Dimas worked with local Scottish commands, kept an eye on the English and the French, while William focused on the Brotherhood.

Three weeks after their arrival, Hughes walked into William's chambers and handed him a one-page report from a Paris brother. On October 13th, two days after William had set sail from London, King Philip had arrested all the Templars left in France. Grand Master Jacques had been in Paris and was caught in the raid. Apparently frustrated that the other kings had not followed suit on their own, a week later the pope ordered all kingdoms to do the same or face excommunication.

Hughes waited for William to finish reading. "The Caesarius Prophecy has come to pass," he said matter-of-fact.

For the next months William saw the spreading out of the incoming Templars to their pre-selected units throughout Scotland, most to Scottish commands, but some to Templar sites. All non-combatants went to some of the eight hundred or so Templar farms and estates. These would soon be passed on to the Hospitallers at least in appearance before the Templar order was abolished by the pope and its properties taken over by Philip and the Church.

Six months later, Brotherhood members came to Galloway from all over, concerned about the Templars, and wanting to provide whatever assistance they could. William held an informal meeting at their humble castle. The membership was most concerned with Philip, and decided to focus on the means to reform England and France's governments, to move the existing parliaments from under the kings and into independent bodies. They had had enough with despots and would concentrate their efforts to get rid of the condition that created them, the concentration of power on one man.

Time went by painfully; as William received monthly reports from the Brotherhood in Paris about the trials, and each time he would send for Hughes and Dimas and read the distressing news aloud. "King Philip and the pope are going through the motions to appear legitimate," William read, "All kingdoms in Europe have obeyed the pope and arrested the Templars in their midst and now they are holding their own hearings and trials."

The writing was curt and dry, apparently written by a lawyer. "The charges are as expected: heresy, sodomy, worshiping the devil and witchcraft; all of which are Nogaret's standard trove of accusations used so successfully in the past against perceived enemies of the crown. On the other hand, the confessions are bringing to the surface what *commanderies* instituted as part of novitiates' training, specifically denying Christ and spitting on the cross, which was done to teach them never to surrender their most sacred beliefs no matter what. This is obviously being misinterpreted, as is the innuendo of an inner, secretive organization with talk of a human head and a black cat involved in secret rites.

"The trials are typical of the Dominican inquisitors: once evidence points toward guilt, which can be a witness or someone merely making an accusation, then it's a question of extracting a confession. The inquisitors would rather torture and kill an innocent man than possibly overlook a guilty one." William paused, shook his head and kept reading. "Those who confess and repent—if their heresy is considered redeemable—are let go after being duly punished with incarceration and daily penance. But those who refuse to confess, or do not repent sufficiently, or whose heresy is considered beyond redemption, are burned at the stake for the good of their immortal souls."

Dimas listened with a frozen expression. Hughes stood with his back to William and stared off into space; William could hear him grinding his teeth.

"All kingdoms, except England, are using torture to help the accused confess, albeit none use it as extensively as the authorities here in Paris."

The reports kept coming. The trials would stop and then continue as the pope tried to maintain some semblance of legitimacy and Philip pushed for expediency. Then in 1310, Philip got his wish, and 54 Templars were burned at the stake. William recognized some of the names. Among them was Maurice. He was one of the bravest and refused to confess to any of the charges and not only maintained the strict Templar code, but also helped those around him remain steadfast. The tale of his heroic death circulated among the Templars, how he cried out for Jesus on his last breath as he was being burned.

On hearing the news, William said a quiet prayer for Maurice, and knew how happy he must have been to die for Jesus, to die as a Templar.

Three years later most of the Templars were eventually released to live on their own devices after confessing to minor charges of heresy, in all countries except for France, where they kept questioning and torturing Templars, sadly including Grand Master Jacques de Molay and his top aides.

In Scotland, the Church rounded up a few Templars and questioned them. Neither King Edward nor Robert de Bruce allowed torture in the lands they controlled, so the Dominicans got very little information, then let the men go.

The trials went on and on, and William thought things could not get any worse, when Hughes walked into his chamber clutching a letter from a spy. "This man says that 'the French king strongly suspects that a good many Templars along with their treasure are hiding in Scotland,'" he read aloud.

Hughes waved the parchment in the air in his clenched fist. "It seems that a French spy followed one of our Templar galleys when we came over here five years ago. King Philip is planning an invasion, in the form of a crusade sanctioned by the pope, to wipe us out and take our money."

William sighed. "I suppose we best prepare to fight him. It'll take him a couple of years to get an army ready."

"I'm not waiting."

William studied Hughes. His face was now a hard and angry mask. William could only guess what Hughes was planning on doing.

That was the last William saw of Hughes for several months. Then one day he found him in the great hall as everyone in the castle was settling down for dinner. A young Scottish knight was sitting next to Hughes, but on seeing William approach, stood and offered him his place.

William waited until a servant had served him the day's portion of salted pork, bread, and ale. "I know you are planning something Hughes, what is it?"

William watched Hughes put down his knife. "I don't know what you mean William, I'm simply minding my spies and gathering information. Nothing else."

But William was certain that his former commander was up to something. He had that energized look about him, the look he had whenever he was on a mission. "See that you take good care, my friend. Please remember to meditate."

"Not everything can be solved with meditation, William." With this, Hughes stood up and walked away.

A few weeks later Hughes and Dimas intercepted William as he was about to leave his chamber for the stables. "William, may we have a word?" Dimas asked.

William nodded and led them back into his chamber of rough stonewalls and wide wooden planks for a floor. One side of the room was dedicated to his bed, a chair and personal effects, and the other side, the area by the only window, to work. William opened the shutters and a gust of wind blew into the room. He sat at his table among the large cabinets containing maps and documents.

"What do we have?"

Dimas moved a bench next to William. Hughes decided to stand on the other side of the table facing them. "We were concerned about the Templar treasure that's been sitting here in the castle's strong room," Dimas said. "Hughes is certain that Philip is making preparations to invade Scotland, and I have strong evidence that Edward II already has an army ready."

"Edward poses the most immediate danger," Hughes said. "If Robert de Bruce can't stop the English, they will storm this place and take all of our money, and of course imprison us."

"Let's talk about the money first," William said. "For the past four years I've been sending part of our treasure—a shipment each month—to Zurich, a city that is now part of the Helvetic Federation." William noticed the surprise in his friends' faces. "In another ten months the transfer will be completed."

"Where is the Helvetic Federation?" Hughes asked.

"It's in the Alps," William said. "Don't you recall Otto talking about it?"

Hughes shook his head.

"In 1292, three forest cantons, or districts, formed a federation, and Otto asked for help from the Brotherhood to fight the Austrians. The city-states of Zurich, Lucerne, and Berne recently decided to join them. Otto is overseeing the entire operation."

"But why send our money so far away?" Dimas asked.

"No one would think to look there," William said. "Besides, the terrain makes it very hard for a large army to invade, and I like the idea of a federation. They have developed a form of government not focused on a single person, but on a governing assembly. Locating the treasure there has empowered the new nation, has made them the focus of financial power, and since it's centrally located, we can move money in any direction."

"Sounds as though you've been thinking far into the future, William," Hughes said.

"I have but a few years left as grand master of the Brotherhood. With the time left I want to make sure we survive, and that a few ideas are implemented."

Hughes seemed surprised. "Why do you say you have a few years left, are you planning on leaving?"

"If Robert de Bruce is able to defeat the English, and somehow we do away with the French threat, then our work will be done."

Dimas leaned toward William. "If you mean the French Scheme, yes. But we'll still have to figure out how to disseminate the Jesus Gospel, right?"

William turned to look out the window to the hills with grazing cattle. He sighed. "Yes. That's something I haven't quite figured out how to accomplish."

"But wasn't that your primary mission?"

"Yes, it was…still is."

"To get back to the Helvetic Federation," Hughes said, his manner friendlier, as though a weight had lifted, "if things collapse around here, that's where we go?"

"That's where we go. In the meantime, Hughes, keep applying pressure on the French in Flanders. I think that's what keeps Philip from invading us. And tell me, how's the French Scheme these days?"

Hughes crossed his arms over his chest. "It's confined to four men. Philip, the pope, Nogaret, and Marigny. No one else outside of the four men has the operational knowledge of the scheme. Of that I'm certain. Some, like the Princess Isabella, knows of her father's ambitions, but is not aware of the specific steps."

"Do you have a plan to stop them?"

"I'm working on it. Like you said, Flanders keeps them occupied, and that gives us time. Unfortunately after I killed Flote they've become very guarded."

William gasped. "Hughes, you are not thinking of killing them, are you?"

Hughes' expression grew cold again. He turned and started toward the door. "I'm working on various plans, William. Just remember, you are the one who ordered me to protect the Brotherhood. You must trust me to decide how it should be done."

From then on William's encounters with Hughes became even less frequent and on the times their paths did cross, succinct. Hughes seemed to talk only as he needed to, and didn't meet William's gaze. One day they met on the castle's stairs. William couldn't take it anymore and blocked Hughes' path.

"Here we are alone, Hughes. Talk to me."

"What about?"

"You know what about. You are avoiding me."

"I talk when the need arises. What else is there?"

William placed his hands on Hughes' shoulders. "We were once brothers. What happened?"

Hughes' heavily lined face contorted into a grimace. "Killing is what happened, William. I have to do it and you find it repugnant."

"I can't ever find you repugnant, Hughes. But yes, killing is taking you away from who you were."

"Don't you think I know that? Don't you think I want to be like you? But someone has to do this awful job and I don't see anyone else volunteering."

"Hughes, the job can be done without killing."

Hughes's face went red. "Did you find an alternative yourself to sacrificing all those brothers to the inquisitors? Wasn't that what you decided, to sacrifice the few for the sake of the many? "

"Yes, Hughes. That's what I did," William said in a hoarse whisper.

Hughes anger melted away. "I'm sorry William," he said with sadness in his voice.

That Sunday after hearing mass, William heard quick footsteps behind him. He turned to find Brother Albert. "Sire, I wonder if you would come with me to meet some friends of mine?"

"What is this about, Albert?"

"Brother William, I know I acted without your permission, but I met four men from the nearby town six months ago. Last month they told me about a church they are forming. They call themselves 'The Truth Seekers' and they follow a man who says that the Church is not following Jesus' teachings. I thought you would want to talk to this fellow."

William's heart sank. *Oh no, he's told people about the Jesus Gospel.* "Interesting, Albert. But what have you told them?"

"Only that you are a knight with a different view of what it means to be a Christian. I also said that you have a kind opinion of working men."

"I'll be glad to meet your friends, Albert. When?"

"Would next Sunday after mass do?"

"Fine. I'll be ready in a week's time."

That following Sunday, Albert was waiting for him outside the chapel. "Ready, brother?"

"I need my hauberk and sword. I'll meet you at the stables within an hour."

William rode with Albert to the nearby town of Dumfries, which unlike English and Norman towns was not insanely crowded and therefore cleaner. Up on a hill stood a single story stone building meticulously maintained, and had all the looks of a public house of sorts.

"This is the masons' guild meeting hall, brother," announced Albert.

"We are meeting masons?" William asked pleasantly surprised.

"Yes, Sire. That's who they are."

"How did you meet them?" asked William as they tied their horses to a hitching post.

"A Templar sergeant mason I knew from Pilgrim. He introduced me."

William entered an ample room with tall windows. A gathering of men sat on benches obviously waiting for someone.

When he walked in with Albert, all those present rose to their feet. A corpulent man with a bushy black beard met William. His eyes shone in cautious greeting from under equally bushy black eyebrows.

"I'm Jack, Sire."

Jack escorted William to the front of the room. "Let's give our Templar brothers a warm welcome," Jack said in a surprisingly cultured voice with a heavy Scottish accent.

The men in the room broke into applause.

Jack stood beside William and addressed the crowd of about thirty men. "We have all heard how our honored guest saved Brother Albert's life by rushing a Turk without his shield or lance. He's also the man who spoke to Albert about the secret teachings of our Lord Jesus Christ.

"May we hear from his lips."

William tried to buy time to recover from his surprise and assess the gathering. "Albert told me only of four men who belonged to a group called 'The Truth Seekers.' I didn't come prepared to meet such a large group. Who may you gentlemen be?"

"We are the Truth Seekers from hereabouts," Jack said. "I apologize. This meeting is all my doing. When the four of us—and Jack pointed to three men sitting in the front row—heard you were coming, we told our friends."

William scanned the room. Eager eyes looked at him expectantly. The faces were beaten by the sun and wind, and big arms spoke of heavy labor. William knew that they apprenticed long years and had to read and write and use complicated calculations to build the cathedrals, bridges, and castles. These were learned men.

"What I'm about to tell you would be considered heresy by the Church," William started to say.

"Sire, forget the Church. We are tired of being told what to think," said a man in the second row, who also spoke in a cultured voice.

"It's not enough that they make us go to church on penalty of prison and fines, but they threaten us with death if we think differently from them," said another man way on back.

"Please, Sire, speak freely, you are among friends," said a short man with a carefully trimmed white beard.

William couldn't tell whether it was the quality of their voices or the communal feeling in the room that told him that he could trust them. "I do have information about what Jesus taught," William began, and he expounded on how Jesus had tried to salvage true Gnosis from what had become a religion, and William described original Gnosticism. He told them about emperor Constantine and the edicts that made the Christian Church, and about the Cathars and their discovery of Jesus' true and complete teachings and how they passed on the information to the Templars' inner sanctum, now intent on preserving pure gnosis, "The Knowing," which William explained in great detail.

The thirty or so Masons listened in rapt attention. They asked questions about "The Knowing," and a couple of hours went by as William first described meditation and then provided instruction.

At the end, Jack asked William to return and meet with them again, that he would bring more people eager to hear his words and learn about "The Knowing."

"And not to worry, Sire, whoever comes will be well known to us."

"You have told us the truths we knew were out there," said the man with the neat white beard, his voice laden with emotion. "A more precious gift no one could have given us."

At those words, the men stood and broke into an applause that sounded more like a celebration.

William decided to return as long as they wanted him.

Riding back to their castle, William realized that the fortuitous meting had surprised even Albert. "I had no idea there were so many," Albert said. William's concern was that word would reach an official of the Church who would feel compelled to notify the Dominican inquisitors.

But that was a risk worth taking. And it occurred to William that he knew a good many Templar masons, all sergeants, who were in the Brotherhood. He decided to encourage them to become members of the mason's guild Truth Seekers' group.

The next time William met with the group he encountered a local nobleman, and on following occasions there were more gentry, causally mixing in with the workingmen. The excitement of the meetings was such that they talked for hours on end about the newfound information, an exhausting process but one that William found exhilarating. The Jesus Gospel was being spread, and all thanks to a humble man with a pure heart: Brother Albert.

That summer William received sad news from London. Lord Ralph Hengham had died the previous month, on May 13, 1311. William stared out his window. Otto was about the same age, but thank goodness the tough old bird was still alive, "breathing my invigorating mountain air" as he had said in one of his letters.

Winters in Scotland were hard. A cold wind would blow from the ocean and freeze everything in sight. William did not dare touch anything metal with his bare hands, and the drafty castle offered no refuge. He wrapped himself in many blankets and lived like that, meditating, sleeping, and working. But then spring was ever so welcome! Then came summer, what back home William would have called spring weather.

And the work was all consuming. The de Bruce brothers were highly skilled warriors and administrators, and honorable men. Scotland had been an excellent choice. But the tension was overwhelming waiting for King Edward's inevitable invasion.

William kept close watch on Dimas and prompted him to meditate with him daily.

News from France was disturbing. William received a letter from a French brother indicating that the Order had been dissolved by decision of an ecumenical council. Officially the Templars were no more, and Philip was moving closer to his goal, the Imperial crown. The campaign started by describing his devotional practices, and his dedication to serving Jesus. He was, after all the grandson of King Saint Louis. Then several miracles were attributed to him. He could heal with his touch. People were now praying to him, and there were stirring tales of how bodies would heal and crops rebound in his presence. Next, intellectuals in Paris talked about how Philip was the logical choice for Holy Roman emperor: The Imperial crown belonged to France by virtue of Charlemagne, a true French king, and the first emperor. And Philip had also proven his mettle, his dedication to the Church, by valiantly taking on the Templars.

The new pope had named ten new cardinals, all French, ensuring that all popes in the foreseeable future would be French. Everything was going in Philip's favor.

In the meantime, Dimas reported that Edward II was still enlarging his army, recruiting recalcitrant barons, borrowing money and hiring more troops. But he already had a large enough army, certainly several times the size of Robert de Bruce's. William imagined that the English king relished making the Scots wait. In all likelihood, his spies would have told him of the instances of Scots breaking down with the tension—fights, drunkenness, and the mass desertions across the border.

William called for a meeting of the Brotherhood for the following spring. Seven years had passed since the last time they all gotten together, and there was much to discuss.

Dimas appeared elated at the news. "My nephew was recently inducted into the Brotherhood this past year, William. Poor fellow, he fought at the Battle of the Golden Spurs in Flanders nine years ago and witnessed the slaughter of his cousin and two friends."

"But he survived? I thought all French knights perished."

"No, a few made it. In his case he says he was saved by a French-speaking merchant who appeared on the battlefield on a horse, picked him up off the ground along with two others, and took them to safety. The merchant then nursed them back to health at a farm."

"That's quite a story. I'm glad he lived, Dimas. You must be proud that he's now a member."

The Brethren came in droves from everywhere, perhaps concerned that things were going to climax in Scotland.

The castle's great hall was filled to capacity, close to a thousand people standing shoulder to shoulder. William opened the meeting with a prayer for all the Templars who had perished at the hands of the Dominican Inquisitors at King Philip's behest.

"Let's also pray for the French king and the pope's souls, so when they realize what they have done and why, they may find answers and peace.

"Most of the English forces in Scotland have been beaten back across the border. There are some castles that King Robert de Bruce and his brother Edward have yet to conquer, but eventually they will.

"We expect that King Edward II will invade us soon, and we are confident that we can defeat him and Scotland will remain free. So far—with our warriors' assistance—the Scots are invincible."

"Grand master, what about the treasure?" Cardinal Massimo wanted to know.

"It's now safely vaulted in a city in the new Helvetic Federation, and our financiers resumed their functions a year ago."

The members responded with applause.

"What about the Gospel, William?" the Cardinal asked.

William told them about the Truth Seekers. "Some belong to the mason guild, but a good many do not, they come from other walks of life; there are a number of noblemen and knights. Their organization has chapters in many cities where they are spreading 'The Knowing.' I understand that a new secret fraternity is also being formed, specifically dedicated to it."

"Are you not concerned that it may become a new religion?" an English bishop asked.

"It might. But if in the process 'The Knowing' spreads, then we have achieved our goal."

"Have you given them copies of the Jesus Gospel?"

"No, the Jesus Gospel remains our secret. I propose that we find a place to bury it in a safe vault, and wait for 'The Knowing' to spread. Eventually people will look at the Church with new eyes, realize that dogma, ritual, and all of the written words are not so important after all, and that there is no need for the Bible and the Koran to be the literal 'Word of God.' Then and only then, can we let the Gospel be known.

The applause started hesitantly, then it increased until the sound in that great hall became deafening.

Then a French duke asked to be heard. "The Truth Seekers sound much like the 'Brethren of the Free Spirit.' They too believe much like us, but are being accused of horrible crimes…"

"That's because they operate in the open, daring the Church," said a Spanish bishop. "One of their leaders, the saintly Marguerite Porete was burned at the stake last year by the Dominicans. There's another group comprised solely of women called 'The Beguines.' They too are in danger."

Cardinal Massimo seemed on the verge of tears. "I can only guess that those groups were started by remnants of the Cathars," he said haltingly. "Let's make certain we counsel new organizations who pursue 'The Knowing' to remain in hiding."

Following the usual requests for assistance and deliberation, the participants dedicated the last day to socializing and alliance making. William sat in a corner, greeting old friends and new members. Dimas came over to introduce his nephew, a tall knight in his early thirties, who bore some resemblance to his uncle, same nose and pursed lips, but his face was bright and lively.

The young man bowed when he met William, brimming with pride. His name was Yves, and he spoke effusively on how important the Brotherhood was to him, and how honored he was to be present. "I didn't know my uncle was such an important man, a close brother of the grand master himself, the most powerful man in Europe."

William smiled and shook Yves's hand as he spotted Hughes coming in their direction with urgent intent.

"William, there's a man…" Hughes began.

Yves turned to look at Hughes and grew pale. "It's you! My God, it's you!" he said excitedly, and then turned to Dimas. "This is the man who saved my life nine years ago in Flanders! Uncle, it's him!"

When Dimas introduced his nephew to Hughes, the young man pumped Hughes' hand and smiled broadly.

Yves turned to William, still clutching Hughes' hand. "I had been wounded along with two of my friends and we were lying on the ground helplessly watching as the Flemish pike men slaughtered our comrades on the other side of a gulch. The pike men had seen us and were coming in our direction, and I tried to stand and fight, but was too weak, and collapsed. All was lost, when this gentleman came out of nowhere on a horse, picked us up like so much kindling, and took us to a farm where he took care of our wounds and looked after us for four days until we were well enough to travel. Then he procured us plain clothing and horses, and escorted us to the border.

"I'll never forget you, noble Sire, my two friends and I have tried to find you ever since."

Hughes withdrew his hand, and stood frozen in place. "Yes, I remember you, young man. You say Dimas is your uncle?" his words trailed off.

William sensed that the encounter with Yves had shaken Hughes, and watched as his hard features softened.

Dimas shifted his gaze between Yves and Hughes. "Hughes, you never told me anything about saving three young knights. My word, man, you do keep things to yourself."

Hughes appeared to be studying the floor. "Yes, I guess I did that. Excuse me please, I must go." And he hurried off.

William stood up. "Excuse me as well, Dimas and Yves, I need to see about Hughes."

William followed Hughes' hurrying figure as he bounded out of the crowded room and into the inner ward.

William finally caught up with him in the middle of the drawbridge leading out of the castle. "Hughes, please stop."

"I… I don't feel well right now, please, I need to go."

"Hughes, what you did took not only courage, but heart, and I understand what you must be going through."

"You do?"

"Yes. You have taken on a task that involved violence repugnant to your soul. You couldn't abide by the violence anymore, and compelled by your compassion, saved the three young knights. You are fine, my friend."

"I am?"

"Yes, Hughes, there's nothing wrong with you. You are a good man, a man of God, and I care for you dearly, my brother."

Hughes stared sadly into the distance. "It's quite a coincidence that out of so many wounded French knights I happened to save Dimas' nephew, don't you think?"

William shook his head. "That's the way things work out sometimes. Life is strange."

Hughes cleared his throat. "You don't know what happened to me William," he then took a deep, slow breath. "As the battle in Flanders was dying down, I went seeking revenge. You see, there was this one French knight I was after who had taken a farmer's daughter by force, and I decided to right that one wrong. But when I reached the scene of the battle, my world came crashing down. The guildsmen were slaughtering those poor boys on the ground with no regard for honor or chivalry, no respect for the fallen warrior. Those were French boys, like so many who served with us in Outremer. I rushed out into the battlefield and I saved three young men. Three out of several thousand, but that's all I could do. Now one of those three turned out to be Dimas' nephew. William, I can't kill anymore."

"I understand, Hughes. In fact I can't tell you how glad that makes me feel."

"But there's still more killing to be done, William. My men did away with Nogaret a few months ago. But the French Scheme will go on with Philip, Marigny, and the pope as long as they are alive. I need to stop them, I have no choice."

William closed his eyes. "No, Hughes. This is your opportunity to trust."

"Trust?"

"Yes, make a solemn oath not to kill again, and I guarantee you that circumstances will change. I know, because that's what happened for me. The French inquisitors have let go of most of our brothers, and that was divine intervention."

Hughes looked old, worn out. "Tell me what to do."

"Kneel down, Hughes. Then swear by the Holy Mother that you will not kill anymore."

Hughes bent down on both knees on the cold ground and closed his eyes. A Scottish knight rode past them quizzically examining the two, then bowed to William.

Hughes opened his eyes and stood up, a far-away look in his eyes. "Very well, William, I made my vow. I don't know how things will work out, but I won't kill anymore."

"Good, brother. Let's see what happens. Let's go for a walk, Hughes."

William watched Hughes. He walked for some time looking down at the ground, his strides slow and tired. When they came to the top of a hill, he stopped. The blustery sea was an angry gray mass some distance away.

"Your men killed Nogaret, Hughes. Tell me what else you planned."

Hughes studied the craggy coast. "From the moment we settled down in this castle, I started my work, William," he said in a somber voice. "I recruited twenty-four of our best men, and I trained them for three years. Then I brought two Venetians, experts in poisons and the means to deliver them, and two of my spies who had volunteered to help: a Frenchman and a Florentine."

"Twenty four? Why so many?"

"I expected casualties."

"But you found your ideal recruits."

"I had to go through five hundred men before I settled on the best suited: skilled, quick, strong, and fast learners."

"And they are now in place?"

Hughes nodded. He looked at the road ahead, stretching among the hills. "They left last spring, a year ago. Eighteen were assigned to Paris together with the French spy, and the other six left with the Florentine for Avignon. Time was of the essence if we were to prevent a French-led crusade to invade Scotland, but patience was necessary for the right moment to execute our plans. Opportunities were few.

"My men observed their targets and planned possible scenarios for each. For Nogaret they had three possibilities, I don't know yet which one they used, but the man is dead.

"Marigny is a harder target, the man varies his routine, and they will have to improvise. The pope presents only one option: poisoning. Philip is too well protected, so they decided to watch him and wait."

"Hughes, please call off your men."

Hughes sighed. "Yes, I will. I promise."

For the next two weeks Hughes made it a point to come visit William in his chambers every week, first with news that his team had indeed pulled back from their intended targets, and then simply to chat, pray and meditate.

On the fourth week, on a Tuesday afternoon, Hughes showed up with an angry look on his face. "Ten days ago, William, on March the 18th, Grand Master Jacques de Molay and his top aide were burned at the stake in Paris." Hughes remained frozen in place, standing in the doorway.

William sighed. "That was to be expected. We knew it was going to happen."

"Let me go after Philip, William. Let my men kill that monster!"

William looked at his friend long and hard. "Hughes, it's not me you should ask, but yourself. However, I would counsel that you wait. Remember when we were on the road to Hafiz Mountain and we encountered the Berbers?"

"Yes, of course."

"And then when we came to the wadi and were able to save the pilgrims with another incredible ruse, and then we figured how everything was working out like magic; how we ended up in the right place but for the wrong reason? We were being guided and protected. You remember?"

"Yes. I do."

"Then when we sailed from Alexandria and the pirates were about to attack?"

"Yes, the wind blew out of nowhere and our boat left the bandits behind."

"Allow the magic to work, Hughes. Wait for the wind to blow."

Hughes nodded and walked out.

For the next seven days William prayed almost constantly for Hughes, the pope, Philip, and Marigny, the last remaining French minister involved in the scheme. He asked for harmony so that events would unfold in a way that would provide all concerned with the best opportunity for the awakening of their souls. By the seventh day, as he sat in meditation and once again visualized all of them, one by one, he perceived each person's outcome of that one drama, feeling in his flesh, heart, and mind, what they were experiencing and the upcoming changes.

He sensed that Philip and Marigny were too engrossed by their evil and their souls clamored for punishment so they could awaken. The pope was already suffering through great remorse; the burning of Jacques de Molay had affected him deeply. All three men were coming to the end of their days.

Hughes was teetering on the verge of an awakening, but was still too emotionally engrossed in the proceedings. After the French Scheme ended he would naturally seek another pursuit to take its place, unless William acted fast enough.

William bowed his head and said a final prayer for all of them.

Two weeks later William received a summons from King Robert de Bruce for that afternoon.

The meeting with the de Bruce brothers took place in Galloway Castle's lone sumptuous room, a sitting chamber on the third floor that rumor had it had been part of the apartments of a beautiful courtesan. The large salon was paneled in wood, the windows had actual glass panes instead of waxed cloth, and there were carpets covering the floor.

They sat as friends would to discuss a common problem: Dimas, Hughes, William, Edward, and Robert in five chairs in a circle with assistants and attendants fluttering in the background.

"Hughes, we need your counsel," began Robert. "We want to hear from you directly how you defeated the French army in Flanders."

"There's no magic," Hughes began, "train the pike men to stay in formation and obey. Make sure they know that the heavy pikes are not lances, but used for thrusting, and have the cavalry and bowmen come to their aid when needed."

"We know all that, Hughes," King Robert said, "but given what you know of our countryside, do you think the pike men will be just as effective here as they were in Flanders against a large army?"

Hughes thought for a moment. "No, if the English come, say here to Galloway, the pike men would not be as effective. But why let the English choose the battlefield?"

Robert laughed. "Because they are the invaders!"

"Then let's make them invade when and where we want them to."

"How do we do that?" Edward de Bruce asked. "Do we bribe one of King Edward's counselors?"

Hughes smiled. "No, the man is making us suffer waiting for his move. He fancies himself a master gamesman. Let's outsmart him. Is there a likely castle he might attack on land best suited for our needs…a place with a boggy field or a broken plain?"

"Stirling Castle," King Robert said right away. "It's in English hands. If King Edward conquers the towns around it, he would have a large chunk of Scotland at his command, with a strong fortress in the center. To get to Stirling you have to go through bog land."

"Excellent," Hughes said. "King Edward can't launch his army in time to prevent us from taking Stirling, but let's make sure he would want to conquer it first thing when he invades."

"We can lay siege to the castle," Edward de Bruce said, "and with some luck we can take it. But how would that help us? The English king can take it back."

"We don't take the castle, "Hughes said. "When Stirling is about to capitulate, we give them an honorable truce."

"You mean they surrender the castle without a fight if we let them go by a certain date?" Robert asked.

"Better than that," Hughes said, "something that would appeal to King Edward's gamesman vanity: they surrender the castle to us by a certain date unless relieved."

"We can make that happen," Edward de Bruce said, "but then what?"

"Then," Hughes said, "King Edward will want to wait until the very last day to relieve Stirling, just to keep up the tension. If we give Stirling until June 24th to either surrender or be relieved, chances are excellent that we will encounter King Edward's army on June 23rd, on the boggy field outside Stirling."

The de Bruce brothers looked at one another, then at William, Dimas, and Hughes. "By God, Hughes, you're worth your weight in gold!" Robert said and stood up.

William walked out with Dimas and Hughes.

"I know what you are thinking, William," Hughes said, "that all I needed was the intent not to kill. This trap at Stirling will work without a single man dying."

Dimas looked perplexed. William smiled. "Hughes, what do you need me for, when you can figure things out on your own?"

"To be my conscience, I guess."

They descended the stairs in silence until they reached the inner ward.

"Thank you, William." Hughes said, and walked away.

"What was that all about?" Dimas asked.

"Oh, Hughes wrestling with himself is all."

A few days later, William was about to leave his chambers for mass, when Hughes came running up the steps. For a man his age, thought William, he was still surprisingly limber.

"William, Philip just killed the pope," Hughes announced trying to catch his breath.

"How do you know? What happened?"

"I just received word from Avignon. I left some of my men watching the pope. Just watching, William, on my word. After Philip burned our Grand Master Jacques at the stake, a change came over Pope Clement. He became withdrawn and was seen studying the Templars' Rules. One of our cardinals heard him say that he was going to abdicate, that he didn't deserve Saint Peter's throne. William, I think he was going to denounce Philip, and the French king got nervous and decided to poison him.

"Pope Clement died a few days ago of an unknown ailment." Hughes was clearly elated. "If this is how your magic works, William, I'm all for it. But I guess we should wait and see what happens at Stirling Castle."

A month later, a Scottish knight brought William the news: the de Bruce brothers had successfully raided Stirling Castle, which had accepted the "Honorable Truce" that allowed until June 24th for the English to relieve it. Past that date, if King Edward and his troops didn't show, the castle would surrender to the Scots.

The following two months were a tense time in Galloway. Hughes kept waiting for news from his men regarding Philip, and Marigny. Edward II kept the Scots guessing whether he would invade or decide to forfeit Stirling Castle. William spent most of the month in meditation, but would check with Hughes every evening after Vespers for news.

One morning, in mid June, as William read a letter from a brother in Spain, he heard a commotion outside. The English had invaded and were marching toward Stirling Castle.

The trap had worked! The only question was, how well?

"All we can do is sit and wait," William said to Dimas and Hughes in his chambers. "Let us spend our time in meditation and prayer. That's the very best we can do."

Ten days later the three were coming out of the chapel after Nones when a messenger told them the English under Edward II had been soundly defeated three days earlier not far from Stirling Castle in what he called the Battle of

Bannockburn. The courier started to give them details of the battle but William stopped him.

"No need, my friend. That's all we care to know. Thank you."

Following the victory there was much rejoicing all over Scotland. Robert de Bruce had won, and had established himself firmly as the new king. The English would not dare intervene again.

William could only hope that the French would be stopped as well, and eventually Hughes delivered the news. The French king had suffered an accident at his hunting retreat at Fointainebleau. "He's lying in bed dying slowly and in pain."

William stared at Hughes. "And you are sure your men had nothing to do with Philip's accident?"

"William, I swore I would not kill."

But William remained with a nagging doubt. There was no way Hughes would lie, but he had become so involved in subterfuge that perhaps he found a way to satisfy his conscience and his need for revenge at the same time...which he most likely rationalized as fulfilling his duty.

A few days later William heard rumors about the French king's accident. One story had it that he fell off his horse while in pursuit of a stag; the second one, the most disturbing, told that Philip had been jousting, his lance broke on impact and a splinter went through his helmet's eye slot, piercing his eye and lodging in his head. The doctors couldn't remove it, and he lay in bed agonizing. That, William realized, had Hughes' imprint all over, for it was the way the Saracen marksmen used to maim Templars in Outremer, by shooting an arrow through the helmet's eye slots, invariably causing long suffering but not certain death.

However way it was that Philip had been injured, William was sure that Hughes had been involved. He was becoming a man with no moral bearings, a lost soul. William resolved to help him become the Hughes he had been once at Hafiz. But Marigny was still alive, and surely Hughes would find the means to do away with him while keeping his oath not to kill.

Three months passed without further developments, until one day in early January, while William was having dinner with Dimas in the great hall, Hughes came and sat next to them. "Philip is dead!" he announced. "But that's not all," and he chuckled. "Last week Philip's son Louis arrested Marigny and accused him of corruption and treason for his handling of Flanders.

"You see, four months ago while Philip lay in bed dying, Marigny signed a treaty with the Flemish that was seen as a French capitulation. Louis accused Marigny of treason and had him executed!"

Hughes smiled broadly. "It's such a relief. You were right, William! I don't know how that worked out, but I'm very glad it did. Brothers, the French Scheme is now over." Hughes slapped his leg and let out a howl. All around people turned to stare at him, but Hughes seemed unconcerned and let out another loud howl. Then he laughed. The other diners—mostly Templars, but also some Scottish and Hospitaller knights—smiled and exchanged quizzical glances.

Hughes appeared full of excitement and scarcely able to contain himself. Perhaps in an attempt to prevent Hughes from howling again, Dimas spoke: "What's next? Do we go about maintaining the Brotherhood?"

William looked around and decided they needed to talk in private. "Let's go for a walk."

"It's cold outside," Hughes said.

"Oh, the walk will warm us up. Let's go Hughes."

William walked in between Hughes and Dimas. He then placed an arm around each man's shoulders. "Ever since the defeat of the English, I have been thinking about our future. I heard from London that King Edward II is going to sign a treaty with Scotland. He is busy with his wife's schemes against him and fighting his barons.

"Philip's son Louis is no threat. Even if Philip told him about the French Scheme, we managed to contain the French everywhere."

As they made their way past the drawbridge, William paused to study the frozen water below. "In fact, the powerful monarchies of Europe will eventually disappear. The new federation in the Alps defeated the Austrian duke, thanks to their well-disciplined pike men. It's just a matter of time before they solidify their independence."

William took careful measured steps down the lane. "I think we are done with the Caesarius Prophecy."

Dimas stopped and held William by the arm. "Was that what it was all about, to get us involved against the French and then as a result accomplish all those things?"

"Yes. I discovered that Otto learned about Philip's plans from a spy named Cantor de Milly, a very capable man whom Philip had entrusted with his daughter Isabella's welfare. But he was a secret Cathar with intense hatred for the French monarchy and the pope. He probably told Otto that Philip intended to destroy the Templars just so that Otto would pit the Order against the French."

Hughes stared at William in disbelief. "Are you saying that the Prophecy was a fake?"

"Otto did come up with the Prophecy, Hughes."

"So Cantor manipulated Otto and that's how come the Brotherhood went to

war against Philip? Then Cantor must have known that Otto was in the Brotherhood. How did he know? Did Otto tell him?"

"Does it matter, Hughes? What matters is that he was one of the many players in this drama."

Dimas shook his head, apparently bewildered. "I can't believe that Otto and
this Cantor made everything up!"

William nodded. "It really doesn't matter that Caesarius was not the Prophecy's author. He might as well have been. Otto and Cantor were just like us,
pawns...of fate. I see the events in the Prophecy as inevitable as nightfall. When
the time is ripe for something...an event, an idea, a book, even the Jesus Gospel...it will be manifested; the author is unimportant, merely a conduit. Just like
the tactics you came up with in Flanders, Hughes. If you hadn't done it, someone else would have, because the time was ripe. That's how things work, and the
Prophecy was no exception. It was real.

"However, like all prophecies, it described a potential. It was up to us, the
players, how we made it come to life.

"Imagine what would have happened had we remained true to our higher
selves and refused to kill. I believe that a miracle would have taken place, another
magical journey, just as it did back then when we were facing the bandits and the
pirates during our Hafiz journey."

Dimas listened intently, his eyes firmly fixed on William.

Hughes appeared perplexed, and he rubbed his chin. "You mean the entire
set of events...Philip, his ministers..."

"Things would have been radically different. Either the individuals involved
would have been different or they would have changed, but at any rate the outcome would not have been the same."

Hughes' gaze was fixed somewhere in the far off mountains. "I can't change
what happened...it's too late..."

"No, Hughes, it's never too late. We can strive to reach 'The Knowing,' which
is what this challenge was meant to do...what life in general is all about."

"Sounds as though that's what you have decided for yourself," Dimas said.

"Yes I have. And I want to ask you two to come with me. We still have a few
good years ahead of us and we need to recover what we lost in this battle of ours.
We should do what my uncle did and leave the worldly struggles to those who
will benefit from them."

"Where would we go?" Hughes said in a hesitant voice.

William slowed down his pace to a gentle stroll. "Hafiz Mountain. I have felt
her calling for the past year or so."

"How do we get there?" Hughes asked suddenly animated. "We can't take the old route and I doubt that at our age we can survive what we went through back then."

"I have already made inquiries through the Brotherhood," William said. "We make our way to Granada in Spain, and from there take a ship to Tunis. Since our visit, several brothers have made the trip to Hafiz Mountain via Tunis. A Berber brother in that city will guide us."

Hughes appeared lost in thought. He turned to William. "When do we leave?"

William smiled. "Next week would be fine."

"But it's the middle of winter," Hughes said.

"No matter, we ride to the English Channel, then through France, and once we get to Spain it'll warm up."

"I have so much left to do!" Dimas said. "Our lawyers are still busy replacing the laws the English imposed on Scotland; three of our financiers in Zurich are establishing money routes to us. Then there is the army..."

"Do you have an assistant?" interrupted William.

Dimas hesitated. "Well, yes, of course. You told me a year ago to name three assistants, one for each aspect of my work. They are very helpful."

"Then let them take over. Hughes' will do the same. My own assistant will call a meeting of the Brotherhood and they will replace me.

"The world will try to keep us here if we let it. We have to cut the ropes that bind us with one swift stroke. We leave a week from tomorrow."

Dimas appeared dumbfounded. Then he smiled. "Very well, so be it. I'll be ready."

They walked for a time in silence. When they reached the top of a hill, Hughes looked back at the castle. "So we are free to go."

"Yes, Hughes, our duty is done." William said. "I'll ask Albert to get our horses and gear ready."

"He's coming with us?"

"Oh, yes. He already knows about Hafiz Mountain and can't wait."

The three stopped when they heard the castle's bells announce Vespers. They turned to look at the sunset, and William could tell from looking at Hughes' face that his former commander was seeing a sunrise over the African desert twenty-five years before on the way back from Hafiz Mountain.

Yes, they were free.